THE HIGHEST BIDDER

Before she knew it, the auction was over, and he was standing beside her, swinging her up into his strong arms. She tightened her body, tried to shrink away from the warmth and hardness of him, but he jostled her slightly until she fell against him, her fingers splayed on his chest for balance. She could feel the strong, steady beat of his heart. Her other hand gripped his arm tightly.

Gwyn closed her eyes, not wanting to think about what awaited her. Then they were in her room, and she was set gently on her feet in front of him. Gwyn opened her eyes and concentrated on looking at his chest. His coat and breeches were expensive; she could tell by the cut and quality of the material. But what was beneath frightened her.

"Hello, my beauty." His voice was soft. Husky. For her ears alone. Gwyn began to tremble as he slowly lowered his lips to hers and claimed her as his own. . . .

D0191690

MORE BLAZING ROMANCES
From Zebra Books

FRONTIER FLAME (1965, $3.95)
by Rochelle Wayne
When her cousin deserted the army, spirited Suzanne Donovan knew that she had to go and get him back. But once the luscious blonde confronted towering Major Blade Landon, she wished she'd never left home. The lean, muscled officer seemed as wild as the land — and made her think only of the rapture his touch could bring!

ARIZONA TEMPTRESS (1785, $3.95)
by Bobbi Smith
Rick Peralta found the freedom he craved only in his disguise as El Cazador. Then he saw the alluring Jennie mcCaine among his compadres and swore she'd belong just to him. When he left his lawless life, he'd leave the enticing captive behind . . . but until then the hot-blooded Rick would have all of his needs fulfilled by his provocative ARIZONA TEMPTRESS.

PRAIRIE EMBRACE (2035, $3.95)
by F. Rosanne Bittner
Katie Russell was shocked by her passionate reaction to her bronze-skinned, jet-haired Indian captor. The gorgeous pioneer reminded herself that he was a savage heathen and beneath her regard, but deep inside she knew she longed to yield to the ecstasy of his PRAIRIE EMBRACE.

PIRATE'S CONQUEST (2036, $3.95)
by Mary Martin
Starlin Cambridge always scoffed that the ruthless pirate Scorpio would never capture her sleek, treasure-laden ship. But one day, the notorious outlaw overtook her vessel—and kidnapped its raven-haired owner. Furious that the muscular marauder has taken her freedom, Starlin is shocked when she longs for him to take her innocence as well!

MEMENTO (2037, $3.95)
by Eleanora Brownleigh
Just one chance encounter with the compelling Gregory West settles Katherine's mind: she knows he is the man for her, even if it means forsaking her rich and comfortable New York City home to travel across the uncivilized continent,. And though the dark secrets of the past ruled out marriage for Gregory, nothing could stop him from savoring Katherine's whole body for a brief, intense fling that would forever be this most cherished MEMENTO.

Available wherever paperbacks are sold, or order direct from the Publisher. Send cover price plus 50¢ per copy for mailing and handling to Zebra Books, Dept. 2133, 475 Park Avenue South, New York, N.Y. 10016. Residents of New York, New Jersey and Pennsylvania must include sales tax. DO NOT SEND CASH.

VELVET FIRE

ELDA MINGER

ZEBRA BOOKS
KENSINGTON PUBLISHING CORP.

To Janet Smart, who started me on this path by giving me my first historical romance. I like to think you always knew it was only a matter of time.

And to Lynne Barbre, who helped shape this novel as only another writer could.

Andrew and Gwyn—owe you a special debt. Velvet Fire is dedicated to both of you, with much love.

ZEBRA BOOKS

are published by

KENSINGTON PUBLISHING CORP.
475 Park Avenue South
New York, NY 10016

Copyright © 1987 by Elda Minger

All rights reserved. No part of this book may be reproduced in any form or by any means without the prior written consent of the Publisher, excepting brief quotes used in reviews.

First printing: July 1987

Printed in the United States of America

*"The events we speak of
took place in a time when
a woman's honor was her single
—and therefore most precious—
possession."*

Book I

"Is your life such a terrible tangle?
Take some simple advice from a friend—
You must trust in your Guardian Angel . . .
Things will come out all right—in the end . . ."

Prologue

Midnight, November 25, 1762
London

The late night wind howled with primal fury as it lashed around the elegant stone townhouse, whipping the carefully trimmed shrubs and tearing leaves off the stately oak. Dark clouds obscured the moonlight and thick fog snaked around the iron fence. The wooden sign above the door facing the narrow alley swayed back and forth crazily, the dark stallion painted upon it seeming to gallop against the wind. It was a world out of control, a night during which anything might happen. A night for witch's revelry, mischief, or simply staring at the moon until one went quite mad.

In the distance, the clang of horses hooves on cobblestones could be heard, along with the rattle and creaking of a lone carriage. The horses pulling the carriage were black, like servants of Satan having risen from Hell.

The driver reined in the nervously prancing animals, soothing them with his low voice. The carriage slowed as it passed the stone house, turned into the narrow alley, and came to a full stop. Afraid of the elements, the horses still shifted in their harness.

Edward Sleaforth stepped down from the carriage, grabbed a cumbersome bundle, and slung it over his shoulder. His pale eyes shifted from side to side, then he scuttled quickly to the back door and rapped on it sharply. Within seconds, it opened, and the dark-haired maid gestured him to follow.

"Put her by the fire. The Mistress won't want her catching cold," she said coolly, with just a hint of a French accent.

Sleaforth complied. The kitchen was a large room, with a massive stone fireplace along one wall. A fire was snapping and popping, giving off small sparks. Two chairs stood in front of it. Without hesitating, he unrolled the bundle he'd been carrying and deposited the girl in a chair. She was dressed in a sheer chemise and one ragged petticoat. Her hair was long, reaching almost to her waist. Wet, it shimmered like dark gold.

"Well, Edward, I see you finally did something right."

He turned, fighting not to let Janet Wickens see the anger inside exposed on his face. She was standing half silhouetted in the doorway, those damn spaniels at her heels. Dressed in an emerald green silk wrapper trimmed lavishly with lace, her dark red hair caught up on top of her head, she had an air of haughty elegance she wore like the finest velvet cloak. Her green eyes narrowed, dark and liquid in her finely boned face, and as she assessed him he felt as if he'd been caught with his breeches down.

"Let's take a look at her." Janet glided into the kitchen. Edward heard the clicking of both dogs' nails on the stone floor. They followed her everywhere.

She knelt by the chair and studied the girl. He watched her face carefully, but she gave nothing away. She was much too clever to let him have any advantage. The spaniels made a move to sniff the girl's outstretched hand, but Janet softly snapped her fingers and they both trotted over by the fire and lay down, panting gently.

The wait seemed to stretch forever, but it couldn't have lasted more than a few minutes. When Janet stood up, Edward steeled himself for what was to come.

"She's drugged." It was a statement, not a question.

He hesitated a moment, then decided not to lie.

"Laudanum."

Janet smiled, but it didn't reach her eyes. "So she didn't come willingly?"

He shifted, nervous. There was a large man standing in the corner. He didn't have any ears. Bearded, bald, tall and muscular, his arms were crossed in front of his massive chest as he watched the interchange. Edward knew whose side this giant was on: Janet never left anything to chance. He felt his nose begin to twitch, a nervous habit he despised.

It was clear Janet could see the agitation on his face. The madam of The Dark Stallion slipped her hand smoothly in the pocket of her wrapper. "What a man won't do for money, eh Edward?"

She was making fun of him, but he deftly caught the bag of coins she tossed. Untying the top, he began to count the gold sovereigns.

"This is less than we—" The giant's eyes glittered, and Edward ceased speaking.

"It's more than you deserve, considering she'll wake up sick and won't be any use to me for a few days. And if she dies, Edward, what is she worth then?"

He hadn't thought that far ahead. Glancing at the earless giant once again, he decided his business at The Dark Stallion was finished. Stuffing the bag of coins into his pocket, he backed away, then turned and walked quickly toward the door and the waiting carriage.

Janet made a small, disgusted noise in the back of her throat. "That's the last business I'll do with you, you sniveling little mouse." Her glance fell on the soaked girl by the fire, and her thoughts turned to business.

"Angelique! Bring a blanket and towels. We have work to do."

The drugged girl was a bedraggled, sodden mess. The chemise stuck to her breasts, outlining them as they softly rose

9

and fell with her labored breathing.

Janet took a small pair of scissors out of her wrapper pocket. Expertly she cut away the wet clothing until the girl was completely naked. She lifted the girl's head and eased the heavy wet hair out from underneath her, letting it tumble to the stone floor before the fire.

She glanced up as Angelique rushed in, carrying several towels and a blanket.

"Dry her off, then wrap her warmly."

While Angelique rubbed the girl's body briskly, Janet took one of the towels and began to dry her hair. It wasn't something she would normally have done, but she didn't trust any of her servants except the French maid. And she wanted to keep this beauty hidden until she regained her strength and could do her some good.

It was beautiful hair, thick with just a hint of wave. The parts already dried sparkled like spun gold shimmering softly in the firelight.

Once her hair was dried, Janet took a comb out of her wrapper pocket and began to untangle the silken mass, her thoughts racing excitedly.

This girl will make me a fortune. Janet studied the pale face, the square jaw with its hint of stubbornness, the high cheekbones and generous mouth. Her eyes had to be blue. They were thickly fringed, her eyebrows beautifully arched.

Her hands and feet were shapely and elegant, her waist small. Her hips possessed the gentlest curve, her buttocks shaped for a man's hands—not too large. Her breasts were superb, large and well-shaped with perfect pink nipples. Men were fools for large breasts, and the girls who were well-endowed received twice as many clients as their flat-chested competitors.

Her legs were long and nicely proportioned, her skin white and smooth. As Angelique moved the towel lower and continued drying the girl, Janet quickly eyed the silken hair between her legs. Her brow furrowed. There, high on her inner

10

thigh, the skin was puckered and discolored. Scarred.

Yet it's small, and by the time a man notices it, he won't care.

The curls between those slender thighs were a darker gold than the hair on her head. Except for that scar, this woman was made for a man's pleasure and satisfaction.

And if she's kept her virtue . . .

Taking the blue blanket, Janet wrapped it securely around the girl. Her orders were brisk. "Go upstairs and start a fire in the rose room. We have to keep her warm."

Angelique returned a short time later and waited until Janet nodded almost imperceptively before she spoke.

"The fire has been started, Mistress, and the room is warm. I closed the curtains and arranged the bed."

"Very good. I don't want anyone to know about the girl— not yet."

"Yes, Mistress."

"You may go now." She could trust Angelique not to gossip.

Thatch stood silently in the corner. Though he had also seen everything that had transpired this night, Janet knew she could trust him not to talk. The same men who had cut his ears off had also disposed of his tongue. She had found him half dead in the streets on the way home from a gambling hell and had brought him to The Dark Stallion. She'd nursed the giant back to health. He was as loyal as her spaniels and, along with his twin whom he had brought to the brothel later, kept an eye on everything that went on in her house.

Janet loved her business, loved every aspect of the brothel, especially the vast amounts of money it brought in and the secure feeling that money gave her. She never rested; she worked feverishly to make the Dark Stallion the most notorious brothel in London. She guarded her business as zealously as any mother would her new babe.

Forty minutes later, Janet ran her fingers carefully through the girl's golden mane. Satisfied it was bone dry, she motioned

11

for Thatch to help her. She watched as he carefully eased his massive hands underneath the still form, then caught her up gently against his chest. Janet followed him up the stairs, her eyes on the shimmering swing of golden hair as the girl's head lolled gently.

Superb. Utterly superb. This girl was a prize. She was sure of it. Her green eyes became cloudy, almost opaque as she lost herself in thought. This girl had just the right quality to entice her jaded clientele.

Angelique met them at the door.

"I used the bedwarmer, Mistress. The bed was cold, so I ran it beneath the linens."

Janet nodded her head approvingly. "Very good, Angelique." If there was one thing she couldn't abide, it was a stupid servant.

Angelique beamed, then after Thatch carefully laid the girl on the bed, she pulled the covers over her.

"Remember, come to me the moment she wakes."

Janet turned and, with her spaniels trotting at her heels, headed for her private rooms.

Once inside, she seated herself at her rosewood desk and took out her ledger. Smiling, she opened it to the correct page and took out a quill. She sharpened it with a pen knife, then carefully dipped it in the inkwell.

With great care and precision, she wrote in the sum she had paid Edward.

What a fool. She could still see Edward's pale, long face, his twitching nose, the thin blond hair. The nervous look in his eyes—he obviously wasn't experienced in this sort of thing. The girl wasn't near death. She'd merely wanted him out of her house—paid the minimum amount of money. He could have asked for much more. With her beauty, he could have asked for a fortune. And if he were right, and she were still untouched . . .

You're a fool, Edward Sleaforth. And she laughed out loud. *I'll have to plan something very special for Friday night.* She

12

ran her fingers lovingly over the pages of the ledger, over the neat columns of numbers representing the vast sums she had earned. She had more imagination than any brothel owner in all of London, and now she possessed one of the most beautiful girls she had ever seen.

Blissfully, she sat at her desk and dreamed of all she could do with the girl who lay sleeping beneath her roof.

As she visualized the girl at her Friday evening gathering, one vision became clear and she smiled.

Perfect. Just perfect.

Nothing made Janet smile like the prospect of making more money.

Chapter One

Andrew Hawkesworth, Earl of Scarborough, lay perfectly still as he slowly awoke, knowing full well where he was and not liking it. When had this game with Lady Belinda turned sour? She had afforded him hours of amusement, had always known exactly what their affair was about. Both had wanted a warm, sensual body. No commitments. No emotions. Nothing to entangle the heart in any way.

Why is it so damn dissatisfying?

"Andrew?" The feminine voice was petulant, used to having her own way. He felt one of the feathery plumes she had worn in her dark hair the night before tickling his nose, and he closed his eyes tighter, not wanting to face what he had become.

"Andrew?"

He opened his eyes and took in her voluptuous body. She was braced up on her elbows, her generous breasts pressed together.

"Yes, Belinda."

"Would you like to have me again before you leave?" There was sharp calculation in her eyes. At first it had amused him, then bored him. Now he was secretly disgusted with himself, but he didn't desire any alternative, either.

Have you is exactly what it is, what with the response you give me.

"What I would like," he said, his voice husky with sleep, "is a moment of peace." He closed his eyes, tasting the aftermath of last night's indulgence. He needed more and more drink to bed Belinda these days.

"Andrew . . ." The tone was seductive, and he felt her hand moving between his thighs.

His eyes flew open. He captured her fingers with his own, then sat up in bed, letting the lacy covers fall away from his chest. "No, Belinda."

"But I haven't had enough of you, darling. I am prodigiously fond of having you in my bed, you know that."

"Let me rest, or I will leave." He turned away from her.

When had it all become such an effort? When had his master plan gone astray? Freedom to do as he pleased with whom he pleased. And Belinda, with her perpetually calculating eyes and tight little smile, had seemed the perfect companion. She had bedded half of London, he knew that as well as anyone. It hadn't bothered him at first; she had suited his purpose admirably. But now he was restless. Searching. There had to be something more.

But I didn't want anything more. Everything has been fine until now. Why do I feel so very empty? He found himself wanting Belinda in his life, then desiring nothing more to do with her. But whether Lady Pevensy was a part of his life or not, he didn't have any answers.

Andrew closed his eyes and tried to rest. The only thing he was certain of was that he did not want to give his heart to a woman. It was a far too vulnerable position to be in.

He would have to squelch these odd early-morning yearnings, put them down to his usual moodiness. Wanting more than Belinda could be dangerous business.

"Andrew . . ." Her hand was creeping up his muscled thigh.

Sighing, he reached for his breeches.

15

"Where are you going? With Jack to that club?"

"It's none of your concern."

"When we're married it will be!" Now her carefully contrived performance was replaced by a flash of anger.

He grasped her chin in his hands and raised her face so she was looking directly into his eyes. "You overstep yourself, Lady Pevensy. When we are married, I will still do as I please."

The false expression returned. "How can you blame me, Andrew, when you give me such total satisfaction?"

You lie even about that. He knew Belinda was false in her responses. How long had it been since a woman truly excited him? He could perform, but that was all. Sometimes when he was drunk enough, he didn't even have to fantasize.

"Don't come back besotted, looking for comfort."

He shrugged into his shirt. "Dear heart," he said softly, a touch of cynicism in his voice, "if I ever desired comfort, you would be the last woman in the world I would seek."

He smiled as he picked up his boots and walked softly toward the bedroom door. With the expertise of long practice, he ducked as the china figurine sailed past his head and smashed against the wall.

Gwyneth opened her eyes and everything blurred. The light hurt her, and any movement sent stabbing shafts of pain lacing through her head. She closed her eyes tightly, wondering suddenly where she was. She couldn't seem to think properly.

Edward took me to London. . . .

Where was Edward now?

The room smelled of flowers, and she could hear a fire crackling softly against the chill morning. Gwyneth didn't know when she was suddenly aware of someone watching her. She opened her eyes and looked straight into an unabashedly curious female face. The face studied her slowly. Assessing. Gwyneth stared back, taking in the glossy brown curls, the large eyes, the delicate features and widow's peak. The stranger's hair was pulled back beneath a white cap, and she wore a blue dress with a crisp white apron over it. She couldn't have been more than sixteen years old.

Perhaps I've arrived at my cousin's friend's house after all. But why don't I remember anything?

The storm. There had been a thunderstorm. And she had gotten into a carriage with Edward. She wrinkled her brow as she tried to remember.

Nothing. Where was she?

The woman with the white cap was still watching her intently, as if afraid she might bolt from the room. Or sprout wings. Gwyneth decided to put her fears to rest.

"I don't believe we've met," she said quietly.

Her statement took the woman by surprise. She glanced toward the door, then back at her.

"No, we haven't."

When nothing else seemed to be forthcoming, Gwyneth offered her hand. "My name is Gwyneth. And yours?" she prompted gently.

The woman continued to stare at her with an amazed expression on her face. A guarded light came into her dark eyes. "Angelique. But all who know me call me Angel."

Gwyneth laughed softly as the woman took her hand and squeezed it briefly. "You seem like an angel to me." Not knowing quite how to ask her next question, she simply blurted it out.

"Could you tell me please . . . I'm so sorry, I don't seem to remember. Could you please tell me where I am? And where is my cousin, Edward? We were supposed to be visiting friends, but after we got into the carriage last night—" She could feel a blush creeping into her face as Angel continued to stare at her. Now there was open amazement on her expressive face, then quick disgust.

"I know you must think I was drinking too much, but I rarely indulge. If you could just tell me where I am . . ."

"*Nom de Dieu,*" the French girl breathed softly. Gwyneth

17

felt her suddenly pat her arm. "You sit here. I'm going downstairs to fetch you some tea, then I'll come back."

Gwyneth watched her as she crossed the room, but the effort she'd made sitting up and carrying on a conversation suddenly caught up with her. Slowly, feeling as if every muscle in her body had been severely taxed, she slid down into the cool sheets and rested her cheek against the silky pillow. Before she could worry about anything else, her lashes slowly fluttered shut.

Angel banged the china cup against the saucer with such an abrupt clatter that Cook, snoozing by the fireplace, jumped up with a start.

"Damnation, girl, stop making such a racket! I have a right to a little rest at my age!"

"I don't like it!" Angel muttered under her breath.

"Don't like what?" Cook asked sleepily. She'd resettled her massive bulk on the chair close to the fire.

"The new one. Upstairs. Gwyneth. She's not like us. She doesn't belong here." Angel punctuated each statement with a jerky movement as she assembled a tray. Some porridge from the pot by the fire. Two slices of bread. And a mug of strong tea.

"Don't get your head involved with something that's none of your business. Let the Mistress take care of her."

"I can't. That cousin of hers should be horsewhipped." Angel filched one of the apple tarts they'd baked this morning for lunch and added it to the already heaped tray.

"You're a good girl, Angel. Don't do anything foolish," Cook muttered. "I thought the same once, but after all my years here, I've accepted things. Can't save any of them. Not here."

Angel picked up the tray and walked out of the kitchen.

She hurried up to the third floor, ignoring the other girls as they walked down the halls. When she reached the bedroom furthest back, she shifted the tray to one hand and pushed against the solid wooden door gently, easing it open.

The girl was asleep. Her hand was pillowed against her cheek, her face serene in repose.

Angel studied her again as she set the tray down on the table by the bed. Then she patted the girl's—*Gwyneth's*, she reminded herself—shoulder and wakened her.

"You'll feel better when you eat this," she said softly. "Then you must rest and regain your strength." Reluctantly, Angel backed out of the room and headed toward Janet's private suite.

None of the other girls call me by my name. None of the others look me in the eye when they talk to me. There was something different about Gwyneth.

"Come on, Andrew! You haven't made the rounds with us in months!" Jack Colborne, the Viscount Lanford, sounded exasperated.

"I don't know if I want to," Andrew replied. Jack sat back in his leather chair, dismayed.

"Whatever happened to Randy Andy?"

"Perhaps he's just tired of the entire game," Andrew said shortly, his dark glance sweeping around the private club. It always smelled the same—overpowering cologne, the reek of wet wool, the pleasant scents of leather and strong tobacco. Some things never changed; they simply lost their appeal.

Andrew's sensual mouth twisted into a grimace and he set his glass of claret down on the table. "Grandfather has decided it's past time I settled down."

"A capital idea! And who's the lucky lady?"

"I was thinking of . . . Belinda."

"Belinda! Andrew, she's nothing more than a—"

"I know what she is and it suits me fine. At least we'll both be getting exactly what we want from each other."

"You've become too cynical, my friend. Especially where the fairer sex is concerned."

"Look at the women in London, Jack, and tell me different."

"I shall get you out of this devilish mood if it kills me," Jack replied, and Andrew saw the grin starting to spread over his open, honest face. "You're not married yet! Surely you can join us at the Dark Stallion for a debauched weekend. You can't get married without one last fling. Come on, Andrew, for old time's sake if nothing else!"

Andrew smiled. He knew his friend didn't have a great deal of experience with women. Jack wouldn't go to the Dark Stallion unless he went with him. It had always been that way, even when they'd been younger. He'd led, Jack had followed.

"All right. For friendship's sake!"

Jack chuckled and sat back in his comfortable chair. "The word's out that Janet has something spectacular planned for Friday. A new girl."

Andrew merely nodded his head, listening politely. He had absolutely no interest in anyone Janet might display.

He signaled one of the servants for another set of drinks, then met Jack's glance and smiled again. This time it reached his eyes. When their drinks arrived, he lifted his and touched it briefly to Jack's.

"To Friday, then."

Three days later, Angel came in to find Gwyneth sitting by the fire in a light blue wrapper with a white shawl tucked around her shoulders.

"Would you answer a question?" Gwyn asked. Though her tone was polite, there was no mistaking the quiet strength in those blue eyes. Angel bit her full lip nervously. She knew what was coming.

Slowly, she nodded her head.

"Edward isn't coming for me, is he." It was a flat statement, not a question.

She shook her head, the slightest movement, not wanting to hurt Gwyneth.

"And this house—what am I doing here?"

Angel looked down at the pattern on the lush Oriental carpet. "You'll have to wait for Mistress Janet to answer that one."

"And who is Janet?"

"She owns this house, miss."

Gwyneth got up and began to pace agitatedly around the room. "When will I meet this Janet?" she asked finally.

"This evening, miss. She's coming to see you." Angel took a deep breath. "I have orders to get you ready."

Gwyneth walked back to the overstuffed chair by the fire and sank down into it. Her legs had started to tremble, more from some unexplainable fear than weakness. Where was Edward? Why wasn't he coming for her? He'd promised her father he would protect her, but if he wasn't coming back, there could be only one reason. . . .

"Edward's dead, isn't he?" she asked flatly.

"That I don't know, miss. Why don't you sit by the window and have a cup of tea while I bring up your bathwater," she suggested hopefully.

But Gwyneth simply stood and stared blindly out the window at the smoky patchwork of rooftops and chimney stacks that extended as far as she could see. A fear she had never felt in her entire life began to slowly wash over her.

Janet would supply all the answers. But somehow she knew they would be answers she didn't want to hear.

"Think of it as something to whet your appetite!" Jack said. He and Andrew had just come back from a ride in the park and were walking away from the mews.

"I don't need my appetite whetted; I have the lovely Belinda."

Jack made a disgusted face. "The lovely Belinda, indeed! Well, *I've* never seen a lady bathe, and I hear this one is superb."

21

"You've never seen a lady undress? Take a bath?" Though he'd already agreed to tonight's entertainment, he couldn't resist the chance to tease back. "Your education is sadly lacking."

They had frequented Janet's house before and knew her to be a Madam who delivered anything a gentleman could desire. Her girls serviced most of London's respectable gentlemen; one could find anything imaginable there.

"This will be amusing," Andrew murmured. "When do we have to be there?"

"Three. And I don't want to be late."

Andrew threw back his head and laughed.

"Your bath is ready," Angel said.

Gwyneth glanced toward the fireplace. A fire was snapping merrily; the room was much warmer than before. The tub was placed close to the hearth, an elaborate copper affair one could lie down in. She'd never seen anything like it.

There was a small table next to it, and a cake of scented soap was placed there, along with a towel and a hairbrush.

"Do you need anything else?" Angel asked.

Gwyneth smiled at her. Though she was terrified of her meeting with Janet—for she knew the woman would tell her the truth—she refused to take her fears out on someone who didn't deserve it. "Thank you, Angel, this will be fine. What time will Janet be here?"

"She said she'd come to see you after dinner. I'll bring up a tray."

Gwyneth nodded, and Angel walked over to the table and picked up the hairbrush. "Turn around. I'll help you with your hair."

"I never really thought you were the peeping Tom, Jack," Andrew teased softly as the two men made their way slowly through the intricate maze of catwalks and false corridors that ran throughout Janet's house.

"Andrew, some of us haven't had the opportunity to savor all the debauchery you have," Jack replied. "Now be quiet; we're almost there."

"I could be spending the afternoon in bed with Belinda."

"We should all be so blessed," Jack replied sarcastically.

Not more than ten feet later, Jack signaled with his hand for Andrew to be quiet. There were several chairs set by various holes in the wall. Three men were already seated. Andrew recognized one as the Duke of Cuckfield and averted his face before the man could greet him. He'd never liked the older man.

He and Jack settled themselves into their chairs. Andrew knew they were viewing the room through eyes cut in the various portraits that hung on the inner wall. Many of the other rooms were thusly equipped. One could watch any of the girls at various activities, the degree of titillation solely up to the beholder.

"Just like the theater," Andrew whispered to Jack, his voice low. "Ah, Jack, the delights you have in store—"

"Will you be quiet!" Jack hissed.

Andrew smiled at his friend, then looked through the peephole. A woman in a maid's uniform attended another woman in a silk wrapper, brushing the longest, most golden hair Andrew had ever seen. It caught the light from the fire as it waved down the woman's silk-clad back.

Beautiful hair, he mused. But he'd known a lot of women and quite a few had had beautiful hair. It was nothing that unusual.

Jack inched forward to the edge of his chair, and Andrew smiled indulgently.

He stifled a yawn and, determined to show Jack he wasn't bored, turned his attention to the scene in the bedroom.

Andrew squinted his blue eyes and studied the woman with the golden hair. She still had her back to them, but the maid had finished attending her.

23

She turned slowly toward them. And Andrew felt his world slowly reeling on its axis, taking an entirely new turn from which he knew there would be no going back.

He felt as if someone had hit him in the stomach with a tightly clenched fist. She was the most beautiful creature he'd ever seen—her face a perfect oval, her eyes deep blue, almost midnight in color and thickly lashed.

"Sweet Jesus," Jack whispered softly. The sound was almost a moan.

Her lips were full, her jawline square, her cheekbones high, almost aristocratic. Her nose was small and straight, her brows darker than her hair and finely shaped.

Andrew caught his breath and stared. *So lovely. It almost hurts to look at her.* His eyes moved lower, taking in the full breasts thrusting against the thin silk wrapper, the feminine curve of waist and hips, the shape of her thighs, long and delicately formed. She was a woman made for a man's loving. Perfection.

She unfastened the sash of her wrapper, and Andrew felt his mouth go dry. As the silk fell away, the most intense, primitive desire washed over him. It was the strongest sensation he'd experienced in his life. Sensual fire licked his entire body, then concentrated in his loins.

If her face had been that of an angel, her body belonged to a goddess. She stood for a moment before the fire, looking down into the tub. Her shoulders were creamy and white, the skin smooth and unblemished. Andrew almost groaned aloud, thinking of what it would feel like beneath his fingers. Her breasts were made for a man's hand and he watched, fascinated, as the nipples puckered and she crossed her arms in front of them.

As she raised one leg and stepped into the large copper tub, Andrew quickly scanned the rest of her body. Her waist was tiny; he could easily fit his hands around it. Her legs were long and slender, the curls between her thighs darkly golden.

Andrew shifted in his chair, imagining what it would be like to press his hand there, lace his fingers through those curls, press his lips against her there and make her moan and writhe beneath him.

She stepped into the tub, letting the water cover her body. Andrew found himself willing her to sit up. He wanted to see more.

And she did, bracing her back against the lip of the tub, the voluptuous tops of her breasts just visible above the water. She sighed and her lips parted, and Andrew imagined what it must feel like to be immersed in that warm water by the fire. And for just an instant he wanted to forget everything and find a way to her room. She might resist him at first, but he would overcome her fears and join her in the tub. Later, he would dry her with a towel, lie her down in front of the fire and . . .

Jack's soft, strangled moan brought him out of his dream and he watched, fascinated by her every move, as she sat up in the tub and reached for the bar of soap.

Her breasts were visible now, gleaming wetly in the fire-lit room. She rubbed the soap between her palms, then set it back in the dish on the table and began to wash her face. Her breasts moved gently, swaying with each movement of her arms. He couldn't tear his eyes away.

She ducked her head underneath the water, wetting her hair. When she came back up, she arched her head so her hair fell cleanly away from her face. As she moved, her breasts thrust forward and Andrew bit the inside of his mouth to keep from making a sound.

For a moment he thought he did moan, then realized it was Richard Trelawny, the Duke of Cuckfield. Though Andrew refused to tear his eyes away from her, he felt a violent anger surge through him at the thought of a man with the Duke's proclivities staring at so lovely a creature.

I have to have her. The thought hit Andrew with the force of a violent storm, ripping through his body and making him aware of his most primal needs. He couldn't bear the thought of another man touching her. For the first time in his adult life, cynicism was overshadowed by intense excitement, caution obliterated by a desire so total it consumed him.

He couldn't even swallow, his throat was so tight. He watched, branding the image in his mind, as she lathered the curls between her legs, then moved her hands over her stomach, her shapely thighs, her slender hips. He moved forward in his chair, wanting to touch her, to take the bar of soap out of her hands and lift her out of the tub. He'd set her on the bed, not caring whether she was wet or not, and slowly part those exquisite thighs, lower himself between her legs, and make her his forever. His eyes narrowed as he thought of all the sensual pleasures he'd teach her once she was his.

When she stepped out of the tub, her back was to them. The maid held up a linen towel and wrapped her in it, then sat her close to the fire to dry her hair.

"That's it, Andrew." Jack's voice was low, and it trembled slightly.

Neither man revealed how he had been affected as they got up and walked down the dark corridor. Andrew didn't even want to look at the other man who had been there. Especially the Duke. Andrew was silent as they continued, but images of the woman he'd seen refused to leave his mind. His manhood was swollen and erect, making movement almost painful. He consciously blanked his mind to thoughts of her and was gratified as he felt his arousal begin to subside.

When both men reached the street, neither looked at the other. What had happened was too powerful for Andrew to joke about. He didn't want to return to the club and have a drink, or waste time in idle talk.

The only thing he wanted was to possess that girl. Completely.

"What time later?" he said, looking Jack in the eye after he swung up onto his black stallion.

"Eight. Janet says she has something special planned for her."

So have I. "I'll be there." He paused for just a second, then said softly, "I mean to have her."

He gathered his reins in his hands and urged the stallion forward, not seeing Jack's amazed expression nor the slow grin that spread across his friend's features.

Chapter Two

Gwyneth sat quietly in her chair in front of the fire as Janet Wickens gave her one last measured look and walked out of the room. The sound of the door shutting had an awful finality.

There was a moment of silence after Janet left, then she heard the door open again. Angel peeked her head around it and gave her a questioning look.

"Are you all right?"

Gwyneth looked away into the fire as tears gathered in her eyes and began to run slowly down her face.

Angel shut the door and darted quickly to her side. She knelt in front of her and took her hand.

"It won't be so bad! Mistress Janet's house is the best in all of London! She only caters to *gentlemen*. Some of them are very nice, and when they see how pretty you are, they won't—"

"Don't. Please." Gwyneth's voice was low and anguished. She pulled away and covered her face with her hands.

How could Edward have done this? Sold her like—like a slave, a horse, an *object*. Janet had supplied the missing memories: how she had ended up at her house, where Edward was.

Did you hate me that much, Cousin? she thought tiredly. *Did you want me out of your life so badly?*

She didn't want to think about what would happen. Janet

had said she had something special planned for her.

It didn't bear thinking about.

"I have to leave this place," she said suddenly, then was surprised when Angel took her shoulders in a firm grip and shook her. Hard.

"You aren't going anywhere!" There was fire in her normally calm brown eyes, and Gwyneth recoiled.

"You wouldn't stop me," she said evenly.

"I would," the maid retorted, lifting her chin.

"You're that loyal to Janet. That determined to see me stay?"

"*Listen to me.*" Angel cupped her face in her hands and forced Gwyneth to meet her serious gaze. "This has nothing to do with the Mistress. Do you have any idea what's out there?" She jerked her hand toward the window and the darkening, purple sky.

"I could find work. . . ."

"After having been inside this house? All the Mistress would have to do is spread the word among her titled friends and nobody would want anything to do with you."

Tears stung Gwyneth's eyes. "I could go back home."

"You have no home. Edward's sold it by now. He wanted you out of the way so he could do what he wanted. Do you understand that?"

"I could—"

"You could do nothing. You are penniless. You have no choice."

Gwyneth's voice broke. "Why are you telling me this?"

Angel opened her mouth then closed it. She glanced away for an instant, then walked over to the window and looked outside at the London skyline, dusky now in early evening.

The fire snapped and hissed, crackling gently. It was the only sound in the room for several minutes before Angel spoke.

"I want to help you, but you must listen to me!" She spread

29

her fingers wide in a gesture of helplessness. "You've been kind to me. You look at me as if there is something inside of me." Angel's deep brown eyes were large and imploring. "There is no escape from this house. Not yet."

"I can't stay here." Gwyneth blinked her eyes rapidly so she wouldn't start to cry again. "Angel, someday I want a husband and a family. Children. A *home*. But I can't have any of that if I stay here."

"Some of the girls have babies." Angel crossed the room and knelt in front of her again. "Listen to me, Gwyn. If you catch one gentleman's eye tonight, he might make you his own. You'd only have to service one man, do you understand? Otherwise, you'll be like Suzanne and some of the others, going from customer to customer and at the mercy of anyone."

"Couldn't you help me escape? I'll come back for you. . . ."

"Bon Dieu, vas-tu m'ecouter!" Angel whirled away and clenched her fists, then turned back and grasped her arm so hard it hurt. "How do you plan to escape? Thatch guards the hallway. Bill, his brother, is at the bottom of the stairs. This room is on the highest floor; if you jump out a window, you'd kill yourself. Janet paid a good price for you and she is not going to let you go!"

Gwyn felt as if she were slowly freezing inside. There had to be a way out of this nightmare. And Angel was her only friend.

The French girl must have seen the fear in her face. Her voice softened.

"Will you listen to me? Will you hear me out before you decide what to do?"

Seeing the genuine concern in her face, Gwyneth slowly nodded.

"I know what people are capable of. I've known since I was a child, because I've been around all types!" Her brown eyes flashed angrily as passion filled her voice. "Most people don't give a damn! And it's worse in the city; you wouldn't last a day. There are people who slit a throat the way you or I buy a chicken.

"My mother died when I was twelve. I had my first man the same year. He put me out on the street, made me work for him and bring back the money. When I didn't make enough, he beat me until I couldn't lie down." Quickly she unfastened her dress and slipped it off her shoulders. "Is this what you want? It's what you will find if you make the streets your home."

Gwyneth sucked in her breath sharply at the ugly scars that crisscrossed the girl's back.

Angel pulled her dress into place and continued talking as she buttoned it. "I tried to run away from him, but he always found me. Each time he swore he'd kill me if I ran again. But I kept running. When I came here, Janet put me to work. You know all I had to trade?"

Gwyneth shook her head, totally immersed in the terrible story.

"This." Angel tugged at her hair. "And this." She smoothed her hands over her breasts and hips. "And it doesn't last long. I knew I had to have protection."

"Angel, I'm sorry."

"I didn't tell you my story to get your pity. Would you be here right now if you had a man's protection? Would your cousin Edward have been able to do this to you?"

"But it's unfair."

"Yes, it's unfair. But it's the way life is."

Gwyneth swallowed, slowly realizing her plans to escape were foolish. Angel was right: She'd grown up in the country, used to a different way of life and surrounded by people who loved her. She'd never survive in London alone.

There was nothing she could do except listen to this woman who had been where she was now—and had survived.

All of the plans she had spun crashed at her feet. Hopeless. Fairy dreams she'd created to keep panic at bay. There was nothing she could do but accept the best of a number of bad choices.

But she couldn't escape.

Gwyneth admitted defeat. Her voice was very quiet as she

31

asked, "What would you do if you were me?"

"First, I'd find out what Mistress Janet has planned for you. And you don't even have to do that, because I already know."

She felt her heart begin to race, a relentless thudding inside her chest. "What?"

"She's going to auction you off. To the highest bidder."

Gwyneth couldn't speak, her throat was so tight with fear.

"No, don't look like that. It means whoever wins you will have money. A lot. And money properly applied can accomplish anything. All my life I've watched it happen."

Gwyneth nodded slowly. "Then what?"

Angel smiled. "I would look beautiful tonight, so the men will go crazy. If Janet gets a high price for you, she'll treat you well.

"And then once I was alone with the man, I'd make sure I kept him happy so he wouldn't give me to anyone else. You *must* have a man's protection."

A rush of color heated her face as she realized the meaning of Angel's words.

"Angel, I—" She put her hand over her mouth and looked up at the woman with agonized eyes. Forcing herself to lower her hand, she spoke the words slowly. "I've never been with a man before."

Angel stared at her, amazed. "How old are you?"

"Seventeen."

"And you've never been with a man?" She sounded incredulous.

"My father . . . he was going to let me pick someone I cared for, and—"

"—and before someone came along, Edward brought you here!" Angel finished her thought for her. "So you have no experience. But that's not a bad thing for a woman, if she is smart."

Gwyneth simply stared. No one had ever talked to her as frankly as Angel had.

"Men!" Angel snapped her fingers and laughed. "They

think they know everything and really they know nothing. They value the woman who is inexperienced in bed. And do you know why? Then she can't tell if he's a bad lover."

Gwyneth was fascinated. "You mean some men are . . . better at . . ." She couldn't say the word, and embarrassment washed over her as she realized just how ignorant she was. Her father had certainly never explained this to her. Her mother had died giving birth to her younger brother when Gwyn was seven. Her infant brother had died within days.

Swiftly, Gwyn found her embarrassment turning to anger. Why hadn't her father prepared her for the world? But as soon as she asked herself the question, she realized the answer. A vicar, he *had* prepared her, as well as he knew how, for the world he had thought she'd be a part of.

Thank God for Angel.

"Some men are not only better—some men are magnificent!"

"Do you—I mean, can a woman enjoy—?" It seemed too personal a question to ask. All her life she had been told the duties of a wife were numerous and never ending. Some—like running a house and raising a family—were considered pleasant. Others—the unmentionable things that went on behind bedroom doors—were simply parts of life to be endured.

Love had been the one blessing Gwyn had counted on to make her transition from girl to woman easier. She had wondered what her bridal night would be like but had never confided these thoughts to anyone.

Angel didn't seem offended by her question. "With the right man. And we have to make sure you get the right man to buy you! Someone with a lot of money, powerful enough to get you out of here. And someone who is good to you when you're in bed so your life has some fun. Someone who won't beat you." Her eyes twinkled devilishly. "I'll teach you some tricks that will make the man *your* slave forever. We'll make you so irresistible he won't know what kind of a spell you've cast over him!"

Gwyneth stared at the fire as she tried to digest all this. Her old life, less than a week ago, was so far away from what this evening would bring.

Andrew lay alone in his bed, thinking about the woman he had seen bathing. The room was quiet, the only sound the soft snapping of the fire. The light from the flames danced across the ceiling. He stared at it, desperate for anything to get his mind off such sensual torment.

He had never felt as strongly about any woman. While growing up, he'd discovered at an early age the effect he had on the opposite sex, and he'd used it to his advantage. But never cruelly. Only with women who knew exactly what was expected. And what was expected was a torrid affair, weeks of splendid lovemaking. But no emotional entanglements.

He knew most of London society watched him, eager to see what outrageous thing he would do next. It was only to be expected, what with the parents he'd had.

There was a portrait of his father and mother at his grandfather's home, but he never looked at it long. He couldn't bear to remember. There had been years when he'd run wild as a young boy, his father dead, his mother locked away.

He didn't want to remember. But it pressed at his consciousness. The unearthly screaming. The supernatural power in her slender fingers, the wild look on his mother's face. And blood. Blood everywhere . . .

He shut his eyes, willing his emotions back under control. Afterwards, once everyone knew and had talked and speculated and been delighted by the tragedy, his grandfather had come for him. After some legal manipulations, Henry had adopted him.

Thus had begun one of the most trying times of his life. As his grandfather tried to "civilize him," as he'd called it, Andrew had resisted every effort. He had run wild through

London, shocking most proper people with his willful antics. No one had looked at the young boy closely enough to see that his incredible energy masked an equally incredible pain.

Jack had been his only close friend. The runt of the litter, fragile and light-haired, the smallest of twelve children, they had met when Andrew saw him being beaten up by a boy twice his size. Two years older than Jack and much stronger, Andrew had been eager to get into another fight. Anything to diffuse the emotions constantly tearing at him. He'd pulled the boy off Jack and beat the bully senseless.

If his relationship with Jack was more hero worship than a true meeting of equals as young men, by the time they both reached their twenties they'd caught up with each other. Jack tried to understand his moods, to joke him out of them. Andrew gave him the Dutch courage to have a few escapades of his own.

Like today, he thought, and another image of the golden-haired woman flitted into his memory.

He groaned and rolled over in bed, pressing his body against the hot sheets. He couldn't get her out of his mind. Exquisite. Lovely to look at. But better still to touch, to hold, to kiss and caress . . .

This woman had reached him. On a purely sensual, visual level, she had reached inside and taken hold of his deepest feelings and pulled them out of him, exposing them for his inspection.

Go there. Buy her. Spend a night with her until both of you are so exhausted you can't even stand. Just get her out of your system.

He rolled over again and stared at the ceiling, then kicked off the covers until only a thin sheet remained on his body. Glancing down, he saw what he'd felt all evening. He could make out a faint outline of his swollen manhood beneath the linen.

He stretched his body, trying to relax. But it seemed his body wasn't his own; no matter how much he resisted the sensual onslaught of her memory it slipped back into his consciousness. Intruding where he didn't want intrusion, making him fully aroused, hard, and uncomfortable.

Go to Belinda. She'll be more than happy to rid you of that. But he didn't want her. He wanted the woman with the golden hair, high, full breasts, slender thighs. He wanted to roll her beneath him, pin her to the bed and take her, again and again, until he ceased to want her. He didn't like the hold she had over his senses, even in memory.

Closing his eyes, he gave up. He moved his hand down his body until his fingers closed around the rigid shaft. The skin was so tender to his touch that his back arched slightly and a groan burst forth from his lips. He waited until his racing heart calmed slightly, then he began to move his hand slowly up and down his aching flesh.

While he touched himself, he imagined it was her. He saw her, bending over his body, her skin glowing with reflected firelight. She teased him with her mane of golden hair, then lowered her head and kissed him intimately. Again and again she touched him, with fingers and mouth, until he was an aching mass of need.

His breathing deepened as he imagined her, his fingers gripped tighter. He could see himself catching that golden mass in his fingers, gently pulling her mouth to him to love him intimately. Then, before the inevitable, he'd pull her up, circle her slender hips with his hands, and position her over him. He would arch his body up and she would be open, moist, and inviting. He would bury himself inside her and she would gasp as he filled her. Her eyes would open, her lips would part, and her moans would excite him further.

Then he would slide in and out of her tight, warm wetness. And she would answer him, move for move, her silken hips undulating against his. Their passion would burn brighter and hotter than he'd ever experienced. She would call out his name when she reached her climax, a sound of pure erotic need.

The thought was all he needed. A ragged moan escaped him, his hips arching as he climaxed powerfully. Then he lay in bed, perfectly still, utterly spent as his breathing and heartbeat slowly returned to normal.

After taking care of his needs, he settled back among the sheets and closed his eyes, consciously breathing evenly. Sleep would come now that he was relaxed. He had needed the release his fantasy afforded him.

He had been shocked he could respond so deeply to a fantasy. If this were what happened when he thought of her, what would truly possessing her be like?

A small smile played around his lips. *You'll find out later*, he thought as he drifted off to sleep.

On that same night, Angel and Gwyn continued to talk and plan.

"Tell me what you know, Gwyn. About what goes on between a man and a woman."

"I've been kissed before," she ventured.

"That's all?" Angel made a face. "*Merde*, I'm making you more nervous. Did your mother never tell you anything?"

"My mother died when I was seven."

"Oh." Angel paused for a moment, then said, "Your father didn't tell you either?"

Gwyneth grimaced. "He said I would find out everything I needed to know on my wedding night."

"Then we'll start at the beginning. I'm going to tell you all of it. Stop me if I talk too fast." Angel took a deep breath. "Most men are the same. First they'll kiss you and tell you how beautiful you are and how much they love you. That's so you'll let them do things to you. Of course, if he's bought you for the night, he won't tell you anything except what to do. Most of the time they won't kiss you. They want to touch you all over, especially your breasts and between your legs.

"Men are much more . . . emotional than women. They can be ruled by what is between their legs. Do you know what I'm talking about?"

"I think I do," Gwyn replied.

Gwyn closed her eyes, trying to block out the thoughts running rampant through her mind. How could she lie naked with him and feel anything but shame?

"It sounds horrible." She didn't bother trying to hide the slight quiver in her voice.

"It can be. Because half the time he's finished before you're even started and most of the time all he cares about is how *he* feels; he doesn't give a damn whether you're having a good time of it."

"Is there more?"

Angel was silent for a long moment, then replied, "There are other things, but I think with you being a virgin and all—and I'm sure the Mistress is going to let everyone know because you'll fetch a higher price—whoever buys you won't expect more than what I told you."

"Does it hurt when—when he—?"

"It can hurt the first time. But everyone's different. Let him know you've never been with a man before."

"Angel, I don't think I can do this." Gwyneth could feel her stomach starting to twist as panic engulfed her.

"Yes you can," she replied comfortingly. "Every woman is scared her first time."

She couldn't answer. So much had happened, so much had to be learned. It was frightening. And exhausting.

Angel was almost out the door before Gwyneth remembered what she'd wanted to ask her all day.

"Angel?"

"Hmm?" She stopped, her hand on the door.

"What can I do for you? I feel like you're giving so much to me and I'm not giving anything in return."

"Gwyneth, you're not going to be here forever. I can smell it. When you go, I want you to take me with you."

"I will."

"Ah, *mon pauvre tresor*, have courage. Things are not as bad as they seem. You will survive this, and much more." Giving

38

her a smile and a wink, Angel hurried out the door.

She watched Angel until the door closed softly behind her, then slid down underneath the covers.

Damn you, Edward, for doing this to me. All her life, Gwyn had been taught to love and trust, to depend upon others for her safety. Now, as each day passed, adjustments in her thinking and feeling were taking place. A wariness was replacing her openness, a different way of thinking was beginning to form. She never fully relaxed as her mind tried to make sense of how quickly her fortune had changed.

When her restless thoughts stilled and her eyes finally closed, the first morning light was breaking softly over the rooftops.

Chapter Three

Friday morning breakfast at his grandfather's was a weekly obligation for Andrew. Sometimes he considered making his excuses, but he knew the older man would miss him. Still, he considered it an ordeal—his grandfather didn't mince words where his conduct was concerned.

"What's the matter with you, Andrew? You haven't heard a word I've said!" Henry Hawkesworth, Duke of Drummond, was a formidable figure at sixty-three. He possessed keen grey-blue eyes, bushy white brows, a sharp blade of a nose, and a strong jawline. Though the skin on his face sagged slightly with age, his movements were spry and alert, his wits fully about him. In his better moods, he'd tease Andrew about what a handful he'd been and how it was a wonder they were both still alive. Nevertheless, the old man's gruffness concealed a great deal of love.

"I'm sorry, Grandfather. I—I haven't been sleeping well."

"Belinda been keeping you up?" The bushy brows drew together in a scowl.

"I haven't seen Belinda since Tuesday."

"And I'd be a lot happier if you didn't see that lightskirt at all!" His grandfather's fist hit the mahogany table with a resounding thump. "Damn it all, Andrew, you can't be serious about marrying that . . . woman."

"Surely you misunderstand her, Grandfather," Andrew replied, sarcasm heavy in his voice.

"I understand that little fortune hunter better than you think. She'd give me the eye if she thought she could gain from it. You're the last of this family, not that that probably means anything to you. . . ."

"You're right, it doesn't." Andrew deftly speared a muffin with his knife and broke it open, then generously spread it with butter and strawberry jam.

"You can't be in earnest, Andrew! Whatever you think, it means something to me!" Henry warmed to his subject, his grey-blue eyes sharp. "She hasn't borne a child yet! Have you given thought to the possibility she might be barren?"

"I have no desire to become a father."

"Damnation, why won't you take your responsibilities seriously? I want a great-grandson! I need to know this family will continue after I am gone!" Henry took a deep breath, his face flushed with anger. "You're twenty-two years old, Andrew, and it's high time you thought of your duty to this family and started acting like a man instead of a fool!"

Andrew calmly bit into his muffin. He did possess a deep sense of family honor and duty, though he would rather die than admit this to Henry. Yet his deepest emotions violently rejected the idea of a home and family for himself. The marriages he had seen had been miserable, painful affairs for both parties involved. He did not want to love that way, to open his heart to more hurt. He had had enough heartbreak for his lifetime.

Belinda would not break his heart. Waking up some mornings feeling empty was a small price to pay compared to uncontrolled emotions he wanted no part of.

There were times he felt all his feelings, indeed his entire heart, had been used up. There was nothing left.

Yet his moods shifted, mercurial and intense. He yearned for something more. The golden-haired girl at the Dark Stallion slipped into his thoughts once again. He had felt

41

passionately alive when he had looked at her.

Realizing his grandfather was staring at him, Andrew pushed the girl out of his thoughts. Tonight he would have her. He would charm her, make love to her, explore these feelings. It would certainly be a pleasurable night.

He took his time eating because he knew it irritated Henry. And he wanted to irritate his grandfather because he was making him uncomfortable. Henry's tirades always forced him to look deeply at his life. Most of the time, he didn't like what he saw.

"I suppose you'll be seeing the illustrious Belinda this weekend? Well, do give her my warmest regards before you give her a tumble." Henry snorted inelegantly and reached for his teacup.

"As a matter of fact, no, I won't be seeing her."

The bushy brows rose. "What are you up to, Andrew?"

"Jack and I are going to the Dark Stallion tonight."

"Well, at least you're finding your whores in a whorehouse as opposed to trying to make one your wife!" When Andrew didn't reply, the older man asked, "Is there some special reason you're going? Or are you just trying to irritate me further?"

Andrew set down his teacup and smiled. "Jack wants to go. One last fling before my marriage, you know how it goes."

"No, I don't. I wasn't as familiar with my bride-to-be as you've been with yours. In fact, I don't believe I did anything in my life with the particular . . . finesse you've given over to yours." Henry glowered for a moment, then continued. "What does Jack have to say about your fiancée?"

"Anyone that makes me happy is fine with him."

Henry stared at his grandson for a long moment. Their gazes met, eyes and features so much alike, before the older man said softly, "She won't make you happy, Andrew. She doesn't care about anything except your money. You'll probably end up raising someone else's brats. She's not the woman for you. Why you persist in carrying on this sham of an engagement is beyond my comprehension."

"Maybe I don't want to care too deeply," Andrew replied with feigned nonchalance. "Maybe I like my life just the way it is."

His grandfather scraped back his chair sharply, rose, and tossed his linen napkin next to his china plate.

"Then you're a damn fool. And a coward." His voice was close to shaking. "I never thought it would come to this, but I'm ashamed to call you my grandson. Go on and consort with your whores, but don't expect me to be happy for you." Henry's voice trembled. "Make no mistake about my feelings, Andrew. I want a grandson, but not one born on the wrong side of the blanket!" And without another word, he left the dining room.

Andrew stared at the delicate rim of gold around the china plate in front of him as he heard his grandfather's heavy tread up the stairs. When a door slammed upstairs, he got up slowly and walked out.

Gwyneth sat in front of the fire while Angel slowly combed her wet hair. Even sitting this close to the flames, she couldn't seem to warm her body. She hadn't slept at all last night, despite the large goblet of wine with her dinner. She'd tossed and turned, knowing it was her last night sleeping alone in her virginal bed.

"Stop fidgeting," Angel commanded quietly. "You're beginning to make me nervous."

"I can't help it." Gwyneth bit her lip, then burst out, "Promise me you'll watch the auction and see who purchases me."

"I promise."

"And if he's truly horrible, you'll think of some way—"

"I promise." Angel continued to comb her hair even though most of the tangles had been worked out. Gwyneth found both her presence and touch comforting. Angel's steady common sense and faith were all that stood between her and total panic.

Earlier, Janet had brought costume after costume into the bedroom and had Gwyn parade in front of her. A shepherdess with a full skirt and staff, a vestal virgin, a sultry temptress. Finally, after draping and tucking several yards of fine white silk in a Grecian style around Gwyn's body, Janet had decided she was fit to auction off.

Gwyneth had been horrified. The silk clung to her curves, to the slight roundness of her stomach, and to her long legs. To her high, full breasts. Her feet were bare, her ankles visible! The expensive cloth was nearly transparent, and she was sure every man would be able to see her body as clearly as if she were naked.

It was too much to bear.

Even though Angel had promised to do what she could, Gwyneth knew her influence was severely limited.

This was something that, ultimately, she would have to face alone.

"Your hair is dry. Mistress Janet wants me to braid some of it around your head and weave in these ribbons."

Gwyneth nodded, staring dully ahead. What a mockery this was. Dressed in white, her hair adorned with silken ribbons. A woman her age should be getting ready for her wedding to the man she truly loved. Instead, she was preparing herself for a night with a total stranger.

She couldn't possibly come out of this experience without being changed forever.

The large room downstairs was ablaze with hundreds of candles. The overpowering smell of burning wax and strong cologne filled Gwyneth's nostrils, making her stomach tighten as if she were going to be sick. Her heart pounded so rapidly she thought her body had to be shaking with the force of it. Her hands and feet felt like ice, her breath was shallow and rapid.

She didn't look at any of the men, though she knew the room

was filled with eager spectators. But it was more than the simple presence of bodies in a space. There was something in the air. A sense of heightened expectation. The smell of excitement.

Gwyneth listened as two whores were auctioned off. Janet had a sense of the perverse. She had hired an actual auctioneer, and his voice was quick and assured as he handled the bidding. There was much bawdy humor, the laughter raucous and coarse. She closed her eyes each time the women squealed, and she knew the men who had bid the highest had come up to the small stage and dragged the women down.

For the fleetest of seconds, hatred burned in her breast. Hatred toward Edward for exposing her to this sort of world and leaving her so vulnerable. Hatred toward Janet for taking advantage of her. Hatred toward all men secure within their smugly satisfied little worlds. Worlds that allowed such things to take place.

The instant before the short, pudgy auctioneer took her arm and helped her up on stage, her eyes met Janet's. Gwyneth gazed deeply into the large green eyes with all the hatred she could muster.

And she had the small satisfaction of seeing Janet look away.

Then she was standing in front of all of them. Her legs started to tremble, but she remembered Angel's advice and locked her knees. Taking a deep, shuddering breath, she looked up above the crowd and fixed her gaze on the brightest candles on the far side of the wall.

Don't let them break you. She smiled a secret inner smile and let the noise and confusion, the blood lust and the scent of burning candles and expensive cologne fade from her consciousness. She looked to the light and silently prayed that Angel would find a way to help her.

"One hundred pounds!" said a portly gentleman in the far corner, raising his hand slightly. The fingers glinted, his rings flashing in the candlelight. The auctioneer acknowledged his bid with a nod of his head.

"One hundred pounds. Do I hear two?"

Andrew watched the golden-haired woman carefully. He'd bid at auctions before, bid for horses and furniture, paintings and crystal. His grandfather had trained him well. He knew how to let an auction run its course, knew to remain quiet until the serious bidding commenced.

She was superb. Full of courage. While the other whores had simpered and played to the crowd, she stood perfectly still. He was sure she had no idea how striking she looked, the candlelight glinting off her hair, the sheer silk moulding itself to her body in a way that fired the lust of every man in the crowded room.

As the bidding continued, fast and furious, he noticed Janet sitting in back of the crowd. Her arms were crossed, her smile satisfied. Andrew was sure she knew when she had an audience under her control.

"Five hundred pounds." The words rang out, the voice deep and clear. A voice used to giving orders.

Richard Trelawny, the Duke of Cuckfield. In his late twenties, he looked older. The slight lines carved in his handsome face were a silent testament to the depravity that had completely ruled his life. His blond hair was lightly sprinkled with silver, his grey eyes were without a hint of kindess. His gaze was fixated on the golden-haired woman.

Andrew knew the Duke to be a man of bizarre and insatiable sexual tastes. Though the Duke had invited him to many of his social gatherings, Andrew had never attended. He knew exactly what happened at those private affairs, and he wanted no part of it. When he thought of taking a tumble with a woman, it had never included anything but the most sensual side of lovemaking.

The Duke's lovers were well-known. They were the ones with bruises on their bodies. The ones with empty, vacant eyes. There were several young women who had never been heard from again.

"Six hundred," Andrew called out, his voice firm and authoritative. The crowd fell silent, everyone shocked he should bid against such a powerful man.

"Do I hear seven?" the auctioneer asked.

"Seven," the Duke answered quietly.

So the true bidding has begun. Andrew smiled grimly. He certainly wasn't going to let the Duke have his way with her.

"Seven hundred and fifty," Andrew replied. The other men in the room had stopped bidding, none of them wanting to take on the Duke. But their love of gambling still won out, and private bets were quickly placed as to whether the Duke of Cuckfield or the Earl of Scarborough would win the golden-haired beauty.

"Eight hundred." The Duke was beginning to look annoyed. Absolute silence filled the room.

"Eight hundred and fifty," Andrew called, quick to answer the bid. He looked at Jack and winked. His friend looked worried.

"Nine hundred pounds," the Duke replied. Andrew could tell by the tightening of his jaw that his adversary was highly displeased. Thus it gave him great pleasure to quickly answer the man and thwart his intentions.

"One thousand pounds."

The crowd began to buzz, unable to contain its excitement. Andrew was instantly gratified to see the golden-haired woman meet his gaze. Her expression was haughty, but there was something in her eyes . . . He gave her a slow smile and she looked quickly away.

A hush fell over the room as the auctioneer waited, gavel upraised. Janet's eyes glistened. The candles cast flickering shadows across the richly paneled room.

And all heads turned toward the two men.

One thousand pounds. God in heaven, what kind of man paid

that sum of money for a night's pleasure?

She glanced quickly at the gentleman who had uttered the words. Alive blue eyes, thick, well-cut black hair, a straight nose and strong jaw. The thrust of his chin was determined. She could imagine him a pirate or a highwayman. He had a ruthless quality about him, as if he let nothing stand in his way.

Then he smiled. Slowly.

Bastard. She glanced away from him, toward Angel. When their eyes met, Angel nodded her head almost imperceptively and smiled.

"One thousand pounds. Do I hear eleven hundred?" The auctioneer was sweating profusely and had to keep pushing his spectacles back up the bridge of his bulbous nose.

"One thousand five hundred pounds," commanded a deep, threatening voice.

Gwyneth closed her eyes, trying to still her violently pounding heart. She recognized the deep, raspy voice from the bidding that had swirled around her. She glanced quickly at Angel again. Slowly, the maid shook her head, her liquid eyes filled with a deep fear.

Gwyneth directed her glance toward that commanding voice and looked into the coldest pair of grey eyes she'd ever seen in her life.

They looked so familiar. Who was he? And if she did know him, why was she so afraid?

"Please don't let the Duke have her."

Andrew barely heard the slightly accented, whispered words. When he glanced down, he encountered a petite girl in a blue maid's uniform and white apron, carrying a tray of drinks. But her urgent eyes were fixed on his face.

He thought quickly, then slid a ruby ring off his finger and handed it to her.

"Take this to your Mistress. Mind you tell her I'll pay the money tonight. In full." Then he turned to Jack, standing at his side.

"She's a sweet, little thing," his friend murmured, staring after the departing girl.

"How much money do you have on you?" Andrew asked abruptly.

"Your grandfather will flog you for this one, Andrew." Jack sighed in resignation. "You must know this indulgence will be all over London by tonight."

"How much?"

Jack had a comically pained expression on his face as he reached into his pocket. "Never let it be said I didn't warn you."

Andrew's attention focused on the dark-haired maid. He watched as she reached Janet's side, whispered urgently in the woman's ear, and slipped the ring into her hand. The madam's green eyes narrowed as she began to walk determinedly toward the auctioneer.

"Sold!" the pudgy man declared. "For one thousand five hundred pounds, to the Duke of Cuckfield."

But before the Duke could shoulder the crowd aside and claim his prize, Janet reached the small stage.

"I want my money tonight," she declared, her hands on her hips.

The Duke's gaze was riveted on the young woman swathed in thin silk. "I'll send my man by in the morning with a draft from the bank," he said, addressing Janet as if she were a bothersome fly.

"No. Tonight." Janet was adamant, and as Andrew watched her, he began to grin. The Duke had many enemies; it was unusual for the man to carry much money. He had extensive credit in all the private clubs and gambling halls. But not with Janet.

Thank God for the little Frenchie. She'd planted just enough doubt in Janet's mind.

"This isn't like you, Janet." Now the Duke was plying his charm. But Janet wouldn't be budged.

49

"I agree. Because this is a very unusual situation. The girl is exquisite—worth coin of the realm, not a piece of paper."

"I'll send my man—" he began imperiously.

"Tonight," she replied, her dark green eyes flashing.

The Duke glanced around nervously, and Andrew knew he was studying the two men standing at the double doors. Janet employed the giants as bouncers. They were enormous, and both had the cropped ears of convicted felons, making them look like vicious fighting dogs. They were well over six feet tall and heavily muscled—and would do anything for Janet.

Up to and including disposing of the Duke.

The crowd was silent, eagerly waiting to see what would happen next.

"Do you have my money or not?" Janet asked quietly.

Angrily, the Duke turned and began to walk through the tightly packed crowd. Voices rose and the noise swelled, filling the room as the angry man moved closer and closer to Andrew.

The auctioneer cleared his throat and banged his gavel to indicate he wanted silence. "The previous bid was for one thousand pounds, by the Earl of Scarborough."

In answer, Andrew deftly tossed a pouch over the heads of the crowd and straight to Janet.

She opened it and quickly checked its contents. Satisfied, she indicated Gwyneth's silently standing form with a graceful hand.

"To the victor goes the spoils!" Her green eyes sparkled and her color was high.

But Andrew, knowing the Duke would want a word with him, waited until the man reached his side, then gazed into those cool, detached eyes. There was a moment of intense silence, but Andrew didn't look away.

"I want her when you've finished." The Duke's voice was slightly raspy, and Andrew knew what it had cost him to lose stature in front of the other men.

"If it pleases you to think so—" He let the words trail off, then watched as the Duke walked quickly out the door. One of the cropped-eared servants followed him, and Andrew was amazed by the grace the huge man exhibited.

"You've displeased him," Jack murmured at his elbow.

Andrew shrugged. "I expect I'll do so again." Then he smiled. "But she's mine now. I won her, didn't I?"

"And emptied my pockets," Jack grumbled.

Andrew clapped him on the back and laughed. "I'll see you get your money back—with interest."

Jack smiled. "Well, go to her then. I'm sure you're already thinking of more interesting things to do than talk to me!"

Andrew fixed his gaze on the woman still standing on the stage, her delicate hands clasped tightly in front of her.

"You're right about that, Jack." He squeezed his friend's arm briefly. "I'll see you in the morning for our ride, hmm?"

"If you don't wear yourself out riding tonight." There was a hint of amusement in his friend's voice.

But Andrew didn't hear his friend. He was already striding toward the stage.

She had wanted to die. When she faced those cruel grey eyes and thought of being alone in a room with a man like that, Gwyneth almost turned and fled.

But the situation changed rapidly. Suddenly Gwyn realized she was at the mercy of the man who was striding toward the stage.

He was tall and well-muscled. She remembered the look in his vivid blue eyes, as if he knew full well what she looked like without any clothes.

Then he was standing beside her, swinging her up into his strong arms. She tightened her body, tried to shrink away from the warmth and hardness of him, but he jostled her slightly until she fell against him, her fingers splayed on his chest for balance. She could feel the strong, steady beat of his heart. Her other hand gripped his arm tightly. Gwyn closed her eyes, not wanting to think about what awaited her.

51

"Janet." His voice was deep and resonant. The sound sent a peculiar trembling to Gwyneth's stomach and she didn't dare open her eyes.

She could smell the expensive floral scent Janet wore and knew she was near.

"I won't be paying one thousand pounds for one night." She held her breath.

"She's yours until you tire of her, then. Angelique will show you to a room, and I'll send supper up."

Gwyn felt the air rush against her bare skin as he walked swiftly out of the room. His fingers seemed to burn against her body, right through the thin silk covering. Gwyneth thought of fighting him, but the silk covering her was wrapped and tucked precariously. She didn't dare chance it coming undone.

Gwyn opened her eyes as he started up the stairs. She saw Angel walking swiftly in front of them, a brace of candles in her hands lighting the way. He carried her higher and higher, to the top floor. They continued on until Angel turned down still another silent hall and stopped in front of a door.

"The fire's lit, sir. Supper will be up directly."

"Thank you, Angelique, for all you did tonight."

Angel smiled shyly, then walked rapidly down the hall away from them. Gwyneth felt him loosen his hold on her. *Now. It's all going to happen now. This night.* Though Angel had smiled, given her approval of this dark stranger, Gwyn's stomach twisted in fear. She grabbed his arm to keep from falling, then felt herself sliding slowly down the entire length of his hard, muscular body.

Once she was set gently on her feet in front of him, she trembled. He was taller, and she concentrated on looking at his chest. His coat and breeches were expensive; she could tell by the cut and quality of the material. But what was beneath frightened her. Gwyn sensed firm muscles, barely leashed male power. The way he had bid for her had shown a strong will determined to have its way.

She started as she felt one steely arm go around her waist,

then his warm hand cupped her chin. He lifted it just enough so their eyes met. His were dark. Appraising. Filled with an expression she knew instinctively was desire.

"Hello, my beauty." His voice was soft. Husky. For her ears alone. Gwyn began to tremble as he slowly lowered his lips to hers and claimed her as his own.

Book II

"As a teacher you'll find me demanding—
Though never, I trust, find me cruel.
But I'll teach you to leave no man standing
Should he give you a challenge to duel."

Chapter Four

His kiss was overpowering, his lips hard and warm against hers, asking for a response. Gwyn was stiff at first, resisting, but as his lips coaxed hers, she softened slightly. He drew her gently against the length of his body. His chest was hard and warm beneath her fingertips, and she could feel the strong thudding of his heart, faster now than when he had carried her up the stairs.

He was coaxing her again, his mouth very gentle, and something elusive in that first kiss made her want to surrender, to simply give in and let him take her on a maelstrom of desire and senseless wanting.

He finished the kiss and kept her close to him. She buried her face against his chest, loathe to look in his eyes and find triumph, dominance—or worse, laughter—in their blue depths. That one kiss had taught her much: He knew what he wanted and let nothing stand in his way. This dark man would be a dangerous adversary, and she could not stop what was to happen.

She kept her eyes lowered as he opened the door to their private room, avoiding his gaze as he placed a firm hand on the small of her back and urged her inside.

She watched him as he walked over to the fire and warmed

his hands. He moved with a fluid grace, and his shadow danced on the wall. Gwyn remained by the door. If she could stay out of his reach, he could delay the inevitable.

"Come here." The words were a command, but his voice was soft. She glanced quickly at him, then looked away. Adjusting the thin white silk against her body, Gwyn padded silently toward him. Barefoot, her feet made no sound on the thick carpet.

A furious blush raced up from her breasts and suffused her throat and face as he silently studied her. The silk wrapped around her naked body was an inadequate covering, and she crossed her arms in front of her breasts.

"What is your name?" he asked.

She hadn't expected that. Her head snapped up, and she met his gaze steadily for the first time. She thought of not answering, then realized if he knew her name, she would be more a flesh and blood woman and less an object.

"Gwyneth," she said softly, her throat still tight with fear.

"Gwyneth?" He smiled slightly, and she caught her breath at the astonishing change in his face. An inner light illuminated his eyes, an inner warmth softened the harsh lines. "It's very pretty. It suits you."

"Thank you . . . my Lord."

"Gwyneth what? That can't be all."

She glanced away, reluctant to reveal her surname and sully her family's honor. "All who know me call me Gwyn."

The silence lengthened, and she knew he was watching her. Studying her. Her body was tense, tight as a bowstring. Unable to endure the silence and the strange feeling that stretched between them, she asked softly, "And yours?"

"Andrew."

She faced him then, backing up as she talked. "Andrew what? There must be something more."

"Just Andrew." His answer seemed to mock hers.

"Andrew." She said his name softly, and something in his eyes told her the sound of it on her tongue gave him great pleasure.

She wondered what to say to this man. What to do. Was she expected to simply throw off her clothing and bounce into the bed? Did he expect her to take off his clothing?

"Andrew, I—"

She was spared revealing her ignorance by a soft knock at the door.

"Come in," Andrew said, and Gwyn was astonished at the change in his voice. This man was used to giving orders and having them obeyed.

Angel appeared silently, a tray loaded with food in her hands. She walked quickly into the room and placed their supper on a small table in front of the fire. She curtsied to Andrew, and when she spoke, her tone was low and deferential.

"Mistress Janet asked me to come and prepare Gwyn for you, my Lord. She will be down directly with some wine, then you will be left alone as you desire."

Andrew nodded, and Gwyn felt Angel take her hand. Her fingers were very warm, and it took Gwyn a moment to realize it was because her own were like ice.

Angel led her behind a screen and, once there, began to unwind and untuck the length of silk. Once Gwyn was naked, she took a wrapper made of rich red silk lavished with lace and held it up.

"Put this on, Gwyn."

Feeling like a puppet she had once seen at a fair, as if her arms were operated by strings, Gwyn slid into the wrapper and Angel tied the sash.

"Sit down. I will loosen your hair."

Gwyn felt Angel's deft fingers unbraiding and brushing until her hair fell around her shoulders and down her back like a golden, gleaming cape. She closed her eyes, wishing with all her heart that she could follow Angel out that door and be done with this entire night.

"Oh, Angel," she whispered. "I would welcome my own demise."

Angel's fingers tensed, pulling her hair slightly and making her wince. "Gwyn." Angel relaxed her hands, then smoothed her palms over the masses of golden hair. "Don't forget your most powerful weapon. You are so very beautiful. What a happy man Andrew will be when he makes a woman of you."

"But I can't—"

"Don't be afraid." Angel's voice was the slightest sound, so it wouldn't carry. "Andrew is a good man; he has no problems with pleasuring women. If you tell him the truth, that you've never been with a man before, he'll be gentle. He's very attracted to you. He'll listen."

A measure of calm began to fill Gwyn's body. Angel would never betray her.

"Will you come to me . . . as soon as he leaves? I—" She stopped, unable to go on.

"I will help you in any way I can, Gwyn." Angel paused as she heard a slight squeaking from the sofa as Andrew shifted his position. Then she turned back toward Gwyn and gave her a fierce hug.

"You'll survive this, Gwyn. At least you aren't out on the street with some brute." She stepped back and put a finger to her lips.

"Now we've got to be quiet and we've got to hurry. I've got one more thing to teach you or you'll be a mother by summer and we can't have that!"

Janet paced her sitting room furiously, her spaniels at her heels. She couldn't banish the final image of Gwyn's face. When the girl had stared at her before stepping up on the stage to be auctioned off, Janet had seen trouble in those eyes.

She won't submit. She'll put up a fight and then you'll be out one thousand pounds. Not to mention the Earl of Scarborough. He'll never frequent the Dark Stallion again, and if he should get word to his friends . . .

All of London's most powerful men had been at the auction

tonight, and for them to find out Janet Wickens auctioned off unwilling girls who gave paying customers the fight of their lives would destroy the business she had worked these many years to build, the business she had nurtured as tenderly as a child.

The girl had to be willing. I should have let Cuckfield have her; he would have taught her who was master.

But Andrew, as good a lover as he is, has a soft spot for a pretty girl. He might listen to her nonsense. . . . He might even believe it.

She had to do something to insure Gwyn's submission. Desperate times called for desperate measures, and Janet never hesitated.

She crossed the length of the room, to an ornately carved Chinese cupboard. The key hung on a gold chain around her neck. No one knew of her knowledge of herbs and the various elixirs she could create. People were too hysterical these days, especially since the damn Methodists had brought up all that witchcraft nonsense again.

Janet carefully unlocked the black and gold cupboard and quickly surveyed the small bottles neatly lined up and carefully labeled. Running her fingers along the smooth wooden shelves, she searched for one particular bottle. Finding it, she went over to her desk where she had already poured two crystal goblets of her finest wine.

Once in a great while she partook, as this elixir had the power to excite the body and inflame the senses. If she took one drop, she was guaranteed a wild night of endless lovemaking before she was finally satiated. She had experimented with two and been told she'd been insatiable, begging for release.

Janet poised the small bottle over the two goblets, and in her mind's eye she saw Gwyn's face. There had been hatred in those beautiful blue eyes. Hatred and contempt.

Don't be so quick to judge me, miss. When your luck runs out, you'll find yourself capable of deeds you never suspected.

With a steady hand, she put one drop in Andrew's goblet. Then she poised the bottle over Gwyn's and counted softly to herself.

"One, two, three. That's my present to you, Miss Leighton. Let it be a night you remember for the rest of your life."

When Gwyn came out from behind the screen, Janet and Andrew were sitting in front of the fire. When Gwyn came up beside him, he motioned her to sit next to him on the sofa.

"Drink your wine," Angel whispered, giving her arm a final pat. "It will help relax you."

Gwyn took a sip. It was sweet, with an aromatic flavor she had never tasted before.

Janet stood up. "If there is anything you need, Andrew, you have only to ring." And she walked out the door, Angel behind her.

Gwyn turned her head and looked at Andrew. They were alone now, and she felt ill at ease and never more aware of her own inexperience.

Desperately wishing she could be any place but where she was, she met Andrew's gaze. What she saw there unnerved her further. Without conscious thought, she drained the last of her wine and set the goblet down.

Angel was halfway down the stairs when Janet's voice stopped her.

"What were you whispering to Gwyn?"

She turned slowly. "Mistress, I merely suggested she drink her wine, as it would help her relax."

"And why, pray tell, would she need to relax?"

Angel took a deep breath. "She's a virgin, and I thought if she had a little to drink, it might go easier with her."

To her complete surprise, Janet smiled.

"You've done very well, Angelique. You may take the rest of the night off. I'll have Peg attend to the extra work."

"Thank you, Mistress." Angel hurried off, but her mind

raced furiously. Had Janet truly not known Gwyn was a virgin? And why should a glass of wine make that much difference?

Why would it make Janet smile?

Janet watched her maid leave, feeling victorious. But she still had work to do. Andrew could suspect nothing until the night was over. Then it would certainly be too late.

One of the reasons Janet had purchased this particular house was the intricate maze of tunnels and catwalks built between the walls. She knew a particular walkway ran behind the room now occupied by Andrew and Gwyn. She would watch them, to make sure everything went smoothly.

But first she had to talk to Andrew.

He was stroking her cheek with two of his fingers. Gwyn swallowed, amazed her blood rushed so hotly beneath her skin, growing warmest where he touched her. Their dinner was untouched. They would not be dining this night.

Andrew shifted on the couch, pressing her into its soft depths. He was going to kiss her. Trusting Angel, she wanted to tell him her predicament.

"Andrew, I—"

She was interrupted by a slight tapping.

Andrew swore softly as he sat up, then strode quickly toward the door, where Janet motioned him to follow her into the hallway.

Gwyn sat back against the couch. Would he believe her? Would he be gentle?

The room was very hot, and she thought of rising and walking away from the fire, but her arms and legs were curiously languorous. A swift heat seemed to be filling her body, swelling it and making her skin feel tender.

She leaned her head back against the couch and sighed. It had to be her extreme agitation, making her senses come alive like this. She seemed aware of everything, of the feel of the silken brocade underneath her, the sensuous warmth of her wrapper. Her bare feet curled into the thick carpet, delighting in the exquisite sensation. She closed her eyes and breathed deeply. Gwyn ran her fingers gently over the sofa and waited for Andrew to come to her.

"I'm sorry to disturb you, m'lord, but I thought there was something you should know about our Gwyn."

"And what is that?"

"She likes to play the virgin. It adds to the . . . delight she experiences in loveplay. It makes the consummation all the sweeter for her."

"Then she's not untouched?"

"I never said she was. A girl that fetching couldn't have kept her virtue long. But she has not had many, m'lord. Just enough for me to find out about this curious habit of hers."

"How many?"

"Only five, m'lord, but none them real men, if you know what I mean."

"Enlighten me, Madam."

"None of them would play along with Gwyn's little game. So if you would, m'lord, I do promise 'twill make the entire night more pleasurable for you."

"And if it's not?"

"Then your money shall be refunded in full. You're a valuable customer to me, m'lord, and I never wish to see you walk away unsatisfied. Now I will leave you to your pleasures, and if tonight you fare ill, ask Angelique to fetch me and I will repay you at once."

When Andrew reentered the bedroom, Gwyn sensed a subtle change in him. He was studying her again, but this time as if he didn't quite know what to make of her. He sat down beside her, not as close as before, and took her hand in his. She felt a deep quiver in her stomach as his fingers covered hers.

He brought her hand to his lips, turned it, and kissed her palm, his tongue lightly flicking out as he did. Then he bit the soft pad below her thumb, just enough so she looked up at him.

As their eyes met, he gently released her hand and began to unbutton his shirt. He'd shed his coat and vest while she and Angel were behind the screen. Now as each button opened, she could see a muscled expanse of bronze skin covered with dark, curly hair. For one wild moment her palm itched to touch him, to feel those hairs tickle her hand. But she balled her fingers into a fist. She *had* to tell him.

"Andrew—" The words stuck in her throat as he pulled his shirt free of his black breeches. Naked to the waist, he let the shirt fall to the floor in front of the couch.

She couldn't stop looking at him. He ignited her blood and she became curiously light-headed. But as soon as that sensation passed, she felt the blood throb in various parts of her body. She was gloriously alive and sensitive beneath her silken robe. Her breasts felt swollen, heavy, and tender. Her nipples ached, tight and waiting. A soft, slightly burning sensation bloomed between her thighs.

"Andrew?" Her tone was curious now, as if he could tell her what was happening to her body. She felt out of control. She wanted to stand up, run to the door and pound on it, demand to be let free. But her legs felt weak, tingly.

He touched her again, his fingers cool against her inflamed body. He stroked her neck, her cheek, smoothed the hair back from her forehead. She leaned into his touch like a cat wanting to be petted, anxious to have him touch her.

When Andrew shifted his weight and began to press her back against the couch, she didn't protest. Her thighs fell apart, muscles lethargic, as he lay over her. It seemed right, somehow, that he was lying between her legs. She arched her back up slowly, delighting in the feel of his rough breeches against her silken thighs.

He pressed her deeper into the cushions, then covered her mouth with his. The feel of his lips against hers made her body catch fire, made the dull throbbing between her thighs quicken. Her hands roved restlessly, until she caught at his hips and pulled him closer. She was vaguely aware of Andrew breaking the kiss and lifting up, supporting his weight with his arms. His expression seemed surprised. But then he smiled, a soft, warm, languorous smile, for her alone. She laughed softly, then pressed her hands into the small of his back, forcing him closer to the warmest part of her heated body.

"Not so fast, little virgin," he whispered, and she felt waves of relief wash over her. He knew! He had seen inside her and plucked the words right out of her thoughts.

He eased himself slightly above her, and she felt his fingers on her sash. It came undone easily, and she watched him through half-closed eyes as he slowly parted the silk wrapper, unveiling her body. There was a powerful, warm gleam in his eyes, and she smiled. Andrew leaned back on one arm, then slowly drew a finger around her throat, down over her collarbone, around both her breasts. He didn't touch her nipples, but continued the slow, sensuous journey down her belly until his fingers cupped the dark blond curls between her legs. He grasped them gently, then pulled. Her head fell back, her breath came out a soft sob. Then she felt his palm against that most exquisitely sensitive place, rubbing her gently as she quietly sobbed out her frustration into the brocade cushions.

But before she could find what she was desperately searching for, he got up off the couch and, taking her hand, pulled her with him so they were both standing in front of the fire. He slipped the wrapper from her shoulders and she felt it slide down her back and pool at her feet. He moved backward, strangely graceful for a man, taking her hand and pulling her with him. She stepped out of the silk, completely naked, feeling as if her entire body had been fed to the fire.

Then he was kissing her, almost savagely, wrapping her tightly in his arms, her breasts crushed against his chest. The crisp hairs tickled her sensitive skin and she would have cried out her ecstasy if her lips hadn't been devoured by his. His thigh parted hers, his hands on her waist slightly lifting her, so she straddled him. She broke the kiss, her breath coming out in deep, sobbing gasps.

His hand closed around hers, guiding it to the front of his breeches, pressing it against his rigid, thick shaft. He began to move her fingers over his heated flesh. Gwyn obeyed his command, completely mindless now, but searching, searching. Surely he wouldn't let her suffer much longer.

"My boots," he whispered, walking backward until he sat back down on the couch. "Take off my boots, Gwyn, and I'll give you your pleasure."

His words soothed her, and she knelt down and began to remove his boots. Several times, flushed and frustrated, she glanced up at him. He watched her intently, and each time their eyes met, he smiled. She managed to get first one boot off, then the other. She stood up, shakily, then sighed as he took her into his arms and pulled her onto his lap, her legs straddling his.

"Now my breeches." But before she could move to obey his command, he looped her hair around his hand and gently pulled her face toward his. He kissed her eyelids, her cheeks, then gave her several long, lingering kisses on her mouth. His fingers still tangled in her hair, he pulled her head back so her body arched and her breasts were close to his face.

Gwyn almost screamed as he took her nipple deep into his mouth, sucking strongly. Pulsations washed through her body; she had no desire to pull away. Instead, she arched further, and heard a muffled groan as Andrew drew his lips away from one breast and concentrated on giving pleasure to the other. He nibbled and licked, even lightly biting the swollen peaks. His hand fell away from her hair and his arms strongly circled her waist, holding her against his mouth.

She writhed against him, her body pleading eloquently. Andrew grasped her shoulders and pulled her up, then found her lips with his. He parted them expertly and his tongue plunged inside her mouth, filling it with the taste of him. Gwyn whimpered as his large hands moved down her back and cupped her buttocks, sending searing waves of desire smouldering along her sensitized skin. She grasped his shoulders tightly with both hands, her fingers digging into his muscles. Those smooth, hot muscles were the only reality in a world composed completely of sensation. Even her mouth had come alive; it seemed strange and hot and alien to her, but she knew she wanted him inside. Her body trembled as she answered him with the tip of her own tongue and heard him groan deep in his throat.

The waiting, the heat, the burning between her thighs was unbearable. Remembering his palm against her, Gwyn closed her fingers over his and eased his hand against her belly. His fingers spread over her skin and pressed against her. Groaning, she pushed his hand inexorably downward.

On fire everywhere he touched, she felt his hand move slowly, steadily, until his fingers were tangled in her wet curls. Gwyn shuddered as Andrew inserted first one finger deep inside, then another. Andrew matched the movements of his fingers with his tongue, and Gwyn felt every nerve in her body scream for release. She felt a pressure, an urgent burning, but before she found release, Andrew stopped and rolled her gently onto the couch beside him.

"My breeches now, Gwyn, and I'll make sure you're satisfied."

Almost sobbing her frustration, she leaned over him. Her fingers fumbled with the buttons of his breeches. So desperate to have his body naked against hers, she tore at the dark material. Andrew groaned, then said softly, "Take it more slowly, my sweet, and we'll both be happier for it." Gwyn began to carefully unfasten the remaining buttons. She felt Andrew's hand caressing her back, moving to her buttocks. She gasped as she felt two of his fingers enter her from behind, then start a smooth, soothing, undulating motion.

"We're almost there, sweet," Andrew whispered as she whimpered, then dropped her head into his lap in utter surrender. He stroked her hair with his free hand, his fingers continuing their delicious ministrations. Gwyn felt she would certainly die if she didn't find what she was looking for. Her body felt poised on the edge, desperately searching.

She raised her head, looking into his face. Andrew kissed her then, and she could feel his hands working his breeches off. She helped him, her eyes closed as she kissed him, and heard the offending garment drop to the floor. His hand caught hers, and for the first time she held his manhood.

His skin was so hot she thought she might be burned. Large and thick, it arched tightly against his stomach. Her hand looked small and white against it, and she could barely fit her fingers around the base. She squeezed slightly, wanting to surround him with her fingers, and he groaned again, the sound anguished.

She lightened her touch and he taught her how to please him, the right movements and pressure. And when he could take no more, his hands encircled her waist and raised her up over him. He was sitting, and she straddled his powerful thighs.

"I'll let you decide, Gwyn," he whispered into her neck. The tip of his rigid shaft probed her, and she sensed this was the only thing that would satisfy the peculiar burning, throbbing sensation filling her body. Andrew kissed her as she straddled him, her knees trembling with the effort. He held her effortlessly, waiting for a signal from her. He was such a powerful man, holding everything he had to give her in check.

"Yes," she whispered, slipping her arms around his neck, then gently thrusting her hips toward him. He lowered her slightly, and she felt him enter her, stretching her. There was a twinge of uneasiness, then a satisfaction so complete she whimpered her relief. As confused and burning as she was, she recognized this was what would release her from her heated torment.

He surged upward slowly and she sighed. She kissed his

66

cheek softly in gratitude and lay her head on his shoulder.

"Wrap your legs around me," he whispered, and she did. She would have done anything he asked, simply to prolong this exquisite feeling. She was surprised when he stood up slowly, and she flinched when the motion caused more of his hardness to slide into her. It hurt slightly and it puzzled her, but before she realized anything more, she felt him settling her onto smooth, cool sheets. His hot, powerful body followed her down onto the bed.

The room was almost dark, the only light coming from the faintly flickering fire. She searched the darkness for his face, wanting to see what was in his eyes. She felt his hands against her thighs, pressing them further apart. Then she felt his body on top of hers, powerful dominant, and all the while he had never left her body.

"Andrew," she sighed his name, utterly content.

He kissed her then, still moving gently inside her. But something was different. Each time he moved, she felt more of him slide inside her, beginning to hurt. She whimpered, trying to lift her head and tell him not to move so quickly.

He kissed her cheek and whispered, "Just a little pain, Gwyn, then so much pleasure. I promise you that."

And then he surged forward, met strong resistance. Gwyn wanted to cry out, but before she could make a sound Andrew moved forward again, plunging his hot hardness into her with a low, guttural groan. She felt him push up inside, opening her. Hurting her. He was too big, too hard. She squirmed beneath him, her hips bucking ineffectually, but his muscled body was so powerful and the weight of it held her down.

She cried out, but it was a muffled cry, easily mistaken for passion. Andrew, completely lost to her needs, pushed in as deeply as possible, then drew out the entire length and pushed in again. Rhythmically, urgently, he opened her virginal tightness completely, and despite the burning sharp pain, she could accept him fully. It was still a very tight, uncomfortable fit, and Gwyn squirmed, moving with a frustrated rhythm as she tried to throw him off her. This seemed to excite him more, and he simply continued to move his strong hips, never still for an instant.

Gwyn moaned softly, turning her head from side to side. Though consciousness had returned to her briefly at the moment of Andrew's first heated penetration, now she wasn't sure what she felt. A part of her hurt. But a part of her, hotly sensual and newly aroused to passion, loved what he was doing to her, craved and needed the feelings he awoke in her.

She was aware of every nuance of their bodies. His muscled legs pushed her soft thighs further apart. His flat, hard stomach burned against hers. His muscles flexed and rippled as he moved, thrusting fiercely, hungrily inside her. And Gwyn's body burned, hot tremors centered where they were joined, filling her entire body.

He moved inside her again and again, and it seemed he wanted some response from her. She felt her body readying, tensing in a final struggle, blindly reaching for a way past this tautly erotic present.

Then she sensed the change in him. Urgent now, his hands grasped her buttocks, his lower body seemed to have a will of its own. His mouth closed over hers and she moaned against him as she felt him swell even larger, then pulsate strongly inside her. He took her over the edge and she felt ultimate, almost painful fulfillment course through her. His back arched against her hands and he groaned aloud, then slowly slid down on top of her and rested his head against her shoulder.

His breath was warm against her skin. She didn't know how long they lay there, both of them utterly spent, without the energy to move. The only thing in the world that mattered was what had just happened.

Her energy returned slowly, and when it did, she smoothed her fingertips over his slightly damp back. Andrew shuddered, then reached back and captured her hand with his.

"No. Please." His voice was low. Exhausted.

Gwyn shifted her hips slightly and was surprised to find he

was still deep within her. Was there more? She had thought they were finished. But even as these thoughts raced throughout her mind, she felt the traitorous warmth begin to steal into her relaxed body again, centering where she held him.

"Oh, Andrew," she moaned softly aginst his mouth. Her hips began to undulate slowly, imitating the movements he had made scarcely an hour ago.

He groaned, then she felt him lift up slightly, balancing his weight on his elbows. His body was responding, moving very slightly inside her. She felt one of his hands steal behind her and press against the small of her back. Carefully, he rolled over so he was on his back and she was astride him, his manhood still imbedded deep within her softness.

"Put your hands on my shoulders," he commanded softly.

She felt his fingers close around her waist and lift her slightly, then place her back down. He helped her until she began to move her hips herself, riding him and feeling the greatest pleasure as she made sure he touched each secret interior place. She thought there could be no greater pleasure, until he began to caress her breasts. They were still full and throbbing, very tender, so each touch made her feel alive. Within minutes, Andrew had eased her forward and taken possession of one of her hard nipples. She closed her eyes as she felt his tongue swirl around the delicate flesh, then realized her own breathing was quickening. Her hips began to move more urgently, and she felt his long fingers close around her thighs as he began to help direct her movements.

He surged upward, and she cried out as he filled her. Lost in a maze of sensual delight, she let Andrew claim her as his own once again.

Janet got up from her chair, then held onto the back as her knees trembled. She had only meant to stay until Andrew had deflowered Gwyn, but their lovemaking had been so erotic she

69

had watched them make love three times.

If he asks for his money back, he's a damned liar! But she smiled to herself. He wouldn't. With Gwyn behaving like a wanton, he'd be back for more. He would never settle for anything less.

You deserved it, Gwyn. If you had been cooperative, less stubborn . . . She had winced when Andrew had first surged inside the girl, because she knew he was better endowed than any other man who frequented The Dark Stallion. Suzanne, who had been Andrew's regular whore, had made this announcement to the breakfast table at large one morning as she had brought a feather pillow to sit on after a particularly playful night. Janet had found her interest piqued, and she had watched them one night and found Suzanne had told the truth.

But he won't be seeing Suzanne anymore, she thought. Her legs steadier, Janet walked through the maze, back to her bedroom.

If I could afford the time, I'd try three drops myself. Gwyn had been out of control, totally insatiable, completely driven by the sensual side of her nature. It had been fascinating to watch. But Janet derived even more satisfaction out of knowing The Dark Stallion was safe.

Three times so far. She chuckled softly. If her own experiences were anything to judge by, neither Gwyn nor Andrew would sleep this night.

Chapter Five

Late the next afternoon, Andrew slowly opened one eye. The drapes were drawn, no candles were lit, so the bedroom was bathed in dusky firelight. Someone must have come in and started it some time ago.

It took him a minute to realize where he was. His head ached, and every muscle in his body felt as if it had been taxed to its limit.

Slowly he sat up in bed and rubbed his hand over his eyes. Then he saw her. She barely made a lump underneath the blanket, and she was as far away from him as possible, almost to the edge of the bed. Andrew gently pulled back the bedcovers. Golden hair sparkled in the dim light, and memories came rushing back, vivid and erotic.

My God, what a night we had! It would have been impossible to forget a woman like Gwyn. She'd been insatiable. Each climax she had wrung out of him had been sweeter and sweeter, made him ache all over. And *still* she had fired life into him. When they had finally stopped making love, it had been well into the morning and they had both simply dropped from exhaustion.

Now he rose slowly from the bed and, not bothering to dress, moved silently over to one of the large windows and pulled back the heavy curtain. London bustled with life, far below.

The sun was just setting, and the deep blue of dusk washed over the great city. Candlelight sparkled in some windows, voices and sounds were muted.

Andrew wrinkled his brow. He wasn't looking forward to confronting his grandfather. No doubt Henry had already learned of his extravagance—and would not be pleased. But what they had shared was priceless. He had thought he knew a lot about making love, had thought Suzanne was quite something in bed.

She was nothing compared to Gwyn.

Such a slight girl to have such inexhaustible energy. He grinned as he remembered. Though his body ached, he welcomed it. He had acted out every fantasy, and she had denied him nothing.

And never will. With the confidence borne of being a member of London's ruling class, Andrew had great plans for Gwyn. As soon as possible he would set her up as his mistress. Perhaps a house of her own. He would marry Belinda and put a stop to his grandfather's nagging, but he would always have Gwyn for his private pleasure.

She pleases me greatly. He walked over to the couch and began to retrieve his clothing. As he dressed, his eyes strayed to the sleeping woman. *Her skin was so soft, she was so beautiful. And the way she received me, again and again and again . . .* He had never experienced such utterly sensual warmth. No matter that she wanted to play games, to call herself a virgin. She could be a virgin every night they lay together if she would continue to give him such great pleasure.

He tucked his shirt into his breeches, then reached for his waistcoat. Once he was completely dressed, he grabbed his greatcoat, then strode softly to the large curtained bed.

She was lying perfectly still. Andrew reached out and touched her hair gently. *So soft, so perfect . . .* He would be back tonight, though he didn't have time to dally with her this afternoon. Yet he wanted to look at the perfection of her body one last time. The memory would hold him until . . .

Slowly drawing back the blankets, he gazed with intense

pleasure at the fullness of her breasts, the slender waist. He drew the cover lower, taking in the slimness of her thighs. There was a slight scar high up on her inner thigh, and he frowned. The ugly, puckering skin ruined what would have otherwise been perfection. But it didn't matter. She was lovely.

Andrew gazed at her for several seconds, then not wanting her to catch a chill, he grasped the edge of the wool blanket.

At that exact moment he saw the dark red, angry stain on the linen. The meaning of that blood came to him with crushing force.

She likes to play the virgin. . . .

Janet had lied. She had *been* a virgin. And he had taken her as though she were a seasoned whore.

A girl that fetching couldn't remain pure for long.

Yet she had.

He knew the madam of The Dark Stallion to be totally unscrupulous. But why had she lied about Gwyn?

Nothing is as it seems. Suddenly Andrew realized he knew nothing about this golden-haired vixen save her name. But why had she kept him up all night? Why had they made love into the hours of dawn? It wasn't something a virgin would do.

His head ached now, more from tension than tiredness. Andrew sat down on the edge of the bed, careful not to wake her. Lacing his hands together and leaning forward, he thought back over the past evening and tried to put the myriad pieces together. Somehow, they had to fit.

So if you would, m'lord, I do promise 'twill make the entire night more pleasurable for you.

He thought of having Angelique summon Janet, of forcing the entire story out of the madam, then reconsidered. Janet's wrath would come down on Gwyneth.

And you've certainly done her far too much harm.

He didn't stop to consider why this girl's fate troubled him so, why he felt guilty at having initiated her in such an excessive way.

Something still isn't right. Why had she pressed her body

73

against his, begging him to continue making love to her? Why had she brought her hand around, begged him to touch her, take her with his fingers? Though Andrew had spent little time with inexperienced women, he knew no virgin would have behaved as Gwyn had.

His eyes fell on the dinner tray, still on the small table. Thoughtfully, he studied it. *But we didn't have any dinner . . .*

Instantly, his dark eyes flicked to the two wine glasses, both empty. Gwyn's still held a few drops. He stuck his finger in the glass, brought it to his lips, and sat back with disgust.

Drugged. Both of them. Though his draught had certainly been lighter, as he didn't remember his wine tasting as sweet.

That explains your desire as well.

The irony of it was they hadn't made love to each other at all, but to amorous, hot illusions spawned from the drug.

Flashes of their night together flitted through his memory. the innocence in those eyes. Normally he steered clear of virgins.

He despised anyone who took advantage of someone weaker. The women he'd made love to had been his equals, players in his game who had known the rules, known exactly what it was he'd sought in their beds.

This woman should not have been in his bed. But if he'd decided to risk the temptation she offered, he should have realized she was untouched. He could have made their night more pleasurable, been gentler. He had hurt Gwyneth, and he didn't like this feeling of shame.

Filled with roiling emotions he had no idea what to do with, Andrew stood and walked slowly out of the bedroom, shutting the heavy wooden door firmly behind him. As he walked down the wide, curving staircase, he spotted Angelique hurrying up the stairs.

"Good day, m'lord." She seemed to be studying him closely, and he was suddenly unnerved. Was she aware of exactly what had transpired last night?

"Angelique."

She stopped instantly, giving him a quick nod of her head.

He had to ask her. "Please see to Gwyn. I'm afraid—" He stopped, not knowing what to say. He couldn't possibly tell a servant girl his feelings. Clearing his throat, he said quietly, "I'm afraid she isn't feeling well." As he watched concern cloud her dark brown eyes, Andrew knew he had found an ally at The Dark Stallion. "I don't want Janet to believe I was anything but pleased with Gwyn. I want you to see to her comfort."

And with that, he hurried down the stairs. He wouldn't go home, not just yet. He would go to the club and think.

Gwyn opened her eyes. Dazed, she sat up slowly and swung her legs over the side of the bed. Stiffness cramped every muscle in her body, pain stung hotly between her legs. She was sitting on the edge of the bed, her head in her hands, when Angel entered the room.

"Ah, you're up!"

Gwyn kept her hands over her face, deeply ashamed.

"Gwyn? Gwyn, did he hurt you?"

She didn't answer Angel, then felt her friend's arm across her shoulders.

"You can tell me. I won't think less of you."

"I'm so . . . ashamed." The words scraped out of her tight throat, raw and painful. As wounded as she felt.

"There's nothing shameful about what goes on between a man and a woman. That Andrew, he has a good heart. He asked after your comfort."

She didn't reply. Her mind and spirit felt battered. Not only had she let Andrew have his way with her, let him do everything possible a man could do to a woman, but . . .

"I'm no better than any whore here," she whispered softly.

"But you are." Angel's dark eyes sparkled. "You're getting out. I'm assured of it now. The way he looked when he spoke of you, Gwyn. You have captured his heart."

75

"In the lowest way possible."

"What other way is there? Come now, I see neither of you bothered to touch your supper. Cook will fix you a beefsteak to bring back your strength. And a glass of wine."

"No wine, please! I've had my fill."

"As you wish. I'll fetch a tray."

Gwyn forced herself to eat, then pushed the plate back and gave Angel a triumphant look. "There. I've done it. Are you happy now?"

"Gwyneth Leighton, what has turned you into a high-strung little witch?"

"Everything happened," she whispered from between her fingers. "And nothing."

"Now what is that supposed to mean?"

"Oh, Angel, I'll never forgive myself." All the emotion she had been holding back began to rise within her. Unable to control herself, she burst into tears.

Angel's arms came around her instantly. "Ah, *mon petite chou,* don't cry so. He cares about you, I saw it in his eyes! You have found your protector, and in only one night! I told you things would go well if you let Andrew know the truth."

"He knew it . . . he knew it without my telling him."

"So he was quite a man, that Andrew?" There was a slightly teasing note to Angel's voice.

"I suppose he was."

"You *suppose!* He's only considered one of the best lovers in London! We used to hear about him from Suzanne all the time. I for one am glad Andrew has fallen in love with you and will no longer play with that spitting cat!"

"Oh, Angel, stop talking nonsense! He doesn't love me. I was nothing but a—a toy for him to play with."

"But even grown-up boys like their toys. *Minou,* he was *worried* about you! There are men who visit the girls and walk out the door the minute they finish! Andrew stayed the night and part of the next day—and you couldn't have spent all that time making love because he knew it was your first time."

Mortified, Gwyn covered her flaming face with her hands. "You *did* say he knew it was your first time?"

"Yes . . . and no. Oh, Angel, please don't make me explain this to you. I'm not sure I understand what happened."

Angel was at her side instantly. "Gwyn, start from the beginning. You have to tell someone; you can't keep it bottled up inside you forever. It isn't good for you."

Gwyn remained silent.

"I'll never tell anyone."

She sighed deeply, and Angel seemed to take this as acceptance.

"How many times did he make love to you?" Angel asked softly.

"Several times," Gwyn whispered. There was silence from her friend, and she slowly looked up, expecting condemnation.

There was nothing but surprise.

"Several times? Gwyn, I don't mean to insult you, but do you know your numbers?" Angel's voice sounded slightly choked, a mere squeak. "How did he—"

"I don't know. He just did."

"Did he—?" Angel seemed to be choosing her words carefully. "Did he force you, make you do anything?"

Gwyn could feel tears building up in her eyes, but she had resigned herself to being honest. "No. Never."

"*Nom de Dieu*, the man is a miracle! Suzanne never said anything like this!"

Building up her courage, Gwyn blurted out, "He never forced me, Gwyn. I—I forced him."

There was another short silence, then Angel said, "*Minou*, I do not understand. How can you force a man? It is impossible!"

Gwyn was so embarrassed she was whispering. "The last few times . . . I . . . he was tired, but I kept . . . encouraging him to . . . make love to me." As this last bit of truth came out, Gwyn felt another torrent of emotion burst deep within her, and the rest of her story came out in a rush.

"I didn't belong to myself, Angel! It was horrible. We would finish, I *know* we were finished, then I would have to have him make love to me all over again! I was out of my head, my body wouldn't obey me! It was so frightening. I've never felt anything like that!"

"There is something not quite right here. Let me fetch hot water for your bath and think about this."

Within half an hour Gwyn was finished bathing. Angel changed the bed and quickly bundled up the old linen, but not before Gwyn had seen the rusty red stain. Humiliation had bubbled up inside her all over again. Then Angel left for the kitchen, promising to bring her up a piece of Cook's pie.

Now as Gwyn lay in bed, shame filled her again. She had been initiated into love in the worst possible way. Angel was only trying to make her feel better by telling her Andrew cared about her. He couldn't. He could lust after her, but that was not what Gwyn wanted.

Andrew had taken her on the bed as if she were an animal, a piece of property.

But that's what you are. Property. He bought you last night, and now you belong to him.

She was suffused with a sense of powerlessness so strong it caused her to tremble. A deep, slow anger built within her, a determination that the rest of her life should not be given over so blindly to the fates.

Never. I will never belong to a man this way. Love is the one thing that is mine alone to give.

Gwyn wanted to believe Angel that somehow the two of them would get out of The Dark Stallion and make a life for themselves. Someday.

"I brought you some of Cook's lemon pudding pie," Angel said as she opened the door and hurried inside. "I don't know if Andrew is coming by tonight, but if he is, we only have a short time to talk."

As Gwyn ate, Angel voiced her suspicions.

"You were drugged. Gwyn, I kept remembering the evening

78

in my mind. The only thing that struck me as queer was that the Mistress gave me the night off. And she *smiled*. Janet never smiles. So I tried to think of what I said before, and I remembered she asked me what we were whispering about. I said I told you to drink your wine, and she was pleased."

"The wine," Gwyn breathed. "Angel, after I drank it I felt so strange! As if—as if I were burning up with fever."

"But the only thing you were feverish for was Andrew."

"Yes." Gwyn's voice was low.

"She must have put something in the wine. I've heard from some of the girls there are potions like that that strengthen desire."

"She must have given some to Andrew, too."

"I would think so."

"So he must be as confused as I am about last night!" She felt better. How could Andrew think badly of her when she was not in control of her body? It helped to know his mind had been clouded as well.

"He will remember enough to believe it was you that gave him his power—and that is good." Angel collected the pie plate and fork. "I don't think he's coming tonight. He was so concerned for your health." A quick grin spread across her face. "And he's probably at home, sleeping off the effects of the wine."

Gwyn squeezed her friend's hand. "Thank you, Angel."

"Ah, Gwyn, you'll be leaving sooner than you think." Angel hesitated. "I wanted to tell you something all day, but you were in such a mood I'm glad I waited until tonight."

"What is it?" Gwyn was apprehensive for just an instant.

"Don't look so worried, *mon ange!* It's just something I heard about town this morning. And it reflects very well on you."

Gwyn sat up slowly in bed. "Go on, Angel."

"You made quite an impression on a number of men, and they were jealous of Andrew having you all for himself. All the talk I heard was of the Earl of Scarborough's Bordello Bride."

"Angel!"

"Gwyn, don't you understand? If Andrew sees many men desire you, he'll keep you much closer. Now, sleep while you can. I think your Andrew will be unable to stay away for long."

As Angel walked towards the door, Gwyn snuggled down underneath the heavy blankets. *He's not my Andrew, for I had no choice. Even if I had, I am nothing to him.* She barely heard Angel's voice as she called out from the doorway.

"Sleep well, my little Bordello Bride."

Andrew toyed with the glass in front of him. He considered another drink but knew Jack would discourage him. Several times he had thought of going to the Dark Stallion, to check on Gwyn.

Why are you so worried about her? She's nothing but a whore. Yet deep inside he knew this wasn't so. There was something about her nature that was more refined. He could picture her huge eyes in that finely boned face, gazing up at him, liquid and trusting.

Too trusting. Look what he had done to her.

"Come on, Andrew, I'm going to take you home." Jack's tone was firm as he rose to his feet. "You're not going to solve anything by getting drunk."

"I suppose you're right." Thoroughly disgusted with himself, Andrew stood and followed Jack around the tables filled with gentlemen. They were halfway to the door when he made out a voice in the smoky crowd.

"Well, if it isn't the Earl of Scarborough. And how is the little mistress today, if I might ask? She looked quite fetching in that white silk last night."

Andrew ignored the young man's gibes.

"Ah, he looks tired. His little whore must have given him quite a ride."

Andrew kept his eyes on Jack, walking steadily ahead of him.

"What did you give her, eh Andrew, besides a taste of that

weapon of yours? I wonder how the little bride feels tonight?" Sarcastic laughter rippled through the small crowd. The man, encouraged by the response, continued. "Once broken never mended, eh?"

Laughter started up again, but this time Andrew turned and looked in the direction of the man's voice. His eyes had a strange, hard expression, and any sensible man would have left him alone.

This fool was far from sensible.

"What did you say?" Andrew asked softly.

"Andrew, this is not the time or the pl—" Jack began.

"I just want to ask this . . . *gentleman* exactly what he said."

"Just making a joke about the little piece. I said, 'Once broken, never mended.'" He began to laugh heartily.

Andrew moved so quickly he had the man by the lapels of his expensive jacket and slammed up against the wall before anyone could stop him. The crowd was silent. Watching.

Andrew's voice was soft and level. "If you ask anything more about the woman in question, I'll break you so badly you'll never have a chance to mend. Do we understand one another?"

"For God's sake, man, I didn't mean any harm. Just a harmless joke about the whore—"

The words were barely out of the man's mouth before he was slammed against the wall again.

"One more remark and I'll have to call you out," Andrew said quietly, his words all the more menacing because of the tone he gave them. "Now, is that what you want, or are you willing to take that tongue of yours and blister someone else with your filthy remarks?"

The man's eyes bulged with fear, and a trickle of sweat slid down his forehead. Andrew Hawkesworth had never lost a duel in his life, either with pistol or sword. He rarely dueled.

But when he did, he was a deadly adversary.

"I didn't mean any harm. . . ."

"Do we understand each other?" Andrew tightened his grip

on the man's jacket.

"Yes. Yes, I understand you. I quite understand." The man babbled as Andrew released his jacket. Turning toward the observant crowd, Andrew spoke in a low tone that carried across the large room.

"Is there anyone else who would like to make a remark?" The room was absolutely silent.

Without another word, Andrew turned and walked out of the club.

As soon as he left, voices erupted all around, one on top of the other.

"Just like his father, I tell you! It's in the blood—"

"—born to be hanged!"

"That son of a whore!"

"—mother was Irish, he gets his temper from her. And remember what *she* did—"

"Bad blood. Too bad his grandfather didn't just let him run wild."

"Someone should geld him!"

"He buys the whore, then fights for her! Explain that to me."

Outside, Andrew strode briskly until he reached his stallion. Once in the saddle, he turned the animal sharply and dug in his heels. The stallion reared and snorted, then shot off down the cobblestone street, hooves clanging.

Jack, ever watchful, mounted his blood bay mare and started after his friend, determined to see him safely home.

"You stupid pimping dog!"

Edward cringed as the Duke of Cuckfield ranted, striding up and down. He watched, horrified, as the Duke lashed out with his ivory-headed cane and smashed a vase off a pedestal. The pieces came crashing down on the marble floor.

"Why didn't you give me the girl instead of the money? I would have considered your debt paid if you had done that! You ignorant blackguard! Instead, you sell her for a paltry sum, and I am humiliated at The Dark Stallion!"

Edward didn't answer. There was nothing he dared say. A gambler all his life, he'd barely managed to stay ahead of his numerous debts.

Until meeting the Duke while playing cards. The man was an expert at any game and frequented the gambling hells Edward adored. He had lost much money to the Duke and still owned him far more than he'd received for Gwyn.

And Edward, never a man to blame himself for his own misfortune, began to think of Gwyn and hold his cousin responsible for his dilemma. If the girl had commanded a better sum, he wouldn't even be here and certainly wouldn't have to listen to this man's ravings.

And his hatred for her grew.

"It isn't enough that I should be bested by Hawkesworth, that low-bred ruffian! On top of that, I have to lose the prettiest piece of flesh I've seen this season! How can one man so be insufferably stupid!"

Edward simply stared at the far wall of the library, at an expensive oil painting above the fireplace. A portrait of a golden-haired lady. The Duke had been angry at him before, but his fury had never reached this intensity. There was something demonic about him today. He was a man obsessed.

"Well, Edward Sleaforth, you'll pay back your debt to me one way or another."

Edward came back to the present with a start. He had been wishing he'd stayed in the country and disposed of Gwyn in another fashion. Then the Duke would have never seen the little slut.

The Duke continued. "You'll meet me here Friday night. I have several entertainments planned, and you'll be one of them."

Edward's stomach started to turn over. The Duke's private entertainments were legendary, whispered about all over London.

"You will also help me with a plan. I want that girl, and I

83

mean to have her. And I'm going to pay Hawkesworth back in full for every moment of my humiliation."

Edward said nothing. He couldn't possibly refuse. He had heard of other men, men who had tried to escape the Duke. Men who had ended up on deserted London streets late at night with their throats slit from ear to ear.

He would do whatever he had to do to stay alive.

And he would make Gwyn pay.

Lady Belinda Pevensy, attired in a lacy dressing gown, sat up in bed when her maid brought her a tray. It was her usual fare, hot chocolate and biscuits. She had developed a taste for the drink. It had been Chinese tea the month before; it would be something different the following month. Belinda liked to follow her whims.

And sleeping with Andrew was one of her favorite whims. Spending his money once they were married would satisfy her even more.

"Tell me what they're saying in town, Laura."

Her maid set the tray down on the small bedside table. "I suppose you've heard about the wench Andrew bought at The Dark Stallion."

"I doubt there's anyone in London who doesn't know about his . . . excesses."

"She's very pretty, they say. Golden hair and big blue eyes. And a lovely little shape."

"Is it true he bid against the Duke of Cuckfield?" Even Belinda had been astounded by this turn of events.

"Oh, yes. The Duke, he was an angry man last night."

"I would think so, with Andrew poaching what he considered his property."

Laura's eyes sparkled, and Belinda knew her maid fully intended to make the most of her moment as center of attention. This was first-rate gossip.

"The Duke bid more for the girl, but the Madam wouldn't

give him credit."

"Is it true Andrew stayed with the little slut until the following evening?"

"That's when they said he left, mum."

"Thank you, Laura. That will be all."

Lying back among the lace pillows on her large, canopied bed, Lady Belinda wrinkled her nose in disgust. Andrew and his whores! She had known about Suzanne, of course. She had contrived to see the girl, and the minute she had, Belinda had known the little tart was no threat to her plans. Suzanne had carrot red hair and her white skin was marred by freckles. Her two front teeth protruded. Belinda had secretly laughed at Andrew's taste, but then had forgiven him. After all, a man had to take his baser pleasures somewhere.

She pretended to enjoy herself in bed for Andrew's sake, priding herself on being quite the little actress. At fourteen, her first man had been the stablemaster. He had taught her much. There was something in the coarseness of his expression, the earthiness of his sexual prowess, that had excited her greatly. But her father had found them in the loft, and the man had been dismissed. The Duke of Pevensy had dragged her into the house and thrashed her with his crop. Though she had been unable to sit down for almost one week, at least she had received a fair measure of his attention.

Her mother had died in childbirth, leaving Belinda alone with her father. Raised by a succession of governesses, she had always longed for her father's attention.

Her father had one all-consuming love in his life. His horses. Never so happy as when he was out at his country estate and riding to the hounds, the Duke of Pevensy treated his blooded hunters with more affection than he gave his only daughter.

Thus, Belinda looked for her affection elsewhere. Now, four years later and easily ten times as many men, Belinda had set her mind to winning the man her father admired.

She knew her father admired the way Andrew sat a horse. Lord Pevensy also had need of his vast amounts of money. Now that her father had spent so much of the Pevensy fortune in foolish investments, it was imperative she wed Andrew.

Her plan had been foolproof.

Until last night. Until the girl with the golden hair at The Dark Stallion.

Belinda knew her appeal to the opposite sex. A full-bodied woman, with dark brown hair and pale blue eyes, she took great care to emphasize her charms. She was careful not to talk too much and tried to make a man feel as if he were the center of her life.

Her smooth brow puckered. Sometimes she had the feeling Andrew was laughing at her behind her back. No, not exactly laughing, but sometimes she had the disconcerted feeling Andrew knew she didn't enjoy his hands on her. When they made love, she had to feign passion. Often she closed her eyes and thought back to the summer she turned fourteen and imagined the stablemaster's hands.

Belinda rose from her bed and walked over to the snapping fire. Warming her hands, she began to think. Surely she could outwit a common whore. She had been fooling Andrew all these months, hadn't she?

All she had to do was wait a little longer, until they were married.

Everything she wanted would be hers.

Suzanne lay beneath the covers of her bed in the dimly lit room. The fire was almost out, but she didn't have the energy to call for Angelique. A sickly sweet, perfumy cloud of opium smoke hovered in the air, and she stared at it, entranced by the swirling, blue-grey patterns. Her mouth tasted as though she'd licked a bar of scented soap, but the opium was already making her feet softer, looser. She was floating, her body relaxed, while images began to flicker within her mind.

Her thoughts were hazy. Andrew. He had left her. She had heard the gossip and had locked herself in her room. Polly, one of the whores who had been her friend since their days in the streets, had come in this morning and told her the details. What Gwyn looked like. How much Andrew had paid for her. How his face had looked when he'd carried her up the stairs in his arms.

How late he'd stayed with her. All night and into the next day. That had hurt the worst. He'd left *her* most evenings, after she'd given him what he came for.

In the light of early morning, it was too easy to see things clearly. Looking in the mirror that ran along one wall, Suzanne could see her skin wasn't as clear as it had once been. Her hair was thinning. If she looked closely in her mirror, she could see a few strands of grey. And small lines fanning out around her eyes.

Andrew would never fall in love with her and take her away from The Dark Stallion. Not now.

In a part of her mind she realized her dream had been a fanciful one. She had been happy just to have him to herself for those hours. In his arms, she had believed she was beautiful, that he loved her.

Andrew had been her brightest hope, her last chance. Now he was gone, and with a frightened sense of despair she knew she would never leave The Dark Stallion.

The smoke eddied and swirled as it danced up to the ceiling, much the way her frantic thoughts swirled through her drug-hazed brain.

Gwyn. Gwyn. If it weren't for her . . .

And on that pale November morning, lying huddled beneath her blankets in the cold, smoky room, Suzanne decided Gwyn was the cause of all her miseries. And she vowed to get even.

Chapter Six

"Gwyn, it's working! We'll be gone by Christmas! They're coming up the stairs now, and there's a carriage in the alley. I've never seen so many things."

Gwyn was up on her feet in a flash, then walked quickly to Angel's side and put an arm around her trembling shoulders.

"Angel, what are you talking about?"

She didn't have to wait for an answer. A man in dark green livery came to the door. "Is this Gwyneth's room?"

"I'm Gwyn, yes."

"We were instructed by the Earl of Scarborough to see you received these." He raised his nose slightly, marched into the suite, and deposited three large bags on the canopied bed.

"But I don't—"

"My men will bring the rest of the parcels up directly," he said, then swept out as another man entered.

The room began to fill with boxes and bags of all shapes and sizes. The stream of men seemed never-ending. As more and more packages were set down, Gwyn became aware of several whores standing back from the door, gazing inside with incredulous eyes.

A short time later, the man bowed stiffly from the waist and walked out of the room, leaving the door open. Gwyn watched him as he left, then her eyes narrowed. Janet had come to the top of the stairs, and the group of whores was slowly, reluctantly, disassembling as their madam came closer.

Pretending an interest in her packages, Gwyn walked to the bed and toyed with a silken ribbon. Everything had been wrapped in elegant paper and elaborate bows. She heard Janet enter the room and close the door softly behind her.

"Well, Miss Leighton, it seems you made quite an impression on the Earl of Scarborough."

Gwyn slowly lifted her eyes to Janet's smooth, unreadable expression. She had done much calculated thinking, for want of anything else to do. With that thinking had come an absolute hatred for the madam of The Dark Stallion and the tentative birthing pains of a will to survive. Angel was right— one did what one had to.

With sudden certainty, Gwyn realized the packages were tangible proof Janet would not be foolish enough to hurt her.

"Yes, I did. Such a pity that in my . . . *condition* I had nothing at all to do with it."

Janet said nothing, but Gwyn caught the faintest change in her eyes. A swift flash of irritation. Gwyn decided she enjoyed this game. If the madam of The Dark Stallion thought her stupid, Gwyn would just have to make her revise that opinion.

"If you ever put anything in my food or drink again, I shall make my displeasure known to Andrew." Taking a deep breath, she decided to tell the first lie she had ever told in her sheltered life. "He wasn't pleased to see me hurt. I am not your property anymore, *Madam*. I belong to Andrew, and he will not be pleased with your schemes."

Gwyn knew her barbs had found their mark by the slight thinning of Janet's lips, the flaring of her delicate nostrils. The woman said nothing, silently studying her as if she were a rare bird she had suddenly found and didn't know what to do with.

"Do we understand each other?" Gwyn asked.

"Your food and drink will not be touched."

Testing her power one last time, Gwyn said firmly, "I would

like you to leave me now."

She caught the flash of surprise, then resentment. But, to her intense gratification, Janet moved slowly toward the door. She stopped as her hand closed over the knob and looked back at Gwyn.

"Enjoy it while you can, Miss Leighton. The Earl of Scarborough has been known to tire of his women quickly."

Gwyn said nothing. Waiting.

"Let me tell you something, from one whore to another." Gwyn almost shrank from the animosity she saw in the woman's expression. She prayed her face wouldn't give away the fear she felt.

"Leave your master something to come back for." There was a malicious gleam in her green eyes. "Don't give everything to him all at once, Miss Leighton. Unless you were so unutterably stupid last night that you already did."

Without waiting for an answer, Janet opened the door and stepped out, pulling it firmly shut behind her.

Gwyn grasped one of the intricately carved bedposts as her legs started to tremble. She closed her eyes, her stomach clenching. She heard Angel clear a space on the bed before putting a comforting arm around her waist and helping her sit down.

"We have to get out now. You know that, don't you?" Angel asked.

Gwyn nodded. "I'm not sorry for what I said."

"No. You were right. And Janet was right, too. You have power now, Gwyn, and you can't be afraid of using it. Andrew is—he has feelings for you. We have to figure out what those feelings are and use them to our advantage."

"And yours," Gwyn said to her gently. "You're coming with me." She was determined Angel should escape with her.

"I'm not as worried about me. Now, we have to work with Andrew. Let's unwrap these presents and see what it is he's sent you."

"I'm not taking any of it."

"Gwyn. What are you saying? Didn't we agree we have to get you out of here?"

"I couldn't help being bought and paid for at the auction. But I won't accept any favors from him."

"Let's open some of the boxes and see what he's sent you before you make up your mind to refuse them. I've never led you astray before. Won't you trust me in this matter?"

Gwyn sighed. "You can open them."

Angel quickly began to unwrap a small box adorned with gilt paper and a large, white bow.

"A fan! Oh, how cunning! Look at the mother-of-pearl handle!" Angel pressed the gift into Gwyn's palm and gazed up at her, her dark eyes sparkling. "I saw a fan like this in a shop window! Oh, Gwyn, he isn't trying to fob you off with oranges or a box of chocolates! Do you know what this means?"

Gwyn silently opened the fan. It was beautiful, hand painted, with flowers—roses—and curling leaves adorning it. They seemed to bloom as she opened the fan; the painting was quite skillful.

"He's *guilty!*" Angel whispered. "And we can use his guilt to your advantage!"

"Why would he be guilty? You told me he came to The Dark Stallion and saw other women. Why would it be any different with me?"

"Gwyn, think! He sees you, he buys you. Not only does he buy you, but he bids against the Duke of Cuckfield! Andrew risked the Duke's displeasure to win you, and not many men have the courage to do that! He took a tremendous risk buying you!"

Gwyn had the fan spread open in her lap and was tracing the delicate pattern with her finger.

"He takes you up here and doesn't even bother to eat supper before—"

"That was the wine—"

"Yes, but Gwyn, whether he knows he was drugged or not, he'll remember how it was with the two of you, and that's what

91

matters! I've watched this unfold *hundreds* of times in this house! A woman can be both pretty and skilled, but if a man ever—if there's ever a time when he can't perform—"

"Why does that happen?"

"I don't know. Men are very curious creatures. But the important thing is that the first night Andrew was with you, he couldn't stop making love. I've thought about why Janet might have used those drugs, and I think she thought you would refuse Andrew."

"She's right. I would have."

"But Gwyn, she did you a favor. If Andrew has no idea the two of you were drugged, he thinks himself a man among men! If he suspects the wine, then *you* are an innocent lamb, because he would never suspect you of doing it! Either way, you win!"

"Why would Janet help me?"

"She'd never help you. Janet Wickens only helps herself. She made money and she wanted to keep it. Do you think Andrew bought you so he could come here and play cards? Janet wanted to make sure he walked away satisfied. And he did!"

"But Angel, the next time he comes here, I'll have to do it all without that potion."

"*You* won't have to do a thing! He's been successful with you, so he will be again! It's that first time that seals a woman's fate, I swear it!"

"But Angel, I don't know if I can."

"You can. You could easily learn to enjoy it with Andrew. He's not like most of the men here, those rabbits! He takes his time and makes sure the woman is pleasured, too. Suzanne told us all about what Andrew does in bed."

"Is Suzanne—is she still here?"

"Yes. And that's why, for now, you stay here. I don't want that cat getting her claws in you." Angel reached for another package. "Don't be ashamed of liking it, Gwyn. My own mother used to say, 'There are no cold women, only stupid men.' And Andrew certainly isn't stupid."

"I'll never like it."

"*Merde!* I think you're still thinking with your head and what you were taught. Men are such fools! They want their woman demure and inexperienced, they *say*. If they do, why are so many of them here every night?"

Gwyn didn't reply but simply continued opening another package.

"They're here to get what they can't get at home! And, Gwyn, they can't believe a woman is capable of enjoying herself, so they make us into two sorts. A bad woman and a good one."

"Which am I?" Gwyn asked.

Angel laughed. "You're just Gwyn. A little of both, like all of us if we're honest. Andrew is thought to be a bad boy, and women like him better for his reputation. I've always thought that was why he could appreciate a good woman."

"Bad? How?"

For the next half hour, Angel told her of Andrew's reputation, and how London watched to see what he would do next.

"And so you see, that's why all the men are talking about you. They wish *they* had had the courage to fight Cuckfield for you. Why, half of them in bed with their 'good women' probably close their eyes and think of you while they're trying to stand!"

"I never thought about what men do or why they do it," Gwyn said softly as she reached for another package. "But they seem to spend a lot of time telling us how we should be."

"And has any of them ever been a woman? Hah!"

"How can they know, Angel? How can they know what we think and feel?"

"That's the spirit I want to see in you! Just use common sense, Gwyn, and most of the things men do to women seem foolish. Come, keep unwrapping. We've got to start making our plans."

* * *

Andrew always thought while he rode, and today was no exception. He had declined Jack's offer of company.

His grandfather was furious. So furious he hadn't confronted him. Their meals together were strained, uncomfortable affairs, the only conversation what was necessary. After meals, his grandfather simply scraped back his chair and walked out of the dining room.

Henry knew about Gwyn. All of London did, so why would his grandfather be the lone exception? He didn't doubt his grandfather also knew he had bid against the Duke of Cuckfield. Cuckfield held tremendous power throughout London and was not a man to cross. It was one thing to refuse to attend his private parties, another altogether to come between him and a woman he wanted. And he had wanted Gwyn, no doubt of that. No man bid one thousand five hundred pounds on a whim.

His black stallion, Mephisto, tossed his elegant head and snorted. Andrew squeezed his legs gently and the horse surged forward, breaking into a restrained canter.

He had spent much money on Gwyn, not delving too deeply into the curious guilt he felt when he remembered those bloodstained sheets. He kept his feelings to himself, determined not to let anyone know he had felt so emotionally toward a woman. Nothing could affect his authority over her. He would not have anyone saying a slender, golden-haired girl had unmanned him. It was simple: He would buy her off, relieve his guilt with money.

A Frenchwoman in one of London's most exclusive shops had helped him pick out the most cunning presents. Gowns, gloves, hats, fans, delicate shoes. When he had bought the more intimate apparel, the silken chemises and stockings, he had not had anyone's company but had relied on his own thoughts and fantasies. Gwyneth would wear what pleased him, as she was his now.

She should have received my gifts by now. And they will go a long way toward soothing any remorse she has about my taking her

94

maidenhead. His feelings were curious. He'd bought her. He *owned* her. Yet he wanted her to be warm and responsive to him.

She had to remain his, and his alone.

She had roused him to heights of passion unknown before their night together, denied him nothing, and that had excited him more. There was such a challenge present within her. She had seemed such a lady, even when she had stood before the crowd at The Dark Stallion and looked out over their heads with an arrogant attitude.

And she had been such a wanton in his bed.

He slowed Mephisto, letting the stallion cool down. The park was not crowded, as it was a gloomy, overcast day. The grey clouds and bitterly cold wind suited his solitary mood. Thus he was surprised to hear hoofbeats behind him, gaining. As he turned in his saddle he expected Jack but was surprised to find the Duke of Pevensy astride his favorite chestnut mare, Athena.

"Good day, Andrew." The Duke of Pevensy was a tall, dark man. He had never given way to fat, having ridden extensively every day of his life. Andrew liked the man, as he was simple and uncomplicated. How he had spawned a daughter as peevish as Belinda was beyond Andrew's imagining.

"Good day, James." Their horses fell in step beside each other along the path. The two men were comfortable with the silence, enjoying a friendship that spanned many years and shared riding experiences.

"Belinda would like to have you dine with us tonight. We haven't seen you for a week, at least."

"I would be delighted to join you and your daughter tonight."

"My daughter tells me you have asked her to marry you."

How like Belinda! Andrew's lips curved into a smile. He had planned on asking her the same day he had first seen Gwyn. But the sight of Gwyn had driven all thoughts of Belinda from his mind. Still, it would be unsuitable to allow Belinda to be

95

caught in a lie. Especially when Andrew knew it was all for the best.

"Yes. I wished to have your daughter's consent before I asked you, wanting to know if the lady's heart was as fully enamored as was mine." Though he knew he was telling James an out-and-out lie, for neither he nor Belinda loved each other, he respected James enough that he did not wish him to see his daughter's marriage as the total sham it would be.

"Very kind of you, Andrew. I also hear you picked up a pretty little filly at The Dark Stallion several nights ago."

"Yes, I did." For some reason, this time it annoyed Andrew that everyone was talking about his exploits, speculating about Gwyn. He wanted to keep her to himself, away from anyone who might fall beneath the spell of her beauty. But he couldn't be angry with James, knowing the older man had no such designs on Gwyn himself. If the Duke of Pevensy could have somehow become one of his beloved horses, it would have suited him admirably.

"Good thing, getting a filly like that. I've heard speculation around town she was a well-spirited and satisfying mount. And from what they say, she's a beauty." He chuckled, then reached down and lovingly patted his mare's neck. "Better not let Belinda find out about your private affairs, son. Make her bend to your will immediately."

"Belinda and I understand each other, James. I'm sure ours will be a most mutually gratifying union."

"Well said, son. I'll see you this evening, at seven."

"Yes, sir." Andrew watched as the Duke of Pevensy galloped off, his mare's hooves flying over the sparse brown grass. Trust Belinda to want the most fashionable things. Late suppers were more and more the rage.

He would just have to make sure he left the Pevensy house in plenty of time to spend a long, leisurely evening with Gwyn.

"You look beautiful, Gwyn." Angel stepped back and

admired her handiwork. Gwyn smoothed her hands over the blue and silver brocaded gown, one of many Andrew had bought her. There had been a note carefully pinned to the bodice of the dress.

Wear this gown when I come to you Friday evening. Andrew.

So that was the gown she and Angel had chosen, along with a pearl-colored silken chemise and petticoats, lace trimmed and threaded with small ribbons. There had been scented soaps and sweet-smelling oils within the packages, and Gwyn had taken a long bath and washed her hair in preparation for this night. Angel had dressed her hair simply. It was pulled back and fell in ringlets down her back.

"I want to achieve a style that will make you seem all the more innocent. We will play on the Earl of Scarborough's guilt."

But now, mere minutes before she was sure Andrew would arrive, Gwyn's hands were ice cold and her fingers tightly clenched. She'd watched the sun set as Angel did her hair, and as the sky had darkened she'd trembled, knowing this night she had to face Andrew alone.

"Angel, help me. I'm so scared."

Angel clasped her ice-cold hands. "Gwyn, you must know that in just looking at you, you're going to give Andrew tremendous pleasure.

"And remember what I told you about good and bad lovers? Andrew Hawkesworth is one of the best! Gwyn, enjoy him!" She gave Gwyn a quick hug and a kiss. "I'm going to leave. He'll be here any minute. Just do exactly as we planned. I have faith in you, Gwyn."

Then Angel was gone and she was alone.

Candles were lit, and the fire was blazing merrily. The large room was bathed in light and warmth, but Gwyn felt cold to the tips of her toes.

The sound of firm steps in the hallway brought her head up. Her heart started to pound, her throat constricted. Praying she didn't look as frightened as she felt, Gwyn composed her features and smoothed her damp hands over the brocaded skirt of her gown.

The doorknob turned. Gwyn watched as the massive wooden door opened slowly and Andrew Hawkesworth, Earl of Scarborough, the man she would spend this night with, stepped quietly inside.

Chapter Seven

She couldn't meet his eyes. Though Angel had told her to look at Andrew directly, she found when she did, memories came flooding back, filling her with the most intense shame she had ever felt in her life.

And so Gwyn waited. Convinced he would simply stride over and take her clothes off. Then lead her over to the bed and—

"Gwyn. Gwyn, look at me."

He was closer now, standing a few feet away from her. Slowly, reluctantly, she raised her eyes, taking in his shoes, stockings, breeches, snowy white shirt, and elegantly embroidered waistcoat. Her heart pounded rapidly as she finally looked at his face.

She had expected lust. Or greed. Something expressing the power he had over her, the fact that he had bought her and could do what he wished. Instead, she looked into the darkest, bluest eyes, surrounded with lashes so thick they were almost indecent on a man.

His expression was absolutely unreadable. Carefully expressionless.

Her heart began to slow its frantic beating. *He's studying me as much as I am him. But at least he has the courage to make us look at one another.* And at that moment, Gwyn determined she would not be afraid of this man. No matter what he did to her, she would not lose her courage. Nor her pride.

"Andrew." She nodded her head, feeling dizzy. Angel had laced her corset snugly, and she couldn't breathe. After having spent days in her wrapper, the corset felt restricting. Whenever she relaxed, the stiff boning reminded her of the fact and forced her to straighten her spine. Severe of cut, the garment shaped her figure and forced back her shoulders, displaying her bosom. Her gown was cut quite low, with an absolutely indecent décolletage, making her feel as if she were on display for him.

"You look quite beautiful tonight. It pleases me you wore the dress I requested."

"And what would you have done had I not?" The words were out of her mouth almost before she was aware of having spoken them. *This wasn't what you were supposed to say.* But for some perverse reason, she wanted to test this man.

"I would have undressed you myself and given you the proper gown."

The look in his eyes convinced her he would have done exactly that.

"Why was it important to you that I wear it?"

"I saw it at the dressmaker's. I thought of you in it. Indeed, madam, you have far exceeded any fantasy contained within my mind."

He's complimenting you. Stop arguing, keep things simple. Gwyn merely looked up at him, not trusting herself. Waiting for Andrew to make the next move.

"Are you hungry?" he asked.

Her smile faltered for just an instant. As she glanced at the canopied bed and thought of the obvious alternative, Gwyn determined to devour their entire supper if it would delay the inevitable.

Remembering what Angel had said, she smiled sweetly and replied, "I waited for you."

Her reply seemed to amuse him—but not fool him. He studied her face for a long moment. Gwyn had the distinct feeling he could see inside her head and knew the sweetness and affability she presented was nothing but a sham. Yet he inclined his head toward the small table set in front of the fire.

They sat down in opposite chairs, and Andrew reached for the bottle of French wine. Janet had spared no expense with their supper tonight.

"If you wish to have anything else, you can simply request it," she said softly as she watched him open the wine bottle.

"I have what I desire at the table with me."

She averted her eyes, staring at the lace of the tablecloth, until she heard the wine being poured. Quickly, not wanting a repeat of the other night, she reached out her hand and covered the top of her wine glass.

"I will not have any, thank you."

"The bottle was sealed. I doubt even Mistress Janet can make her potions go through glass."

She stared at him, dumbfounded, as she felt hot, angry color wash up her neck, flush into her cheeks. *He knew.* He knew and yet he sat there, as comfortable as if what had happened that night had been hardly more than a quick kiss on the cheek.

Forgetting her modesty and anything Angel had taught her, Gwyn felt her temper flare. "I fail to see how what happened the other night can be such a source of amusement to you, *m'lord.*" She felt triumphant as his expression changed to annoyance. He wanted her to call him Andrew, that much she knew. But annoying him in little ways was pleasing to her, and she determined to continue.

"I can see you have decided that one night shall stand between us forever."

She didn't reply, realizing instantly this man had a very short fuse—and she had already ignited it.

"I won't have it, Gwyn. We will start fresh this night, as if the other never happened."

"Is that possible?" She didn't protest as he filled her wine glass.

"Difficult—but possible. Now, what do you desire?" he

asked, his attention seemingly turned toward their supper.

She swallowed. "I should like to talk with you concerning how we are to forget what happened the other night. Have you already forgotten—Andrew?" She bit out his name reluctantly, not wanting to goad him further.

"I remember everything about that night. Indeed, Gwyn, it sustained me over the next several days." The expression in his blue eyes was hard. "I could have come here and claimed my rights the very next day, as I'm sure you are aware. But I didn't want to contribute to more discomfort on your part."

Her cheeks flamed again at his frankness. She wanted to dislike him intensely, yet had to admit he had been considerate of her. He had waited a week. And in that time, she had made the delicate adjustment in her mind from girl to woman.

"I sent you gifts to give you pleasure. You must know I value your companionship. I don't think I am asking too much if I desire an evening with you." His tone was slightly sarcastic, and Gwyn knew this man would ask for nothing.

She couldn't reply. Instead, she looked away again, at the silver and sparkling crystal on the small table.

"Am I?" His tone was firm, the tone of a man who would brook no disobedience.

"No, you are not," she whispered.

He set the fork down, all pretense of enjoying their supper forgotten. "Why are you so reluctant, Gwyn? Is what passed between us before so disagreeable to you? I seem to remember—"

"Please. No. I cannot bear to think of—" She pushed back the chair and stood, then would have walked away from the table if Andrew hadn't quickly stood up and blocked her.

"Gwyn?" She felt him grasp both her hands in his, and as she heard the sharp intake of his breath and felt the warmth of his fingers, she realized he must have felt how icy hers were. Suddenly she felt boneless, without any will of her own, and she resisted him only slightly as he led her over to the small sofa closest the fire.

"Sit still for a moment," he said softly as he settled her among the cushions. When he returned, he held her glass of wine in his hand.

"No, please—"

"Drink this. It will warm your blood. Gwyn, your hands are like ice!" He sounded incredulous. "Are you truly so afraid of me?"

Miserable, and for a fleeting moment conscious of the fact none of this was according to Angel's plan, Gwyn quietly downed her wine, then burst into tears.

Andrew surprised her, pulling her into his arms and holding her tightly as she sobbed. The scents surrounding him were comforting, reminding her of home. Tobacco, leather, the slight smell of horses. He held her so closely her face was pressed against his fine shirt front. Gwyn was aware, after the worst of her tears had been spent, that she had ruined the front of a very expensive shirt.

Afterwards, he kept her on his lap as he handed her a handkerchief. Gwyn quickly wiped her eyes and blew her nose as delicately as possible. Wincing, she attempted to remove herself from his lap.

"Gwyn, what's wrong? Are you in pain?"

"No, I—" Shame overtook her again. Within the course of two nights, she was more familiar with this man than any other. What could he possibly think of her? "My corset hurts." She slowly raised her eyes to his.

Gwyn was surprised to see amusement in their depths. "Then we should remedy the situation as soon as possible."

"I can call for Angel and—"

"Nonsense. I'm perfectly capable of relieving your discomfort."

She hesitated for a moment, perfectly aware of the *double entendre*. Was he belittling her? Amusing himself?

"I don't mean to hurt you, Gwyn, or make fun of you. Here now, let's take care of your problem."

Within seconds he'd assisted her to her feet, turned her

away from him. His hands were as adept as Angel's as they quickly unbuttoned the back of the blue and silver dress. She hesitated for just an instant as the gown began to slide off her shoulders, then realized how foolish she was being. He had seen her naked before hadn't he? She had the feeling he was not the sort of man who had ever had to resort to taking unfair advantage of any woman.

Andrew would take the time to win her, conquer her sensual nature completely. That scared her even more.

The dress was a pool of shimmering brocade at her feet as she stepped out of it. She hesitated, wondering if he knew how to unlace a corset. But his fingers were already beginning to work at the offending garment.

She took a deep breath as the boning loosened and felt immediately better.

"You don't like to be restrained in any way, do you, Gwyn?" There was something in his voice she couldn't quite define.

"No, I don't. It goes against my nature, as it does yours, I am sure."

He laughed then, his fingers deft and sure. "I certainly had no idea you were such an interesting woman when I first saw you on the auction block."

"Would you have bought me if you had?"

There was a smile in his voice. She couldn't see his face. "Gwyn, with beauty such as yours, I should have purchased you if you had the disposition of a shrew."

Quickly, before she lost her courage, she decided to voice her feelings.

"I feel we are alike that way, loving our freedom. I feel we have that in common."

Gwyn knew she had angered him by the silence that greeted her words. When he spoke, his voice was soft. "We may feel alike, but freedom is different for a man than for a woman."

The subject was closed. For now.

When the corset fell to the ground, she was clad in only her chemise, her petticoat, and her stockings.

Slowly, she turned to face Andrew.

"Madam, I had thought the dress would do you justice, but I'm discovering I like you better in deshabille." She was conscious of his thorough perusal of her body, his gaze lingering on her breasts and legs.

"I don't ever want you to be restrained with me, Gwyn. Do you understand my meaning?"

She bristled at the assumption, but knew that, for the time being, she could do nothing. Her fighting would have to be more subtle, or she would never win any skirmish with this man.

"Come." He held out his hand and she gave him hers. He led her over to the sofa and they sat down.

"How did you end up at The Dark Stallion?" he asked quietly.

Gwyn met his eyes. "None of that matters now." And as she said it, she was surprised to find she meant it. Edward had sold her, nothing could change that. Andrew had changed her further. Though she was still frightened by what lay ahead this night, she didn't want Andrew to give her back to Janet and have to face the madam's wrath.

My life begins at this moment and with this man. There is no looking back, ever again. The thought sustained her, gave her a quiet calm as she gazed at the man who was now her master.

"You didn't come here by ordinary means, I'm convinced of that."

She didn't reply.

"Was it against your will?" he asked gently.

"What does it matter?" she replied. "I'm here now. What I would have wished for does not enter into it."

"What would you have wished for?"

She was dangerously close to tears again, thinking of how her life had gone askew. Only two weeks before she had been home, surrounded by people she had known since she was small. People she trusted and loved.

Until Edward, and his overriding greed.

"It doesn't matter." When she saw concern darken his eyes, she rushed on. "But I would tell you what matters now."

"Go on." He took one of her hands in his, seemed to be studying the delicate fingers.

"I would ask you for your protection. The madam in this house dislikes me, and I would like to believe you will—" She stopped, not sure if she should go on.

"I will what?"

"That you will not tire of me. Or if you do, I would implore you to help me leave this house."

"I will, but on one condition."

"What is that?"

"You must tell me how you came to this place."

Gwyn moved away slightly. "In time. But not now." She found the tale of her life this past fortnight too sordid to put into words. The only bright spot had been Angel. And now Andrew. He seemed understanding, but . . .

But he is still a man.

Andrew tightened his grip on her hand and gently pulled her closer to him. "It's time to start over, Gwyn. There will be nothing between us, no false illusions."

She began to tremble before he touched her further, and he stopped.

"Why are you afraid of me?"

"I knew nothing of men until my night with you."

"I know." When she didn't answer, he said quietly, "I saw the blood on the sheet. You were a virgin."

"I was." This last was said so softly she wondered if he heard her. How could Andrew possibly understand what he had taken from her? It was something more precious, more emotional than merely the physical change in her body. He had altered the course of her life forever.

Shame flooded her. When he did not reply, she began to speak, her voice quiet and controlled. She had to try and make him understand. A man's prowess, his sexual initiation, was cheered and encouraged with delight and pride. But a woman's . . . It was always so different.

"I know Janet. What she put in my wine was to ensure my obedience to you. But it cost me dearly. Do you understand, Andrew, what it means to wake up in the morning and not want to face yourself?"

She thought she detected a hint of sadness in his expression. "I think I passed that mark quite a long time ago."

"But do you know what it does to a woman?"

"The women I've lain with have never had the feelings you have; but then, they knew what it was all about."

"And I was brought to you against my will."

He cupped her chin in one of his hands. "Sweet Gwyn, you will have a life far better than most wives. Do you realize many married couples have not talked the amount we have tonight?"

"Then how could people possibly stay married to each other?"

"You *are* an innocent! The marriages I have seen have been misery for both parties concerned. I think you've idealized the relationship between men and women. What you talk of has no place in the world."

"I cannot believe that."

"I cannot force you to. But it's the truth." His fingers loosened their light grip on her chin and feathered down her neck. Gwyn shuddered and flinched from his touch, a part of her surprised he should affect her so strongly.

"Potion or not, you possess a most sensual nature."

"No," she breathed softly, all the while afraid he spoke the truth.

"I have given you time, Gwyn. I have talked with you and tried to understand your fears. I think you are afraid of lying in that bed with me, and there is only one cure for that."

"Andrew, please—"

Gwyn stood up and would have moved away, but she felt his hands grip her shoulders and stop her. They were facing the large bed now, and she closed her eyes.

"You cannot tell me you don't respond to my touch."

Without waiting for an answer, he began to massage her shoulders, the movements slow and soothing. When she didn't say anything, she felt his fingers touch her neck, then felt one against her collarbone. She flinched gently, and he laughed. It wasn't a laugh filled with triumph or amusement. It was a low, masculine laugh that told her he knew his instincts had been correct.

"Come with me, Gwyn. Let me show you how good it can be between us." His voice seemed to be caressing her, and before she could reply, she felt his lips touch her bare shoulder. It was as if the flames from the fireplace leapt to her body and kissed it where he did. A slow, soft velvet fire began to fill her. Her eyes flew open and she jerked away from him, frightened of her feelings.

"Andrew—"

"Open your eyes, Gwyn. Don't be afraid of me, for I will never hurt you."

She did as he asked, in time to see his face near hers. She closed her eyes again as he kissed the side of her neck.

"Take your clothes off for me," he whispered.

She hesitated, then sat on the bed and took off her shoes. As she rolled down her silk stockings, she concentrated on her task. If she thought herself alone in the room, her fingers didn't tremble quite as much. But it was impossible; Andrew's burning gaze was as palpable as a touch. With clumsy fingers, she unfastened the ties on her petticoat and slipped it down over her hips.

Now there was nothing left but her chemise. The silk molded itself to her body, and she knew she was as good as naked in Andrew's eyes. Yet she was afraid to take that last step, to leave herself naked to his gaze.

"Before you take that off, I'll have to catch up with you." She watched, covertly fascinated, as his deft fingers unbuttoned his shirt and pulled it off, over his head. Gwyn caught her breath as she saw the play of taut, clearly defined muscles in his chest and arms. Strong arms. At that moment, she knew there was no escape from what was to happen this night.

Next his shoes, then his stockings. When he began to unfasten his breeches, she looked away. The soft thud told her they had joined the other clothing on the floor. She felt Andrew's arms come around her, then he was easing her down on the bed.

"Don't think, Gwyn," he whispered, his voice husky. "Just feel. Feel everything I'm going to do to you."

She thought he was going to kiss her, but he didn't. Instead, he simply ran the palms of his hands gently over her shoulders and down her arms, the smoothing, soothing motion making her skin grow warm and tingly. They were on their sides now, on the large bed, the room ablaze with light from the numerous candles and the fireplace.

"Andrew, could you . . . the candles . . ." For an instant she thought he would refuse her, but then he sat up. She closed her eyes, not wanting to see his nakedness. When she felt the mattress give beneath his weight as he joined her in bed, she opened her eyes.

Darkness. Not only had he extinguished the candles, but he had pulled the heavy curtains shut around the bed.

They were encased in a world of their own. Gwyn shivered for an instant. Tonight she would be conscious of everything he did to her.

"Cold?" Andrew pulled back the blankets on the bed and she eased herself underneath, grateful for some covering, no matter how scant. But then it didn't matter as he slid in beside her and fit his masculine body against hers. He was so warm and hard that his presence in the bed seemed to warm the sheets and turn the bedclothing into a snug cocoon.

She started as she felt one of his hands smooth over her leg, then up over her hip underneath the silk chemise. The other hand supported her as he gently rolled her over until she was straddling him.

"I think we can do away with this," he said as he grasped the hem of the chemise and slowly pulled it up over her head. He tossed it to the side of the bed, then pulled her down so she lay full length on top of him.

She stiffened, as if by making her body rigid she wouldn't have to touch his. But as his large hands moved slowly over her back with deep, long strokes, she felt herself relaxing against him. Her body began to soften, and when she put her cheek against his chest and sighed, he stroked her hair back from her forehead with a gentle touch.

"Better?" he asked.

She nodded. Suddenly, words bubbled up inside her. What frightened her most was the feeling of being powerless, of her destiny being completely out of her control. Their previous night had defied her at every turn. Would it be the same without Janet's potion? She was afraid of her lack of control from this fire he brought to life within her body, and some primitive, protective instinct warned her against such terrible vulnerability.

"It will be good for you, my beauty. I promise you that." He kissed her neck, and she blurted out the words racing through her mind.

"I just wish I were a man."

She was surprised when he threw back his head and laughed, deep laughter that shook his muscled body and made her jiggle gently astride him. When his laughter died down, he stroked her cheek softly and said, "I'm certainly glad you aren't."

"But if I were—"

"If you were, you would never have gotten into this situation."

"Exactly. A man isn't as vulnerable as a woman."

"In some ways. In others, a man is certainly more vulnerable. We don't have the advantage you do of being able to keep our feelings hidden." As he spoke, one of his hands closed over hers, and he guided it down his chest, over the crisply curling hair until she felt the heat and masculine hardness between his legs. "I have no choice but to be truthful, Gwyn. I want you. And soon."

110

It felt strange, touching him there. His hand taught her how to caress him, and all the while Gwyn wondered how he could say such strength was vulnerability. But then, as she touched him, she felt his body tense and arch slightly, and she knew she controlled his pleasure. Emboldened, she began to touch him freely and was shocked to find a part of herself *wanting* to explore his masculine body and learn its every secret.

She was surprised when he gently stopped her exploration and rolled her over so she was pinned beneath him, his body hot and hard against hers, his weight balanced on his elbows.

"If you were a man," he said as he gently kissed her cheek, then her temple, "you would no doubt be an impertinent rascal." Gwyn drew her breath in sharply as she felt his tongue trace an erotic pattern on her collarbone, then move tantalizingly closer to her aching breast. "And if you were a man, I'd no doubt have to call you out. To demand satisfaction, as it were." His mouth closed over hers, his lips easing hers apart and his tongue darting deeply inside. Gwyn moaned deep in her throat at this intimate invasion, and she felt pure, white heat invade her loins. She had thought so much of her reaction had been from Janet's mischief. Now she knew her response had been to Andrew.

It was too late to protest, to ask him to slow his relentless, erotic path. Each thrust of his tongue pushed her deeper and deeper into a vortex of complete sensation. Her mind receded, to be replaced by the clamorings of her body, aching and insistent. He was never forceful with her; he simply coaxed and urged, letting her dance toward the flame of passion at her own pace, but never allowing her to elude it.

Andrew broke the kiss. "We would meet at dawn, and each be given our weapons," he said softly, for her ears alone.

"I don't have any," Gwyn whispered.

"Oh, you do. More than you know. This," he said as his hand traced her cheekbone. "And this." He outlined her lips with a gentle finger. "This." His hand caressed her neck and moved lower. "And most certainly this," he said as his hand moved over her breast lightly, with just enough pressure to ignite the skin his fingers traced.

"Andrew." His name was a low, ragged moan on her lips as he covered them. This time the kiss was more passionate, as he cupped the back of her head with his hand and gently moved his mouth against hers, rubbing, nipping, enflaming. He caught her lower lip with his teeth and gently bit it, and Gwyn arched herself against his warmth and strength, sensing completion in the hardness of his body.

She broke the kiss this time, turning her head to the side on the soft pillow and panting for air, for something, anything to replace the wild sensations invading her body.

Gwyn almost cried out, the sensations were that intense. He touched her intimately, and she grasped his muscular shoulders, desperate for something to cling to, anything to make what was happening more bearable.

His lovemaking began in earnest then, and Gwyn could do no more than respond. Her hands moved restlessly over his body, settling on his shoulders, where her fingers dug into the strong muscles. She tried to prevent herself from crying out countless times. His mouth and hands worked magic, moving quickly over her burning, sweat-sheened skin.

She was mindless as his lips closed over her breast, drawing the hard, tight nipple into the warmth of his mouth. He took his time, exciting her to a frenzy before she felt his warm breath between her breasts and knew he was moving his attentions to the other. They seemed to swell and grow harder as he licked and kissed them, and Gwyn was powerless to do anything but bend her body to his will.

He kissed his way down her stomach, and her hips bucked in sharp surprise as his hands forced her thighs farther apart. His lips swiftly claimed that most sensitive, secret part. Unerringly, he found the heart of her femininity, and this time Gwyn did cry out, muffling her quick, sharp sobs deep within the feather pillow. Andrew was as urgently masculine here as ever, opening her. Gwyn could feel herself responding to his touch, the secret rhythms within her body powerful and deep. His erotic heat was the sun, blazing and powerful as it rode through the sky. And she was a rose, tightly budded; but as the dazzling fire of the sun warmed her, each petal opened, slowly, and soon she was fully in bloom, turning toward that powerful heat, unable to resist.

His tongue probed deeply, exactly as it had within her mouth, and Gwyn cried out, in the throes of an ecstasy deeper than any she had ever experienced. Her fingers became tangled in his hair and she was pulling, pulling, urging him up and over her, accepting his mouth hotly over hers, arching her hips against his and silently, eloquently, pleading with him to end this sensual torment.

With one clean thrust of his powerful hips, he entered her. She felt a moment of discomfort as her body sought to accommodate his power, then a pleasure so intense she cried out against his shoulder. He began to move, long, smooth strokes meant to arouse and excite, and Gwyn knew her resistance was gone, replaced by an aching, primal need that overrode all else. All sensation was centered where she and Andrew were joined together, where his hot, silken maleness touched her burning wetness.

Her hips began to answer his, and she heard him groan as she surged up against him. Their lovemaking was urgent, taut, relentless, as they moved closer and closer to that ultimate, passionate goal. Gwyn could feel the muscles flexing and bunching beneath her fingers as she touched his shoulders and back, then her fingers closed over his buttocks and held him tightly. His hands moved to her hips, his fingers dug into her flesh, but nothing mattered except that this should continue, this blinding sensation that left her oblivious to anything else.

Her head fell back, her eyes closed tightly. Her body tightened, every muscle urgent, compressed, anxious. Waiting. Waiting for something on the brink of happening.

When it did, she heard someone scream. As she felt Andrew's mouth come down over hers, she realized it had been *her* scream. Her body burned with heat, sensation pushed out from that most intimate place all the way to her fingers and toes and up out the top of her head. Andrew continued to move within her, his powerful strokes becoming faster and deeper, as did his breathing. Soon his entire body shuddered, then she felt him pulse deep within her trembling body. He broke the kiss, his breath coming out in a low, anguished moan as he lowered his head and buried it against her hair.

It had all stopped now, and he felt heavy and warm on top of her, but she didn't mind. The weight of his body kept her from trembling, flying off the bed, exploding into a thousand glowing stars. They lay, arms and legs entwined, for what could have been minutes or hours. Finally, Andrew slowly raised his head and levered his body off hers.

"Gwyn?" His voice was raspy. Anxious.

Something deep within her heart burst with happiness as she heard genuine concern in his voice. He had to care for her, otherwise why should it matter to him how she felt?

"I'm all right, Andrew."

"Did I hurt you?"

"No."

"You're sure?"

She had never heard his voice sound so soft. So caring. Moving her body closer to his, she whispered, "A little. But it's no matter."

"It sounded like I did. The sounds you were making."

"You sounded the same way."

He laughed then, a low, satisfied laugh, and she felt his arm come around her shoulders and pull her tightly against him.

"No more fear of my bed, I trust."

"No. Now I . . . understand why people would want to do this."

He laughed again. "You are the most interesting woman, continually saying what's on your mind."

"I'm not usually this way."

"Only with me, hmm?"

"You bring out that side of me, m'lord."

"*Andrew.*"

"Yes, m'lord." And she laughed, the sound of sheer delight filling the curtained bed.

Andrew rolled her over slowly, then gave her a long, lingering kiss. When he finally lifted his head, he said softly, "Madam, I cannot promise you a night like our first, but I can assure you your pleasure this night is far from finished."

Chapter Eight

Gwyn opened her eyes slowly, aware of the warmth and strength next to her in the feather bed. She moved her head slightly so she could see light spilling in the window. The room was warm. Someone had come in during the morning and lit the fire and opened the bed curtains.

In the light of day, her actions the night before were scandalous. She had cavorted in bed with Andrew, urging him on, laughing at his murmured words. They had been enclosed within the bed curtains, safely tucked away. He was the only man in her world, certainly the only man she would let take the liberties he had.

How far you've come in so little time. Andrew was an excellent instructor in the art of seduction; there wasn't a part of her he hadn't explored, admired, loved.

Loved. He doesn't love you. He doesn't even know you. She shifted her eyes to the canopy above, not wanting to look at the erotic mural on the far wall. Her vision blurred, and she cursed her weakness. *Angel was right. I could never have survived in the streets. I can't even control myself in his arms. The minute he kisses me, I'm lost.*

She melted in his arms like a candle against a flame. And he was the expert, the master, the all-powerful lover who had her beneath his complete control.

I don't know what to do. She blinked her eyes rapidly, still staring at the canopy. The turns her life had taken seemed so unfair, everything thrown at her so quickly. More than anything she wished she could escape her confused emotions and try to understand what these trials were meant to teach her.

But not this. All I'm learning is how to be a man's mistress. She glanced over at Andrew. He was lying on his back, sleeping soundly with one of his arms flung above his head. The other was wound tightly around her, his fingers beneath her breast. She studied his large, strong hand, dark hair feathered over the wrist and up his arm. He was a powerful male animal, perfectly aware of the pleasure and mindlessness those fingers could induce. She had been at the mercy of his hands and lips and body, and especially his—

She stopped the thought but couldn't stop her eyes from wandering down the length of the covers. They were pulled halfway up his muscled chest. Her gaze stopped where she thought his thighs were, where he was most powerfully male.

The night she had been drugged was receding in her mind. Last night had been shrouded in darkness.

Now, though she fought a hard battle with what she had been taught a woman should think about, Gwyn was curious.

What does he look like there? In the darkness, that part of his body assumed larger-than-life erotic power. But what did it look like? She had touched it, taken it inside her own body, yet she had no idea.

She glanced at him again, assuring herself he was still deep in slumber. Slowly, carefully, Gwyn extricated herself from his grasp. Even in sleep, he protested. His fingers moved higher, closed around one of her breasts. Gwyn bit her lip against the sensation.

Moving a little at a time, she managed to loosen his hold. She shifted gently in bed so she was lying next to him and could see his face.

There was something unguarded about Andrew in his sleep,

117

and Gwyn suddenly realized why. A constant tension was present in his face and stance when he was awake, as if he were always prepared to fight.

And where does that come from? she wondered. For a moment, her eyes stung again. *How little we know about each other.* It was a total paradox, and one she wanted to rectify.

Working carefully, she lifted the blanket and lowered it so his body was exposed. She had seen his chest before, and the muscled flatness of his stomach.

Gwyn held her breath. There was a queer little ache in her stomach as she moved the blanket lower still. . . .

Andrew shifted his legs and she stared. What had brought her so much pleasure last night was lying softly against one of his thighs. It seemed incredible that so much power could be stored in something that looked so totally defenseless. She reached out and touched it gently. It felt different, not smooth and hard but soft and tender. Vulnerable. She cupped it in her hand, her fingers closed over the soft skin, and wondered at her discovery.

"So curious so early in the morning?" he asked softly, then lowered his head and gently bit her shoulder. Desperately, Gwyn willed her body to go rigid. She hadn't intended this to happen!

She turned her face away from his, tried not to respond as she felt his lips caress the soft skin beneath her ear.

"Come with me, Gwyn," he urged softly. "Send me home with a smile on my face and thoughts of you."

His casual words were her undoing. She started to cry, long, shuddering sobs that wracked her body. She felt his fingers closing over her chin and found herself staring up into his face.

"Gwyn?" He seemed truly concerned.

She tried to form the words. "No. Please."

He shifted off her, slid to her side, and put his arms around her. He held her until she was still, her face buried against his chest. It seemed strange she should seek comfort in the arms of the man who had caused her such emotional pain.

"Gwyn? Tell me what bothers you." He lifted her in his arms so she was sitting across his lap, the blanket pulled up around her shoulders. "I don't want any secrets between us. Tell me why you have tears in your eyes."

"I'm so . . . *ashamed*," she whispered.

"Ashamed?" He was incredulous. "You have nothing to be ashamed of. You've given me great pleasure."

"I behave like a whore in your bed. I'm not any better than any of the girls here."

"You're considerably better—more than you know. Many feign their pleasure, while you give freely of yours. When you show me I am pleasing you, it heightens my own."

The shock she felt must have shown in her eyes, because he continued. "Don't think a man doesn't realize. Though many of the men who frequent The Dark Stallion don't care."

"They . . . the girls here pretend?"

"It's a job to them, Gwyn. It has nothing to do with the joy of the body."

"But I . . . my father said—" She couldn't go on.

"Tell me what your father taught you about the way a woman should behave."

"Why should you want to know?"

"You . . . fascinate me. I can't figure you for a whore." His dark blue eyes seemed to burn into hers, and Gwyn felt herself looking away again.

"I'm going to make you tell me how you came to The Dark Stallion. Everything about you interests me, Gwyn. You belong to me now, and that makes you my business."

His words angered her, and she could feel a fine tension in her body.

"Don't test me on this point, Gwyn. I'm a reasonable man, but I don't share what is mine."

"There are people who would say you are wrong, that one person can't own another."

His eyes widened. "Have I bought myself a rebel? A sharp mind disguised by such beauty?"

119

"Do you believe you can own me?"

"I don't believe it. I know it."

She took a deep breath. "And if I asked you for my freedom? If I asked you to see me safely back to where I came from?"

"I would ask you for one thousand pounds."

"I see." She had had a quick glimpse of the temper that simmered beneath Andrew's cool, controlled facade, and she did not wish to try him further. But she had to ask.

"And if I gave it to you?"

Something in the way his body tensed told her she had pushed him too far. "Don't think of trying to earn any money while you're here. I won't have you consorting with any other man."

She opened her mouth to reply that that had not been her intention, then quickly shut it.

"Tell me what goes on in that mind of yours," he said quietly.

"I think of home."

"And where is that?"

She remained silent.

"I'll find out soon enough, Gwyn. Tell me what your father taught you about men. And what a good woman is meant for." There was a slight edge of sarcasm to his voice, and she was stung by it.

"Certainly not for this, to be some man's mistress!"

His calm statement of ownership still smouldered within her breast.

"So you think if you had followed the path your father had laid out for you, you would be happier?"

"I—my father is dead."

"I'm sorry." His voice was soft, tinged with regret.

She wasn't sure she had heard him correctly.

"What happened?"

"He was—he was visiting with a neighbor. They—the husband and wife—had just lost a child. He stayed later than he should have and was caught in a storm on the way home.

120

Lightning hit a tree near the road, his horse bolted. He fell, and his head hit a stone." Her voice was flat, devoid of all emotion. She had loved her father deeply and missed him so very much.

"Your father was a giving man."

"He was a vicar. He would have gone out in any storm if he'd thought he could offer comfort."

There was quiet amazement in his tone. "And how did a vicar's daughter come to The Dark Stallion?"

She pushed her hair off her face and sighed. "It doesn't matter. Not now."

"Yes it does."

She met his gaze and consciously changed the subject. "My father wanted me to marry a good man. We would build a life together, raise children. I would have been a good wife, Andrew. Before . . . this."

When he finally spoke, his voice was very quiet.

"You will never be intimate with any man but me. How is what we have truly different from marriage?"

"My father didn't bring me into this world to service a man in a bordello." She wanted her words to hurt him.

"Perhaps he was unaware of hidden talents you possess. A more apt pupil would be hard to find."

She stared at him, incredulous he should want to mock her so cruelly. It was several moments before she found her voice.

"I don't consider what I do with you a talent."

"You've adapted very well."

She could feel tears gathering in her eyes as she studied him. Gwyn took a deep breath. "Who taught you how to be so exquisitely cruel, *m'lord?*"

"You did." He slid off her lap and rose to his feet. "I find this conversation displeasing. Either we change the subject or I will leave."

"As you wish."

"I wish to change the subject."

"Yes, m'lord." She took perverse pleasure in the little ways

121

she could annoy him.

"Yes, *Andrew*," he said quietly.

"Yes, Andrew." She could feel his eyes on her.

"Now, what did your father tell you about men?"

She lowered her gaze to the carpet, sure he was going to laugh at her. "He told me I would find out everything I needed to know on my bridal night, in my husband's arms."

"And weren't you curious?"

"No."

"You were curious this morning."

Color stung her cheeks as she looked up at him. "I never meant for you to see—"

"But I did. And you *were* curious."

"I—" Words failed her. She had been curious after her talk with Angel about men's bodies, but she couldn't tell that to Andrew!

"Why don't you believe you should enjoy yourself in my bed?"

The question shocked her, going to the heart of her emotions. Realizing she had already lost whatever respectability she could hope for, Gwyn decided to be honest with him.

"I've always heard there were two kinds of women. . . ."

"Good and bad," he finished for her.

"Yes."

"And which do you think you are?"

"Now?" For some perverse reason, she wanted to hurt him. "Certainly bad."

"I think you're very good."

She studied his face, wondering if he was teasing her. "Surely you don't mean—"

"Yes, I do. Let me add to your education. There are plenty of respectable, married women in London—your good women—who have never hesitated to let me know they're available to share my bed if I so desire."

She stared at him, shocked.

122

"There are quite a few of your good women who never hear a word of any sermon and are like mares in heat when it comes to selecting the man they want to bed."

"What does that make you?" The words were out before she considered them.

He laughed. "I know exactly what I am. And what people think of me. But for all that, I've never taken a woman to bed against her will." His eyes were strangely expressionless. "Before you. And I can assure you, Gwyn, I felt just as taken advantage of by the wine as you."

"But afterwards, you still came to my bed. . . ."

"I'd already robbed you of your maidenhead and claimed you as my own. You'll never want for anything, Gwyn. I'll see to your happiness."

She spoke very quietly. "I don't know if I can be happy with such an arrangement."

"You will be. I can promise you that in a year's time, you'll realize you have a better life than most women."

They were interrupted by a soft knock at the door.

"Come in!" Andrew called as he slid beneath the bedcovers.

Angel poked her head around the door. "M'lord, we have the tub your requested, and the water is heating. Shall I bring it in?"

"Thank you, Angel, that will do nicely."

While Gwyn stared, Thatch carried in the big copper tub she had bathed in before. Three maids followed him, laden with towels, scented soaps, and oils. Comprehension dawned as Thatch set the tub by the fire and the maids clustered around, depositing their burdens.

Once they were alone, Gwyn asked, "Am I to take a bath in front of you?"

He smiled. "No."

"Then I am to bathe you?"

"No."

Her stomach tightened as she held in her desperation. She didn't like the strange, sensual power he had over her.

"I wish to take a bath with you."

It seemed a strange command. "Why?"

"I want to indulge a fantasy I've had for a long time."

Gwyn knew better than to refuse. He was like a violent summer storm, wreaking havoc in her life. She had seen the aftermath of such storms, the scattered pieces of trees that refused to bend. Only those that yielded before such power survived. She remained quietly in bed beside Andrew as Angel and her small fleet of maids reentered the room with buckets of water. When they finished, after two trips, and left them alone, she turned to Andrew and looked up at him, unable to conceal the glint of defiance in her eyes.

He ran his fingers underneath the covers, touching the swell of her breasts gently. She fought the urge to close her eyes and sway toward him.

His soft laughter infuriated her even more.

"Don't fight yourself, Gwyn. Yield to me."

"No."

He eased the bedcovers away from her body. She closed her eyes.

"I would like you conscious again tonight, beauty." There was a peculiar hunger in his tone, and she opened her eyes, curious.

He was already aroused. She couldn't avoid seeing his maleness, but then she glanced quickly away.

"What, not curious any longer?"

She couldn't endure the amusement in his voice. "Please, Andrew, don't make fun of me."

"Make fun of you? Is that what you think I'm doing?"

She was silent.

He gathered her into his arms and she felt his hot arousal against her stomach. "I won't make fun of you, Gwyn. I want to make love to you."

She cursed herself as she realized even the low sound of his voice made her tremble.

He led her over to the tub and helped her in. She stood,

waiting, her hands crossed in front of her breasts, as he stepped in. Andrew lay back so his shoulders were braced against the lip. Still holding her hand, he gently pulled her down until she straddled his thighs. Catching her hair in his fingers, he pulled her face close to his and kissed her, his lips firm and warm.

She felt her body loosening, blooming beneath his expert ministrations. When his lips moved to her breasts and grazed the tight pink buds, she moaned softly.

"That's right, my beauty. Give to me. Don't be afraid. Give me all of you . . . I want all of you."

And then she stopped thinking and slipped into total sensuality.

"You can trust this woman?" The Duke of Cuckfield had an edge to his voice, and Edward Sleaforth knew he had to tread carefully. He didn't want to rouse the Duke's wrath. He was at the Duke's house and they were sitting in the immense library.

"Yes. I've promised her a way out of The Dark Stallion. All she has to do is give me information about Gwyn and Andrew."

"That black Irish bastard. I'll see him dancing on air at Tyburn before this is finished. What did the tart tell you?"

"He's been spending most of his time with the girl. He barely leaves her room, except to go home and change his clothing. He even eats most of his suppers with her."

"What did they do tonight?" Edward noticed the Duke of Cuckfield stared at him with a peculiar intensity, as if he wasn't really there. The man had retreated into his mind, deep inside his peculiar fantasy world.

"He ordered a bath sent up, and they—they bathed together. Afterwards, he had her again."

The Duke scowled, furious. "He'll wear her out before I have a chance to have her."

"From what I hear, my cousin has taken to a whore's life with ease. She's completely captivated him."

Cuckfield took a small sip of Burgundy, then set the crystal goblet down on the table. "She won't find me as easy a keeper. I mean to have that girl, whether he tires of her or not. How long was Andrew with this other woman?"

"Almost five months. I've heard that was a record of sorts—for him."

"I can't wait five months, Edward. We'll have to devise a plan."

Edward remained silent. He had barely survived the debauchery at the Duke's last private orgy and had no desire to participate again. If he kept himself in Cuckfield's favor, perhaps he could escape more sexual service.

The Duke tapped his fingers thoughtfully against the table. "Perhaps a way to dispose of Andrew. Once that little beauty has no protection, she'll be easy to capture."

"I think that's a capital idea," Edward said, knowing he would verbally agree with anything the Duke decided on.

The Duke abruptly changed the subject. "Will you be coming to my holiday revel? I'd like to count on your participation."

It wasn't an invitation. It was an order. Edward felt his stomach clench in revulsion. But gazing into the cold grey eyes across the table, he knew he had no choice.

"Of course I'll attend."

"Good. Good." The Duke's fingers tapped lightly together, forming a steeple. He tilted his head back, deep in thought. Edward simply waited. He'd been with the Duke long enough to realize these fragmented ideas and bits of conversation would eventually coalesce into a whole.

When the Duke finally spoke, Edward's eyes were heavy, a combination of too much wine and too many late nights.

"What did you say this woman's name was?"

"Suzanne."

"And you're sure she can be trusted? I don't want anything to interfere with my having Gwyneth."

"Suzanne will obey me."

"Perhaps"—and here the Duke leaned forward, flecks of interest finally lighting his cold grey eyes—"perhaps your whoring little cousin can be persuaded to join us over the holidays?"

Edward nodded his head. "I'm sure I can arrange it. Just let me talk to Suzanne."

Gwyn lay on the chaise, wrapped in a blanket, staring into the fire. Andrew had left this morning, after another sensual night. Their lovemaking knew no bounds. After he had carefully bathed her—and had made her bathe him—he had lifted her, wet, out of the tub and taken her in front of the fire. His lovemaking had had a fierce intensity to it, and Gwyn had been powerless.

But afterwards, looking at his face as he slept, she had wondered at his need to be so physically close to her. He was an expert at physical intimacy, but she suspected the path to his heart would be much harder to find. Yet he seemed to have need of this closeness, and lovemaking was the only way.

He had taken his time exploring her body, had even asked her about the scar high up on her leg. When he had first touched it, she'd flinched away. But he'd reassured her and had insisted she tell him.

"I was burned as a child, Andrew. I don't remember much about it; I was too young. But I have always been a little afraid of fire."

Especially the one you raise in me.

He'd spent the night with her, woke her with a kiss, and walked out the door. Leaving her only her memories.

She didn't even turn her head at the slight tapping at the door.

"Gwyn?" She heard Angel shut the door, then her brisk footsteps as she came quickly into the room. "Gwyn? Are you feeling poorly?"

She nodded her head, not trusting herself to speak. When

Angel sat down on the chaise next to her, she looked at her friend, knowing her anguish was clearly reflected in her expression.

"*Mon petit chat*, it cannot be so bad. He cares for you, I know it! He spends so much time with you, is so enamored—"

"He likes to dominate me."

"That is not so! He is a *gentleman*, Gwyn, and you can depend on him to help you. . . ."

"I'm never going to depend on any man. Ever again."

Angel sighed, then took one of her hands. "I think you are getting crazy, trapped in this room. Come with me; I want you to meet a friend of mine. Let me fix your hair, and we can pick out a dress. You'll feel better if you get out for a time."

Twenty minutes later she was following Angel down a winding hallway. Despite her earlier depression, she was intrigued by the prospect of getting away from her prison, if only for a few hours. When Angel stopped in front of a door, Gwyn had to admit she was curious.

"Lily! *Pouvons-nous entrer?*"

"*Oui*, Angelique, *Entrez donc.*"

When they stepped inside, Gwyn smiled in spite of herself. The woman who was lying back on the canopied bed was dressed in a sheer silk wrapper. On the brocade bedspread was a box of chocolates, and the tiny papers littering the bedspread gave evidence to the fact she had already enjoyed several.

"*Avancez, avancez!* Hello, Gwyn. Angelique has told me so much about you." Her English was precisely pronounced, her choice of words painstaking. She was making such an effort to make her feel welcome Gwyn couldn't help but respond.

"Hello." She held out her hand. "I'm very happy to make your acquaintance." There was something about this woman that made a person absolutely sure they were going to have fun. Glossy black curls were piled high on her head, held in place with a pink satin ribbon. Her features were delicate, her mouth slightly pouting, her bright green eyes half closed. Her nose was a mere snub on her oval face, and her eyelashes were thick, black, and spiky.

"*Asseyez-vous; je vous en prie et prenez des chocolats—*"

"Lily, Gwyn doesn't speak French."

"Ah, I see! Well, then you will have to endure my English, as bad as it is."

"It's much better than my French," Gwyn admitted. She had to smile again when Lily laughed. It was an infectious, tinkling laugh that filled and warmed the room.

"She is so precious, this one! Just like you said!" She glanced at Angel, then picked up the box of chocolates and handed it to Gwyn. "Take one. Fat George, he gave them to me! Such a generous man!" She rolled her expressive eyes. "And he should be, that rabbit! He jumped on top of me and was done before I even knew what he was about!"

Angel dissolved into a fit of giggles, and Gwyn watched as Lily twined one of the maid's dark curls around her slender finger and yanked it gently.

"And then," Lily said, restraining her laughter, "he said"— and here she puffed out her cheeks into comically fat jowls and lowered her voice—"'Oh, Lily, we still have almost an hour. Could I have you again?' And I said, 'not unless you bring me a box of chocolates!' And he did!" She lowered her voice. "Even sending him out for chocolates, I still had time for George again!" Lily laughed and waved her hand at Gwyn. "Take another one, *mon petit chou!* You can afford to; you have a beautiful little body!"

She leaned over toward Angel. "I'm thinking of giving George to Madeleine. What do you think?"

"I think George would have a seizure!" Angel replied.

"I don't think I would want Fat George, if he's still the rabbit you say he is!" Gwyn looked up as another woman silently entered the room. She was slender, her figure almost boyish with slim hips and a flat chest. Her fair blond hair was cropped closely around her head, and her eyes were the brightest blue Gwyn had ever seen. She was dressed in a black wrapper, and to Gwyn's eyes she looked terribly sophisticated.

"Madeleine! You finally meet the Bordello Bride!" Lily was triumphant as she handed her friend the box of chocolates. Gwyn looked up, startled, but Lily took her hand and squeezed it. "Don't take any of us seriously, *mon ange*. We laugh so we don't go crazy in this madhouse, you know?"

Gwyn was aware of Madeleine studying her. When the short-haired woman finally spoke, her words startled her.

"Is it true your cousin sold you to Janet to pay his gambling debts?" Though she still had a slight French accent, her English was flawless.

Gwyn looked quickly at Angel, feeling betrayed.

Angel shrugged her shoulders eloquently. "I never told her a thing. Madeleine has a way of knowing everything that goes on at The Dark Stallion."

"I make it my business," Madeleine replied softly, reaching for a chocolate. "You are always protected if you know who your enemies are"—Her huge blue eyes flashed—"and what they are up to."

There was something in her expression that made Gwyn believe this woman had led a hard life. Realizing Madeleine's knowledge of her was not going to be used in a malicious way, Gwyn decided to trust her.

"Yes. It's true."

"I heard about the auction. The Duke of Cuckfield was furious when Andrew bid against him. He was fascinated by you. You'd best be scared of that man, Gwyn," Madeleine said with assurance. "You have an enemy in a high place. He can hurt you."

"Hah!" Lily waved a hand in the air. "He's a handsome one. I think he just needs the right woman to tame him, like Gwyn is taming Andrew."

"Not the Duke, Lily," Madeleine warned. "The things I know about him would make your blood freeze."

"Fat George walking in my door makes my blood freeze," Lily teased. "Come, Gwyn, tell us your story."

She quickly related the events, telling Angel's two friends of everything but her intimate evenings with Andrew. She knew even Madeleine couldn't know about her wine being drugged and about the first night she'd spent with Andrew.

"He is a stallion, that one!" Lily leaned back against the masses of lace cushions on her bed. "I've had dreams of making love with him since Suzanne came down to breakfast and had to sit on a pillow!"

"Suzanne," Madeleine said slowly, unwrapping a chocolate carefully, "is one of your enemies at The Dark Stallion. She bears you little affection. Stay away from her."

"Why?" Gwyn asked.

"Because you stole Andrew away from her."

"I didn't steal him! He *bought* me! He made the decision!"

"You also," Madeleine said, studying the chocolate in her hand, "have to know how your enemies think. Suzanne thinks you stole Andrew away from her. He used to see her all the time, for a long time. His patronage gave her status—power—among the whores. Now she has nothing. So she hates you." She popped the chocolate into her mouth.

"What should I do?" Gwyn asked.

Madeleine thought as she savored the chocolate. She finished the sweet, then said quietly, "Stay away from her. She's the sort who will destroy something before she'll let it go. She can't destroy Andrew, he's too powerful. So she'll try to destroy you." She touched Gwyn's arm. "She's a cowardly thing. A pathetic creature. Stand up to her once and she'll leave you alone. Just be aware."

"So," Lily said, a mischievous smile on her mouth, "how are things with Andrew? Is he as wonderful as Suzanne says?"

"I don't know." Gwyn hedged, not wanting to reveal any of the intimacies she'd experienced with Andrew. "I haven't ever been with another man."

"So you *were* a virgin! Ah, Gwyn, you will have a hold on his heart now. Men are funny about that, being the first, you know?"

"I've heard that, yes."

Lily pouted prettily. "You are not going to tell us anything, *non?*"

Gwyn smiled, feeling more at ease with this group. "*Non.*"

Madeleine laughed and reached for another chocolate.

"You must find out all about Andrew, *mon ange*, because he is as much a threat as Suzanne," Lily said quietly. "Men and women fight for different things because they feel so differently. I will help you with your fight. Angelique likes you, and anyone she likes, I like. Madeleine can tell you anything you want to know about Andrew. It will help you . . . handle him. Understand his moods. He is a moody one, eh?"

"He's only in one kind of mood when he visits your rooms, Gwyn." Madeleine reached for another chocolate.

"Why is he so . . . distant?" Sensing Madeleine could help her, Gwyn warmed to her subject. "I feel he's with me in the room—but not with me."

"You wouldn't have heard any of his past, growing up in the country." Madeleine settled back on the bed next to Lily.

"That Andrew, he has a tragic, romantic past," Lily interjected quickly. "It is all in his brooding eyes. You can see when he is thinking how his expression changes. . . ."

"It wasn't romantic; it was a bloody mess," Madeleine said. "I know what really happened because I talked with one of the servants in the house at the time. Maura's maid. I met her at the lacemaker's. Andrew's father, Geoffrey, fell in love with Andrew's mother, but she was already married to a *very* powerful and cruel man."

"The Earl of—"

"Lily, it doesn't matter! There are too many details. If you tell it like that, we'll be here all night!" She shifted her attention back to Gwyn. "Andrew's mother became pregnant and gave birth to a boy—Andrew—but his stepfather didn't know the child wasn't his until he caught his wife in Geoffrey's arms. He called him out the same night and locked Andrew's mother, Maura, in her rooms."

132

Gwyn felt a strange chill settle over her. She was certain the outcome of this story was not going to be happy.

"They were both excellent swordsmen, and battled up and down the hall of the huge estate. The entire time Maura kept pounding on her bedroom door, begging to be let out so she could stop the fight."

"How old was Andrew?" Gwyn asked quietly.

"Five, if I remember that old servant correctly. Both men had agreed that the first to draw blood would be the winner. And Geoffrey drew first blood. He put down his sword, and the Earl ran him through. He killed him."

Gwyn felt sick. What a horrible thing for a child to bear. She thought back to her own childhood, especially her father. He had always been there, making it easy for her to learn to trust and love.

Andrew, though he was born to privilege, had never felt secure, had never been surrounded by the type of love she had always taken for granted. She thought of how he always seemed tense, ready to fight. And she couldn't imagine living her life that way, alone and not trusting. Something softened in her heart as she came to understand part of what drove him.

"It was a huge scandal!" Lily broke in, picking up the threads of the story. "Maura went completely mad, and her husband, *l'affreux*, kept her locked up. Andrew was allowed to run wild, like a little animal. Then one day, when the mother was getting dressed, she asked her maid, 'How could Geoffrey have been killed when he was the better swordsman?'"

"I thought she was insane," Angel said.

"She was," Lily replied. "This was one of her—how do you say—clearer moments in the head."

"Or maybe he just locked her away," Gwyn said quietly, thinking of her cousin Edward.

Madeleine continued. "The maid had been in Maura's family for years, and she told her mistress the truth. She had been hiding behind one of the curtains in the hallway when the duel began, and she peeked through the folds and saw the Earl break his promise and kill Geoffrey. So when she told Maura, she escaped her rooms and went to find her husband." Madeleine's voice was quiet, utterly devoid of any emotion. "She found a knife and slit his throat. Then she killed herself."

Gwyn was holding so much emotion in check that her chest hurt. Twice her eyes had filled, her nose stung. She wasn't sure why she should feel so strongly about a man who kept her captive and continually dominated her.

But thinking of Andrew as a small, helpless child was her undoing. Remembering his face in sleep, his expression peaceful. So beautiful. No wonder he never let himself relax, except in sleep.

"What happened to Andrew?" Gwyn's voice was low.

"His grandfather came much later and adopted him. And raised him as best he could." Madeleine, finished with her story, reached for another chocolate.

"And they say," Lily said dreamily, "that the ghosts of Andrew's father and mother still walk the grounds during the witching hour. But they never meet. And when you hear the wind sighing through the tree branches, it is that they are talking to each other and saying how much they still love each other."

But Gwyn's thoughts were far from romantic ghosts. She couldn't stop thinking about Andrew. How could you ever explain something like that to a five-year-old boy?

No wonder he keeps a certain part of his emotions in reserve. No wonder he is so very careful to reveal as little as possible to me.

"She is thoughtful, *mon pauvre tresor*," Lily observed.

Angel reached over and squeezed Gwyn's hand, jarring her out of her thoughts. "We had better get back," she said. "Andrew will be coming soon."

Gwyn nodded. "Thank you for the chocolates, Lily. And thank you, Madeleine, for the warning and the story."

Madeleine rose to her feet, the movement quiet and graceful. "Stay and chat with Lily, Angelique. I'll make certain Gwyn gets back to her room safely."

Once outside in the hallway, the two women walked quickly back to Gwyn's rooms. Madeleine stepped just inside the bedchamber with Gwyn and closed the door carefully behind them.

"Gwyn?"

"Yes?"

"If you're ever offered a glass of wine you don't see being poured from a bottle in front of you, dip your finger in it first and taste it. If it's sweet, it's one of Janet's potions. If it's bitter, it's poisoned."

Gwyn stared at the short-haired woman. "How did you know?" she finally whispered.

Madeleine smiled. "Survive in this world as long as I have, and you'll learn." She touched Gwyn's hair gently. "You're smart. You're going to survive." She paused for a moment, then said, "Can I ask a favor of you?"

"Anything."

"Help me watch over Lily. She's—she dreams too much, and I worry it will be her downfall."

Gwyn reached for Madeleine's hand and squeezed it reassuringly.

"I promise."

"Now enjoy that man of yours tonight, and make sure you keep his protection." Madeleine smiled quickly, her large blue eyes friendly. Gwyn watched as she turned and slipped silently out the door.

Chapter Nine

The days passed, and a pattern was established. Though it was a pattern Gwyneth wasn't particularly comfortable with, there was nothing she could do. Thatch stood silently in the hall, his eyes ever watchful. In her heart she still wanted to escape, but any such plans proved impossible.

Andrew came to her room almost every night, and if he did not, he sent a message. Gwyn found herself looking forward to his visits, though she was still uncomfortable about her ardent response to his lovemaking.

He was her one link with the outside world, indeed her only evidence such a world still existed. He was an intelligent man, a complex person. And Gwyn was determined to get beneath the calm, composed facade he presented her with and find the man beneath.

Mornings were the worst. She had to lie in her bed and face herself and what she had become. As the weeks passed, her life in the country seemed farther and farther away. Almost like a dream.

Did I ever live that life? Gwyn thought one morning as she lay in bed, Andrew beside her. His muscular arm was thrown possessively over her waist even in sleep. She didn't struggle to move away from him anymore. There was something comforting about his warmth and strength. At first she had been surprised when she woke each morning to find herself tight against him. Sometimes one of her arms was even around him, the palm of her hand resting against the dark chest hairs curling around his nipples. She could remember feeling the slow, steady beating of his heart. It had touched her deeply, until she realized with a start that the rhythm of her own heartbeat matched his. She had pulled her hand back, disturbed by a feeling she could not put into words, and had rolled carefully away from him to stare at the ceiling and wonder at the fates that had put her in this position.

This morning, she lay quietly studying his face. Even in sleep, Andrew was beautiful, a distinctly male beauty that had the power to move her to tears. His intense eyes were hidden beneath shadowed eyelids, and he looked tired. His profile was relaxed, his dark skin a startling contrast to the linen.

There was something different about him. Now, in repose, he looked oddly vulnerable. As her gaze flicked over his face, she wondered what secrets he contained and if she would ever know them.

As if sensing her attention, Andrew's eyes slowly opened. For the barest instant, he didn't seem to know where he was, seemed to be struggling between dreaming and waking. At that moment, her heart went out to him.

What could it be like, to see his face open and unguarded, looking down at me? What if there were no barriers? And if we had met in a different way?

That first instant Andrew had wakened, his eyes had possessed a yearning, vulnerable quality. And in that instant, seeing the smallest part of the man beneath the tightly controlled facade, Gwyn responded. She wanted to touch him. This was the man she wanted to be close to.

On impulse, she leaned forward and placed her fingers against his cheek. His skin was warm beneath her touch, with just the faintest rasp of a beard.

She watched him, almost giving in to tears as she saw the guarded look coming back, his eyes slowly becoming unreadable, his face tensing so slightly. The Andrew she had seen for an instant that morning might never have been.

Her throat tightened. Her emotions this morning surprised her. She wished he would let her see inside him, share that most closely guarded part of his heart. When they shared this bed, they revealed everything to each other physically, held nothing back in their responses. But there was another sort of intimacy she longed for. If they were to be intimate, she wanted true intimacy, a sharing of hearts and minds as well as bodies.

Yet you keep a part of yourself hidden as well.

Everything had happened too fast. They had been thrown together in a most peculiar way. Now it was as if they had to go backward and slowly discover what they had not had time to find before.

She would do as women have always done, and wait for a time. And hope she might see more of this man than he chose to reveal to her.

"You're supposed to see your grandfather this morning for breakfast," she reminded him. During the course of their evenings, she had managed to find out about what family he had left. Henry Hawkesworth, Duke of Drummond, obviously played a very important part.

"I'm supposed to do a great many things," he replied softly, and she could feel his eyes on her, his gaze sensual and disturbing. "But I find none of them as necessary as lying in your bed. . . ."

The sun was much higher in the sky when Andrew finally left her, and Gwyn buried herself deeper beneath her covers. But sleep proved elusive.

She hated having no control, trapped within the walls of this room like some exotic beast waiting for her owner to come and pet her. Sometimes, when she was alone, Janet's words came back to haunt her.

The Earl of Scarborough has been known to tire of his women quickly.

What would happen to her then? She was sure Andrew would provide for her handsomely, probably even set her up in her own house. Yet that wasn't what she wanted. While she was no fool about financial security, what she longed for more than anything was to be with a man who would love and respect her.

It seemed destiny did not have that in store.

She heard the door open and welcomed Angel's company. She could rid Gwyn of her blackest thoughts.

Within seconds, she realized it couldn't possibly be Angel, because her friend always announced her entrance immediately upon stepping inside her room. Sitting up quickly in her bed, Gwyn was startled to see an unfamiliar face. The woman had reddish hair and her front teeth protruded slightly. She was dressed in a pale yellow wrapper, and she held a chamber pot in her hands.

Gwyn swiftly jumped from the bed even as the foul contents of the pot were flung across the still-warm linens.

"You nasty little slut," the red-haired woman said softly, starting to circle the large canopied bed.

Gwyn kept her eyes on the stranger, but as she did she reached for the blue wrapper that had fallen to the side of the bed the other night. With quick, precise movements, she donned the garment and knotted the sash firmly about her waist.

Suzanne. This had to be Suzanne.

She ducked as the woman threw the chamber pot, and it made a dull thud as it hit the wall behind her. Then the red-haired woman jumped up on the bed and began to walk across its foul surface. Gwyn backed up, then turned and raced for the protection of the large sofa.

Angel would be up soon. Until then, she would have to defend herself from this woman.

They circled the furniture like two wary cats with their

backs up. Gwyn studied her opponent carefully, and she remembered what Madeleine had told her.

She'll try to destroy you.

Never looking away from her opponent, Gwyn formulated a plan. She had never physically fought anyone in her life, unless she counted her ineffectual struggles against Andrew. Suzanne would know how to fight. All she could do was stay out of her way until Angel came up.

Unless you make enough noise to bring someone else into the room.

The woman's face was angry, contorted and tight. There was no time to waste. Gwyn picked up one of the china figurines on a nearby table and sent it sailing against the heavy wooden door. The crash was loud and extremely satisfying. She was surprised to find her arm trembling from the effort, as if that simple motion had unlocked all the emotion she'd been attempting to keep under control.

Her eyes were still on Suzanne, her feet keeping her just ahead of her swiftly moving opponent. She heard the door open.

"*Nom de Dieu,*" a voice breathed softly.

Angel.

Gwyn ducked as Suzanne hurled a silver snuff box perilously close to her head. It crashed against the far wall. Then the woman turned wild, picking up and throwing anything within her reach. Her thin white fingers grasped the empty wine bottle from the night before and shattered it against the small table in front of the fire. Still holding the bottleneck, she stared at Gwyn with hatred in her pale eyes.

"I'm going to cut up that beautiful face of yours so Andrew will never wish to look upon it again." There was a dull flush in her freckled cheeks, and her hands shook with rage.

Gwyn watched the woman carefully, her entire body tense as she waited for Suzanne to make her move.

Gwyn sensed the woman was going to attack just before she vaulted up onto the couch, and she ran back across the room to

140

the bed. Suzanne just laughed.

"So Andrew has a little coward for his bedmate? At least give me a fight! You're nothing but a whore like the rest of us, even if you did come to him a virgin."

Gwyn swallowed against an onslaught of panic. Where was Angel? Wasn't anyone going to come? Before she could complete another thought, Suzanne raced toward her, bottleneck in hand. The woman jumped up on the bed and began to laugh.

"I thought Andrew liked spirited women! And here you are, a weak little piece if I ever saw one. It should be easy to take you out." She began to laugh, a high-pitched, slightly hysterical sound.

Where the idea came from, Gwyn was never to know. With strength born out of desperation, she grabbed at the heavy counterpane and yanked it sharply. There was a look of complete surprise on Suzanne's face as she lost her balance and fell back against the soiled bedding. Gwyn took advantage of her surprise and jumped up on the bed, rolling her tightly in the quilt and off the bed.

Suzanne screamed with frustration and rage as she hit the floor with a thud, and at that exact moment the door burst open. Angel rushed in, Thatch at her side. The giant took one look at the situation and went swiftly to Suzanne, who was spitting and cursing like a wildcat. Thatch's massive muscles barely bulged as he lifted the squirming woman.

"She has a bottle—" Gwyn began.

"Thatch! She has a weapon," Angel said sharply.

Gwyn watched with a sick sense of fascination as the cropped-eared servant unrolled Suzanne from the soiled counterpane and jerked her to her feet. With one quick twist to her wrist he secured the bottleneck. Suzanne cried tears of frustration and rage, and strands of her red hair were wetly plastered against one of her cheeks.

At that moment, despite what the woman had almost done to her, Gwyn felt pity. What could it possibly feel like to be replaced in Andrew's affections?

"Suzanne," she began, stepping forward toward the sobbing woman.

"Gwyn!" Angel shouted the warning and reached for the back of her wrapper.

"Bitch!" Suzanne's hand flashed out, catching Gwyn's wrist, and she clawed her as deeply as she could with the nails on her other hand.

Gwyn pulled away, her action reflexive, her left hand coming up to hold her bruised wrist tightly. Tears filled her eyes, but she refused to let them fall.

She watched as Thatch bent Suzanne's arms cruelly behind her back. The woman flinched, then smoothed her expression into one of haughty disdain as Thatch prodded her sharply in the back and forced her to walk out of the room.

"Gwyn!" Angel reached for her wrist. "Oh, Gwyn, you can't feel any pity for a bitch like her! You have to protect yourself!" She studied the bloodied wrist. "She's scratched you badly. You wash it and I'll get you a bandage. Knowing where that *chat* has been, you might get a fever."

"She scratched her?" The Duke of Cuckfield's voice was low and gently modulated, but Edward still shrank back, knowing the exquisite control the man was capable of just before he struck.

"On the wrist." Edward rushed his words, not wanting the Duke to blame him, then force him to endure more punishment. "I told Suzanne she was not to hurt the girl, only to listen. I'm afraid, my lord, that the whore's temperament is weak. She allowed her passions to rule her."

The Duke leaned back in his chair, tapping the ivory-headed cane he always carried gently against his knee. "You will see to it that nothing more happens to the girl. I don't want her further damaged before I have her."

"Yes, my lord. I will see Suzanne tomorrow and warn her

she is not to lose her temper again."

"You will go now."

"Yes, my lord. Of course."

"And you will come back here after you are through. I'm having a few friends over for dinner. I think you will find them most entertaining."

"Yes, my lord. Of course." Even though his stomach recoiled with fear, Edward knew he had to agree. This was his punishment for letting something happen to his cousin. He was no match for the Duke. The man was obsessed with having Gwyn. Edward knew there were moments when his master relived the auction in his mind, remembered every detail of Gwyneth's face and body. It seemed to excite him greatly, and Edward was surprised he found anyone more fascinating than himself. The Duke was a vain man; there were many mirrors in his house. His clothes, his food, his servants, even the section of London he lived in, all served to enhance his person. Edward sensed the man felt he'd found perfection in Gwyn; he knew the Duke wanted her badly.

And he wasn't willing to wait much longer.

"Do you have any ideas concerning how we can transport your cousin to our Christmas revel?" The Duke's question cut through his thoughts, and Edward's reply was calm.

"That cropped-eared monster guards the hallway constantly, but I think I can create a disturbance to distract him. Then it's simply a matter of getting her into the carriage with the other whores."

The Duke closed his eyes, and Edward knew his session with the man was almost over. He was beginning to dream again, of what he would do to Gwyn once he had her. Edward knew he wouldn't be needed much longer.

"Arrange it, Edward. Be certain nothing goes wrong. I mean to have her by Christmas." A smile crossed his features, a smile that made Edward ball his hands into fists to keep from shaking.

"I'm going to give myself a special Christmas present this

year," the Duke said softly. "A present I've wanted for a long time."

Edward had no doubt that present was Gwyn.

"Where is your mind wandering today, Andrew?" Henry was impatient with his grandson. First, Andrew had missed breakfast. Now, this afternoon, he was sure his grandson hadn't heard a word he had said.

His mind is on that whore. Henry was worried. All of London was abuzz with his grandson's affair. He had heard about the auction from a well-meaning friend. And from the beginning he hadn't liked the fact that Andrew had let nothing—not even the Duke of Cuckfield—stand in the way of his having the girl.

"I saw James in the park this afternoon," Henry began once more. "He told me you haven't been to see Belinda in quite some time."

He noticed Andrew shifted restlessly in his chair, then glanced at the clock on the mantelpiece.

His patience tried to its limits, Henry didn't bother to hide what he was thinking. "It's that whore, isn't it?"

Andrew remained silent, but his grandfather saw the subtle signals. The tightening of his jaw. The tension in his body.

"Get her out of your system, Andrew. If I thought Lady Pevensy was not suited to you, this whore is even less so."

"She's no whore," Andrew said softly.

"You're the laughingstock of London, what with the amount of money you paid to share her bed and the time you spend with her."

"I think not." Andrew rose slowly to his feet and even Henry could sense the tension in him. He loved the boy. Yet Andrew had inherited his father's rashness when it came to making decisions of the heart. He wasn't—he *couldn't* be in love with the little piece. But he was fond of her. Protective. That could be even more dangerous.

For years Henry had felt guilty about the turns his only

grandson's life had taken. Much of what he had given Andrew had been an attempt to make up for the desperate unhappiness of his younger years. Now he was frightened, because he saw Andrew's life taking the same strange turns Geoffrey's had taken.

Like father like son. He couldn't let that happen.

"I think not," Andrew repeated softly, then met his grandfather's gaze head on. "I think I'm the envy of any rational man. There's not one who wouldn't want to be in my place."

"In her bed?" Henry asked quietly. He so desperately did not want bad feelings between them when Andrew left, yet he couldn't seem to stop asking questions.

Andrew stared past his grandfather, and Henry knew he was looking at nothing substantial but instead seeing images in his mind.

"She's beautiful," he said softly, and the older man knew total despair.

Get his mind off the whore.

"Will you be having dinner at Belinda's tonight?" he asked, but even as he spoke, he knew the answer.

"No." Andrew focused his intent gaze on his grandfather, then smiled, a heartstoppingly beautiful smile. "I have other plans for this evening."

"With that—"

Andrew held up his hand, silencing his grandfather. "I don't want to fight. Let me leave your house with good feeling between us."

Henry sighed. "Go on, then."

He sank back in his chair and wearily closed his eyes as he heard his grandson stride out of the room. Impossible. This situation was impossible. It was one thing for a gentleman to frequent a house of prostitution in order to take care of his needs. It was quite another to set up one of the girls as his personal whore and shower her with presents and affection.

And time. He spent all his time with her. Though Andrew

145

might not see what kind of tragedy could result, Henry could.

Andrew had humiliated the Duke of Cuckfield, not a man to take such a thing lightly. Many people in London were fooled by the Duke's charming manner, but Henry had watched him long enough to know of his truly evil nature. He would be Andrew's enemy now, and the boy didn't seem to care.

And the whore. What did she want with Andrew? Did she mean to work her way up through society on her back? She had to be secretly laughing at Andrew, now that he had run through so much money and bought her such expensive gifts. She had Henry's grandson in the palm of her hand.

He heard the front door shut soundly and knew his grandson was going out into the evening to consort with that—what did they call her? Henry gritted his teeth.

The Earl of Scarborough's Bordello Bride.

If he had thought Belinda was a tragic match for his grandson, this . . . *Bordello Bride* had to be far worse.

Yet you were the one who wanted Belinda Pevensy out of his life. He smiled, a tired, self-mocking smile, as he remembered an Arab proverb he had read once.

Be careful what you wish for. You might receive it.

As Andrew opened the door and walked quietly into her room, Gwyn looked up, surprised. He was early. And she was still in her bath.

She couldn't scold him for being early, so she simply slid deeper into her bathwater.

"Beautiful," he said softly. He stripped off his coat and unbuttoned his waistcoat, then rolled up the sleeves of his white shirt. His eyes never left hers.

Gwyn heard the door open, then saw Angel enter the room.

"You may go," Andrew said softly.

Angel turned and left the bedchamber. They were alone.

She watched as Andrew pulled a chair over to the side of the tub and sat down. Her hair was pinned up, so his hand easily caressed the back of her neck. The skin felt vulnerable to his touch. Then he lowered his head and touched his lips to hers.

She felt the faint, now-familiar quivering begin within her body, and her lips parted helplessly, allowing his tongue to flick inside and caress her mouth. The kiss had a gentleness, a tenderness to it, but she knew how quickly Andrew's kisses could heat her blood and send both of them hurtling headlong into deepest passion.

"Ah, my Gwyn, you taste so very sweet." The words were soft, for her ears alone.

She smiled slightly. Her lips felt warm and full from his kiss.

"I'm glad I came by as early as I did." He took the fine, French-milled soap in his hands and worked up a lather. "I wish to bathe you."

"My lord—"

"Andrew."

"Andrew, I am perfectly capable—"

"Do you remember what happened the last time we bathed together?" His tone was as seductive as his touch. "Sit up a bit, and let me see you, Gwyn."

She couldn't disobey him. Gwyn slid up slowly in the large copper tub, then gasped as Andrew's soapy palms slid smoothly over her breasts. Her body responded instantly to his touch, her nipples tightening into hard pink buds.

"So beautiful," he said softly as he cupped water in his hands and rinsed the bubbles off. "I want you to take your bath later, Gwyn, with me. We have other needs to attend to. Give me your hand and let me help you out of the tub."

She did as she was told, and he brought her hand to his mouth to kiss her palm.

It was then that he saw the ugly scratches.

The room seemed unbearably still. A moment ago it had been filled with that powerful sexual tension only Andrew could produce, but now all Gwyn could feel was his anger, a palpable force, growing hotter and hotter.

"Who did this to you?" His voice was perfectly calm, but

Gwyn could feel the rage behind the words.

"I—no one." Her words sounded like the lie they were.

"I won't have you lying to me. Now, who did this to you?"

She remained silent, afraid of what he would do once he found out.

"Someone has to know." Rising to his feet, he strode angrily over to the bellpull and yanked it sharply. Within seconds, Angel entered the room. Gwyn knew from the expression on her friend's face that Angel sensed the tension in the room immediately.

"Who did this, Angel?" Andrew held up Gwyn's wrist and turned his gaze on the French maid.

Angel kept her voice perfectly impassive. "It was Suzanne, m'lord. She came in this morning and had a fight with Gwyn. Thatch restrained her, but Gwyn tried to—to talk to Suzanne, and she scratched her."

"I see." He gave Gwyn a hard, assessing stare. She looked away.

"Stay with Gwyn while I take care of this matter," he said quietly.

"No!" Gwyn rose from the tub and grabbed Andrew's arm. "Please, don't do anything. . . ."

"Don't argue with me, Gwyn. Stay with her, Angel."

"Andrew, no!" But then she felt Angel's hand on her arm, restraining her.

"Let him go," Angel whispered. "It will do Suzanne good to know you have a man's protection."

Chapter Ten

Edward had just finished his dalliance with Suzanne—which had included some of her opium—when he heard a door flung open further down the hall.

Something's amiss, he thought sleepily. He turned over in bed, away from Suzanne. The woman was so easy to seduce it was laughable. Afterwards, he always felt faintly disgusted with her.

When the door to their room crashed open, he was so surprised he fell off the far side of the bed.

"Damn you!"

He recognized Andrew's voice immediately.

"Andrew!" Suzanne sounded truly frightened. "What are you—Andrew, stop! Let me go!"

As scared as a mouse cornered by a hungry snake, Edward slowly peeked out from behind the bed. Andrew had both of Suzanne's wrists in his grip. His face was taut with anger; it blazed out from his blue eyes. As Edward had no wish to turn any of this wrath in his direction, he promptly slunk back out of sight.

"The little bitch is lying! She'll do anything to hurt me! What did she tell you, that I hurt her? I haven't even *seen* her. *You* never allow her out of that room."

"Woman, *be still!*"

And amazingly, she was. Edward still cowered behind the bed, but his attention was riveted on the couple.

"I'm giving you fair warning, Suzanne. If you do anything to hurt Gwyn, you will answer to me. You know I'm not a man to make idle threats. Do you understand what I'm saying?"

"I didn't hurt her. If that nasty little slut told you anything, you can't believe her."

"Gwyn didn't have to say a thing."

Edward risked another peek, and saw Suzanne's mouth slack with shock, her eyes filled with tears.

"Why don't you ever come to my room anymore?" The whore's voice was tremulous. She pressed her naked white body against Andrew, and Edward recognized the open invitation in her pale eyes. "We used to have such good times, Andrew. You used to tell me—"

"I never promised you anything, Suzanne, and I won't have you believing otherwise. I will not be coming back here again— unless you give me reason to. Touch Gwyn and you won't enjoy the consequences."

Edward closed his eyes in disgust as he heard Suzanne whimper softly.

"Andrew—" She was beginning to sob like a little girl deprived of her favorite doll. "I'm better for you than she is. I always let you do anything you wanted. . . ."

"Do you understand what I said? About Gwyn? That's all that matters."

This brought fresh sobs from Suzanne, and Edward crept back behind the bed in disgust. How could he have thought Suzanne was intelligent enough to help him?

He heard Andrew pressing Suzanne down on the mattress. Edward didn't dare risk taking another glance. Andrew was too close.

"I don't want to hurt you, Suzanne. I will have no choice if you touch Gwyn. Promise me you will leave her alone."

Suzanne's voice was choked with sobs. "I—I *hate* her! I *hate* her for what she did to us! You *loved* me. I *know* you loved me, and if you had never met her, you would have stayed in my bed! You love her, don't you?" Suzanne said in a defeated voice.

Edward sat up and paid attention—any weakness on Andrew's part could be used to destroy him.

There was too long a pause.

"You *do* love her! I knew that was why you left me! From the moment you saw her at the auction—"

"Suzanne, that is none of your concern."

"But you do! You *do!*" Edward heard the bed frame creak as Suzanne rolled over. Now her sobs were muffled by her pillow. He wondered what Andrew was doing, but he didn't dare make his presence known.

"Don't hurt her, Suzanne. I don't want to have to hurt you."

"Andrew—" Now it was a wail, and Edward despised Suzanne all over again for the weakness she displayed.

"Good-bye, Suzanne. I wish you well—as long as you don't hurt Gwyn."

He left—Edward could tell from the sound of the door closed quietly. He waited a minute, then crawled back up on the bed. Suzanne huddled in the covers, sobbing brokenly. Her skin was blotched with vivid stains of color, her eyes were red-rimmed. She reminded Edward of a rabbit he had once tried to catch, those same wild, timid eyes.

"Oh, Edward!" She reached out her thin, freckled arms, grasping at comfort. Though he was totally disgusted with her, Edward Sleaforth realized he still needed an ally at The Dark Stallion. Perhaps Suzanne's very weaknesses could bind her tighter to him, and she could be of some use.

"There, there," he said softly, smoothing her damp red hair away from her face. "Andrew may not love you, but I do."

Gwyn had dried herself and put on her wrapper by the time Andrew returned. She stood perfectly still as he walked in the

151

door. She and Angel had heard faint wailings from down the hall, and she knew he had confronted Suzanne and exacted a promise from her. But Gwyn had been frightened by Andrew's anger. She was beginning to understand some men were far more protective than others.

His first words were directed at Angel. "Get your mistress."

With the smallest nod of her head, Angel darted swiftly out the door.

Gwyn found her voice at last. "Please don't do this, Andrew."

"Don't do what?" His blue eyes were blazing. "See to your protection? What kind of man do you think I am?"

"It will only cause more trouble. . . ."

"If there is any more trouble in this house, I'll move you to another one."

She opened her mouth to reply, looked at his face, and thought better of it. Gwyn bit down on her lower lip. Now was not the time to lose her temper.

Janet entered the room within minutes, her expression furious.

This will be something to watch, Gwyn thought. She wondered who would best who, then knew she had no doubts Andrew would triumph.

"Is this how a man is treated when he invests good money in your house, Mistress Wickens?" Andrew asked.

"I cannot control the behavior of my girls at all times," Janet said quietly, Her dark green eyes shot venom at Gwyn.

"Are you saying it was Gwyn's fault Suzanne came into her room and attacked her?" Andrew's voice was very quiet. Gwyn didn't envy Janet having to face him.

"All I know, m'lord, is that I have never had such trouble in my establishment until this one came to stay."

"But she brought you a goodly sum."

"And trouble to match."

"Then you would not object if I moved Gwyn to another house."

"Not at all."

"And you would not object if several of my friends heard of how I was treated at The Dark Stallion. I think they would be most interested."

Gwyn watched Janet's face carefully. Her delicate nostrils flared and her eyes widened. Gwyn could feel her displeasure.

"Andrew," Gwyn began quietly, knowing if she didn't tell this white lie things would only grow more difficult between her and the madam, "I have no desire to move from this house. There is a good lock on my door, and I can certainly use it."

"This doesn't concern you, Gwyn," Andrew said.

Her body froze as if he had slapped her. Though she stood very still, emotions warred within her. *It is my life! Of course it concerns me!* She clenched her hands into fists, willing herself not to say anything she would regret, then turned and walked toward the bed. If she heard anything more, she would scream at both of them.

"I want a guard at the door at all times. Not just in the hallway."

"As you wish, m'lord."

"I will not be as lenient the next time."

"Yes, m'lord."

"I would greatly prefer one of your cropped-eared fellows."

"That can be arranged."

Gwyn looked over at Angel, standing quietly by the door, waiting for either her mistress or Andrew to permit her to take her leave. Angel must have seen the anger in her eyes, for her own were imploring. Gwyn recognized the silent appeal for her to remain quiet. She directed her gaze toward the fire and took a deep breath. The voices continued, a buzz in the back of her angry emotions.

"If anything like this happens again, you will greatly wish it had not."

"I do understand you're upset, m'lord, and I promise to see that in the future you and your friends have no reason to take your business elsewhere."

After what seemed an eternity of tension, Janet finally left, Angel following in her mistress's wake. The door closed, and Gwyn was left alone with Andrew.

He walked over and put his hands on her shoulders. "Did someone call a surgeon?" he asked.

"Andrew, it's only a small scratch. Angel washed and bandaged it for me. I'm feeling better; I need no more attention."

"Do you wish to have supper?"

She couldn't believe this was the same man who had so curtly ordered her out of the earlier argument.

"No."

"What is it you wish to do?" He was smiling down at her, and Gwyn realized with amazement he had no idea of how insultingly he had dismissed her. Anger swelled through her, and she was determined to let him know how damning she thought his actions were.

"I don't know, m'lord. I doubt I am capable of making such a difficult decision. Why don't you make it for me? You seem to have no trouble ordering every other part of my life."

He was silent, and she took it as a signal to continue.

"What do *you* want, not what do *I* want! What *I* want has never mattered since Edward brought me here. . . ."

"Who is Edward?" he asked.

She could have bitten her tongue off. If what he had done to Suzanne was any evidence, he would tear Edward limb from limb. Though she was furious with Edward, she didn't want him involved with her cousin's evil ways.

"No one that matters." She stepped out of his embrace, then walked over to the fire and sat down in one of the chairs. "What would you like to do tonight, m'lord? Perhaps I could take off my clothes and dance on top of the table for your amusement. Or maybe I could take another bath."

"Gwyneth—"

"I am nothing but your little trained dog, am I not? You feed me a treat—whether from your table or your body—and I

154

respond with a trick. Well, m'lord, tell me what I am to do for you tonight."

"First, control your waspish tongue."

"Why? Do you find it so difficult to hear the truth?"

Anger was beginning to brighten his eyes, but Gwyn refused to back down. She had reached a peculiar place within herself where she had nothing to lose. She wanted to test him, to see his anger unleashed upon her. Gwyn wondered what it would be like to battle with Andrew. In the temper she was in now, she would be a worthy match for him.

"The truth is," he said slowly, walking toward her, "I treat you far better than any other woman in this establishment. Had I not bought you, you would have serviced hundreds of men by now, and I can assure you, madam, what you would feel about yourself after time in their hands is far worse than anything you are feeling now."

"I'm your whore now, and what I feel at your hands disgusts me." The angry words were out before she thought, and she watched the change in his face, the tightening of his muscles, the tautness of his strong jaw. He *was* angry now, but she was still too emotionally volatile to care.

"Disgusts you?" he asked, his voice dangerously soft.

"*Disgusts* me."

"Then you are saying that my treating you with gentleness and concern is no different than what the other women in this house experience every day."

"Yes."

"You have a lot to learn, my beauty."

"Surely you'll teach me."

The firelight was behind him. For a moment she couldn't see his face clearly and it frightened her. But she resolved to continue.

"And now, m'lord, what do you wish to do tonight?"

"If I took you the way most men would, you would not enjoy it. Is that what you want?"

For some perverse reason, now she wanted to cry. She had

155

wanted to make Andrew see how she felt and realize she wanted some say in how her life was to be lived. That right had been taken from her the moment she had woken up in her bed at The Dark Stallion.

She couldn't back down now.

"I don't understand how either way makes much difference. The end result is still the same."

"You are very ignorant of the ways of men."

"How I feel afterwards is the same. Why should any difference before matter?"

This time she *had* pushed him too far. His eyes were the deepest blue as they swept over her. Taking her arm, he pulled her to her feet.

"As you wish, Gwyn. I will give you one last chance to reconsider this mistaken idea of yours. Do you want to?"

"No." She would not be the one to break.

"Very well. You are mine to do anything I wish with."

"I wish to have supper now. And I do not wish you to wear any clothing."

Andrew . . . The words she longed to say froze in her throat. How could this man be the same person who had treated her with such gentle consideration? Why hadn't she simply told him how she felt, without making her argument an attack? Why had she wanted to arouse his anger in the first place? Gwyn would have given anything to have had Andrew, the tender lover, take the place of this harsh stranger.

"Take it off."

"Andrew—"

"*Off.* Come, Gwyn, this is what you would have faced if I hadn't bought you. The thought of my touch disgusts you. I am a man who cares nothing for your desires, remember? Why shouldn't we get on with our evening?"

She looked wildly around the room, desperate for some escape.

"There's nothing you can do. Even if you scream, we will be left alone. Janet wouldn't want to face me again."

"Andrew, I don't think I—you didn't understand what I was trying to say to you."

"How touching. Now you want to make amends. Come, Gwyn, show me some of the spirit you displayed earlier. Or now that it's time to pay the piper, have you lost your courage?"

She backed away, watching him carefully as she spoke. "I don't want this to happen between us, Andrew. I would like us to talk again, as we did the other night. I would like to come to know you better."

"I think not." His tone was very calm, a calmness that bespoke of terrible anger. "I don't think you are capable of knowing what you want, and I think you want me to choose for you. Isn't that what you said earlier?"

"I said many things, Andrew. I thought you cared nothing for my feelings."

"I see." But he continued to walk slowly toward her, stalking her. She backed away, trembling.

"I know now—I know that isn't true. You *don't* treat me badly, you *do* protect me, you want what is best for me."

"And how touching you've come to this conclusion at this time." He smiled, and before she realized why, she felt her back bump into the wall. He was upon her in three steps, then pressed her body against the first surface with the hard, muscular planes of his own.

"I want you out of that wrapper, Gwyn. I wish to see your beauty."

She felt his fingers doing battle with the tight knot she had made earlier. Seconds before his temper flared, she sensed it, felt his fingers come round the back and yank the silken garment away from her body. There was a ripping sound, and the wrapper parted, torn off her body until she was naked from the waist up.

"Is this what you wanted all along, Gwyn?" he asked roughly, and she could feel his heart pounding as rapidly as her own. "Is this how you want to be treated?"

She couldn't answer him, could only stare up into his angry face. She had hurt him deeply by telling him his touch disgusted her. Disgust had not been the right word. His touch terrified her, astonished her, shamed her. She was confused by the responses he forced from her body.

"Most men wouldn't have kissed you, wouldn't have seen to your comfort. Is that how you see me?"

She shook her head, too frightened for tears.

He continued speaking to her, his voice low and slightly shaking. "They wouldn't kiss you all over or tell you how beautiful you are. They would have barely brought you into the room before they would have been out of their breeches and upon you." He took a deep breath, and she was surprised to feel his body trembling against hers.

"I never forgave myself for the way I took you that first night, but then I came to realize neither of us was responsible. That second night, I tried, Gwyn. I tried to make it good for you. I know you responded to me, I *felt* your response. Why do you tell me I disgust you?"

"Not disgust," she whispered.

"I want you to know what you would have been up against. He would have brought you in here and barely waited for supper. No one would have come running if they had heard your screams. He would have thrown you on the bed, or on the sofa, or had you up against the wall like this. He might have kissed you once if you were lucky, might possibly have seen to your pleasure if he'd thought it would add to his own. But he would have had you immediately. Like this."

She felt his hands move down and roughly part her thighs. Gwyn could feel the scratchy wool material of his breeches against the softness of her inner thighs as he pushed one of his legs between hers, then pinned her more tightly against the wall. Her throat was so tight she could barely breathe.

"If you think this way of me," Andrew said roughly, "it matters not how I treat you. Good or bad, I'm damned in your eyes."

"Andrew—"

He swung her up over his shoulder, her legs tangled in the torn wrapper. Gwyn clenched her hands into fists and brought them down as hard as she could on his back. She would not make this easy for him, would fight him until his anger cooled and she could make him see reason.

But she hadn't counted on his superior strength. All breath left her as she was flung down on the large bed. He followed her, his body heavy atop hers, and there were none of the light, arousing, seductive touches he usually bestowed in the beginning. His hands were firm, his grasp rough as he caught both her wrists in one hand and pulled them up over her head.

"I want you naked beneath me," he said quietly, his lips grazing her ear. There was a savagery to his tone, and Gwyn knew with a terrible sense of finality he'd meant everything he'd said. He truly meant to dominate her. She had been so foolish, thinking he already had.

The rest of her wrapper was torn from her and she was naked. His body pressed hers down into the mattress. His free hand caressed her breasts, cupping them roughly with no thought to her response, no delight in any pleasure she might display. Gwyn held her body rigid, tried to turn away from his touch. But he was heavier, stronger.

Her breath caught as he pulled her to a sitting position and placed both her palms on his shirtfront.

"Unbutton my shirt," he said.

Fingers trembling, she unfastened his shirt and pushed the material off his shoulders, baring his chest. Each muscle was clearly defined in the firelight, his whole body held in a state of tension.

"I should have treated you this way from the beginning," Andrew said softly, his eyes hard. "I should never have permitted you to lash me with that tongue of yours. I gave you too many liberties, Gwyneth. You are going to learn there is one master in this bed. You will never answer me shrewishly again, and you will do exactly as I say."

Tears stung her eyes. She looked down at her hands, wondering what he would have her do next. She did not dare deny him anything.

"Take off my boots."

She divested him of his boots and breeches, her fingers clumsy and trembling. Convinced he was going to throw her back on the bed and take her roughly, she was surprised when he lay back, his fingers tight around her wrist as he pulled her with him.

"Now pleasure me," he said. "Show me why I bought you and why I should keep you. And if your lovely mouth can do anything besides infuriate me."

His words shocked her, froze her inside. She could only stare at his face as her eyes began to fill. His angry expression blurred, and she ducked her head, looking anywhere but at him.

She felt him grasp her hair tightly again, this time pushing her down his body, past his chest until her lips were almost touching him intimately.

It was the ultimate invasion. What she had given him freely before filled her with revulsion. She couldn't move, could only lie still, her cheek against his stomach, his fingers tight in her hair.

"This is what any other man would have had you do," Andrew said.

"You are not any other man," she whispered, her throat painfully tight. "Please, Andrew—"

"Then you must pleasure me another way." He let go of her hair, grasped her wrists, and pulled her up until she was lying on top of him, her face mere inches from his.

He dragged her to her feet. Her eyes swimming with tears, she faced him, hatred in her eyes.

"I will never," she said, her voice trembling, "never give in to you. You can do whatever you wish with me, but you will never break me."

"Get on that bed."

And knowing what she wanted to do would push him beyond all endurance, Gwyn brought her hand up and slapped his face as hard as she could.

He exploded with fury then, and if she had thought his temper frightening before, it was as if misty rain turned to a violent thunderstorm. He lifted her up and threw her on the bed. Before she could struggle up, she felt him pushing her legs painfully apart. Then he was between her thighs, and she cried out as he thrust his shaft into her. There was unleashed violence in the way he drove into her, again and again.

Her nails raked his back, she bit his shoulder and struggled beneath him, but nothing seemed to penetrate his relentless, driving thrusts. His hands slid down and grasped her buttocks painfully, forcing her against him.

Then he shuddered, great racking shudders that pulsed through his body. She felt him swell even larger inside her, desire urging him mercilessly, until his release burst deep within her.

She closed her eyes as he slid off her, his body damp with exertion. Gwyn turned away from him, curled herself into a tight little ball, and pressed her fist against her mouth. But she couldn't stop the soft, openmouthed sobs torn straight from her heart.

Her back was to him, so she didn't see his hands trembling as he pulled on his boots, or the agonized expression in his blue eyes as he gazed at the vulnerable line of her back.

"Damn you, Gwyn," he whispered hoarsely. "You cannot tell me you would have rather learned about it that way." He took a long, shuddering breath.

She was still crying, great wrenching sobs that shook her entire body.

When he spoke again, his voice was quietly resigned.

"I've failed you, Gwyneth. I meant for you to find happiness in my bed. With God as my witness, I never meant to hurt you."

She had no strength left in her body, but she forced herself
to turn over and look at him. Gwyn watched through her tears
as Andrew picked up his greatcoat and walked quickly toward
the door. As she buried her face in her hands she heard the lock
turn, the door open.

And then he was gone.

Book III

*"Though you've learned very much, ma petite chou,
Don't imagine your knowledge complete.
You'll find love is a gamble, ma minou,
And sometimes, to win you must cheat . . ."*

Chapter Eleven

Gwyneth did not sleep that night. She could not remain in her bed, so she took a blanket and huddled on the sofa near the fire. Long after Andrew left, she stared at the glowing coals.

What we pushed each other to. Andrew had been right about many things, the most crucial being she did not know much about men. Had she known the temper he possessed, she would never have continued the argument—and would certainly have never slapped him.

And had she known how sensitive his lovemaking had been, she would have never helped ignite the violent side of his nature.

You have been shut up like an animal in a cage. Perhaps that is why you acted like one, and Andrew followed your example. Her world encompassed four walls. There were times she had paced the floor, desperate to escape, all the while knowing Thatch stood on the other side of the heavy door.

All these feelings had erupted the instant before she'd slapped him. She had wanted to best him, win their argument, make him understand she could not endure this life much longer. No matter what he thought of what her place in his life was to be, he could not ignore her feelings forever.

Why do you have such violent emotions toward him? The

question made her uneasy, and her mind kept returning to the scene that had been played out this night.

What he did . . . There is no excuse . . . Her fingers clenched the soft folds of the blanket as she silently acknowledged both of them had been completely out of control. It was a side of her nature she had never given rein to. Her father had encouraged the sweetness in her temperament and had been shocked by any willful display of temper.

But what Andrew did . . .

There was something each ignited in the other, whether in passion or anger. And the emotions were certainly different, as there had been nothing loving in his brutal possession. Only dominance, a silent struggle for absolute power . . .

She wrapped the blanket tighter around her shoulders as the room grew cooler.

And what is on the other side of that hatred I felt for him?

She pushed the answer to the back of her mind, then rose from the couch and padded barefoot to bed. The candles had almost completely melted down, the wax spilling over and twisting onto the lace-trimmed tablecloth. She lay down slowly, the blanket still wrapped tightly around her cold body. Gwyn wanted darkness, a darkness so complete she would not have to examine her feelings too deeply.

She didn't know how much later it was when she heard the doorknob turn and the heavy wooden door open slightly.

"Gwyn?" She recognized Angel's whisper.

"Yes." Sitting up and swinging her legs over the side of the bed, she reached for her wrapper.

"Make the bed ready," Angel whispered. "We're bringing Andrew in."

Gwyn quickly pulled back the bed linen and plumped the pillow, then raced to the door. She caught her breath sharply at the sight that greeted her.

Thatch and the other giant, Bill, were carrying Andrew. He was unconscious. Bill had his arms, while Thatch had both his legs. The men walked quietly into the room despite their formidable size. Gwyn watched, her hand over her mouth, as they gently deposited Andrew on the bed. Both of them nodded to Angel and strode silently out of the room.

"What happened?" Gwyn asked as she knelt down on the bed next to Andrew. She felt his face. It was flushed and slightly damp.

"I was having a cup of tea in the kitchen when I heard a noise on the stairs. He was out on the back steps trying to get into the house. I called Thatch and Bill and asked them to help me."

Gwyn smoothed Andrew's hair back from his face. As she did, the unmistakable smell of liquor assailed her.

He was drunk.

"I'll help you get his clothes off," Angel offered. Gwyn blessed her friend for not being the inquisitive kind. She certainly wasn't ready to talk to anyone about tonight or why Andrew might be in this condition.

"Let's get him tucked in," she said quietly.

The women worked efficiently, divesting Andrew of his clothing, then they tucked the covers up over him.

"I could brew him one of Cook's herbal concoctions," Angel said. "He's going to feel horrible in the morning."

"Should I wake him?"

"I think you'd be doing the man a kindness."

Once her friend left, Gwyn curled up next to Andrew. He looked horrible, his face pale and exhausted, his hair disheveled. She smoothed it with her fingers, then gently stroked his cheek.

She was surprised when one of his eyes slowly opened, his expression confused. Slowly, waveringly, his other eye came open, bloodshot like the first. Gwyn continued stroking his cheek until she felt his arm carefully move up and out from underneath the covers. He grasped her wrist, and the lack of strength in his grip made tears sting her eyes.

"Oh, Andrew, why did you do this to yourself?" she whispered.

His lips moved clumsily as he attempted to form words.

"Forgive . . ." The words trailed off, and he licked his dry lips.

Oh, Andrew, forgive me.

"Forgive me," she whispered. "I was so wrong to do what I did."

"No." His brow wrinkled slightly, and she knew the effort it cost him to say the words. "Gwyn, forgive me . . . for . . . hurting you."

Her eyes stung again. "You tried to stop it, Andrew. I didn't—"

"No. Our first . . . night. I didn't . . . know. I would have made it different. And tonight—"

She touched his cheek. "That first night was a long time ago, Andrew. You have been very caring toward me since that time." She took a deep breath, then rushed the next words out before she lost her courage. "I played a part in what happened tonight, and I cannot be proud of it."

"It . . . doesn't make me . . . any less ashamed."

"Andrew—"

"If there was one thing . . . in my life I could . . . take back and do over, tonight . . ." He coughed.

"Please don't talk, Andrew. I want you to rest." She could feel herself dangerously close to tears. "I just want you to get better."

His blue eyes were full of a pain she had never seen before. Tonight it was as if one of the masks had been dropped, and she was seeing inside this man's soul.

Andrew closed his eyes and took a deep, rasping breath. Gwyn moved her hand from his cheek to his chest, and she could feel the steady beating of his heart.

"If you could . . . I'd bet you would take back any trust . . . you had in me. It was your first time . . . and I frightened you. And tonight—"

"My father used to tell me I frighten too easily. Maybe I do."

"The . . . lesson you learned from me . . . is that love can be painful. It was a . . . terrible thing for me to teach you. I should have been . . . stronger for you." He opened his eyes again, and they were agonized.

"I think we still have time to learn a great many more things."

"I've hurt you . . . more than that night."

"Hush."

"I'm not a very good man. Not for . . . you."

"Andrew, don't—"

"I know . . . I'm not good for you, but I . . . can't seem to let you go."

"Shhh."

"I don't want you to . . . ever leave me."

She felt his hand come up and cover hers, pressing it against his heart.

"Now where would I go?" she asked softly.

He closed his eyes, and she could see exhaustion etched into the deep lines around his mouth. When he spoke again, she had to lean closer to catch the words.

"Everyone . . . I've ever loved . . . has left me."

Then he was still.

His words pierced her heart as she thought of the life he'd endured. Gwyn didn't stir when she heard the door open or when Angel walked over to the side of the bed and placed a tray on the bedside table.

"It's nasty stuff. Do you want me to help you get it down him?"

"I'll do it later. Thank you, Angel."

After Angel left, Gwyn snuffed out all the candles, carefully climbed into bed beside Andrew, and put her arms around him. She pressed her body against his, determined to warm him. Even in sleep, he turned toward her, and she felt the slight roughness of the stubble on his cheek against her breast.

She had left the bedcurtains slightly open, and as she cradled Andrew in her arms, she watched the shadows the fire spilled across the ceiling and wondered about the man she held against her heart.

He woke once in the middle of the night, and she managed to make him drink two cups of Cook's brew. She was sure it tasted foul from the expression on Andrew's face. Afterwards, he lay back beneath the covers and she curled up beside him.

He is full of emotions he has no idea what to do with. In his tortured confession, she had seen another side of Andrew tonight. There was no doubt he thought he had hurt her badly. He was a sensitive man who buried his feelings deep. Gwyn wondered at the child who had become the man sleeping soundly in her bed.

If a child lives with fear or hatred or sorrow . . . She thought of what Madeleine had told her of Andrew's upbringing and contrasted it with her own. Her father, as vicar for the small village she had grown up in, had always had the time to listen to anyone's problems. Many times, when she sat down with him for their evening meal, he had been exhausted. She could still remember the kindness in his face. He had possessed a great generosity of spirit he had tried to pass on to her.

"It's in the talking that they find peace," he had said more than once. He had never turned anyone away, believing he was doing God's work, helping his people. As Gwyn remembered her father, she wondered what he would have thought of Andrew.

A lost soul. She studied Andrew many times when he wasn't aware of it. She saw the tension around his mouth, the guarded expression in his dark blue eyes. He didn't let many people close to him. Angel had told her he had a friend called Jack. She knew Andrew lived with his grandfather somewhere in London. She didn't know if he had any other people close to him.

And as she thought of this, her heart ached for him. How different they were, how different their lives had been. She had loved her father intensely, had mourned just as fiercely when

168

he'd suddenly died.

Her mother's memory was more distant; as a child she had sometimes mixed up her memories. There was the mother who had died giving birth to her little brother, and this woman had dark blond hair and brown eyes. Yet there was another woman who frequently came to her in dreams. The images of this light-haired woman with blue-grey eyes, laughing and running through a field of wild flowers, were vivid. Gwyn woke from these dreams with a feeling of sadness. When she had asked her father about them, he had hugged her and cautioned her not to let her dreams run away with her.

"Your mother loved you very, very much. You must always remember her and have faith that she is happy and at rest with the angels."

Who had directed Andrew? He had been allowed to run wild after his mother's death, until his grandfather had come to claim him.

He tries to be close—the only way he knows. She shifted deeper beneath the blanket, stretching her legs out as they began to cramp. *And he is sorry for what happened and does not try to place blame elsewhere.*

At that moment, she forgave him everything and determined they should start again. She did not want to belong to another man while at The Dark Stallion. As she studied Andrew sleeping, Gwyn knew that despite what had happened, there was goodness in this man.

Yet there were moments when the lovemaking was over and he drifted off to sleep beside her when she felt . . . empty. She was waiting for something that had never happened.

A look in his eyes, tender words from his lips. Something that would make me believe what we share in this bed is more than lust. Something that might make me believe . . .

A soft groan from the bed broke into her thoughts. Andrew's eyes were barely open, his expression totally miserable. She wondered if he had any recollection of their evening together after he had gotten drunk. Not stopping to think on this now, she took one of his hands.

"How are you feeling, m'lord?" she asked softly.

In answer, he closed his eyes.

She spoke softly, knowing he probably had a terrible ringing in his ears. "Andrew? Would you like a cool cloth on your brow?"

He nodded, the slight movement obviously an excruciating effort, and Gwyn fetched a cloth, dampened it, and laid it across his forehead. "I'm going to summon Angel and see if Cook has made anything you might be able to eat."

In answer, he groaned.

Within fifteen minutes, Angel had brought up a bowl of beef broth and several slices of freshly baked bread. He ate almost half the broth and one slice of bread, then burrowed back beneath the covers with a sigh.

"Gwyn? Would you—I would like you to lie next to me."

That he had almost asked her was enough. She untied her wrapper and took it off, gently lifted the bedclothes, and slid in beside him. He reached out and touched her, his fingers pressed against her hip. His grip tightened and she moved closer. As she looked up at his face she realized he had dropped off into an exhausted sleep.

Her heart went out to this man lying next to her. Somewhere deep inside her, as inexorable and compelling as the tides, Gwyn knew she would always help Andrew, be available to him if he needed her, and care what happened to him. He was a part of her now, this darkly emotional man. Even if she were to ever go back home, she would carry images of him in her heart and mind. Nothing would be able to burn them out of her memory.

He had changed her life forever.

"You cannot hurt her. You cannot do anything to her. Suzanne, do you understand me?" Edward was agitated. The whore seemed deaf and dumb when the subject of either Andrew or Gwyn was brought up.

"Why do you protect her?" Suzanne's voice was petulant, her pale eyes hostile. She was lying in the midst of the rumpled bedclothes.

"I am not protecting her for me. I am protecting her for . . . the gentleman who employs me."

"And who might that be? Why should I be afraid of some man I've never met?" Her voice was steadily growing more shrill. "If I want to harm Gwyn, who are you to stop me?"

Edward could feel the sweat beginning to pop out on his brow. The punishment he would endure because of Suzanne's mischief was mild compared to what the Duke of Cuckfield would do if Gwyn, his obsession, was harmed again.

He strode over to the fire, his hands clasped behind his back.

"Am I not good to you, Suzanne?"

It was almost a minute before she answered, and he was silently incensed.

"Yes. You are." The reply was almost forced out of her.

"Do you not care for me the tiniest amount?" He held his breath, knowing her reply would be crucial.

"I am somewhat fond of you."

The little bitch. "Could you consider this a personal favor that no harm will come to Gwyn for the next week?" By that time, right before Christmas, the Duke would have Gwyn safely in his possession. And he would be able to leave London and the hateful man forever.

"And how will I benefit?"

"Remember what I brought you last time?" he said, turning to her and smiling. Suzanne was rapidly becoming an opium addict.

"Yes. You will bring more?"

"You have my word."

"Then I will not harm the little slut—for a week."

Bitch. "Good. Now, what information do you have for me?" Edward was all attention. If he could bring the Duke back some news, things might not go as badly for him.

"Let me think." There was a slight pause, then Suzanne

said, "Andrew rarely misses a night. He comes to her room at nightfall and leaves in the morning. There is talk around London that his grandfather is furious with him."

"Good. Anything else?"

"When Andrew is with her, Thatch does not guard her door as closely. At times I have managed to steal into the hall and press my ear against the door."

"Have you heard anything?"

"He calls her 'my beauty.'"

"Excellent."

"They make love more than once a night, of this I am sure."

"Go on." Edward decided he would not tell the Duke this bit of information.

"He likes to watch her bathe before the fire."

"Can you remember anything else, Suzanne? You are pleasing me greatly.

"He has demanded she call him Andrew all the time, and never m'lord."

"Excellent. I will bring you another present tomorrow, as you have been most agreeable this evening. I am glad we have reached an understanding on this matter, Suzanne. Trust me, my dear. You will hurt Gwyn far more by helping me than you ever could alone."

Suzanne smiled at this, a satisfied expression in her eyes. "You'll come to see me tomorrow, Edward?"

He walked over to the bed, picked up her hand, and kissed it. "Nothing would give me greater pleasure. Is there something I might pick up for you before my visit?"

"I should like another box of chocolates, and also some tea from that little shop you visited before. And, Edward, you will not forget the other?"

"You shall have that, too."

Edward let himself out of her room cautiously, and walked swiftly down the wide staircase toward the door leading to the back alley. He wasn't certain Gwyn was ever allowed out of her room, but he had no desire to come face to face with his cousin.

He heard laughter, the beating of a drum, and the melodic strains of a flute wafting out from the main parlor, but he did not stop. He had to return to the Duke and make sure their plans were finalized.

Once Gwyn was in the Duke's possession, his worries would be over.

Once outside, he walked quickly away from the bordello and was silently swallowed by the fog.

"I will not be coming back this evening, my beauty."

Gwyn watched Andrew as he tucked his shirt into his breeches, then reached for his waistcoat. It was dark outside the small window; she had watched him sleep the greater part of the day away.

"My grandfather is having a birthday celebration and I must attend. You don't mind being alone tonight?"

"I think a night with your grandfather will be very good for you."

"You didn't answer my question, Gwyn."

"I will miss you, of course. But I would not want to be responsible for depriving your grandfather of his grandson's company."

He laughed as he shrugged into his greatcoat. "You're quite the little diplomat."

"Will there be many people there? Do you have other relatives living in London?"

"Only grandfather." He glanced in the mirror, then quickly smoothed a hand over his hair. "Do I look as bad as I feel?"

"Oh, much worse." But she smiled as she said it, and he laughed again, then walked over to her chair and pulled her to her feet. Andrew kissed her with a hungry urgency, his hands sliding down her back until they rested on her hips. He pulled her against him as he kissed her, and she could feel the solid strength contained within his body.

He broke the kiss gently. "You know I'd much rather spend

the night with you."

"You haven't seen your grandfather in a long time. I think it is good of you to go." She took a deep breath. "Will your mother and father be there?"

He stared at her. It was all she could do to look up at his face with a totally innocent expression. She wanted to know this man, wanted him to stop shutting himself away from her.

"No. They will not." There was something in his tone that quietly forbade any further questioning. Tension hung in the air for a moment, then Gwyn placed her hand on his arm. She felt the muscles relax.

"I hope your evening with your grandfather is pleasant."

She watched him as he strode out of the room. Once she was alone, Gwyn went to one of the chairs in front of the fire and sat down. Picking up a book, she opened it and tried to read.

Within minutes, she heard a soft tapping on her door.

"Come in."

Lily poked her head around the door, her dark eyes sparkling. "Hello. Would you like company?"

Gwyn had to smile. She had heard Madeleine and Lily argue many times about Lily's refusal to speak English when she could use her French. Gwyn knew the French girl was making an effort to speak her language.

"I would love company," she admitted.

"Where is that Dark Stallion of yours tonight?" Lily asked as she sat down. She giggled as Gwyn felt her face grow warm.

"Oh, I do not mean to embarrass you, Gwyneth. I wish I had someone to protect me like Andrew protects you. I think he is a very—how do you say?—gallant gentleman."

"He is," Gwyn admitted.

"So, you are beginning to care for him? He is a man desperately in love, I think. Maybe he will even give you a house of your own, and Madeleine and I could visit you."

Gwyn had to smile. Lily, like Angel, was determined to leave The Dark Stallion before another year passed. "You can come visit me anytime, no matter where I live, Lily."

"Angel, she told me you were very sweet and she was right. I am glad I am in this house if only to meet you."

"Thank you, Lily."

Lily stretched her hands toward the fire. "What shall we talk about now?"

"You decide."

"*Mon ange*, something is bothering you."

Gwyn was quietly amazed at Lily's perceptiveness. She had been convinced she was hiding her emotions carefully, yet Lily knew she was upset.

"It is Andrew, *non?*"

She nodded.

"Perhaps I can help. Problems are always smaller when you talk to a good friend."

Gwyn sighed. She turned, facing Lily more fully on the sofa. "Do you remember when you and Madeleine told me about Andrew's mother and father?"

Lily nodded.

"Andrew never talks about himself. I want to know him better, try to understand him. But I can't get close to him, and I don't know what to do."

Lily nodded again. "That one, he shares his feelings with no one. That is why he broods. But if he would talk to anyone, he would talk to you. Men do not talk to other men the way they talk to a woman. They go to their clubs and they drink and gamble, but when it comes to matters of the heart, they need a woman. And you are just the woman for Andrew!"

"Do you think so?"

"You are very sweet and untouched. Andrew, he has seen too much bad in the world. You are like a—" She paused, searching for the word. "You are like the innocence he lost a long time ago. You heal his heart. He is a very sad man in many ways."

Gwyn's throat tightened. "I know. My father used to say the same thing, that problems were less when they were shared. But Andrew, he can't share that way."

175

"He doesn't know how, *cherie*. If you love him, you will have to teach him."

"How can I do that?"

"I have a plan. You will have to tell a little lie, but I am sure God will forgive you because you mean no harm."

"What?" Now Gwyn was intrigued.

"I know a little bit of how Andrew thinks and I know a lot of how men think." She grasped Gwyn's hand and squeezed it. "I'm going to go to my room and get something, and we are going to prepare you to make Andrew tell you everything!"

Gwyn wondered at that, but she remained sitting on the sofa as Lily went back to her room. In less than a minute, the French girl returned, a conspiratorial gleam in her eyes.

"Have you ever gambled before, Gwyn?"

"No, I—my father didn't allow cards in the house."

"I am going to teach you." Before Gwyn could reply, Lily reached into her wrapper pocket and pulled out a sealed pack of cards. She set them on the sofa.

"Do you have any playing cards here, Gwyn?"

"I've never looked."

"Let me check." Lily hunted through the room and finally found two packs in one of the drawers of a small table by the window.

"When Andrew suggests the two of you gamble, look for the cards as if the thought never entered your mind, but you will know they are here."

"And how will I convince Andrew to gamble?"

"I will explain that in a minute. First, you must learn to play." Lily seated herself on the sofa. "Pass me the deck."

Convinced Lily was absolutely crazy, Gwyn handed her the playing cards.

"Andrew is possessive. He will never let you play cards with another man, and he has no interest in another woman. You cannot play whist, you need four. Or ombre." She laughed. "That takes three, and Madeleine and I play sometimes when we entertain the same gentleman. You need a game for two, and I have just the one. Piquet."

"Piquet?" Gwyn asked uncertainly. "Lily, I don't think—"

But Lily was already unwrapping the cards. "There are fifty-two cards in the deck, but you have to cut it to thirty-six. You must take out some cards. We will get rid of the twos, threes, fours, and fives." As she spoke, she did exactly that, and Gwyn watched in amazement as Lily's small hands worked deftly.

"Lily, I don't see how Andrew will agree to this. . . ."

"You keep the ace, six through ten, and the three courts. This is the queen, this is the king, and this is the knave. They are not hard to recognize, *non?*"

"Lily—"

"Now, Andrew will assume you know nothing. He will shuffle, like this." Lily proceeded to demonstrate, and Gwyn watched, amazed by her dexterity. "And then you will cut, like this." She cut the cards. "Now you do it, Gwyn."

Gwyn complied.

"And now he will deal. Twelve cards to you, twelve to him, and twelve in the middle." The cards flashed out on the sofa face down. Lily set the remaining cards in a neat pile between them. "Pick up your cards, Gwyn."

She did as she was told. What could be the harm in playing a simple game of cards? Especially if it helped her understand Andrew. She wasn't sure how Lily had decided she was supposed to persuade him, but she decided to go along with this plan.

"Now, do not arrange them, because you must make him think you are ignorant. And do not let anything show in your face. You have a very expressive face, Gwyn, and it will give you trouble when you gamble. You must not let Andrew know what you hold in your hands."

"Lily, *I* don't know what I have."

"Aha! I have a good hand."

"Lily?"

"Ah, yes. You are trying to get cards in order. How do you say it in English?"

"In a sequence?"

"Yes. Perfect. The higher the card, the better the sequence. If Andrew, for example, gets a nine, ten, and knave, you must get a king, queen, and ace to top him."

"I have an ace here, but it has a mark on it."

"Let me see." Lily looked at the card. "That has nothing to do with the card. The duty ace is always stamped. That means tax has been paid on this desk of cards."

"The king taxes playing cards?"

"I would if I was king, the way you English love to gamble. It makes him a lot of money. Now, do you see any sequences you could make?"

"Not right now."

"The same for me. So we draw from the pile in the middle. I will go first." Lily picked a card and studied it. She added it to the fan of cards in her hand and discarded another card, face up, next to the pile in the middle.

"Now, Gwyn, you may either pick it up or take another from the pile. Can you use the card I put down?"

"No."

"You may not use it, but you must remember it. It was the six of hearts. Once that card is in the pile, neither you or Andrew have it. And he does not have any of the cards in your hand. If you watch the cards during the game, you may be able to guess what he has. And you *never* put down a high card."

"I understand." Gwyn picked another card, studied it for a moment, then added it to the ones in her hand. She discarded a seven of spades.

"Non, non, non!"

She looked up, startled.

"Ah, Gwyn, you looked like you knew too much. To fool Andrew, you must do it like this." Lily proceeded to pick up a card. The expression on her face said most clearly she didn't know what to do with it. Puzzled, she slipped it into her cards and discarded another, then looked up at Gwyn as if asking if she had done the right thing.

Gwyn couldn't control her laughter. She set her cards down and leaned back on the sofa, her arms across her middle.

"You think he will not believe you, *non?*"

She gasped and wiped the tears from her eyes. "Oh, Lily, I can't do it! I know I'll laugh! You were perfect, just perfect!"

Lily smiled. "My aunt on my mother's side was a very famous actress in France. I am sure I inherited something from her. But I am going to watch you and train you this night until you are perfect. When you win the card game, Andrew will be shocked!"

"How are you so sure I'm going to win?" Gwyn asked, picking up her cards.

"Because, my little innocent, we are going to cheat."

Several hours later, and many games of piquet, Gwyn looked up with a guilty start as the door opened. She half expected Andrew to walk in unannounced and find her up to mischief with Lily. But it was Angel.

"Lily, what are you doing corrupting our Gwyn?" But amusement laced her voice as she set the tea tray down on the table.

Lily didn't take her eyes off Gwyn as she watched her reaction to picking up another card. "I have a plan, Angel. I am helping Gwyn with Andrew."

"By teaching her to gamble?" Angel had clearly been through schemes like this before with Lily, and Gwyn could tell she was waiting for an explanation. But she was still amused.

"Let us finish this game while you pour the tea and slice the cake. I'm sure Gwyn has a third teacup here somewhere."

"In the carved chest by the screen," Gwyn said as she discarded another card.

"Perfect! Your face was perfect! He will never know you know what you are doing!"

"*Who* will never know?" Angel asked from the back of the room. "Lily, if this is another of your—"

179

"Ah no, Angel. I am helping. This is going to work because Andrew is an honorable man."

Over tea and gingerbread, Lily outlined the last part of her master plan.

"What does Andrew do when you ask him of his past?"

"He gets very angry," Gwyn admitted.

"But he is warmer and less like a bear after you have been nice to him in bed and when he first wakes up in the morning."

Gwyn could feel her face heating again. "Yes, he is."

"Ask him then. See what response you get."

"He will demand to know of my past as well."

"Ah!" Lily rubbed her hands together. "That is the moment you must suggest a contest of some sort. Make it very playful, and he will go along. No man ever believes a woman could be clever enough to beat him at anything. And you are very sweet and innocent in his mind. He will never suspect you of any tricks."

"I have one question," Angel said, her mouth full of gingerbread. She swallowed. "What happens if Gwyn loses? She has to tell him about her past, correct?"

"She's not going to lose," Lily said smugly.

"And how can you be certain?"

"Because I am going to mark the cards for her."

"Oh, Lily! Don't you think Andrew will be able to see through that? He will probably insist on a sealed pack."

"I am going to reseal them, too."

Angel stared at her friend, clearly amazed. "How are you going to do that?"

"Did I ever tell you about Charles, my gambling friend?"

"No."

"He taught Madeleine many tricks, and she taught me. When we entertain men together in the blue silk room, many times we play cards and they never know how we are so clever. They don't care how much money they lose when we are nice to them at the end."

Angel slowly smiled. "Lily, you never stop surprising me."

Lily patted Gwyn's arm. "I want this one to be happy. Andrew has always been kind to me, and he deserves Gwyn, whether he knows it or not."

Gwyn felt a warm glow fill her. "I cannot thank you enough, Lily."

"One thing you must learn, little one, is that men are very stupid in matters of the heart. It is up to the woman to help them and provide them with what is good for them. And you will be very good for Andrew."

Chapter Twelve

Andrew could not remember being quite as bored with an evening in a long time. It was all well and good to see his grandfather. Even though Henry was rather stiff and formal with him—and he knew his spending so much time at The Dark Stallion was the reason—there was still a great deal of affection between them.

Henry invited Belinda and her father to his birthday celebration. Lord Pevensy didn't annoy Andrew, but the proprietary attitude Belinda displayed irritated him to no end. She insisted on talking about their wedding, and Henry joined right in, his enthusiasm evident.

Apparently even Belinda is better than a woman at The Dark Stallion, Andrew thought much later in the evening. The party had been over for almost two hours and he was upstairs in his bed.

To his utmost annoyance, Henry had insisted Belinda and her father stay overnight. A chilling December rain had been slashing down in torrents for most of the evening, and his grandfather had been quite clever in appealing to Lord Pevensy's protective manner toward his horses.

And so Belinda and her father were firmly ensconced in the guest rooms down the hall.

And here he was in his rooms, restless. Unable to sleep. He'd grown used to having Gwyn next to him at night. When he woke, he always had his arms around her. Even in sleep he felt she was as insubstantial as a dream and might disappear in a puff of smoke if he didn't hold her fast. The deep, even rhythm of her breathing soothed him on the occasions he came awake in the middle of the night. He liked falling asleep next to her after they had made love. And he loved waking up with her and coaxing her into his arms once again.

He groaned as the memories affected his body. *Just this one night, then you'll see her. You can wait.* Determinedly, he closed his eyes and let his frustration and tiredness wash over him. He could feel his body relaxing, and he half smiled as he buried his face in his pillow.

Tomorrow . . .

His dreams were vivid, dark red and swirling. Passionate images flashed before him, images of Gwyn. He was sliding slowly over her, parting her slender thighs with his hand, cradling his body between her spread legs and sheathing himself tightly in her pure, smooth heat. . . .

He groaned softly. The sound eased him out of the dream; he was between sleep and waking. He didn't have the strength to sit up. Everything, all his energy, was concentrated at the juncture of his thighs.

"Gwyn . . ." he groaned, her name inaudible. There was a moist heat and erotic pleasure around his swollen, aching arousal, yet when he slowly turned his head from side to side, both his hands were by the pillow. Suddenly his eyes opened wider as he saw long brown hair spilled over his stomach.

Belinda!

He raised himself to his elbows, all grogginess gone, grasped her hair and pulled sharply. For a moment her lips closed more tightly around his aroused flesh and he winced, then he was staring into her face. She looked extremely satisfied with herself. Her eyes were bright, and when he loosened his grip on her long hair, she threw her head back haughtily, her large breasts jiggling.

"Hello, darling."

"In the name of God, Belinda, what the devil are you doing in my bed?"

"Andrew, I'm sure you know what I was—"

"Don't play games with me. I want an answer."

She pursed her lips prettily and smoothed her hair back from her face with one hand. It was a calculated gesture, causing one of her breasts to jut out.

"I miss you in my bed, Andrew. I know I'm a wanton for admitting it, but you haven't paid much attention to me lately." She reached between his legs, her disappointment evident. "Don't you want me, Andrew? You were quite lusty only minutes ago."

He opened his mouth but didn't know what to say. He could bed her—if he thought of Gwyn the entire time. But the prospect struck him as sordid. Belinda's lush curves looked overblown when he compared them to Gwyn's slender figure. There were signs of dissipation in her face, greed in her eyes. Gwyn's innocence and beauty would affect him on a more profoundly deep level than this woman ever could.

"Belinda, I have had a lot on my mind. . . ."

"And quite a lot of activity in your bed if I am to believe the gossips."

"What exactly do you mean by that?"

"That little golden-haired whore at The Dark Stallion. The one you bed every night, spend every evening with." Her voice rose slightly. "Even my father has started asking questions, Andrew, as to why you never come to visit anymore. You did ask me to become your bride; I deserve a little more consideration. . . ."

"I never *asked* you. You took care of everything by mentioning our engagement to your father. But that isn't the point of this discussion, dear heart." He gave her the endearment a sarcastic inflection and could tell by the way Belinda's mouth tightened that she had understood. "Our marriage was never supposed to be anything but a business

184

arrangement, and you knew that from the start. Who I spend my evenings with and what I do are simply none of your business—and it will be none of your business after we are married. Am I making myself clear?"

"Perfectly. But you have no right to make a fool of me by being indiscreet. Everyone in London knows about you and that whore and the amount of money you paid to bed her." Her eyes narrowed. "I trust you are clever enough to enjoy her in armour, as I would be quite displeased if you were to catch a poisonous infection. . . ."

His hand tightened around her upper arm, and he was disgusted to see a gleam of arousal in her dark eyes. From what he had heard about town, Belinda liked her pleasures on the rough side. He let go of her arm abruptly, resolving not to lose his temper.

"That's quite enough, Belinda. It would be wise if you returned to your room."

"But I'm not finished. The little slut has you far too enraptured with her questionable charms."

"I said, that's *enough.*" It was one thing for Belinda to berate him, quite another for her to attack Gwyn.

"But I've heard she was quite well-used at another house before she came to The Dark Stallion. In truth, a friend of mine heard she lifted her skirts for men when she was barely twelve—oh, Andrew, what—let *go* of me, how *dare* you—"

He pulled her toward him, all control gone. When she was firmly positioned over his knees, he held her down with one hand and applied the other smartly to her buttocks.

"Andrew, I—*ow!* How dare you—*no, ow, you're hurting me!*" He spanked her soundly, her yelps of distress evoking no mercy in him, until his hand began to tingle and grow hot. When he finished, he rolled her off him and stood up, leaving her sprawled on the large bed.

"Andrew," Belinda whispered urgently. "Andrew, please. Now. I promise you it will be good. . . ."

He was thoroughly disgusted with both her and himself.

185

Seeing the robe she had discarded on the floor, he picked the garment up. Tossing it toward her, he turned his back on the sight of her and reached for his breeches.

"You disgust me, Belinda. Cover yourself and get out."

"Andrew, it will be good. Better than with that—"

"Get out."

After a moment of silence, he finally heard her leave. When he was certain she was out of the room, he sat back down on the bed and stared out the window.

The sky was just beginning to lighten, turning dark violet. Evening stars twinkled in the sky. He knew he wouldn't sleep anymore this night. Belinda had taken his emotions and twisted them around until he had reacted in a way that shamed him. He had vowed to never abuse another person—especially a weaker woman—as he had been abused by his loathsome stepfather.

His appalling conduct with Gwyn had shocked him. Now, even if Belinda had provoked him past all endurance, he couldn't feel good about what he had done.

And to sit at breakfast with her and have her act as if nothing at all had passed between us during the night. It was an abominable way to begin the day.

He continued to stare out the window as the sky lightened further. When he finally stood up and started to dress, he was smiling.

He would go to Gwyn. She would cleanse him of this shameful feeling. He felt soiled because Belinda had been naked in his bed, had used her talented mouth.

He quickly tied the stock of his shirt, shrugged on his waistcoat, and pulled his boots over his breeches. He ran his fingers through his unruly hair impatiently, then walked out the bedroom door, his footsteps quick and almost soundless.

Gwyn was dreaming, deep, erotic dreams that disturbed her sleep and caused her to wake exhausted. It was always Andrew

186

who took her higher and higher into a glorious velvet fire, the soft flames consuming them both as they burned hotly within her body. She moaned softly, then buried her face in her pillow. The dream had been so emotionally and sensually real it had pushed her into a half-awake state.

Her eyes opened as she heard the door creak softly. She sat up slowly, trying to orient herself in case it was Suzanne, sneaking in to do her harm.

When the curtains surrounding the bed parted, she saw Andrew. He smiled, then sat down on the bed and began to remove his boots. Gwyn, clad in a white lace-trimmed nightgown, softly touched his arm.

"Andrew, why are you here this early?"

"Did you miss me last night?"

She blushed, scandalized at the thought of what he would think if he could see inside her head to particular dreams. "Yes," she admitted softly.

Now his boots and waistcoat were off, and he was rapidly removing his shirt. She did not often spend time with him during the day. Gwyn studied his body as he stripped off his shirt and dropped his hand to the fastening of his breeches. His chest was powerfully muscled, his body that of a man who enjoyed hard, physical work. Black curling hair covered his chest, then arrowed down toward a flat stomach.

Gwyn turned her head as she heard his breeches drop to the floor. She felt him slide into bed beside her.

"Come here." His voice was strangely rough, not with command but with a sort of emotion she couldn't quite fathom.

She went to him, and he simply held her. She could feel the warmth of her body start to penetrate the coldness of his, and she wondered at the fact that he had ridden over in the middle of a bitingly cold, wet morning to be close to her. His hair was still damp, his lips cool as he kissed her neck.

"It was a foolish idea, spending the night without you," he said. She felt him take a deep breath, felt the muscles in his arms relaxing. Surprised, for she had assumed he wanted nothing more than to lose himself in her, Gwyn opened her eyes and looked up into his face.

There was a faint stubble along his strong jaw and shadows beneath his closed eyes. His mouth was slowly losing its tension, and as his breathing deepened, she realized he was falling asleep. He sighed and moved closer to her, one hair-roughened leg sliding over both of hers.

His face looked supremely vulnerable. There was no chance of his waking for a time, as he was clearly exhausted. She wondered what had transpired at his grandfather's house.

And she wondered at his need of her. As she closed her eyes and drifted toward sleep secure in his arms, Gwyn decided that if needing wasn't the same as loving, it would have to do for now.

Andrew woke shortly after noon to find Gwyn sitting next to the bed in a chair, concentrating on her embroidery.

She made quite a pretty sight in a rose silk gown. Her hair was styled in loose curls, pulled back with rose ribbons, and she looked fresh and innocent and very, very young.

Before he could say anything, she moved gracefully to the table by the fire and poured him what looked like a cup of tea.

"If you drink this, you'll feel better. It was quite cold out this morning."

"What is it?" he asked as she handed him the cup. Though he wouldn't have admitted it for the world, he liked her fussing over him.

"One of Cook's specialties. She assured me it would take the chill out of your body. Warm white wine with spices."

"What kind of spices?" But he was already lifting the cup to his lips.

"Pepper and cinnamon, I'm sure of that by the scent. She won't reveal the rest. You know Cook."

"She's quite protective of her recipes, isn't she?" He liked this, talking with her in the morning about anything and everything.

"She's a dear when you get around her gruffness."

He watched as she poured a half cup of the warm wine for herself, then sat down in the chair by the bed.

"And how did you endear yourself to Cook? She seems the type to bite off heads."

"I help her in the garden. I used to take care of the kitchen garden we had at home, and I offered my help when she was organizing the pantry."

He frowned, not liking the thought of her having to work. "You don't have to do any of that."

She set her cup down on the bedside table. "I enjoy helping her."

"What else do you do?" He was suddenly curious of how she spent her time when he was not with her.

"I sew. I talk with Angel. And Lily. I read—"

"You can read?" He was amazed by this revelation. "Who taught you?"

He could see the desire for privacy at war with something else in her expressive face. For whatever reason, she decided to trust him, and he felt a slow warmth begin to creep over his body.

"My father."

Now her eyes registered pain briefly, and he wished he hadn't asked. But at the same time he felt a need to know more.

"Where is your mother?"

"She died when I was seven, giving birth to my brother."

"You have no living relatives?"

The pause before her answer was too long, and he knew she was about to lie.

"No."

He set the cup down. "No one knows you are here?"

This time her answer was too quick. "No one."

"How did you come to The Dark Stallion?"

She gathered up both cups and saucers and carried them over to the tea tray. "It doesn't matter, now that I'm here. What would you like to do today, m'lord?"

Find out more about you. But he knew the subject was closed—for now.

"I should like a bath. Later I have some business to attend to, but I will be back this evening. If you would wear the gold brocade gown I bought you, that would please me greatly."

He watched her as she rang for Angel, went to the large wardrobe, and took out the requested gown. Her movements were graceful and elegant, and Andrew felt himself becoming curious all over again.

A vicar's daughter at The Dark Stallion. A woman who could read, who had a way of reaching people, even crusty old Cook. A woman who moved like a member of the aristocracy, whose face was fine boned and elegant. He sensed a mystery within her, and just as he had been determined to uncover the powerful sensuality she possessed, he now determined to discover who she truly was and how she had come to this place.

Andrew stretched, then slowly swung his long legs over the side of the bed. Time was on his side. He had no plans to leave London for the holiday season, and Gwyn would remain right where she was, safely guarded in her room.

"Hello, my lovely." The Duke of Cuckfield talked to his roses daily. He enjoyed taking leisurely strolls through the glassed-in conservatory he'd constructed specifically for his pleasure. Braziers were kept lit round the clock so he could enjoy the flowers in the middle of winter. It was a hot, humid room, and it suited him.

The roses. Their color, shape and texture soothed him. He couldn't smell their fragrance, as he had almost no sense of smell. But that didn't bother him. He worshipped beauty, whether in a flower, a piece of furniture, or a person.

And as he was a particularly vain man, the beauty that gave

him the greatest pleasure was that of his own face and form.

A small black boy no older than ten trailed behind him, and as wilted petals fell to the floor, he collected them. Cuckfield had bought the blackamoor almost a year earlier. He was as graceful and clean as a little black cat. Dressed in harem pants gathered at his slender ankles, a skillfully embroidered vest, and a turban, he added an air of the exotic to his household, which the Duke found particularly pleasing.

The blackamoor was his favorite servant, with his smooth black skin, sharp cheekbones, and obsidian eyes. The boy existed to provide the Duke with comfort, whether by fanning him on a hot summer day or trailing after him as he did now, picking up delicate petals as they drifted to the marble floor.

"This one is quite lovely, don't you agree?" the Duke asked, his voice barely a rasp. He didn't expect an answer as his fingers caressed the full, red petals. The blackamoor knelt down, and the Duke watched as he picked up yet another faded flower.

It terrified the Duke, growing older. As each year passed, he lived at a faster and more violent pace. Younger and younger lovers were used in a desperate attempt to hold time at bay. Each encounter was more important than the last. Time seemed to be closing in on him, as if demanding retribution for the life he had led.

But the roses calmed him.

"Some mint tea, perhaps, would do me good," he murmured. The blackamoor vanished, his red felt slippers noiseless on the cool marble floor.

The Duke continued to stroke the red flower, and he watched with silent satisfaction as the petals trembled. His mind was filled with images of the girl at The Dark Stallion. Edward had reported back to him last night, and now it was only a matter of time before he would capture her. Her face was exquisite, more beautiful than any he had seen in a long time. Her features affected him like no other woman's ever had. There was something about her, the way her face was shaped,

191

that moved feelings primal and deeply potent within him.

The blackamoor returned and placed the silver tea set on a table near the door.

"You have done very well," the Duke said. "Now fetch me the scissors I keep in the chest."

The boy disappeared, then returned shortly, scissors in hand.

"Leave me. I no longer desire company."

The boy bowed, his dark eyes expressionless. He turned and left the room.

As the Duke surveyed his flowers, a smile briefly touched his lips. He could see the golden-haired girl in his bedroom, there for his pleasure alone. As he thought of what he would do to her, his grey eyes clouded over and the slightest of smiles touched his sensual mouth.

For he and Gwyneth Leighton would most certainly be together before this year ended.

"What would you like as a Christmas present?" Andrew asked as he sat forward in the large tub. The water was hot and soothing to his tired muscles. He could feel Gwyn's hands, soft and infinitely pleasing, as she washed his back.

She didn't reply. She simply rinsed his back. He wondered at her and thought of the countless women he knew who would have had an entire list ready and waiting.

"Come, there must be something I can give you."

"There is, m'lord, but I fear it will not please you."

He turned his head and indicated with his hand for her to sit on the stool next to the tub. He watched her as she removed the linen towel and the glass of wine he had been drinking and set them on a nearby table. She settled herself on the chair.

He was pleased by her lack of artifice. Taking her hand, he kissed her palm. "Now what is it you wish to ask that you believe will displease me?"

She hesitated, then said quietly, "I should like to go to Church."

He should have expected this from a vicar's daughter. As he let go of her hand and sank down into the bathwater, Andrew didn't see how he could deny her the comfort of attending. As much as he feared having her any place outside this room, he would have to grant her wish. And as he thought of her request, he realized how different she was from any woman he had ever known.

She asked so little from him. And it was clear his answer was important to her.

He glanced back up at her face. There was something in her eyes, a soft resignation. With a guilty start, he realized she expected him to deny her request.

"Why do you wish to go?" he asked, trying to forestall the inevitable.

"It would give me great comfort."

"I would not have you go alone."

He could tell by the softening of her expression she was beginning to hope. "Lily was planning to attend services Sunday. I could go with her."

He could not attend with her, thus drawing attention to who she was and exposing her to hurtful gossip. Besides, he had given up on salvation many years ago.

"If Thatch is willing to accompany and protect you, you have my permission."

"Thank you, Andrew." Her arms came around his wet shoulders and she gave him the sweetest kiss, filled with emotion. It touched him, and he held her closely, not wanting her to see any sign of weakness or need for her in his expression.

"And I must talk to Lily beforehand."

"Yes, Andrew."

"But I'm certain something can be arranged."

The smile she gave him was all the thanks he could have asked for.

"Ah! The gold brocade is perfect! You will look like a

princess in a fairy tale." Lily carefully inspected Gwyn's dress, then admired the delicate silk chemise and petticoats also laid out on the bed, both trimmed with French lace so delicate it looked like cobwebbing. She fluffed out the brocade skirt of the gown once more and eyed it critically. "I wish I had a man who would buy as many things for me as Andrew does for you."

"Lily, are you sure you think this plan—"

"Ah, *petite*, I know the mind of a man. He will not resist a challenge so easily won—so he thinks." She laughed, her dark eyes bright. "Now, I am going to have you do a little needlework on your chemise."

"What?"

"All part of my plan. Can you take out the seams or move the straps so it is big on you?"

Gwyn nodded. "But I don't even have to do that. There's one in the wardrobe that's too large."

"Put it on."

Gwyn slipped off her wrapper and did as Lily asked, then stood in the middle of the room feeling rather foolish. "I meant to take my needle to it, but I didn't have the time—"

"It's good you didn't. It will save us work." Swiftly, Lily folded the other chemise and bundled it back into the wardrobe. "You will wear that one tonight."

"But what good—?"

"Ah, Gwyn, you must do as all good gamblers have always done and distract his attention. And how could a man like Andrew not be distracted when he thinks your chemise is about to slide off your shoulders?"

When Gwyn began to protest, Lily put her finger to her lips.

"You will mention, when Andrew comes in, that you are feeling rather warm. After dinner, ask him to help you out of your dress and corset so you can put on a wrapper. Then you will conveniently forget the wrapper."

"Lily, usually after supper, Andrew and I—"

"But your stomach is feeling delicate this evening, is it not? And he is not such a cad he would press a lady in distress."

Gwyn pushed the strap of her chemise up on her shoulder.

The garment was too large, and the straps constantly slipped down off her shoulders.

"Perfect! Now sit, I am going to put a beauty mark on your face." Lily rummaged through the small bag she had brought with her as Gwyn obediently sat down in front of a large mirror. When Lily came up behind her, the French girl squeezed her shoulder reassuringly.

"Do not look so frightened! Nothing will go wrong. Now listen closely, because we do not have much time. . . ."

When Andrew arrived, Gwyn was sitting prettily on the sofa as Lily had instructed.

"Would you like a cup of tea or coffee?" she asked as she stood up and took his coat.

"No. But I am rather hungry and would like supper soon."

Her fingers trembled as she hung his coat behind the screen. "I asked Angel to send it up as soon as she saw you on the stairs." She remembered the first part of the plan and said softly, "It is rather hot in here, don't you think?"

"No. But then I just came in from outside. Are you feeling ill?"

"No—"

"You're flushed."

Before she could say anything more, he was standing next to her, his hand gentle on her forehead.

Nervous, she caught his hand in her own and smiled up at him. "I'm sure it's just the heat. Would you like some wine?"

"With dinner, perhaps."

There was a light tap on the door. After Andrew bade them enter, Angel and three other maids walked in, each carrying a huge silver tray.

"There's more. I'll be back directly, m'lord," Angel said, then the four women vanished.

When they were alone, Andrew said, "What's that on your face?"

"What?" Gwyn touched her cheek.

"Next to your mouth. That mark."

"Oh. Lily gave me a beauty mark."

"Take it off. It doesn't suit you."

His manner irritated her. "You don't like it? I find it quite attractive."

"I would like you to take it off."

Remembering what Lily had said, Gwyn smiled slowly, shyly. "Couldn't you pretend to like it, just for a little. For me?"

He stared at her for a long moment as if she had suddenly gone mad. But Gwyn refused to back down. If his mood was such that he wouldn't accept a simple beauty mark, he would never agree to a game of cards.

She was surprised when he relented. Twice in one day. First, permission to go to church, and now her beauty mark. He would have to agree to the card game.

Angel knocked again and entered with one other maid. Two more trays joined the first four. As the women walked out, Andrew said, "We will not be needing any further assistance this evening."

"As you wish, m'lord," Angel said. She walked quietly out the door.

Dinner was torturous. Gwyn was convinced Andrew watched each morsel she ate, when all she really did was push her supper around on her plate. She sipped her wine slowly, wanting to keep a clear head for what was to come.

"You've barely eaten. Are you ill, Gwyn?"

"No. It's just . . . terribly hot."

"It does seem rather warm." He made a move to refill her wine glass.

"No, thank you. I haven't finished what I have." She picked up her goblet and took a small sip.

Andrew was looking at her with the most curious expression on his face. Gwyn, not quite sure what to do next, decided she had to direct things.

"Would you help me with the buttons of my dress? I think I

shall feel much better once I am out of it."

His fingers were skillful, and soon the dress was back in her wardrobe, along with her corset. Gwyn was hesitant about parading out in front of Andrew in just her chemise. She put on a dark blue wrapper, then joined him at the table.

"I'm worried about you, Gwyn. I'm going to send for a surgeon."

"No. Please. I would not want to waste his time. I simply have an upset stomach. If I am quiet for a short time, I shall feel much better." The words came out of her mouth quite easily, and Gwyn realized that without too much effort it would be easy to become an accomplished liar. It was the waiting that made her nervous.

"Lie down, then. Here, let me help you."

He was very considerate of her, pulling back the counterpane on the bed and assisting her into it. He tucked the cover around her, then pulled one of the chairs up close to the head of the bed.

"Do you want me to see if Cook has something for a sick stomach?" he asked.

For just an instant she wanted to cry. How could she deceive this man, willfully trick him this very night? He was being kind to her. Gwyn had done much thinking since their last argument, and more and more she was realizing Andrew was far from an ordinary man.

Yet if there is any hope for the two of you, you must understand what drives him. And that can only happen if he talks to you. She had asked about his past several times, and each time he had changed the subject. Lily's plan seemed a relatively painless way of obtaining information in order to understand him.

"No. Please don't bother Cook."

"Gwyn." His deep blue eyes were worried. "I don't like you feeling like this."

Something in his expression warned her he was going to say more. She remained quiet, and he continued.

"Perhaps I have been . . . wrong. Keeping you shut away

197

like some exotic bird in a cage. Gwyn, you must know you are very special to me, and sometimes I am afraid for you. Beauty such as yours can be a dangerous thing."

She squeezed his hand and wondered at what he said. It was true. Edward had sold her to Janet because he had known she would command a good price. And then she had been sold again at auction, bringing in even more money for the madam of the house. Beauty could be looked on as a curse.

"Perhaps keeping you here is making you ill. I should have looked after you more carefully, made it possible for you to have time outside this house."

"No, Andrew. I don't think that's true. Besides, I'll be going out Sunday with Lily."

He bent his dark head and kissed her hand. "Is there any other reason I should know about?"

It took a minute before the full import of his words affected her, then she blushed all the way up from her breasts, the bright color stinging her cheeks. She wondered what Andrew would do if he knew she had been deliberately preventing any possibility of a baby.

"No. I'm sure it's not that."

"Would you tell me if you thought you were?" His expression was anxious, and it touched her.

She squeezed his hand again. "Of course I would."

He was silent for a moment, then stood up and walked over to the door. She turned her head just enough to see him let himself out. As soon as the door closed behind him, she sat up quickly.

Where could he have gone? She couldn't run down the hall after him, not if she was supposed to be feeling poorly. She lay back down in her bed, feeling frustrated and knowing she could do nothing but wait.

He came back shortly, and from the herbal smell wafting from the teapot, she knew Cook had concocted another remedy.

"She said it might taste bitter, but it's excellent for the stomach." Andrew deftly poured a cup and handed it to her.

Gwyn appealed silently to her sense of the ridiculous and slowly sipped the vile brew. It was strong and had a distinctive, pungent taste, but she couldn't place what herbs made up Cook's blend. *Nothing in anyone's stomach could survive this*, she thought grimly as she finished her cup, praying all the while she wouldn't be sick in the morning.

Andrew would have poured her more, but she shook her head.

"Would you lie beside me until my stomach stops hurting?" Now she felt no guilt about her deception because her stomach was, in fact, feeling queasy.

He did as she asked, and she found a sort of comfort in pillowing her head against his chest.

Ask him now.

"Andrew, where did you grow up? With your grandfather in London?" She prayed silently that he wouldn't simply lie as a means of evading her questions.

"Why all the questions when you should be resting?" He didn't sound annoyed with her, but she admired the skill with which he dealt with her inquiry.

"Talking helps me keep my mind off the pain." There was a pain now, and she was sure she had Cook to thank for it.

"Why does it matter to you?"

"I began thinking on it when you asked me questions about my childhood. I wondered about your parents, where they are and why they no longer live in London."

"I should still like to know how you came to The Dark Stallion."

The stakes were high.

"Perhaps we could share with each other. You could tell me about your past and I will tell you how I came to be auctioned off."

"A vicar's daughter in a brothel in London. It has made me

199

wonder. As for my background, you could talk to anyone in London, or in this house, and hear pieces of the entire story for yourself."

"But I don't care to hear it from a stranger. I would much rather hear the truth from you."

"You won't find my life either illuminating or admirable. I wonder if I care to have you know any of it. You're different from most people in that respect, Gwyn, and I should like to keep things as they are."

This was going to be difficult. She'd have to help things along. "I would never think less of you, Andrew. I'm simply curious, the way you are about me." She took a deep breath, praying her voice would remain steady. "How should we decide who is to first confess?" She smiled up at him. "We could make it less serious. A game of chance, perhaps."

"And what kind of game would we play?" He seemed amused.

"I would leave that decision up to you, m'lord, as I am not at all familiar with most games."

"Perhaps it would be entertaining." She could feel him responding to the challenge. Lily was right: Andrew was so certain he would win, he was going to agree to her terms.

"Have you ever played cards before?" he asked.

She shook her head, crossing her fingers beneath the counterpane and praying for forgiveness.

"I'm sure Janet had put a deck in this room somewhere," Andrew said.

Gwyn knew exactly where Lily had put the deck, but she said nothing as she watched Andrew quickly search throughout the bedchamber. When he opened the desk drawer where Lily had placed the marked deck, she bit her lip. Would he know the cards had been opened and resealed?

"A new deck." He quickly unwrapped it and threw the paper into the fire. "That way neither of us can cheat."

She could feel her face flushing and knew she had to do something about the situation. "Andrew, would you help me out of bed? It is so warm beneath this cover, I fear I shall faint."

He was at her side in an instant, cards forgotten.

"Perhaps we'd best postpone this game for another night."

"No. No, I feel much better now that I'm not covered." She refrained from putting on a wrapper and looked up at Andrew.

"You're certain, Gwyneth?"

She nodded her head.

He helped her to her chair, then sat down across from her, the cards in his hand. He began to shuffle them, and she couldn't help watching his long, skillful fingers.

"As there's only two of us, we'll have to play piquet."

Chapter Thirteen

Gwyn let Andrew win the practice game, all the while familiarizing herself with the subtle marks Lily had made on the deck. When Andrew gathered all the cards together and began to shuffle for their first game, she offered up a silent prayer that she was doing the right thing.

And that she would win.

"We'll play two out of three. Those are fairer odds for you, my beauty, since you have no experience and one game is hardly sufficient practice."

"Thank you, Andrew."

She was silent while she played, concentrating on the various expressions Lily had advised her to use. She could feel Andrew's silent amusement from across the small table. Gwyn was careful to hold her cards so he couldn't see what she had. She was calm now, her heart beating slowly and steadily. Somehow, she knew she was going to win.

"I'm sorry, Gwyn. This is hardly fair." Andrew laid his cards down on the table. She looked at his sequence. Eight, nine, and ten of clubs.

"Andrew, I am not entirely sure, but—" She fanned her cards out clumsily on the table.

Knave, queen, and king of hearts.

His expression was so comically shocked that for one horrible moment she had the most irresistible urge to laugh.

Instead, she concentrated on looking at him as if seeking guidance.

After a short moment of silence, he gathered up the cards and shuffled again.

"A stroke of beginner's luck," he said, but he seemed more concentrated and less amused.

This time, even though she knew he had drawn no high cards, she positioned her arms as Lily had instructed, letting the subtle action lift and press her breasts together above the lace trim of her loose chemise. It did not go unnoticed by Andrew, and he actually dropped a card face up on the table as he picked it from the small pile between them.

Gwyn glanced quickly at the pile, as covertly as she could. The next card up was not a high one.

"You can pick again if you'd like." Her voice held just the right amount of soft innocence.

As the card he had dropped was the seven of spades and Andrew had no need of it, she was certain he would pick again. It was a good maneuver, one Lily had cautioned her to use.

"You must seem fair and generous, innocent and quietly helpless," Lily had said as she applied the beauty mark near her mouth. "Then he will feel like a cad if the thought of your cheating crosses his mind."

He picked the card, and though he didn't change his facial expression at all, she could sense his displeasure.

Lily must have bewitched the cards as well as marked them, Gwyn thought as she saw what card was coming to her. She would have her spread with her next turn. To soften the blow, she let the strap of her chemise slip down off her shoulders, then struggled prettily with it until it was fully in place. She could feel Andrew's gaze upon her and knew she looked like anything but the cheating gambler she was.

"Your turn," Andrew said. He was worried.

She picked the queen of spades, discarded a low club, and fanned her cards out on the table, making sure she dropped one.

Lady Luck, thy name is Lily.

Queen, king, and ace. She knew there was nothing in Andrew's hand to top her. Gwyn had thought about letting him win the second game, but she simply couldn't take that chance.

Andrew was dumbfounded. He kept staring at her cards as if they had lives of their own and at any minute were going to pop up and dance around the table.

"Unbelievable luck," he muttered quietly as he gathered up the cards. "Would you like to play one last game?"

She nodded, knowing she had already won their gamble. She let him win, as much to lead him off the scent as to restore the shreds of his masculine pride. He didn't seem pleased with the victory.

"If I didn't know better," he said softly, "I'd have sworn you wore that damn chemise to distract me."

She blushed, hoping against hope she looked charming and not as guilty as she felt. *It's all for a good cause, keep thinking that.*

"I meant to take this in, but I didn't find the time." At least that part was true. "I'll make sure I finish it this week."

"There's no need. Lady Luck determines the draw of the cards, not a loose chemise." Andrew stood, then came around to her side. He grasped her hand and gently pulled her up from her chair. "Perhaps you would rather rest tonight."

In answer, she curled her fingers into his hair and tugged gently, guiding his lips to hers.

She closed her eyes as he commenced his erotic persuasion, felt his hands slowly span her waist as he nudged her in the direction of the bed. When the backs of her knees touched the soft mattress, she consciously relaxed her legs and allowed him to tumble her onto the bed.

"It's a very becoming fashion," Andrew said as he drew one of the straps down her shoulder, following its progress with a kiss. "I might insist you wear it all the time, as it is much more becoming than the gold dress."

She surrendered to him completely, knowing he needed to make love to her and become physically vulnerable before he could risk his emotions. When his lips and tongue began their loveplay with her taut, aroused breasts, she felt something shatter deep inside her. Gwyn moved closer to everything Andrew promised to give her before the long night was over.

When she woke later in the night, the bedchamber was totally dark, the fire out. She could feel Andrew next to her, and as she snuggled closer, she knew he was awake.

She touched his cheek, then kissed him gently.

"You don't have to tell me anything." And as she said the words, she knew it was true. Her feelings for him were growing more and more tender as the days passed.

"No. I won't back out of our agreement. But I must confess I'm surprised you won. I thought certainly I would be the one lying here waiting for you to tell me how you came here."

She waited, knowing whatever he was going to tell her would have to come out of him in his own way, with no questions from her. Gwyn slid her hand across the thick hair on his chest until her arm encircled him. She could feel the slow, steady beating of his heart increase slightly.

Don't be scared. I know the worst. I only want to try and understand why you keep so many of your deepest feelings locked away in a place I can't reach.

He didn't say anything for a time, yet she knew he was going to.

You told me once you didn't want me restrained with you. I wish I could ask the same. Nothing you say tonight will change the way I feel about you. Believe in me, Andrew. Believe I have strength for us both.

"I'm a bastard." His voice was flat, totally devoid of emotion.

She waited, lying perfectly still.

"My mother fell in love with my father long after her father arranged an advantageous marriage for her. She was married to Sir Reginald Newsome for six years before she met my father.

205

It was a loveless marriage. Reginald was a sadistic man, and he enjoyed hurting my mother. The earliest memories I have are of her crying."

Gwyn's hand tightened slightly against his chest, as if by that simple gesture she could shield him from the pain of remembering.

"He thought she was a brutal woman, flawed and Irish. Why he ever wanted to marry her is something I'll never understand. She was a beautiful woman, and he took that beauty and destroyed it."

Andrew took a deep breath, and Gwyn felt the tense muscles in his chest.

"She met Geoffrey. I'm not sure how. I found a diary of hers that explained some of it to me. She and my father were . . . wildly in love, even though it was forbidden."

He sighed, and the sound was so sad it tore at her. "I was born ten months after they met. I believe she probably approached her husband a few times so he would not be suspicious. I have no doubts my mother attempted to protect me the best way she knew."

Such a different story from Lily's and Madeleine's, when one of the people involved tells it. She wished she could simply hold him tightly against her heart, but she knew she couldn't. He would perceive it as a sign of weakness and pull further away. Gwyn sensed they were on a precipice and that much would be decided of their future relationship this night.

"I was told he enjoyed hearing her screams as she gave birth to me and would allow no one to attend her but her maid. The woman knew nothing about birthing a child, and my mother almost died she bled so badly. Reginald wanted my mother out of his life from the moment I was born. I think he suspected all along I wasn't his but he wasn't completely sure. He and my father were acquaintances, but he didn't suspect he was my mother's lover.

"I never felt close to my stepfather, even when I thought he had given me life. I'm sure he was upset because I looked exactly like my mother, with her Irish coloring. He could see no trace of himself in me. Only my mother. He hated her for that as well."

Gwyn felt his quickened heartbeat beneath her hand and ached for the effort it took him to tell this story.

"My mother was . . . pure love in a very dark world. She was always there when I needed her. She would simply smile and I could carry that smile with me for days if I needed to."

So sad. To learn of such sorrow so very young.

"It was a . . . cold house. I have few memories of being happy, except when my mother and father managed to find time to be together. They included me in the world they created."

Gwyn could hear the slight smile in his voice as he remembered.

"Geoffrey taught me to ride. He gave me a bulldog pup when I turned four. On my fifth birthday he had a pony delivered to the house. Reginald ignored me, and I was just as happy he did. He did not look upon me with great pleasure. But my father . . . my father used to carry me up on his shoulders. We would play a game where I tried to touch the sun. Whenever he was with us, my mother would laugh and smile, and I always loved him for that."

Gwyn closed her eyes. It was horrible, knowing where this story inexorably led. The words were twisting and turning down a dark path, and Gwyn would have given anything to be able to make things right.

"My stepfather found out the truth about my parentage one afternoon when he came home unexpectedly and caught my mother and father in her bedroom. There hadn't been a true marriage between them for years, and he had several mistresses both in the country and the city. Why he wanted my mother so badly I'll never understand. He lashed out at her with his tongue whenever he could."

He paused for a moment, and Gwyn knew he was gathering strength to tell the rest of his story.

"He locked her in her room. While they were arguing in the hallway, I had slipped into my mother's bedchamber and hid beneath the bed. Reginald locked her in, then challenged my father to a duel. They were to fight until one drew first blood. The bastard said he didn't want either of them to lose their lives over an Irish whore.

"They fought up and down the long gallery, smashing vases and destroying furniture. But my mother . . ." His voice faltered for an instant, and Gwyn almost cried out to him not to continue his story and relive such pain.

"My mother was like a wild thing, clawing at the door, screaming. She knew Reginald was part devil and had never intended to keep his agreement." He took a breath, and it seemed to Gwyn he was fighting to pull air into his lungs.

"My father wounded him. He drew first blood. He lowered his sword and Reginald ran him through. He killed him. And I watched my mother die that day. Geoffrey was everything to her, and when she lost him, she didn't have the heart to go on. Reginald finally broke her."

He stopped talking, and Gwyn tightened her arm around his chest.

"He locked her away for two years. And each time I saw her, she seemed to drift further and further away. Sometimes she called me Geoffrey. Other times she didn't know who I was. She never smiled. She just sat in her chair, facing a small window, and stared at the moors where she used to walk with my father.

"A few years later, while her maid dressed her, she was in a more lucid mind. Some days were . . . better than others. She asked the maid how Geoffrey could have been killed when he was such a fine swordsman. The maid had watched the entire duel. She told my mother the truth, that her husband had waited until Geoffrey set his sword down and then killed him.

"She broke away from her maid and escaped her prison. No one knows where she found the knife. My mother went to Reginald's chambers and slit his throat. Then she turned the knife on herself."

Gwyn felt as if her heart were slowly breaking into jagged, painful pieces that pierced with each breath she took.

"I had been out riding my pony. When I came back none of the servants were about. I followed the direction of the weeping and walked into my stepfather's private rooms. They were both on the floor. When I looked at my mother's face, I knew she had found peace at last."

Gwyn could hardly breathe.

"Then I spit on him. I was so glad she killed him."

She couldn't imagine what went through a boy's mind when he saw the mother he had adored lying dead by her own hand.

"The brute used to beat me until I was bloody. For anything. I still hear his damnable voice in my dreams. 'Lord Scarborough, is that any way to address a servant?' 'Lord Scarborough, I heard you took the grey pony to the back pasture. I thought I expressly forbid you to ride that animal.' He was the devil who had bloody well told the groom to saddle the pony for me! He used to beat me until I couldn't move my legs. I used to dream of killing him. I hated him with a complete and total fury."

She heard Andrew take one long, last shuddering breath. "I always knew she would kill him. It was in her eyes. If she hadn't, I would have. With great pleasure."

He was silent for a time, and Gwyn lay next to him, her arm around his chest, her head pillowed on his shoulder.

She felt him swallow, then he continued.

"My grandfather came to take me back to London several times while my mother was confined, but the bastard liked to keep me around as his whipping boy. After he was murdered, Grandfather paid off someone in Parliament and managed to become my guardian."

She could feel the tightness in his chest.

"He was a complete stranger to me. I hated him, hated London after living in the country. I couldn't bring my pony or my dog, and I didn't want to go to school after having run wild through the country. I'm surprised he didn't send me away. But my father had given him a note shortly before his death telling him I was his . . . love child."

He took another breath, then continued to speak. Now his words were hurried, the story almost at an end. "Grandfather was obligated. He loved my father deeply. He'd lost another son and a daughter to smallpox when they were children, so my father was everything to him. And I was a link to the man my father had been.

"He had his hands full with me. The only time Reginald had ever bothered with me was when he punished me. I was a dirty, unkempt little savage."

"Your grandfather must have loved you very much." Gwyn was surprised her voice didn't tremble.

"He must have. The first night I was there, I behaved like an animal."

"You were a scared little boy. He sounds as if he understood."

"He never laid a hand on me." Andrew's voice was thick with a wealth of repressed emotion. "There were a few times when he gave me a good spanking, but I had pushed the poor man beyond all endurance. But he never raised his hand to me the way . . . *he* had. As a child, I knew Reginald enjoyed it.

"My Grandfather hated to lay a hand on me. If he had to, afterwards he'd be as shaken as I was."

"But you survived each other."

"He used to try to make me talk to him. I hated that the most. All I wanted was to smash things, escape outside, and run until I couldn't think or feel anything more. But he persisted. I can tell you this: If my grandfather wants something, he's relentless until he accomplishes it. He asked me, the second week I was with him in London, if there was anything in the world that would make me happy and wipe the sullen look off my face. I was a cheeky thing, a brash little bastard. I told him, 'I want the pony and the dog you made me leave behind.' I was confident I had finally challenged him with something he would never be able to do."

"He brought them to London, didn't he?" Gwyn was smiling now.

"He paid far more than they were worth. Reginald's brother bled him for every pound he could. When my grandfather called me back to the stable, I couldn't believe they were there. I . . . cried. My father had given me both the animals. Having them with me was like having a bit of my parents back."

"Andrew, don't tell me any more." Gwyn was worried. He seemed exhausted, as if all the energy he possessed had been expended in telling the tale.

"There isn't much more. Grandfather kept me out of school and hired a private tutor. I was painfully stupid. He worked with me until I caught up, made me see I wasn't dull, that my schooling had been neglected. He didn't send me away to school until he felt I wouldn't make a mess of it. Then I met Jack, and the rest of it . . . most of the rest you know."

They were quiet for such a long time she thought he was asleep. But then his voice floated lazily into the darkness. His tone was amused, and Gwyn knew she had seen beneath Andrew's careful guard and now it was back in place.

"Did that satisfy your curiosity?"

She simply turned her face into his shoulder.

"There must be something more." Now he was teasing her. She had to ask one more question.

"Why do people talk about you so?" It made her angry, the constant stream of gossip she heard about Andrew, none of which seemed to have anything to do with the man she knew.

"Ah, Gwyn, I've never understood it. It seems to me if a man is happy enough with his own life, he won't take delight in another's miseries. It doesn't bother me anymore. It did when I was small, but then I decided I just didn't give a damn."

She was surprised at his serious answer, half expecting him to tease. Gwyn thought he was finished until he spoke again, this time so quietly she barely heard him.

"You, my beauty, have a dangerous way about you of getting

211

a man to reveal his innermost secrets." His tone changed again, ever so subtly, and she knew his guard was dropping for another instant. "I never told my grandfather I saw my mother right after . . . I've never told anyone."

She tightened her arm around him fiercely, wanting to shield him from all further pain.

"Sometimes I dream. Everything is real. I can smell the blood and hear her maid sobbing. I feel as if I'm swimming through a sea of bodies until suddenly they part and she's there, lying on the floor. Sometimes I see her eyes, just before I wake up. But always blood, everywhere. And I wonder if I will ever find peace within myself."

She was surprised when his arms encircled her, then he gently rolled her over on her back. She reached up and touched his hair with trembling fingers. Something new had been born this night, out of the blood and terror of Andrew's past. Feelings were stirring in her heart. She had seen his vulnerability; he had been unafraid of sharing it with her. Compassion and sorrow mingled with something further, something she'd never felt before. . . .

"Kiss me, Gwyn," he whispered. "Kiss me and help me drive the bitterness out of my heart. When I'm with you, a part of you, possessing you, the demons in my soul are quieted."

Her fingers still trembling, she laced them through his hair as she lifted her face to his kiss.

Sunday was overcast, grey, and drizzling. Andrew sent a carriage for Gwyn and Lily, and they attended the Temple Church. It was a different sort of church from her father's. The minister, a threatening sort of man, shouted his sermon to his people. He did not speak simply, as her father had. The sermon was entitled, "Set thy house in order, for thou shalt shortly die."

"He is not usually that gloomy," Lily said as they sat in the carriage together on the way back to The Dark Stallion.

"He didn't seem to believe we would understand unless he shouted." Gwyn rubbed her fingers against her temple, feeling the beginnings of a headache. It had been stuffy in church with all the people, the windows closed to keep out the chill winter air.

"Are you afraid to die, Gwyn?"

Lily's question caught her off guard for a brief second, but Gwyn could understand how her friend's thoughts had progressed since the service.

"My father always said God would call me home when he was ready and that I shouldn't be afraid to go."

"But do you feel you have been a good person?"

"I have always tried to be."

Lily touched her arm, and she took the French girl's hand, squeezing it gently. Lily's hands were very fragile. She was the smallest of them all.

"I will not see you after we die, Gwyn. You will be in heaven, and I am sure I will be in hell."

"Oh, Lily, the God I believe in is a merciful God. I never see you that you aren't trying to help. I can't believe He would not see what I see."

"But I have done terrible things."

Knowing Lily respected her opinion, Gwyn chose her words carefully. "Lily, when I lived in the country with my father, I was very sheltered. And ignorant. There was one woman in town who used to . . . entertain men. I'm ashamed to say this, but I used to think I was better than she was."

She could see Lily's eyes, huge and dark in her delicately boned face. She appeared childlike at that moment, as she looked at Gwyn with her heart in her eyes.

"I grew up knowing I was going to have to work like that."

"But can you see, Lily, I was protected! You and Angel and Madeleine did not have the life I did. You had to take care of yourself from the time you were a girl."

"I should be like you, Gwyn. I should find a man to take care of me, and then I could afford to be good, *non?*"

213

"Lily." Gwyn patted her hand. Her friend was so worldly and wise one minute, so childish the next. "I think—" And here she thought of Andrew, talking quietly in her dark bedchamber. "I think men need to be taken care of, too. Remember how you told me some of your customers come to your room and just want to talk?"

Lily nodded.

"I think you are helping them. Where else would they go?"

Lily nodded. "Sometimes I don't ask them for money. They look so sad when they leave, even after they tell me their troubles."

Gwyn reached up and smoothed a wayward curl from Lily's cheek. "And I think we have to take care of each other. If Angel had not helped me, things would have gone much worse. You and Madeleine helped me. I cannot tell you how much the three of you mean to me, and I will count you as friends always."

"Even after Andrew sets you up in your house?"

Gwyn flushed, then pulled her hand away. "I am sorry. I should not repeat what I hear from people."

"What have you heard?"

"I know Andrew is looking for a house closer to his grandfather's. I know he intends to keep you there."

To keep you. For a moment, she felt anger flash through her body, raw and white-hot. To be kept, like a performing monkey in a cage.

Lily touched her arm. "Do not be mad at me."

"I'm not."

"Do not be mad at Andrew. He is doing what he thinks is best. It will be your task to tell him what you truly want."

Gwyn knew Lily was worried she'd upset her. Her problems could wait. Forcing down her anger, she said, "Do you have any more card games up your sleeve?"

When Lily started to laugh, she knew she had made the right choice.

For now.

The pounding on her door brought Suzanne upright in bed.

"What do you want?" She had a headache. Edward had brought by the presents he'd promised, and she had indulged in all of them. She was in no mood to be disturbed.

Polly poked her head in the door, her ginger hair loose and tumbling down her back. Her wrapper was barely fastened, and she was tying the sash as she spoke.

"He's given the little miss her own carriage so she can go to town. Fancy that!"

"Polly, leave me be." And Suzanne pulled the frayed blanket over her head.

"The golden-haired slut you hate. She's driving around in fine feathers now, looking pleased as can be. Andrew never gave *you* a carriage, and I'll bet you were better to him in bed than that little miss with ice water in her blood." Polly snorted.

"He gave her a carriage?" Suzanne was wide awake.

"Aye. It's pulling into the alley. Four fine dappled greys and a man to drive them! Come, I'll show you."

Not bothering to don a wrapper over her thin nightshirt, Suzanne jumped out of bed and walked quickly after her stocky friend to an upstairs window overlooking the alley.

She watched as Gwyn and Lily alighted from the carriage. The driver handled both women as if they were ladies, offering his hand in assistance. Thatch stood beside him, watching Gwyn carefully. Suzanne narrowed her eyes as she watched Gwyn pull her blue wool cloak more tightly around her. It was trimmed with white fur, and Suzanne's insides twisted with envy and frustration.

"I bet she wouldn't be sitting so high and mighty if she knew about Lady Belinda," Polly whispered. "Donald told me last night Andrew's going to marry her."

Suzanne could feel the warm glow of satisfaction steal

215

through her. It gave her some comfort, knowing if she couldn't have Andrew, neither could Gwyn.

"I wonder what would happen if she found out about Belinda?" Polly said.

Suzanne smiled. Edward hadn't said anything about talking to the little tart. What she had planned wouldn't leave its mark.

"I do believe you're right, Polly. It would be a kindness to set her straight."

And both women laughed.

Gwyn was glad to reach the privacy of her room. She had been cloistered there for weeks and had forgotten how different London was from the country. The streets had been crowded with people, horses, carriages, and men carrying sedan chairs, which enabled swift travel throughout the city. She saw several children scurrying through the streets dressed in tattered rags, and her heart had gone out to them. The December sky was windy and overcast, constantly threatening rain. A pall of stale smoke hung over everything, and she couldn't help but long for the sweet, clean air outside the city. She had been nervous and felt constantly on her guard.

People had stared at her even though she had worn the hood of her cloak up as Andrew had requested, covering her hair and most of her face. She couldn't help but wonder if they suspected who she was. Gwyn was sure if the people of London connected her with Andrew, she would be the object of speculation and gossip. She had recognized blatant interest in several men's eyes and an entirely different emotion in the women's, causing some to thin their lips and avert their eyes.

Perhaps she had been shut away from the world too long. Her life had an unnatural quality to it. The only people she saw with any regularity were Andrew, Lily, Madeleine, and Angel. Other than that, she was alone.

She took off her cloak and draped it across the back of the

sofa. Angel had seen her come in and had promised her a cup of hot tea. Gwyn sat down in front of the fire, glad for the warmth.

When the door opened, she assumed it was Angel.

"Well, hello Gwyn. I thought I would come by and see how you were feeling."

The familiar voice brought her head up. Suzanne. Gwyn stood, keeping her eyes on the woman.

Suzanne laughed, her hands on her boyish hips. "Don't fear for your safety. I'm not going to risk Andrew's wrath coming down upon me. You've got your protector."

Gwyn said nothing, wondering why the woman had come to her room.

"It's a nice carriage and pretty horses he's given you. But then I'm sure you earned it."

Gwyn found her voice. "Leave me."

"You're a very understanding woman. I don't know if I could be the same, being Andrew's mistress while he is pledged to wed another after the holidays."

The whore's words ripped through her. *Andrew to wed?* She could see Suzanne standing just inside her door, her front teeth protruding as she grinned delightedly.

"I admire you, Gwyn. I'd have kicked and screamed and scratched his bloody eyes out if he tried to convince me he needed another woman in his life." Suzanne slowly pleated her torn nightshirt between her thin, white fingers. "But you're a more loving and generous woman, are you not?"

Only the whore's obvious delight in giving her such hateful news gave Gwyn strength. "Suzanne, why should we continue this charade? Neither of us is fond of the other. I don't enjoy playing the hypocrite, and I'm sure you feel the same."

Suzanne's smile faded, to be replaced by a look of puzzlement. This was obviously not the response she had expected.

"Now, as I have no desire to spend time in your company, I would appreciate your leaving."

"You didn't know, did you? No matter how high and mighty

217

you act with me, the truth is you're still only his whore!" Her eyes gleamed with feral hatred, but Gwyn stood her ground, knowing the woman was too clever to risk a confrontation with Andrew.

"I will not ask you again. Get out of my room."

"He will tire of you!"

"Do not talk of things you know nothing about. For that is the surest sign of an ignorant person."

Suzanne stepped back, almost standing in the hall. Gwyn was about to shut the door in her face when Suzanne lashed out verbally for the last time.

"Ask him, then! *Ask* him if you don't believe me! Ask him to explain who Lady Belinda Pevensy is and why everyone in London is talking about their wedding! Belinda is having a bridal gown fitted, and her father and Andrew's grandfather are gifting them with a new house. . . ."

Gwyn shut the door in the furious woman's face, refusing to give her the satisfaction of slamming it. She locked it, then slowly slid down until she sat on the floor.

Her legs were trembling. Biting her lip against the urge to cry out, she buried her face in her hands.

Married. What would her place in Andrew's life be once he was wed? Would he still consider her his, still come to her rooms and confidently assume their intimacy would continue? That would be adultery in God's eyes.

Married. He'd said nothing of this to her, yet several nights ago he'd opened his soul to her. She'd felt as if they were the only two people in the world, tucked away in their lover's bed.

Even after Andrew sets you up in your house. Lily's words came back to haunt her, everything falling into place with brutal clarity. Once he was married he would not want her here. He would want a more private place. Then they could continue with their affair in secrecy . . .

How could I have ever fallen in love with such a man? As soon as the thought entered her head, she sat very still, her body numb.

Love. How bitterly ironic she should realize her feelings for Andrew at this moment. But it was true. If she hadn't cared about him, the news of his impending marriage would not affect her. She wouldn't feel as if everything in her world were coming to an end.

There was nothing left.

Upon first arriving at The Dark Stallion, she'd believed her life had ended. Angel had convinced her to survive. It had been a raw, brutal time. She'd thought she would never survive, could not be that strong.

And yet she had.

But that pain was the lightest of burdens compared to this. In opening herself to Andrew, she'd exposed her soul to his touch. The night he had told her of his past, she'd never felt closer to another being.

He brought her deepest feelings to the surface—her passion, her hatred, her laughter.

And now her despair.

The jiggling of the doorknob brought her attention back to the present.

"Who is it?" she called, having no desire to face Suzanne again.

"Gwyn? Are you all right?" It was Angel.

She unlocked the door. Angel would know what to do. But when Gwyn opened her door and looked at her friend, the words on her lips died. Angel was exhausted. There were dark shadows beneath her eyes, and her mouth was tight with strain.

"I brought you tea," she said quietly, then walked into the bedroom and set down then silver tray.

Who takes care of Angel? In that instant, Gwyn resolved not to burden her friend with her heartache.

"Sit down. I'll pour you a cup."

Angel gratefully complied, sinking down into the sofa. Her hand shook as she took the filled cup out of Gwyn's hand.

"Ah, this is what I needed. Cook has been running my feet

out from under me."

After she had finished her cup of tea, Angel stood up and dusted off her apron front.

"Did you enjoy church?"

"The minister was a bit gruff. Would you help me out of this dress, Angel?"

"Of course."

Angel's fingers were deft as she unfastened the buttons. As Gwyn stepped out of the pale violet brocade gown, Angel went to work with the fastenings of her corset.

"Lily is intent upon getting her house in order, did she tell you?" Angel said conversationally. "I think the bastard scared her. All she talked about was finding a man like Andrew to take care of her. There you are," she said as the corset fell away. "Get a wrapper on quickly; it's chilly."

Gwyn walked back behind her screen and slipped into one she'd left hanging there. She came around the screen and smiled, her lips stiff.

"Are you feeling poorly?" Angel had a shrewd eye, and she hadn't overlooked the too-bright smile.

"I think I'm just tired."

"I probably won't see you before tomorrow. Have a fine evening with Andrew." And Angel efficiently picked up the tea tray and left.

Gwyn walked over to the window and pulled the curtains tightly closed. Her bedchamber was dusky now, and she went back to the bed and picked up one of the blankets. Still moving slowly, she brought it over to the couch. The fire burned brightly as she wrapped the blanket around her and lay down full length on the sofa in front of it.

She stared into the flames for a long time before she fell asleep.

Chapter Fourteen

Gwyn was still asleep when Andrew entered the room. He'd had a vile day, full of Belinda's bickering and his grandfather's admonishments. Now, all he wanted was the sense of peace and serenity he found with Gwyn.

When he saw her asleep on the couch, he felt an overwhelming tenderness wash over him. Ever since that night when she had astounded him with her luck at cards and he had told her of his past, there had been a difference in the way he felt about her. It frightened him, because long ago he had decided never to care with that fierce intensity. His logic had seemed simple and irrefutable. Allow no one too close to him, and he would never be in danger of caring again.

He had broken all his rules, removed all his barriers. Because of her.

She was a part of him now, he had known it the night they had made love after his confession. He felt closer to her than any other person in his world, and he wanted to hide her away. He did not want anyone to see how vulnerable he felt when he was with her. These feelings were too new to share. He was still confused by them. He wanted to keep her in this private room until he thought of a way to temper the power of what he felt, to control and conceal those feelings.

To reveal any vulnerability to the world was madness.

Andrew shrugged out of his greatcoat, then tugged off his boots. He quietly turned down the covers on the large bed, then walked over to the sofa and gently eased his arms beneath her. As he carried her to the bed, he thought there wasn't a more delightful way to begin an evening with Gwyn than by making love to her.

She felt light kisses on her cheek and turned her head away. The slight rasp of stubble tickled her neck, and she smiled, then stretched. Warmth was stealing over her, light and soft, filling her with a tingling, tight sensation. Her eyelids seemed heavy; they wouldn't open.

She felt warmth skim over her breasts, and her eyelids fluttered. This was stronger than a dream. She felt she was floating on the softest of clouds as it scudded across an open sky. Her eyes opened slowly, and she looked up into Andrew's face.

"Andrew?"

"Shhh," he whispered. She closed her eyes as she felt his lips come down over hers.

It began again, the sensual magic, the velvet fire that filled her body and caused it to become taut with longing. Her hands touched his shoulders, and she was filled with a fierce desire to touch his hair, his face, make sure he was really here. He kissed her with urgency, just a little harder, opening her mouth. He took possession with ease, and the wildfire that streaked through her body and made it grow hot woke her completely.

And she remembered what it was she had wanted to confront him with.

"Andrew," she whispered sharply as his mouth left hers, but before she could form another word, she felt his lips close over one breast. She tensed under him, determined not to respond, then she felt his tongue scrape softly over the taut peak. She felt mindless, as if struggling up from warm, primal depths. Yet she still tried to resist, afraid of giving herself over to him now.

222

She could feel her body responding to what Andrew was doing to her, her breasts seeming to swell at the touch of his lips and tongue. She felt his teeth close gently over a tight bud, stroking it. Without volition, she moaned and pressed herself against him. She felt the last of her resistance fall away as her body flamed, warm and open and responsive to anything he might want to do to her.

She wound her arms around his neck, urging him on. Her hips lifted, moving against him in a purely sensual way. She could feel his need, hot and smooth, burning against her thigh. There was leashed masculine power in every muscle of his body; she could feel it burning into her and knew nothing could stop him from possessing her completely.

She felt his lips move down her stomach, and her thighs parted in answer. He was kissing her hip, moving to her inner thigh. She closed her eyes as he bit the soft skin gently, shuddered as she felt the soft scrape of his chin as he moved further up. She couldn't think of anything but what she was feeling as he began to open her intimately with his tongue. He had her erotically enslaved. She tightened her body in one last attempt to deny him, but felt his lips move unerringly to the heart of her passion, kissing her softly.

"No." The word came out a ragged moan, and she tried to turn away. His long, hard fingers grasped her bottom and he held her; she was powerless against his sensual assault. She was burning there, burning with a need for him to continue his caresses, and it frightened her that such passion could build between them so quickly.

"Andrew—" She moaned his name in warning, but he simply grasped her more tightly, his caresses deeper, more driving. There was a ruthless quality to his lovemaking, a total possession. Higher and higher, hotter and hotter, he knew unerringly where to touch her, how hard, how much. Her thoughts receded, replaced by white-hot fire.

She went suddenly wild, her control snapping, and she grasped his hair. She reached for his shoulders, telling him more eloquently than words ever could that she was nearing that precipice without him.

But he kept loving her that way until she writhed, lifted her slender hips, could resist his sensuality no longer. Great panting, sobbing breaths were forced out of her body. The velvet fire between her thighs was building as if he were stoking it with lips and tongue. There was an agonizing moment when everything peaked, then she went rigid with ecstasy and a cry escaped her lips. Waves of hot pleasure washed powerfully out from where he was kissing her, and she knew no matter what happened she was his forever, bound to him inexorably. She belonged to him now, heart, body and soul.

It could have been minutes or hours later. She was still floating softly, her body aching from the power of her response. Andrew lay between her thighs, his dark head resting intimately on her stomach. When she lifted her head and looked at him, he smiled and kissed her stomach.

An overwhelming wave of tenderness washed through her. She answered his smile, then her hand drifted downward and stroked his hair gently. She closed her eyes and lowered her head to the pillow. Her body was filled with a languid warmth; he had kindled her desire merely by looking at her.

She felt his fingers against her inner thigh, then he was stroking her there, slowly, so slowly. Her thighs trembled. She sighed and stretched her arms above her head, all thoughts and cares driven from her mind, the only reality the man lying between her legs.

The stroking continued, moving slowly upward until she felt him touching her where he had kissed her before. He opened her gently, sliding first one finger in, then two.

"Please," she whispered softly.

"Please what?" she heard him answer, and she knew he wanted to hear her say it; the words would excite him further.

It aroused her to know she had such power over him that mere words could be so erotic.

"I want you inside me." Passion flared within her as she watched his eyes darken, his face tighten with anticipation. With a strong, swift movement he was suddenly above her, and she felt him lift her, his large hands beneath her bottom as he drove into her, sheathing his full length as he pulled her up to receive him. All she could feel was centered where they were intimately joined; she was filled with him completely. He was still for a moment, letting her adjust to his size and strength, then he slid out almost the full length until just the tip of his hardness teased her.

"Andrew," she moaned, and as her voice faded in the quiet bedchamber, he pushed his hips forward and sheathed himself again. It was slow, erotic lovemaking as he drew back, all taut control, then pushed forward. He lifted her, forced her tightly against his arousal, then pulled back and thrust into her again, his movements almost savage. The wildness in his lovemaking demanded a response from her, and Gwyn answered his erotic demands. Her body was all shimmering heat and feminine fire as she pushed upward, meeting each of his thrusts with her own. She didn't want him to be gentle now; she wanted him to push them both over the edge into blazing fulfillment, and she reached up with her arms and locked them around his neck. As he thrust forward again, her fingers tightened in his hair, then moved frantically again, gripping his powerful shoulders tightly. She thrust against him, demanding more, demanding everything he could give her.

Her body blazed hotly, flames licking her relentlessly, shimmering through her, so heated she feared she would be consumed by them. He began thrusting faster, driving himself into her, and she arched her hips, inviting him deeper.

He kissed her, his dominance and strength making her face still under his, then nipped at her swollen lips softly with his teeth, his rhythm relentless as he buried his hard arousal in her softness. She was crying out against his mouth now, begging him to set her free, release her from her fiery cage, when she felt the blood flush race up her breasts and into her face. She was all shimmering heat and pulsating feminine power as she raked her nails across his back, pulling him deeper and deeper. A corner of her mind heard him sharply cry her name, then she felt his release. His body trembled violently against hers, his fingers crushed her buttocks. He buried his face in her shoulder and she turned her cheek against the softness of his hair.

After a long, shuddering moment, he was still. She loved the crush of him against her, his hard male body absorbing the trembling within hers. There was a part of her that loved knowing she couldn't possibly move him. She lay very still, soft beneath him now. She could smell the rose perfume she used mingled with his masculine scent, and that blended with the smell of sensuality. It all mingled, teasing her with a suddenly sensitive scent that kept pleasure trembling through her in soft, gentle waves.

"Are you hungry?" he asked later.

She stretched, and he leaned over and kissed the corner of her mouth. It was a light, teasing kiss, the kiss of a lover well satisfied and proud of his prowess.

"That depends on what we have," she replied, then sat up in bed, letting the covers fall away from her. Angel had brought them supper, and studying the silver tray, Gwyn realized she was ravenous.

After they ate, they dressed and played cards. Gwyn was glad she had hidden the marked deck and replaced it with another, and now she and Andrew were more evenly matched. He taught her ombre, and he played two of the hands while she kept one. She laughed at the sight of him trying to juggle two different sets of cards, and he seemed pleased with her good spirits. He also explained a little of whist and primero.

"Now, if you are ever at a party where they need another

card player, you will be sufficiently prepared."

She was gathering the cards together in preparation for another game when Andrew said, "When are we going to gamble again so I might satisfy my curiosity about you?"

"You would have to have something that I want," she answered quickly. "Something to bet against my past."

"Is there anything you want to know?"

The words tumbled out of her mouth before she thought to restrain them. "I should like to know about Lady Belinda Pevensy."

She could have bitten her tongue off at the black look he gave her. Then, without further comment, he pushed his chair away from the table and stood up. She stayed calm as he looked down at her. Shuffling the cards into a neat stack, she set them down on the table and put her hands in her lap.

"Where did you hear about Belinda?" he asked, and she knew by his quiet tone that he was angry with her.

"One of the whores told me."

"Suzanne?"

She saw no reason to lie. "Yes."

He swore softly, then walked over and sat down on the couch.

As she couldn't possibly make him any angrier, Gwyn decided to confront him. "Are you going to marry her, Andrew?"

"Yes."

His answer stunned her. Because of the emotional and physical intimacies they had just shared she had anticipated his saying no.

"I see." She tried to keep the pain out of her voice, deliberately attempting a cool and detached tone.

"No, I don't think you do."

Gwyn stood up and walked over to the fire so she was closer to him, but not close enough for him to touch her. She wanted answers to the questions she had held in her heart from the first moment he had carried her up the stairs so many weeks

227

ago. She had remained silent for too long.

"Andrew, I wish to ask you a question. The answer is very important to me."

He was staring at her, and her heart sank as she noticed the remote expression on his face. How different from the man who had looked at her with such passion in his eyes.

"Ask me."

She took a deep breath. "Tell me of my future.'

"Your future is with me."

"Until after the holidays when you marry?"

"That little bitch told you the date?"

She sighed, feeling utterly weary. "I cannot . . . I cannot come to you once you are married. That would be adultery."

"If I told you the marriage was one of convenience, nothing more? What would you say to that?"

It shocked her that he could think so coldly and calculatingly about something as sacred as marriage. "Why are you marrying her if you do not care for her?"

"Surely you can't be that innocent, Gwyn. Marriages are arranged for mutual benefit all the time."

"I am aware of the practice. But I have heard of some love matches that worked." She forced the next words out. "My father always hoped I would marry for love. Someday I will find a man who will love me enough to give me his heart—and his name. And I will gladly bear his children and make him a comfortable home."

She could feel his anger, just below the surface. "With your past? Do you think any man is going to want you now?"

His words were deliberately cruel, as only a lover's could be. Gwyn sensed he felt backed into a corner, but she had to continue. It was time to bring everything out into the open. With as much dignity as she could summon, she answered him.

"I believe love makes all things possible. I can only pray that someday a man will see beyond the circumstances of my life and want me for *me*." She raised her chin defiantly, daring him to contradict her, refusing to lower her eyes and back down.

"You make too much of this. It is merely a ceremony to me. It means nothing."

"It means something to me that you should take marriage vows so lightly." She pushed the next words through a tight throat. "And what are your plans for me, m'lord? Suzanne has let me know her opinion. Soon you will grow tired of me and cast your eyes elsewhere. I can only hope you will be kind enough to do so while I am still young enough to attain another man's protection."

"If you even look at another man, I'll make you wish you hadn't."

"You wish to have a wife and keep me as well? Could you please tell me what I have to look forward to? Are you asking me to be your mistress?"

He stood up angrily and paced to the far side of the room. "I don't understand you, Gwyn. I have been looking for a house for you. I was going to move you before the holidays." He jammed his hands into the pockets of his silk robe in frustration. "Any other woman would be happy with this arrangement."

"You know me not at all, then, for I am *not* any other woman!"

"You will lack for nothing. . . ."

"I will not be *kept* like a bird in a cage for you to take out when you fancy some entertainment! I want a husband and a home and children. . . ."

"I can give you a child."

She stared at him, incredulous. When she spoke, her voice was raw with pain. "I cannot believe you think this arrangement will be enough for me."

He raked his fingers through his thick black hair in frustration. "You make things difficult when they don't have to be, Gwyn."

His utter blindness to what she was feeling proved to be the final spark that ignited her temper. "Oh, Andrew, you told me what it was like when you were a child, being treated as if you

229

had no feelings, whipped and abused. You were handled as an *object*, as someone who had no feelings. Andrew, I *know* you are fond of me. Why do you find it so very hard to afford me the respect you were denied as a child?"

"Gwyn, you go too far. . . ."

"I don't want to be a small part of a man's life, to be hidden away in a house! I want to work hard beside him, be his partner and helpmate. I think you know this is wrong, else why would you hide me as if you were ashamed of me? Either let me go and find a man who will love me, or—" She stopped, now knowing the other was impossible.

"Or what?" His tone was cold, his jaw tense.

She closed her stinging eyes and turned her back to the sight of him. "Andrew, let me go. I'm begging you. I will never interfere in your life or tell anyone of the time spent here with you. You can have back everything you gave me. I don't want any of your money. Those things you told me about your past will go with me to my grave. Please don't do this to me."

"Madam, you make me out to be the villain in this piece. . . ."

"And quite justifiably so!"

"Might I give you a bit of advice? If you don't want to vex a man, you should be less stubborn and trust he is looking out for your best interests."

It was too much. She whirled on him, her voice rising. *"My best interests! Your best interests!* You foolishly think we will come to some arrangement this night, and that cannot be when what you are proposing goes against all I believe!"

"Madam, with the greatest respect—"

"Respect! You don't know the meaning of the word! Am I supposed to be *honored* you've chosen me for your mistress? I'd rather stay here and scrub floors! What did you think, Andrew, that I was going to fall into your arms and *thank* you?"

"You will come to understand and prefer this arrangement—"

"I think not. I think you prefer it for me."

"Gwyn, *listen* to me!" He was at her side in an instant, holding both her arms in his strong hands so she could not move away from him.

"There is not one married man I know of in London who does not have a mistress."

"That does not make it right for me."

"Madam, I am asking you to hold that tongue of yours." Something in his tone warned her to do as he said.

"A man's mistress is the woman he treasures. Do you want to marry some man to have him come to your bed one night a week and push up your nightgown while you lie back and submit to him?" He was studying her face intently now, and his voice softened. "I know your nature, Gwyn, and it is a passionate one. You were born to grace my bed. How is what I am asking you to do any different than what you are doing now? Why are you upset when I am giving you your own house and anything else you could want? I will spent far more time with you than I ever will with Belinda. We could have children. I would provide for them, make sure they were brought up properly." He gathered her into his arms and she stiffened, trying to keep some distance between them.

"Gwyn, there is not one woman here at The Dark Stallion who does not wish to leave. I am offering you that chance. We'll spend time together, and I promise you I'll cherish you as long as I live. Do you understand me now?"

He was treating her indulgently, as if she were a spoilt child crying for a peppermint.

"No." Her voice broke as she continued to speak. "What you've described is exactly what I would wish my marriage to be. But if you cannot commit to me in the eyes of God, how can you call anything we have together by any name but what it is? If you love this woman, then marry her, but *leave me alone!*"

His hold on her tightened. "I have been too lenient with you, bending to your every whim. This is one time you are not going to have your way, my beauty."

"Don't make me do this, Andrew."

"You will understand with time. And you will look back and see it was the best solution."

She took a deep breath. "You will understand with time that this situation you propose is impossible."

His eyes darkened. "Come to bed, Gwyn. Perhaps I should work harder on getting you with child. You have spirit and would give me a strong son."

She looked up at him, then deliberately jerked her arms out of his grip. "I'd give you a daughter with a tongue as sharp as mine, and when some ignorant man proposes she be *his* mistress, I'll laugh in your face! I will *never* have your child, Andrew! Is this what you want, to have our child know its mother is a rich man's whore?"

"Gwyn, come to bed. I'm tired of this discussion and wish it to end."

"As you wish, Andrew. It's over." She went to the bed and pulled off one of the blankets.

"What are you doing?" He was clearly not amused.

"I feel a little faint," she said defiantly as she threw the blanket on the sofa. "I will sleep here."

"You will sleep with me." His voice was taut with repressed fury.

"*I will not.* You can drag me into your bed, but unless you tie me down I will not remain there."

"Gwyneth, you will bend to my will in the end."

She didn't reply, simply waiting until he blew out the last candle before she let her tears finally fall.

He took her to his bed the next morning, and when she was cold and unresponsive to his kisses and caresses, he swore softly, dressed, then left her. Gwyn huddled back beneath the bedcovers and closed her eyes, exhausted. She had not slept well on the couch, and it had required every bit of her strength to keep him at bay. She knew he would return tonight, and she didn't know what to do.

It was still early in the morning. Angel would not be up with breakfast for another hour. Wearily, feeling utterly defeated, Gwyn closed her eyes and determined to lose herself in sleep.

"Why did you summon me here in the middle of the night, Suzanne?" Edward Sleaforth was furious. He had returned home from a private party at the Duke's and found a message from Suzanne requesting his presence at The Dark Stallion. Now the stupid chit was sprawled out on her bed. Her skin had a certain pallor, and she seemed thinner than he had last seen her.

"First I want what we agreed on."

"Take it." He tossed the small packet on the mass of tangled bedcovers and disgustedly watched as she scrambled over the bed, her thin fingers eagerly grasping and unwrapping the package.

"Thank you, Edward. This will do very nicely. . . ."

"I didn't get out of my bloody bed for you to act like the queen of—"

"You weren't in *your* bed at all, were you Edward?" She looked at him with an amused expression that made him want to squirm. He suspected she was aware of exactly what he was forced to do at the Duke's private entertainments. She seemed to see inside him, and he wondered if she suspected he was beginning to enjoy parts of it.

"You nasty little slut! I won't have you playing games with me. . . ."

She was unconcernedly reaching for the long, thin pipe, and it infuriated him.

"I told your little cousin," Suzanne said slowly as she filled the bowl of the pipe, "that Andrew is engaged to Lady Pevensy and they are to wed after Christmas."

He wasn't following her but didn't want to reveal that fact.

"Go on." He feigned interest and wondered if he would have to go back to the Duke's tonight. It was cold, rain was coming

233

down in torrents outside, and he wanted nothing more than to go home to a hot cup of tea and his own bed.

"She was upset."

Damnation! This was going to last the entire evening. Suzanne loved a captive audience.

She smiled and lay back on the bed. "I crept to her door this evening and heard quite a row."

"Andrew and Gwyn?" This would certainly please the Duke. He would go to his house directly afterward.

"She was shouting at him loud enough to take the roof off the house." Briefly, she told him the details of the argument, and by the time she was finished, Edward was ecstatic.

"You've done very well, Suzanne. Now, what can I do for you?" His black mood was forgotten now that he knew his cousin was having a difficult time.

"I should like her to take my place in one of the Duke's carriages tomorrow," she said.

Edward could feel his eyes almost bug out of his head. "And how do you propose to accomplish this?" For a moment he thought Suzanne had gone completely out of her head.

"My friend Polly has a plan." And she told him, step by step, what she and Polly intended to do.

"Excellent!" Edward rubbed his hands together. The Duke would be pleased by his cleverness when he reported back to him and informed him of *his* plan. Not this Polly's. "I will be out at the monastery for several days joining in the holiday festivities, but the moment I arrive back in London, I will visit you and bring you anything you desire."

"I am content with this." She waved her pipe lazily. "But when it is gone, I will expect more."

"As you wish. Now, are you sure you can persuade her into the carriage?"

Suzanne laughed, and the sound made Edward uneasy.

"She'll be in it. Tell the Duke to expect her tomorrow night."

* * *

When Angel came into the bedchamber, Gwyn was up, washed, and dressed.

"Would you have a cup of tea with me, Angel?"

"I would with pleasure."

Once the tea was poured, Gwyn decided she had to come to the point.

"Andrew has asked me to be his mistress."

Angel's expression was wary, and Gwyn knew her friend expected no ordinary reaction from her.

"And what did you say?"

"I refused."

Angel sighed and set down her cup. "Gwyn—"

"I will not be swayed on this matter."

"Gwyn, I don't believe you understand that you cannot afford to be virtuous any longer. Be thankful you only have to sleep with one man. And can you honestly tell me you find Andrew not to your liking?"

Gwyn set down her cup and reached over to grasp Angel's hands. "I am asking you a single favor, Angel. Can you get me a horse within the hour?"

Angel jerked her hands free. "Are you mad? And what would you do, escape into London?"

"I am going home."

"Gwyn, be reasonable! You'd probably be unseated the first time the animal spooked. Then you'd be lost in the city. . . ."

"I can ride. My father taught me. Lily told me we are on the outskirts of the city. I already know what direction to head in. If I follow the sun I can be home within two days."

"And what would you do at night? A woman alone! You wouldn't be safe."

Gwyn kept her voice calm. "I borrowed money from Lily this morning. I will find an inn for the one night, and by the next day I'll be home. Don't you see, Angel, it's my only chance! Andrew would never find me. Please, Angel."

The struggle within Angel was plain. She was looking down at her skirt. Gwyn crushed the black silk of her wrapper between her fingers as she waited for her answer.

Finally, Angel lifted her head. "Andrew will be furious."

"Andrew will find another woman who will strike his fancy within a fortnight."

"Do you really believe that?"

"Yes," Gwyn said, not wanting to admit how the thought hurt her.

"If you are caught, you cannot tell anyone Lily and I helped you. We would both be put out on the street. Andrew will be furious with Janet, and if she knew, I wouldn't want to think about what would happen to us."

"I will never betray you, Angel."

The French maid stood and began to gather the tea cups. "I'll do what I can. But I'm asking a good friend of mine to go with you. You need a man's protection. Put on one of your warmest dresses and the cloak with the plain collar. You don't want anyone on the road thinking you have money. Meet me in the garden within the hour. And Gwyn?"

"Yes?"

"Can Dick tell me where you are once he sees you safely home? One day Lily and I could come visit. Maybe Madeleine, too."

Gwyn enfolded her friend in a fierce hug. "I will send you money as soon as I am able to earn some," she whispered, her throat suddenly tight at the thought of not seeing this woman who had become her dearest friend. "I won't forget you, Angel, and I'll try to come for you as soon as I can."

"I have never doubted that. Now eat those eggs and rolls, and wrap some sausages for later when you get hungry. And remember, within the hour at the far corner of the garden!"

As soon as Angel left, Gwyn began to dress. She picked out one of her plainest dresses, sturdy shoes, warm stockings, and petticoats. The simplest of her cloaks joined the pile, along with a warm scarf and gloves.

She thought of Andrew's face when he came to the room and found her gone. Would he be sorry she had left? Or would he simply take up with Suzanne again and be glad she was no longer a thorn in his side, prodding him with her sharp tongue? She pushed the deep, painful emotions down. What was the good of loving Andrew when there was no chance of his loving her back? Life would be like a small, paddleless boat, swirling with the current and totally out of control. Gwyn knew she could never endure that kind of insecurity.

She thought again of their argument, as she had all through her long night on the sofa. He didn't like it when she answered him back. But Gwyn knew she could never be docile, meek, and smiling when asked to do something against her strongest beliefs.

It would be good to finally go home.

Before the hour was up, she was seated on one of the stone benches in the far corner of the garden. Thatch let her go willingly enough, as she usually helped Cook several mornings a week. The rain last night had washed everything fresh and clean, and weak winter sunshine flitted down between soft grey clouds. She could only hope the roads weren't quagmires.

When Angel approached her, she stood. Her friend's face looked tense, and Gwyn's heart began to thud slowly, heavily.

"Dick can't come until the end of the week," Angel said. "But then he can bring two of his fastest horses and accompany you."

"But if Andrew has moved me by then—"

"Gwyn, you cannot go alone!"

"But I can't see Andrew tonight!" The thought of being naked and helpless in his strong embrace was unbearable now. "Is there somewhere I can hide until Dick arrives?"

Angel shook her head. "Andrew would tear London apart looking for you." She lowered her voice. "You cannot be caught, Gwyn. I know Andrew is a fair man, but he will beat you if you defy him this openly."

"I do not intend to be caught."

Angel touched her arm in reassurance. "Let me try another

friend. Perhaps we can have you on your way before Andrew arrives tonight. Stay here, and I'll be right back."

And as Angel hurried toward the side door, Gwyn sat down on the cold stone bench and rearranged her dark blue wool skirt. But the fine trembling that passed through her body had nothing to do with the cold.

"She's not in her room, and the next carriage leaves in minutes!" Polly said as she burst into Suzanne's room.

"Damnation, Polly, can't you see my head is ready to come right off?" Suzanne opened her eyes, still half asleep.

"Get out of bed, you lazy thing! You've got to help me find her!"

Reluctantly, Suzanne obeyed. She pulled one of the dingy blankets around her, then padded out into the hallway after Polly, barefoot.

"I thought you told me she spent all her time in that bloody room!"

"She does." Suzanne yawned. "When she's not helping Cook. Sometimes she sits in the garden." She followed Polly as she raced down the hall toward a window overlooking the small plot.

"There she is, Polly, right on the bench. Now, do you think you can persuade her into the carriage?"

"If I have to hit her over the head and throw her in, that little troublemaker will be out of here by nightfall."

"Hello. Are you waiting for the carriage?"

Gwyn glanced up and encountered a pleasant-faced woman. Her ginger-colored hair was pulled back in a neat bun, and a grey wool shawl covered her shoulders. Attired in a dark green, simply cut dress, she was the sort of woman who would always look like a child because of the roundness of her face.

"No. I am simply enjoying the sunshine." She couldn't

reveal she was waiting for Angel.

"You don't want to go on the Christmas pleasure ride then?" There was a note of disappointment in her voice.

"What ride is this?" Gwyn was intrigued. Angel had told her nothing of a pleasure ride. If a carriage was already hired to journey into the country, why couldn't she be on it?

"Some of the girls come here from the country, so on a splendid day like this we pool our pennies and hire a coach and four. Then we go out for a day in the country, just south of here. It does the spirit good to commune with nature, if you know what I mean, Miss. I don't believe we've met. . . ."

"Gwyneth."

"And I'm Phoebe. Now, would you like to be a part of our little picnic?"

Gwyn glanced toward the large stone house. There was no sign of Angel. This might be her last chance to leave today. She wished for one instant she could trust this woman to give Angel a note, but that would be dangerous. Yet she knew her friend would worry terribly.

I will write to her as soon as I can, she thought, then turned to Phoebe.

"Oh, I *do* hope you will join us, Gwyneth."

"How much should I contribute?"

"I think five shillings should do the trick. You can give them to me, and I'll escort you to the carriage."

The coach waited a short distance down the alley, out of sight of The Dark Stallion. Phoebe walked briskly, and Gwyn had to trot to keep up with her. It was an elegant coach, and Gwyn noticed almost every seat was filled.

"You're a lucky one, Gwyneth. You don't have to wait for the next coach."

"Thank you, Phoebe. You have been most kind, and I shall not forget you for it."

Once securely inside, Gwyn watched as Phoebe gave the

239

driver the signal to leave. She heard the sound of a whip cracking, a horse snorting. The carriage jolted and began to move, swaying back and forth. The horse's hooves clopped as they picked up speed.

The women inside were a varied lot. Most of them were attired in older, worn clothing. One woman, a blowsy blonde with a stained pink satin dress, was snoring, her mouth open and head bobbing as the carriage bumped along the cobblestone street.

Gwyn discreetly glanced out the window, then fastened the leather flap. There was no use tempting fate and having anyone see her who might report back to Andrew. She couldn't entirely understand her emotions. She missed him already. But she was also glad she had left before they'd hurt each other further.

She settled back in her seat, bracing herself against the rocking and swaying of the carriage. This was the beginning of her new life. She would look forward, not backward, as this carriage took her to her future.

Chapter Fifteen

"Gwyn?" Angel called softly as she came back out into the garden. "Gwyn, are you there?" Had the cold, crisp winter air forced her back to her room? She'd never be able to endure the journey if just sitting outside chilled her.

"Gwy—" She stopped as she reached the stone bench. Gwyn's scarf, a soft pile of knitted wool, was next to one of the bench legs.

"Might I be of help to you, Angelique?"

She glanced up into Polly's eyes. The older woman never failed to call her by her French name, reminding her she had not forgotten the days when "Angelique" had been the star attraction on the street.

They were days Angel wanted to forget. "I was looking for Gwyneth Leighton. She was sitting here not ten minutes ago." She knew she was taking a risk. If Gwyn had done anything to arouse Polly's suspicions, she was damned as well.

"She's not here now," Polly said cheerfully. "Why, look at this. The poor lamb dropped her scarf. And on such a bitterly cold day. Why don't you take it back up to her?"

"Did you see her go inside?" Angel asked sharply. She silently cursed herself for seeming too concerned. Polly was smart. Cold and calculating, the woman had survived at The Dark Stallion by using her wits.

"Pray tell, where else would she go?"

She knows. Angel felt fear curl its cold fingers around the pit of her stomach, but she forced a smile. "She must have been cold without her scarf." Averting her face, she knelt down and picked up the scarf, then slowly stood.

"Good day, Polly."

"And you, Angelique."

Something is not right. Angel walked slowly back to the kitchen, aware of Polly's eyes on her every step of the way.

Gwyn was jarred awake when the wheel of the carriage hit a deep rut in the road. Her hair, so carefully pulled away from her face this morning, was coming loose, and tendrils framed her face. It was stuffy inside the carriage, but no one wanted to open the leather flaps and let the cold winter air inside.

She felt groggy and took a deep breath to rid herself of the sleepy feeling. As she slowly began to notice her companions, she was aware of their intense scrutiny.

"Ain't you Lord Scarborough's little girl?" one woman asked. She had bright red hair, massed in tight ringlets, and two of her front teeth were missing.

Gwyn didn't know whether to answer or not. When this woman returned to The Dark Stallion after their outing, would she tell anyone she had seen her in the carriage? Hopefully by then it would be too late.

"Course she is! I saw you at the auction. Oooh, the way Lord Scarborough looked at you that evening, you prob'ly couldn't sit down for a week!" This came from the blonde with the stained pink satin dress. "Why's a pretty little thing like you in this carriage with the likes of us?"

Gwyn was confused for an instant, thinking the woman was referring to the disparity in their ages. "I thought it would be a rather fun outing," she replied. She wanted them to believe she was going on the picnic, rather than leaving to find another carriage that would take her home.

"A fun outing!" This from a woman with ruddy hair. Her skin was slightly puffy and all the rouge in the world couldn't conceal the poor color in her face. She stared at Gwyn with an incredulous expression.

"Yes. I thought a day in the country would do me good." Gwyn stared back, daring the woman to challenge her.

"We're not going to a blooming garden party!" the woman exploded. "Miss Fancy-britches here is going to 'partake of a little country air.'" She mimicked Gwyn's soft tones. "Bloody hell, these young ones don't know when they have it good! If I was younger and managed to entice the Earl of Scarborough into *my* bed, I'd have the good sense to keep him there!"

Gwyn turned her head and stared at the woman. "What I do is none of your 'bloody' business!"

"Why *are* you with us?" asked red ringlets. "By the way, I'm Jane, the blonde is Molly, and the rude one is me friend Beverly. The other two, they had hard nights; we'll just let them sleep."

"Gwyneth," Gwyn said grudgingly. She didn't like the way Beverly was studying her.

"Well?" Jane asked.

"Well what?"

"Why are you here?"

Gwyn was rapidly becoming frustrated with this entire discussion. A combination of her sleepless night, the fight she'd had with Andrew, and the endless tears she'd cried on the sofa were rapidly catching up with her.

"I wasn't aware I needed permission to go on a Christmas picnic."

"Christmas picnic!" Beverly and blond Molly broke into laughter, and Gwyn glared at them.

"I paid my five shillings like everyone else." She took a deep breath, then said heatedly, "I have just as much right to be in this carriage as you do, so stop making fun of me!" This last part she directed at Beverly, who suddenly stopped laughing.

"Five shillings?" Beverly asked. All humor had been wiped

from her face. "Who collected your money?"

"Phoebe."

"There's no Phoebe works at The Dark Stallion," Jane said, puzzled.

"No, but there's a Polly, and whenever something starts to smell like fish Cook's kept out too long, you can bet she's behind it," Beverly said. "Did she have ginger-colored hair and a full-moon face?"

Gwyn nodded her head.

"The nasty slut!" Beverly leaned back in her seat. "She tricked her. And Suzanne's in on this as well, mark my words! Once you're disposed of, she can go back to warming Lord Scarborough's bed!"

"No," Gwyn said suddenly. "I wanted to come."

Now Beverly was staring at her as if she had sprouted horns. "Do you have any idea where this carriage is going?"

"To the country. Southwest of London."

"This carriage is going to a Christmas party all right, but it's no picnic. Do you know of the Duke of Cuckfield?"

For a moment Gwyn's mind refused to work, then she remembered the auction. Two men bidding. And one of them, with cold grey eyes and a raspy voice. A very clear image of his face appeared in her mind, and she shuddered.

Beverly grasped her hand. "This carriage is going to the Duke of Cuckfield's private . . . celebration. He invites many men and women out to his property, and then . . ." Beverly dropped Gwyn's hand and leaned back in her seat. "No woman should have to go to one of the Duke's private parties until she knows what it's about."

"What are you trying to tell me?" Gwyn wanted to scream the words, but they came out small and frightened.

"It's a . . . pr—private club," Molly stuttered. "Men and women and—"

"It's an orgy, Gwyn," Beverly said quietly.

* * *

244

"She's on the carriage!" Polly began to laugh, her ample shoulder shaking as she sat down on Suzanne's bed.

Suzanne, filling her opium pipe again, grinned slowly. "Did you have any trouble getting her on the coach?"

"The stupid little sod *paid* me!" she wheezed. "Five shillings!" She took the money out of her pocket and threw it on the bed.

Suzanne lit her pipe with a candle near the bed. She inhaled deeply, and the smoky, sickly sweet odor filled her small room. "Thank you, Polly. Your plan was . . . masterful."

"You're sure Edward can get me everything I want?" Polly's voice was sharp.

"Anything. I can make him do anything. He's the weakest man I've ever met." The opium was relaxing her; she was drifting into her favorite dream: Andrew, setting her up in her own house, where they would spend quiet evenings together. She would have anything he wanted. Wardrobes full of gowns. Cunning shoes to match each outfit. Chemises and petticoats of silk and spun lace.

And a warm cloak with white fur trim around the hood.

She wasn't even aware when Polly left.

The Duke of Cuckfield had been restless for several nights. Waiting. Anticipating. He would have her soon, this very night.

He had been amazed dull little Sleaforth had the intelligence to come up with a plan. He had rewarded Edward, for the whore Suzanne had done a good job. But he didn't want to think of Edward now; his mind had no room for anyone but Gwyn. She was his glorious, golden-haired obsession. Once Andrew knew he had possessed Gwyneth, the man would never want her again.

His carriage slowed, and the Duke unfastened the leather flap and peered outside. The sight of the old monastery he had bought more than ten years ago never failed to amuse him.

That a place once housing the holiest of men now bore silent witness to most unholy acts satisfied him immensely. He had started his journey as soon as the sun had come up, unable to sleep because his excitement was so acute.

Tonight. Nothing will stop me tonight. He closed his eyes and lost himself in dreaming of her.

"She's gone."

Angel was truly afraid now. She had looked for Gwyn everywhere in the brothel, searching first the kitchen, then Gwyn's room, then racing down the hall to the rooms Lily and Madeleine shared.

"Polly knows. The way she looked at me, spoke to me. She *knows*. But I can't ask her. I feel"—quick tears sprang to her eyes—"something terrible is about to happen. And I don't know how to stop it."

"Polly knows? You're sure?" This from Madeleine. Her huge blue eyes dominated her face, and Angel knew she was frightened. But Madeleine was also angry.

"I know it. I felt it in the garden."

"Let me try," Madeleine said quietly, "to see if she will tell me anything."

Polly was lying in bed eating chocolates. She laughed softly as she remembered the innocent look on Gwyneth's face. How could one girl be so impossibly stupid? What could Andrew see in her? It was all so amusing, and she was proud of her hand in it.

When her door flew open, she sat up with a start. Madeleine entered the room, Thatch behind her. The giant closed the door and crossed his muscled arms in front of his chest. He stood silently. Waiting.

Polly glanced first at Thatch, then Madeleine. She knew Madeleine had come to find out about Gwyn. But she could bluff with the best of them. It was all too splendid, Andrew's virgin whore off to spend the holiday with the most debauched man in London.

"Where's Gwyn?" Madeleine asked.

"Am I her watchdog, Madeleine? Pray tell, why should I know where the child is?"

"I think it's time you stopped lying and told me what happened in the garden."

Now Polly could feel herself starting to sweat. Madeleine had a reputation for knowing everything that went on at The Dark Stallion. She had never tangled with the whore before, but that didn't mean she didn't fear her.

"I don't know what you're talking about."

"Polly." Madeleine walked silently to the side of her bed. Something about her, a quiet self-assurance, told Polly she would not be thwarted. "You're not a very wise woman."

Now she felt her face flush bright red. How dare Madeleine come into her room and make these pronouncements!

"I would like you to leave."

"Where's Gwyn?"

"I don't know where the bloody little bitch is now! Get out!"

But Madeleine simply smiled, and Polly suddenly realized she had told her everything.

"This will be the second woman you've destroyed."

Fear began to softly gnaw its way into her stomach. "What are you talking about?"

"Clare Reynolds." The brilliant blue eyes mocked her. "Or should I say, *Lady* Clare?"

She could feel her wrapper sticking damply between her breasts. How in the name of God had Madeleine found out about that?

"I wasn't the one who killed her," she blurted out.

"But you were there. You and several others. And you did nothing to help her." Madeleine studied her nails. "Her son is still looking for clues as to who murdered his mother. I think he would be quite interested in hearing your part in the sordid

247

little mess. Don't you?" Her smile was genuinely bright now, and Polly hated her.

"*Where's Gwyn?*"

Polly glanced nervously at Thatch. "I'd like to cut out *your* tongue, Madeleine."

"I'm sure Garrett Reynolds will be quite—"

"It doesn't matter now. It's too late. She's at the monastery. At the Duke's." She wanted her next words to cut deeply. "She's with your old lover, Madeleine."

The blue eyes flickered. "You put her on the carriage?"

"She thought it was a picnic. She paid me five shillings for the privilege!" She picked up the coins from her bed and tossed them at Madeleine's feet.

The woman didn't move. "You'll be gone when I return. And you'd best run fast, Polly, because I intend to see Garrett tonight and tell him everything. You'll be lucky if he leaves you alive."

"Bitch!" Polly sprang up from the bed, but before she reached Madeleine, she felt Thatch's strong arms come around her waist in a crushing grip. She flailed out at Madeleine, her fingers clawing wildly, but the woman was kneeling, gathering the bright coins.

"Be gone when I return, Judas," she said as she tossed the coins on her bed.

Andrew was staring into a glass of West Indian Rum when he realized the usual buzz at the club had stopped. He glanced up and saw two women running ahead of the man who regularly stood watch at the door. And they were headed straight for his table.

"It's the Frenchie!" Jack exclaimed. He slid his chair back and stood.

"No whores allowed here!" the man chasing them bellowed. "Come on, you girls know the rules!"

Madeleine spoke quickly, as soon as she reached Andrew's

table. "It's Gwyn, m'lord. She's in trouble; there's not much time. . . ."

All amusement faded, replaced with the quickening beat of his heart. "Where is she?"

"At the monastery. For the Duke of Cuckfield's—"

Andrew felt his insides starting to freeze. *Not Gwyn. Not there.* "I know of that place. When did she leave?"

"This morning. She was tricked by one of the whores. It wasn't her fault."

He might already have her. He took the whore's hand briefly and squeezed it. "Thank you."

"Just get her home safely, m'lord."

He was out the door, running behind the club to the adjoining stable, then vaulting onto Mephisto's back and grabbing the reins. Nudging the stallion with his knees, he narrowed his eyes against the sharp, biting wind. The stallion leapt forward with a surge of its powerfully muscled body.

He would bring her back. Or kill the Duke.

"Take your clothes off quickly or they'll do it for you," Beverly whispered.

"Don't call attention to yourself," Jane whispered as she stepped out of her tattered petticoat. "It will go the worse for you if you do."

With numb fingers, Gwyn began to peel her clothing off. As each layer dropped to the cold stone floor, she felt more vulnerable. Soon she felt the chill air of the monastery against her naked skin. She wrapped her arms around her breasts and rubbed the gooseflesh on her arms.

"Circle round her, girls, or the guard will take her to the Duke directly," Beverly muttered.

Gwyn was touched beyond words as the three old whores surrounded her, using their broad bodies as shields.

"Stay perfectly still," Beverly whispered. "Don't do anything to call attention to yourself."

Beverly had already scooped up dirt as they were herded inside and rubbed it through Gwyn's hair. "It's too shiny; that golden color is like a candle flame in a dark room. You can't be noticed," she'd whispered.

And Gwyn, knowing she had no recourse, trusted the woman.

Another man walked in, carrying an armful of garments. He threw them on the floor.

"Go get something for Gwyn, Jane," Beverly instructed.

When Jane returned, she handed Gwyn a loosely cut garment of a coarse, woven material. "Quick, lovey, pull this over your head." She handed the same sort of garments to Beverly and Molly.

Gwyn was so anxious to cover her nakedness that she barely felt the scratchy material scrape over her skin. It was only when she glanced at the other three women that she realized what she was wearing.

Every woman in the large chamber was attired in a nun's habit.

"Listen to me," Beverly whispered. "The Duke is a sick man, and this is his way of laughing at any goodness in the world. The women dress as nuns, the men as monks. There is a courtyard out back, and within minutes we will all converge there. Adjoining the courtyard is a garden and a maze of hedges. Follow me, Gwyn, and keep your head well covered. I'm going to try and guide you to the edge of the maze. You must hide inside."

"What if the Duke sees me?" Gwyn asked. Her heart was beating so furiously she thought it might burst. She had never known fear like this, not even up on the auction block.

"Stay close to me. Jane and Molly and I will try to conceal you." Beverly squeezed her hand. "Pray, and hope God hears you."

His only hope was that he could travel faster on horseback

than she had in her carriage.

Mephisto was his fastest stallion, and once Andrew reached the outskirts of London he gave the animal its head. The horse broke into a furious gallop, his long, powerful legs eating up the miles. Andrew rode him relentlessly.

And as he rode, he cursed himself for not taking Gwyn from The Dark Stallion sooner. If he had refused to listen to her nonsense and simply moved her to a safe, private house, none of this would have happened.

Changes will be made in the way I handle her. She does not know what is good for her. He refused to let the other fear enter his mind and heart. He could not believe the Duke had her, for that would lead to an agony of madness.

The moon was full, and he thanked the fates because it enabled him to see the road ahead in silvery light. He was less than an hour from the monastery now. If Gwyn could only elude the Duke . . .

His mind worked furiously as he devised a plan. He would have to risk everything to save her, but his heart did not shy away from danger. He would not allow her beauty to be destroyed by the Duke's debauchery.

Hold on, Gwyneth. Just a little longer . . .

And as he galloped over the country road, he was surprised to find himself praying.

Gwyn saw the Duke the instant they were herded out into the courtyard. It was bitterly cold, the stone courtyard freezing against their bare feet.

Beverly directed their little group, and she edged them to the farthest corner. The Duke, dressed in the brilliant red robes of an archbishop, jerked the covering off one of the more slender whore-nuns. Gwyn saw the look of frustration on his face as the hair that spilled out beneath his fingers was a bright, coppery color.

At that moment, she realized he was looking for her.

"Keep moving!" Beverly hissed. "Gwyn, when I tell you to run, stay close to the hedges; conceal yourself in the shadows. Head straight for the maze, the entrance farthest left. Go straight, then right, left, right, and left again. Hide yourself within the middle and make not a sound. Wait until daybreak and I will come for you. Go now! He's looking the other way!" Beverly gave her a fierce push.

Gwyn ducked into the shadows, blessing the nun's habit for the concealment it gave her. Looking ahead as she ran, she dared not think what would happen if she were seen.

A sudden noise almost made her stumble, then quick tears filled her eyes as she heard a familiar voice float out into the night air.

"Get your bloody familiar hands off me, you filthy slut! I'm not partial to your type of desire!" It was Beverly.

The woman had created a disturbance, thus all eyes would be diverted from her desperate flight. Gwyn took a ragged breath and forced her legs to move faster.

"You bloody bitch, I wasn't touching you!" Now Jane joined in, her voice indignant as she screeched.

Their mock-fight reached its climax as Gwyn darted into the shrubbery maze. Her heart pounding, she remembered Beverly's quick directions.

Tears rolled down her cheeks as she thought of the two old whores being punished for the fight they had staged. She moved quickly through the silver shadows, all the while cursing herself for ever disliking their company.

Andrew moved cautiously through the throngs of people. He knew he dared not catch the Duke's eye, or he would be considered a prize of another sort. The scratchy material of the monk's habit irritated his neck. He had kept his clothing on underneath, knowing the Duke allowed the men to wear their boots while he delighted in making the women run barefoot.

He hasn't found her yet. His heart had surged with a fierce happiness as he had studied the Duke's countenance from afar. He still had the look of a wild animal on the scent of its prey.

Andrew continued to move through the crowd, glancing quickly at each nun's face. He walked through groups of naked, writhing bodies, and disgust tightened his stomach as he witnessed acts of depravity. He was a man who loved women, and the men here certainly could make no claim to such feelings.

He was on the edge of the courtyard when he felt a hand on his arm. Turning, he saw a heavyset nun.

"Lord Scarborough?" she asked softly.

He debated whether to reveal his identity, knowing the Duke would relish forcing him to participate in debauchery. Yet there was something about her voice . . .

"It's old Beverly, m'lord. I know where the little one is."

His heart began to slam within his chest. "Is she safe?"

"Aye. In the maze. I will take you to her. Grab my arm and pull me away, as if we are off to find a private place."

Beverly had always been a clever one. She had been the first whore he had had at The Dark Stallion and had taught him well about the many sources of a woman's pleasure.

"She's just ahead, m'lord." Quickly, Beverly repeated the same directions she had given Gwyn. "Can you find your way out?"

"Back the way I came," he replied.

"Don't take the chance, m'lord." She told him how to journey deeper into the maze and end up at the far corner. "There is a hole there, if you simply bend back some of the stronger branches toward the bottom of the hedge."

He smiled down at her puffy, lined face. "You know I never forget a favor. You may ask for anything, as I am greatly indebted to you for helping my Gwyn."

She slowly smiled back. "M'lord, what I would want you would have no desire to give, what with that pretty little one

253

you have. Now get to her before she catches a chill."

She was curled up tightly by the side of the hedge, totally concealed in shadow. The cries and moans that had filled the air shortly after she had fled into the maze still rang in her memory. The sounds were too raw, too agonized to forget. Now she lay huddled, the scratchy wool nun's habit tucked around her bare feet.

The hand on her shoulder startled her. She would have screamed, but another hand swiftly covered her mouth. She bit it, then began to fight silently, not wanting to bring any others to her hiding place. She determined he should kill her before she would submit to his degradation. Her attacker was dressed in monk's robes, and she prayed he was alone.

But he was too strong for her, and she felt him grasp her hands in his and yank them over her head as he straddled her body.

"Damnation, Gwyn, be still!"

Her mind had to be playing tricks with her, as crazed with fear as she was.

"Andrew?" she whispered.

He reached up and yanked the cowl off his head.

"Andrew." Her body relaxed, she closed her eyes and went totally limp beneath him.

"Are you all right?" he asked.

"Yes."

"No one—"

"No one, Andrew. A woman named Beverly helped me. And her friends, Jane and Molly. But for them—" A shudder tore through her body.

His arms came around her, and she could feel his heart beating rapidly against hers.

"We must leave directly, Gwyn. It will not take the Duke long to discover you have escaped, and we must be far from here by then."

She nodded, and he got to his feet, then gave her his hand to help her up. She followed him unquestioningly as he began to walk further into the maze.

She lost track of where they were and how long they had been walking. And she wondered at Andrew's skill. Her feet were almost numb, yet when she stepped on a small, sharp stone, she cried out softly and stopped.

He was next to her immediately, cursing softly as he saw her bare feet.

"Did you cut yourself?"

"No." She rubbed the sole of her foot. "It was nothing, just a stone."

"Get up on my back," he said, turning away and kneeling down.

"Andrew—"

"Do as I say."

She did, her arms wrapped around his neck and her legs firmly around his waist. He patted her feet with his hands, then closed his warm fingers around them and rubbed, attempting to warm them.

They walked further into the maze, and Gwyn leaned her cheek against his shoulder and prayed they would escape the Duke.

The girl cringed as the Duke ripped her head covering back. But the hair that cascaded down was ebony black, not the golden blond he sought.

He cursed, then pushed the girl away. She fell on the stones at his feet and several men swarmed over her.

The Duke didn't give her a second glance. He simply strode through the courtyard and into the garden. Naked bodies glowed in the moonlight, and whenever he saw a flash of blond hair or an elegant pair of breasts or thighs, he stopped, grasping the unfortunate woman by the hair and yanking her face clearly into the moonlight.

But none of them were Gwyn.

She was on the coach. Where could she be hiding?

As if in answer to his silent question, his silvery gaze fell on the opening of the maze.

The slut thinks she can escape me. How amusing that she has unwittingly set up a little entertainment. It will make her capture all the more enjoyable for me.

First, he would have the guards surround the maze to ensure her capture. Then he would begin his hunt.

Andrew pushed back the stiff branches at the far corner of the maze. Beverly had been right; someone had already cut a hole there, and it was almost big enough now for Gwyn to slide through.

His head jerked up when he heard the bells pealing, and his heart began to race.

"He knows you're here, Gwyn. Quick, through the hole."

She obeyed blindly, wincing seconds later as she watched him force his larger body through the small opening, the sharp branches tearing at his clothing. He had discarded the hateful monk's robes within the maze.

Once he was through, he gave her his black cloak as further protection against the chill.

"We have no time now, Gwyn. You must obey me." He put two fingers to his lips and whistled sharply. A dark form appeared swiftly out of the night, and Gwyn moved closer to Andrew. A black stallion galloped toward them, then slowed. Whickering, the immense animal butted his nose against Andrew's shoulder.

"Stand, Mephisto," Andrew whispered, and the stallion froze in place, the only movement his mane and tail ruffled by the winter wind.

Andrew mounted the horse quickly and held his hand down for Gwyn. "Use my foot as a stirrup."

And Gwyn, taught to ride by her father, quickly swung up behind Andrew. She could hear harsh, masculine voices ringing out commands, and she tightened her arms around Andrew's waist and closed her eyes, her cheek against his shirt. Her bare feet were warm tucked against the stallion's belly.

"Come on, boy," Andrew said softly. Gwyn could feel the power within the animal as the stallion sprang to life and galloped away from the high hedge. Andrew bent low in the saddle, and she followed his example, keeping her body pressed against his. She could hear a blur of angry shouts and excited exclamations, but she closed her eyes tighter and held fast to Andrew as the dark stallion swept them away into the night.

"An excellent plan, indeed!"

Edward tried to control his rising fear as the Duke paced his small suite of private rooms at the monastery.

"This is the service I receive for trusting something this important to the likes of you!" The Duke threw his glass of claret against the fireplace and rounded on Edward. "The slut escaped! Tell me, Edward, how does it feel to be outwitted by a mere woman?"

Edward ground his teeth in silent fury. His partnership with the Duke grew more and more dangerous by the week. Some of the Duke's private entertainments were so brutal he counted himself lucky to survive.

"You will pay for this, Edward, every day the little bitch is not in my possession. You were given a chance to prove yourself, and you failed. I shall not trust you again."

Edward winced as the Duke raised his cane and swept it across the crystal decanter and goblets that had graced the small mahogany table. "Stupid idiots! I am surrounded by idiots!" He continued to lash out with his cane, shattering figurines and a small clock.

Edward merely stood, eyeing one of the broken figurines

with a strange sense of sympathy; and knowing his eventual punishment promised to be far worse.

The thick branches of the trees overhead cast shadows on the moonlit road, and they flickered past with amazing speed. It was cold, and Gwyn's face quickly grew numb. She hated to think what punishment Andrew was taking, and she was thankful for the warmth of his strong body ahead of her.

She could feel the fine lather of sweat against her bare feet. Andrew slowed the stallion to a walk, and she sensed he was listening.

The road was quiet.

She was about to say something when he pulled gently on the right rein and Mephisto obediently followed his master's command. The bushes around several huge oak trees parted, and Gwyn pressed herself against Andrew, not wanting her body to be whipped by branches.

They were on a small, rough trail, difficult for more than a single horse to navigate. Mephisto picked his way carefully as they traveled deeper and deeper into the thick forest and further away from the main road. Every so often Andrew would stop the stallion and listen, but Gwyn heard nothing and apparently neither did he.

They traveled this way for several miles, and Gwyn was about to ask Andrew where it was they were going when the trees around them seemed to fall away. In a clearing in front of them was a small, squat building. Its roof was thatched, and dark beams gleamed against the pale walls. A sign hung above the door, but the lights coming out of the windows were muted, and Gwyn could not see what it said.

As Mephisto clip-clopped slowly into the clearing, Andrew gave a short, sharp whistle, and a young man in pants and shirt that looked too small for him shot out from the side of the squat building.

"Good evening, Lord Scarborough."

"Good evening, Brendan. Rub Mephisto down well; he's had a tough time of it tonight. Keep him quiet tomorrow."

"Aye, sir. I'll take as good care of him as if he was my own. Go on inside; Bridget was just saying she hasn't seen you in—"

As Gwyn slid off Mephisto's broad back, he stopped talking.

Andrew said nothing to fill the uncomfortable silence, and Gwyn was very much aware of him as he slid off Mephisto. She kept her eyes downcast as he stepped in front of her, then followed him as he walked toward the inn, wondering all the while what lay inside.

Chapter Sixteen

The room Gwyn was given was just beneath the eaves and faced the back courtyard. Smelling of horse, chilled to the bone, her body aching, Gwyn wanted nothing more than to lie down on the bed and indulge herself in a good cry.

It would have been easy for a blind man to have seen the relationship between Andrew and Bridget. The Irish girl's face had lit up like so many candles at the sight of him. She was beautiful, with thick, curly black hair, a classically heart-shaped face, white skin, and dark blue eyes.

And she obviously had been much more than a friend to Andrew in the past.

Gwyn lay down on the bed, still wrapped in Andrew's cape. So much had happened since she had given Polly the five shillings and climbed into the carriage. . . .

A serving girl returned with a supper tray. She set it down on a small oak table by the bed, then smiled shyly and said, "Lord Scarborough told me to bring you hot water for a bath after you finished your supper."

The thought of hot water against her aching muscles was a pleasure she couldn't resist.

"That will be fine."

When the serving girl left, Gwyn examined her food, her stomach growling. Chicken pie, several slices of freshly baked bread with sweet butter, and a large tankard of ale. Deciding to appease her hunger before she did any more thinking, she sat down on the bed and picked up a slice of bread.

I should stay away from her bed all night and let her wonder. Andrew was in a foul mood now that he had eaten supper and had had a chance to collect his thoughts. Madeleine had told him Gwyn had been tricked into the carriage, but what had she been doing out of her room? How could he possibly protect her from the Duke if she made things so difficult?

"Would you like anything more, m'lord?" Bridget's tone and the way she leaned over just enough to show him the generous swell of her breasts left him with no doubts as to exactly what she meant.

"I should like," he said suddenly, deciding upon a plan of action, "to know when the lady upstairs is taking her bath."

The hot water soothed away the numerous aches in her muscles as Gwyn luxuriated in her bath. She was pleasantly surprised by the small inn and all the comforts it provided. French soap that smelled of roses and clean linen towels. Hot, hot water. Now, her stomach comfortably full and her body warm, she drifted lazily. She would soak just until the water cooled. . . .

The door opened and she tensed, then sat up quickly, sending water sloshing over the rim of the tub.

Andrew closed the door, walked slowly into the room, and sat down on the chair across from the tub. She felt strangely vulnerable with him fully dressed and her naked.

"Was supper to your liking?" he asked quietly.

She nodded.

"And the bath?"

She tried a smile and found her mouth trembled. "It—my legs were sore, and my arms. The heat has soothed me."

"Gwyn, why did you leave The Dark Stallion?"

She had no desire to lie to him. As jealous as she was of the way Bridget had looked at him, this was the man who had saved her life. He had helped her escape the Duke's hateful monastery, and she owed him a truthful tongue, if nothing else.

"I thought—Polly told me the carriage would take me to a Christmas outing. A day in the country."

"During the winter?" He wasn't angry, and somehow, in a way she could not define, that made it worse.

"I thought—" She sighed, then sank down lower in the rapidly cooling water. "I thought I could find another coach and go home." When he did not say anything, she said, "You know how I feel about continuing . . . what we have. I cannot believe it is right."

He stood up and walked to the foot of the tub, looking down at her. "As beautiful as you are, Gwyneth, no man wants a woman who fights him at every turn."

"Then you would be willing to let me go?" Why did the thought of never seeing him again suddenly depress her?

"I think I have no choice, as you seem hell-bent on destroying yourself if I do not give in. Come, the water is getting cold." He helped her out of the tub, briskly dried her, and bade her wrap herself again in the blanket.

"Sit in front of the fire and I will dry your hair."

It was exquisite torture as he slowly dried her hair, then took the wooden comb the maid had provided and began to untangle her waist-length mane. His hands were sure and strong; there was something different in the way he touched her. She sensed it would be wise not to disagree with him this night.

He didn't say another word until her hair was completely dry. Gwyn felt like a cat lying in the sun, ready to curl up in bed.

"I thought," said Andrew, "since you are quite fond of cards, you might grant me one last game."

Her mind was cloudy, sleepy, and she wasn't sure she heard him correctly.

"A card game?"

"Piquet. Just one hand. For very special stakes. If I win, you agree to tell me how you came to The Dark Stallion."

"And if I should win?" She was looking directly at him now, and his eyes were very dark.

"You have your freedom." He took a deep breath. "I will see you back safely to your home and never ask anything more from you."

She didn't want to play this game. Not for such high stakes. *Either way you lose.* The only thought she had was to stall him. Perhaps they could come to another sort of agreement. But not this.

"It seems a trifle unfair, m'lord. You are wagering the one thousand pounds you paid for me against a simple answer to a question."

He smiled. "You think I should ask for more, do you?"

"No. I do not think we should play any card game when we are both clearly tired."

"This needs to be decided upon. But, my beauty, you are smarter than I thought. I will ask for more." He watched her as he said the next words, "If I win, you will also agree to be my mistress. You will move into the house I buy for you, and you will agree to my protection. You will not defy me, publicly or privately, ever again. Do I make myself understood?"

She stared at him, dismayed. "M'lord, I am tired and in need of rest. Could this not be put off until later when we will both be refreshed?"

"I have bent to your will too many times, beauty. This time, it shall be done my way. Tonight."

Her dismay must have shown on her face, because he stroked her shoulder lightly. "I am not a cruel man. Lie down and rest while I find a deck of cards."

The door closed slowly after him, and she stared at it with

dismay. Andrew would not be thwarted in this matter, and she had neither a loose chemise or Lily's cards to protect her.

Andrew intended to leave nothing to chance. He had deliberately requested that the maid serving Gwyn send her up a large tankard of ale. Then a warm bath to relax her further. He knew she was exhausted, and the small amount of sleep he intended to let her steal would only befuddle her further.

But in case Lady Luck refused to visit him this night, he was going to use a marked deck.

He felt slightly ashamed of his deception, but he was also angry with Gwyn. She had risked her life trying to escape him, and he couldn't have that happen again. She had no idea how delightful she was going to find the position of mistress. Her stubbornness would give way amid an onslaught of pleasure so intense she would be powerless to resist.

"Bridget," he said, well aware she was of a mind to give him anything he wanted, "I should like a deck of cards."

Gwyn woke as soon as she heard the door scrape open. She sat up in bed, deeply tired, but when she saw Andrew arrange a small table and two chairs in front of the fire, her heart began to race.

There was a soft knock on the door, and Andrew strode over to answer it. When he came back to her bed, he handed her a nightshirt, and she pulled it over her head.

If you keep your wits about you. If you remember everything Lily taught you . . . There was more than a chance she could best Andrew at this game. Fortune could smile on either of them. Getting to her feet, she walked over the table and chairs. She sat down on the seat closest to the fire, then put both her hands on the table and offered up a silent prayer. The outcome of this game was within the hands of a higher power than herself, and she would abide by the cards' decision.

264

Andrew sat down across from her and set the deck between them.

"Are you ready, Gwyn?"

She nodded her head.

He shuffled the cards smoothly, and she watched them with a sick feeling in the pit of her stomach, knowing her fate would be determined by the spades, diamonds, clubs, and hearts.

He set the deck down in front of her. She cut it, amazed her hand did not shake, and handed it back to him.

He dealt the cards with a swift economy of motion. When he placed the remaining cards between them, she picked up her cards and fanned them out in her fingers.

Not a bad hand. But certainly not a good one. It was up to the cards she picked. She glanced at Andrew. His face looked beautiful in the firelight, all masculine planes and hollows. But he had a totally unreadable expression, and it maddened her.

He nodded at her, indicating she pick first.

She drew the top card. It wasn't anything she could use, but to prevent him from suspecting, she smiled and tucked it into her hand. Carefully selecting one of her useless cards—and there were a few—she placed it face up next to the pile.

Andrew didn't pick it. He drew from the pile, and she waited in an agony of suspense as he added it to his hand and threw down another.

She couldn't use it, so she picked another from the pile.

It went like this for a time, their movements precise and economical. And Gwyn began to fear that Andrew might win. Her hand was muddled; there seemed to be no clear direction her cards were taking.

Andrew drew another card. His face remained expressionless as he laid his hand down on the table in front of him.

Ace, king, and queen of hearts.

Gwyn slowly laid her cards down, her mind completely numb. The hearts on his cards blurred, and she blinked back her useless, frustrated tears. He had won her again as surely as he had won her the night of the auction. Now there was no other life for her but with him.

But never a wife. Never a true home. Never a marriage in the eyes of God.

Andrew gathered up all the cards. With a graceful flick of his wrist, he sent the deck sailing into the fire. Gwyn watched as the cards fanned out over the flames, as the edges began to blacken and burn.

And in the midst, the queen of hearts seemed to stare at her. She couldn't tear her eyes away as the card slowly burned. The woman's face blackened and she looked away.

Andrew was watching her. As she gazed up into his dark eyes, she knew her time of reckoning had finally come. There was no escape.

His eyes were implacable.

She took a deep, steadying breath. "My cousin Edward took me to London. . . ."

Within the hour, Andrew was back downstairs, nursing a tankard of ale. He was completely unaware of Bridget buzzing around him; there were too many other thoughts running through his head.

A vicar's daughter. Gently reared. And her own cousin, Edward Sleaforth, had drugged her and sold her to Janet Wickens, the most notorious brothel owner in London.

He couldn't banish from his memory the anguished expression in her eyes. Nor the words she had softly spoken at the end of her story.

Andrew, I was raised to be a wife and mother. It's all I have ever wanted since I was a little girl. Please, please don't do this to me.

But he couldn't let her go.

She will adjust. She will learn it is a far better thing to be a mistress than a mere wife.

Determined not to look back, he drained the last of his ale and set the tankard down with a thud. Placing a few coins on the table, he stood and headed for the stairs.

When he let himself into their room he noticed she was sprawled across the bed asleep, her face blotched and her nose bright red. Andrew sat down gently in one of the chairs and began to remove his boots.

She's cried herself out. Her breathing was slightly raspy, further evidence of the tears she had shed. Something tightened in his chest at the thought of her so desperately wanting to be free of him.

He removed his waistcoat, shirt, and breeches. The bed was narrower than the one they had shared at the Dark Stallion, but there was still ample room for two. He slipped his arms beneath Gwyn and eased her beneath the blankets.

She stirred, mumbling something incoherent. He watched, smiling, as she buried her face in her pillow.

Drawing the curtain against the bright light at the window, Andrew returned to their bed. He was tired as well, their desperate night ride catching up with him.

They could do worse than rest here for a few days. And he could begin to teach Gwyn exactly what delights lay in store for her as his mistress.

Gwyn came fully awake from a fitful sleep to the sound of horse's hooves clattering against cobblestone.

She was alone.

She thought of the card game last night, and a sense of desperation threatened to overwhelm her. She was his now. Yet she knew if what Andrew had proposed had been totally against her deepest feelings, she would have fought him still. It disturbed her that a part of her, before she had surrendered to sleep, had been glad he was not forced to give her her freedom.

Whatever the outcome of the cards, they would not have changed her feelings for him. The pain came out of the knowledge that, to Andrew, she was as much his property as his horse or his house in London or any of his servants. That she could be nothing more was what hurt her.

267

She hadn't slept well. She'd dreamed she was running through a maze, Andrew chasing her, and had taken a turn in the silvery hedges and raced straight into the Duke's arms. The look on his face, in those cold grey eyes, had jolted her awake.

She had touched Andrew's hair, his cheek, had felt his arm tightly around her before the terrifying feeling of being trapped had slowly ebbed away.

Unable to sleep, she'd thought of her father. He had often reassured her she could not always see God's higher purpose. "Most things happen for a reason," he had told her. "You may not realize it for weeks or months, even years. But you must understand your life is part of a higher plan, and you cannot always understand as quickly as you might wish."

The memory of his words comforted her, and she closed her eyes and prayed she might be granted patience until she understood what part of the plan had determined she become Andrew's mistress. She had curled herself closely against Andrew and finally slept.

Now fully awake, she thought of Andrew. She was alone in their bed. Where was he?

She glanced around the small bedchamber, surprised to find the nun's habit gone. There was nothing for her to wear but the nightshirt she had on presently. She was sitting in bed, pondering her predicament, when the door opened. Bridget walked in, a tight expression around her mouth.

"Lord Scarborough asked me to give you these." She had an armful of clothing, which she unceremoniously dumped at the foot of the bed.

The emotions warring in the Irish girl's eyes told Gwyn that Bridget was spoiling for a fight, and with a certain sense of perversity, she decided to make sure the girl was denied that pleasure.

"Thank you." She said nothing more, waiting for the woman to leave.

"Well, you're an improvement over the other. She had red hair and freckles, and teeth that stuck out. I never understood what he saw in the likes of her."

Gwyn, deciding not to answer, got out of bed and began to examine her clothing. A blue wool dress, quite plain but looking new and clean. Warm shoes and stockings. Quilted petticoats and a knitted shawl. The chemise was made of linen, not silk, but the stitching was even and the material wasn't worn. She wondered where Andrew had managed to find clothing for her.

"He's going to marry that lady in London after Christmas. I guess you'll be installed in a fancy house of your own. But I'm sure there will be other women; Andrew isn't the type to be satisfied with one or even two."

Not wanting Bridget to see how her words were hurting her, Gwyn turned her back to the Irish girl and pulled her nightshirt over her head. She slipped on the chemise, pulled on her stockings, then reached for her petticoat.

"But," Bridget continued, "with a man like Andrew, I would think a woman would have to be content with the little she had of him. He likes a life of variety. . . ."

"Would you help me with my buttons, Bridget?" Gwyn asked sweetly. It was tearing her apart to be civil to the woman, but she would die rather than reveal the true state of her emotions.

Bridget's fingers were quick as she fastened the buttons, and Gwyn sensed the girl wanted as little to do with her as possible.

She heard footsteps on the stairs, and remembering her resolve to be patient and see where this would all lead, Gwyn walked quickly to the door. When Andrew opened it, she made sure her expression was serene.

"Good day, m'lord," she said softly, and was pleased to catch the gleam of surprise in his eyes. He seemed unaware of Bridget in the room as he bent to kiss her. It was anything but a quick kiss, and Gwyn knew he wanted her. In a distant part of her mind she heard the sound of quickly indrawn breath. Bridget. She smiled against his mouth and consciously opened her lips to deepen the kiss, letting herself relax within the circle of his arms.

When they broke apart, she knew she was flushed. A smile

curved her lips at the thought of how their kiss must have looked to Bridget. Whatever the woman might say about Andrew, whatever she might predict, she could not deny Gwyn was the woman in his arms.

Andrew seemed to notice Bridget for the first time. "Bridget, I should like you to pack us a lunch. I'm taking Gwyn riding this afternoon."

"Yes, m'lord," the girl said quietly.

After Bridget left, Andrew said, "You look quite fetching in that dress."

"I thank you for it, m'lord."

"Andrew."

"Andrew." She was determined not to fight with him. Gwyn had no doubts they would have plenty of arguments once they returned to London. She wanted to remember their time in the country as different.

In London early that same morning, Angel was hurrying back to the kitchen with a basket of eggs when she heard a horse snort. She turned, then recognized the blond rider. Jack. She had met him twice, the first time the night of the auction and the second when she and Madeleine had rushed into the men's club to find Andrew. She had noticed his blond good looks the first time and had been touched by the way he had come to her aid at the club. He had escorted both her and Madeleine home, and she had decided she liked him very much.

"Hello, Angelique." He smiled down at her from atop his mare's back, then dismounted.

Something in the way he said her name was different from the way Polly said it. A warmth and friendliness. Genuinely glad to see him, she smiled.

"Hello, m'lord."

When he stood next to her, she barely came to his shoulder. He smelled good, his cologne spicy but not overpowering. And his riding jacket was cut so it lay smoothly against his broad shoulders. The winter wind ruffled his fine blond hair away from his forehead. His grey eyes, she decided, were quite kind.

"I have a message from Andrew. He asked me to deliver it in person as he thought a note might make things uncomfortable for you."

She nodded, touched by Andrew's thoughtfulness.

"Gwyn is safe with Andrew. They're going to remain in the country for a week. When they return, he will move Gwyn to another house. He asked me if you might consider moving with Gwyn and tending to her needs."

It was all she could have hoped for. "Ah, thank you, m'lord. When you send him a message, would you please tell him I am quite interested."

Now that he had delivered his message, Angel thought he looked a little uneasy. He folded his arms across his chest and said, "What is it you are doing?"

She glanced down at the basket of eggs, thinking it was quite obvious. Then, sensing again that peculiar nervousness, she decided to see if she could persuade him to relax. She had the feeling Jack could be quite a jolly companion if he weren't so self-conscious.

"Collecting eggs for Cook, and she will have my head if I don't give them to her soon!" She smiled up at him. "I would love to continue our talk, but I am afraid I have to get back to work."

"You mean you don't—" He flushed bright red, the scarlet color creeping quickly up his neck.

She took pity on him. It was a natural assumption that if a woman lived in a brothel she was a whore. "No, I do not. I am a maid here, nothing more or less."

"I'm sorry, Angelique."

She was deeply touched that he though he should apologize to her. "Don't be. It is an easy mistake." She glanced back at the kitchen, nervous now that someone might see her with him. "I must go."

"Perhaps—perhaps we might see each other . . . again." He seemed to be forcing the words out, and she realized he was truly shy.

"I would like that." She lowered her voice, conscious all the time that many windows overlooked the garden. "I have Tuesdays free. Perhaps we could go for a walk. Or to a coffeehouse. I can pay for myself," she added proudly.

"That would be fine," he said, rushing the words out. "I'll meet you here at ten."

"Wait for me around the corner in the alley. I'll be there." Then she turned and walked swiftly into the kitchen, her feet skimming over the well-trod path. Two pieces of good news within minutes! She was leaving The Dark Stallion with Gwyn, and she might be seeing Jack. She had liked him since she had first seen his face at the auction. It had been a long time since she had thought of being with a man. Once out of the life, she had found she had no physical desire. She couldn't easily trust men, having been exposed to the worst in their natures while on the streets.

She set the basket of eggs carefully on the kitchen table next to Cook, half listening as the older woman complained about the two new girls Janet had hired. Jack's words kept skimming through her memory.

He asked me if you might consider moving with Gwyn and tending to her needs. She had known this moment was coming. Now that it was here, she had to pinch herself to believe it.

She was finally leaving The Dark Stallion.

"Lord Cuckfield, will you take your ground?" The man's voice was slightly distanced as he addressed the Duke.

The Duke turned and took ten paces, turned once again, and faced his opponent. Lord Staverton was barely a man; he looked as if he didn't even shave. But there had been angry words spoken at the gambling hell last night, and in the end the boy had been so enraged he had called the Duke out.

Hyde Park was fairly deserted at this hour of the morning. Thin wisps of fog curled up from piles of brown leaves. The sky was a leaden grey, the sun hidden behind clouds. Large oaks towering over them had born silent witness to countless duels.

"Lord Staverton, will you take your ground?" the voice droned on, and the Duke watched through narrowed eyes as the young man walked off his ten paces, turned, and faced him. There was an angry flush in his cheeks, a sparkle in his eyes. He was full of righteous wrath, even though his brother had begged him to reconsider.

The boy was right, Cuckfield thought. *I was cheating. His mistake was in calling me out.*

A wiser man would have known better.

"Lord Cuckfield, are you ready to receive Lord Staverton's fire?"

"Yes," the Duke said shortly.

"Lord Staverton, cock your pistol and prepare to fire."

The Duke didn't even flinch as Lord Staverton's pistol seemed to explode in his hand. The young man dropped the weapon, shaking his hand rapidly. When he spoke, his words were rapid, desperate, one blurring into the next.

"I can't understand it! I don't know what happened! This pistol must be faulty—I—it must have been loaded incorrectly! Why, I must have another. I don't understand how—"

"I'm sorry, Lord Staverton, but you must first stand your ground and allow Lord Cuckfield his turn to fire." The voice floated out into the still winter air, slightly bored.

He's probably cold and wants to go back to his bed, Cuckfield thought with amusement. Lord Staverton was staring at him in horror now, fully understanding the implications of his rashness the previous night. Cuckfield smiled as he saw dawning comprehension in the young man's eyes.

"Lord Staverton, are the rules quite clear to you?" the man overseeing the duel asked.

"Yes," he whispered. The boy couldn't take his eyes off the Duke.

"Very well, then. Lord Cuckfield, cock your pistol and prepare to fire."

The Duke held the moment out, enjoying the young Lord's fear. Even at this distance, he could see the fool's legs were shaking. He watched as Lord Staverton brought his hand up to his mouth, and the Duke wondered if the boy was going to be sick.

Then all thoughts were replaced by the sweet rush of satisfaction as he cocked his pistol and fired. The bullet flew cleanly, hitting Lord Staverton squarely in the chest. The force knocked him over, and as the Duke lowered his smoking pistol and watched Lord Staverton's brother run to his side, he noticed the dark red stain spreading across his opponent's fine linen shirt.

But he didn't see Lord Staverton's face. All he could see was Andrew.

Gwyn was enjoying their time in the country. She allowed herself to be lulled into a sweet suspension of time, forgetting both her past and future. There would be plenty of opportunity to face her problems once they returned to London.

She had missed living in the country, with opportunities for long walks and solitude. Andrew surprised her by allowing her to go off by herself, and Gwyn found the time to be healing. She began to come to terms with her life.

You are his mistress now, she thought as she walked along the bank of a small stream.

Mistress is not the same as wife. But she was beginning to question this. All she had done since finding herself at The Dark Stallion was question everything. He was close to her, she knew that. He said he would treasure her for all the days of his life. She knew him better than to doubt his word. And she knew he did not find peace with Belinda.

He will marry her. There were times when she thought he fooled himself. She did not dare confront him with the knowledge. They had fought too often in the past; it was time to love and heal. Gwyn always felt closer to God surrounded by his handiwork, and here by the stream she knew she would find a moment of peace.

You can accept the fact you are his mistress, and you can love him the way he needs to be loved. Like a true wife would. The thought slipped into her mind so easily Gwyn knew it to be a deep truth. Everything within her stilled at that moment, and her confusion and fear seemed to flee.

Anyone can call you anything. And they probably will. But you know who you are, and no one can take that away from you.

She had been fighting against convention as bitterly as she had fought Andrew. There were many rules and restrictions she had talked to Angel about, many things she had assumed to be true that, upon careful inspection, made absolutely no sense.

I love him. And I am good for him. I never would have found my way to him in the country. Perhaps that is why . . .

If there was ever a man who needed to be loved, it was Andrew.

How he would laugh at me if I told him I thought he needed me. Needed to be loved by me.

It was enough, for now, that she knew.

Book IV

"Though he'll bluster and crow of his duty,
And insist you are not meant to wed,
He'll heel like a hound to your beauty
When he finds duty won't warm his bed . . ."

Chapter Seventeen

Gwyn was lying in bed that same evening when she heard the door open softly. She didn't have to turn her head to recognize Andrew's footsteps as he came inside.

She sat up in bed slowly. They were journeying to London in the morning, but Gwyn would have been content to stay in the country forever. She had loved these last seven days, alone with Andrew. She couldn't remember a time when they had been closer.

"Gwyn." Andrew lay down and stretched out in bed beside her. He tilted his head back against the headboard and closed his eyes. "You will not be going back to The Dark Stallion."

Somehow she had known this was coming. She said nothing, waiting for him to continue.

"Are you going to miss the place?"

Gwyn was touched he thought of her feelings, when this was something he had most clearly wanted from the start. She knew Andrew had a distinct need to isolate her from other people, especially men. Moving her to a private house would accomplish exactly that.

"I will miss Angel," she admitted. "And Lily and Madeleine. But I cannot truthfully say I will miss the place itself." She looked up at him and was suddenly scared at the hardness around his mouth. She wondered what he was thinking.

"Angel has agreed to come to this new house. And Lily and Madeleine may visit if you wish."

"Andrew, what is disturbing you?" She knew just talking about moving her to a new house would not bring on this tightly coiled tension within him.

"I have had people making inquiries in the city. It seems your cousin Sleaforth has made the Duke of Cuckfield's acquaintance."

At the mention of her cousin's name, Gwyn felt a chill settle over her. Ever since she had told Andrew her story and had admitted Edward's part in it, she had known this moment was coming.

"They are good company for each other, two evil men," she said.

"They are dangerous to you."

"Not if I am hidden. They will never find me if we are careful." But she already knew what he meant to do, and the knowledge chilled her.

"It has to be stopped, Gwyn. When we return to London—"

"No, Andrew." She laid her hand on his arm. "I ask nothing from you, m'lord, except that you are as careful with your own protection as you are with mine."

He covered her hand with his own. "Nothing will happen to me, Gwyn. I merely intend to frighten the man into leaving you alone."

"But you say he is friend to the Duke. That makes me more afraid for you, m'lord."

"You should be afraid for yourself as well. The Duke still wants you, Gwyn, and he needs to be warned."

"You cannot be thinking of taking on both men!" Now she was truly afraid, remembering the determination and bloodhunger she had seen in the chill grey eyes.

"I will do what has to be done. I would have acted sooner, but I didn't have your cousin's name and didn't know of his relationship with the Duke."

She couldn't control the fear building inside her. "Andrew,

I fear for your safety. Please do not do this. I wish I had never told you how I came to The Dark Stallion."

"It has to be done, Gwyn, otherwise you will never feel free."

"I have no desire to feel free if it means endangering your life!"

"I don't want you to worry." His arm had come up around her, and now he dropped a gentle kiss on her forehead. "Come, let's not spoil our last night in the country."

Usually when he kissed her she felt nothing but his touch and the fire he raised within her. But tonight, no matter how she tried to respond, Gwyn could only see a pair of cold grey eyes.

As she lay in his arms and desperately kissed him back, she knew with utter certainty why she had been afraid of returning to the city.

Something terrible was going to happen. And nothing would ever be the same.

Angel spent her spare time in Gwyneth's rooms, packing and straightening. She had no desire for the madam of The Dark Stallion to know she was leaving until she was out the door and on her way to the new house. Andrew would waste no time once he returned to the city, and she wanted to be ready.

It took time, finding the trunks Andrew had given Gwyn and packing away all the dresses, chemises, petticoats, shoes, fans, ribbons, and laces. She folded the garments carefully, packing them as quickly as she could. She'd asked Cook for dried lavender and rose petals to freshen the inside of Gwyn's trunks, and as she packed she listened for the sound of Janet's footsteps.

She wondered what her new life would be like. Andrew would be a fair employer. She had only to work as hard as she had all these years at The Dark Stallion to be assured of that. Janet was another matter. The woman had never praised her work, though Angel knew she was worth three other girls. Maybe four. She was a hard worker, because anything was preferable to going back to what she had been.

She heard footsteps in the hallway and quickly stood up. The trunks were behind the large screen. Darting out from the hiding place, she rushed silently to the large bed and began to strip the bedclothes.

Her caution served her well. The next moment, the door opened and Janet stepped inside.

She stood surveying the room, her striking face totally impassive. Angel continued to strip the bed, working industriously.

"Who were you talking to out in the garden, Angelique?"

"Jack Colborne, the Viscount Lanford. He is a friend of Lord Scarborough's. He came by to let me know Gwyneth was safe and would be returning within the week."

"And that is why you are cleaning the room?"

She prayed the madam would not find it necessary to investigate behind the screen. If she saw the trunks neatly lined up . . . "Yes, mistress."

"But he came by again."

"Yes."

"And may I ask why?"

Angel feigned embarrassment. "He came by to see . . . me."

"It would please me if you would save such talks for your own time."

"Yes, mistress."

"When is Gwyneth returning?"

"I believe he said tomorrow, mistress."

There was a slight pause before Janet said quietly, "I should be very disappointed if you were to leave this house after all I have done for you."

She is guessing. She cannot possibly know. Angel willed her hands not to tremble as she folded a heavy wool blanket.

"I trust you remember where you came from."

"Yes, mistress."

"And where you could easily find yourself again."

Angel merely nodded her head.

"Come to my rooms when Gwyneth arrives. I should like to know the exact hour."

"Yes, mistress."

And then she left.

Once her footsteps faded, Angel sat down on the bed, her legs trembling. Janet could do nothing to stop her from leaving. But once she left The Dark Stallion, the madam would never take her back.

She had escaped the street and was determined never to return. Now, on the eve of leaving the brothel, Angel found herself suddenly afraid.

The Duke sat in one of the front circular rows. He was afforded an excellent view of the pit. Voices hummed around him as money exchanged hands and viewers speculated. But his attention was concentrated on the pit.

The two men entered the fighting area from opposite ends. Both had birds with them, and the murmur of approval rose steadily as the crowd surveyed the fighting cocks. They were armed with silver heels, the better to bloody each other. Each man set his burden down, and Cuckfield sat forward in his seat. This was the part he enjoyed.

The cocks flew at each other. Feathers were torn out as they darted closer, and the noise swelled as first blood was drawn. Money flew from hand to hand, spectators laughed and cheered. And all the while, the Duke sat forward, seeing the cocks but not really seeing them.

The cocks continued fighting, mangled and torn as they were. Silver heels flashed as they attacked each other in a desperate frenzy. Great gouts of blood began to cover the mat, and Cuckfield watched as one of the cocks staggered, then fell. The other jumped on top of its opponent and ripped it savagely, the silver heels gleaming in the candlelight.

And again he thought of Andrew and knew he could wait. Soon. It would happen soon.

Angel rushed inside the kitchen door. She had said good-bye to Jack in the alley and had been surprised when he hadn't even tried to kiss her. They had enjoyed a most pleasant morning, going to a chophouse for breakfast. They had sat over coffee for almost two hours, talking. She had been right about Jack's shyness.

He was a sensitive man, and she suspected he had few friends. She wondered at how he and Andrew had come to know each other and decided they must have met as boys because they were far too different as men. He held his friend in the greatest esteem, without thinking he had much to offer in return.

But he does, she thought as she raced up the stairs, hoping she would not run into Janet this morning. *He is gentle and quiet and shy, and very sensitive. He will make a good friend.* She pushed the thought of anything other than friendship out of her mind. It was impossible, of course.

They had stopped on the way home and she had bought Lily some pink ribbon to trim her new dressing gown. Now she decided to go to her friend's room and give her the ribbon, then tell her she was to be leaving The Dark Stallion.

But when she approached the door, she recognized both Lily and Madeleine's voices as they argued in French. It shocked her, as the two women were the closest of friends and rarely disagreed. But this argument was highly emotional, and Angel couldn't help but overhear.

"You can't do this, Lily! Not with everything you know about him! He will tear you to pieces!"

"And what am I staying here for? You have Charles, he will take you away. Gwyn will be leaving soon, and I know Angel will go with her! And it will be Lily—*Lily* inside this house all alone! There is no one coming for me, Madeleine! *No one!* I have to do it this way! I cannot keep on, knowing I am nothing but an old whore waiting to die so someone else can take my bed!"

"But not with *him!*" Madeleine's voice was anguished, and Angel would have left then, except Madeleine never showed any kind of emotion. It affected her deeply.

"Because he was your old lover?"

"I care *nothing* about him! I care about *you!* Lily, he will destroy you! Please, you must listen—"

"*No!* I must set my house in order! If he asks me to leave, I will go with him. Madeleine, please, you must not cry. It is the only way out for me."

Angel silently backed away, then turned and fled down the hall. She slowed when she reached Gwyn's old room, opened the door, and slipped inside. Leaning against the wall, she panted softly, taking slow, deep breaths as she tried to still her racing heart.

Minutes later, when she looked down at the pink ribbon in her hand, the delicate trim was crushed.

Gwyn and Andrew reached the outskirts of the city by afternoon, and they set off to the new house. It was further into the city, set back from a quiet street. The houses were older and seemed more solid.

Once inside, Gwyn had a quick impression of large rooms, quietly decorated. Furniture was already in place, and paintings graced the walls. Andrew led her straight to the bedroom. A fire was burning, and the curtained bed in the center of the room looked comfortable after their exhausting journey.

"You'll be safe here until I return," Andrew said.

"Where are you going?"

"To The Dark Stallion. Jack and I are going to fetch your things and bring Angelique back."

"Be careful, Andrew." She hadn't been able to dispel the

dark feelings engulfing her as they had neared the city. Coming back had been a mistake. But nothing could have dissuaded Andrew.

"Nothing is going to happen," he said. "Thatch is at the door; he will allow no one inside."

She wondered what Janet thought of this, losing two servants in one day.

Gwyn lay down on the bed as he left and knew she would not stop praying until he was safely in her arms again.

The Duke caressed the rose softly, barely aware of the blackamoor behind him, picking up petals.

It had been a stroke of pure genius to become acquainted with the little French whore. Lily. He knew, from what Suzanne had told Edward, that she was a friend of Gwyneth's. Wherever the golden-haired slut was hiding, she was bound to be foolish enough to tell her friend. And it would only be a matter of time before he would make her reveal Gwyn's whereabouts.

Which one to kill first, he mused. *Andrew or Gwyneth?* It was a decision he relished making, as it afforded him endless pleasure in contemplating the final results.

If Andrew first, then she will be terrified that she no longer has a protector. I could draw out her torture for several days.

If the whore goes first, then he will fight all the harder and killing him would be all the sweeter.

Either way would afford him great pleasure. He knew she was back in London. He could feel when she was near him. No other woman had ever affected him this strongly. There seemed to be a bond between them, something so strong it would only be severed with her death.

He smiled as he reached out toward the flower. *So beautiful.* It was hard for him to pace himself, to move slowly when he wanted Gwyn now. First, he would remove the French whore from The Dark Stallion and delude her into thinking he cared for her. Then he would wait until she went out on her own and have her followed. Eventually he would dispose of her. But not just yet. While she still served a purpose, she would be allowed to live.

He had no doubts she would lead him straight to his heart's desire.

Angel lay back on her small bed and closed her eyes, fighting back tears. How could so many things have happened in a single day? She had gone to Lily's room later and her friend had been quiet and withdrawn. Though part of the ribbon had been crushed in her hand, Angel had managed to salvage it. Lily had thanked her, smiling tiredly.

"So, you leave with the little one today?" she had asked.

And Angel had nodded her head. As happy as she was to leave The Dark Stallion, now that she knew some of her friend's darkest fears, the joy left her. She wished more than anything she could bundle Lily up and take her with her. Madeleine would survive. Lily had always been more childlike and needed someone to protect her. She was afraid for her friend and was about to say something when Lily laid a finger on her lips.

"Don't you stay here because of me," she said as she patted Angel's cheek. "I have a surprise up my sleeve." She lowered her voice. "There is a gentleman who wants to set me up in a house of my own. I will have a fine house and a carriage and I will come and visit you and Gwyn and we will play cards and drink chocolate. . . ."

"Who is this man? Do I know him?"

Lily lowered her lashes. "I am sure you have heard of him. He has a hard heart, some say, but I think he just needs someone to care for him, like Gwyn cares for Andrew." She shivered. "I could not go on if I thought this was to be the end of my life, living here. . . ."

"Lily, stay a little longer. Andrew is paying me well; I can

284

send for you. . . ."

"Ah, no Angel. I cannot ask that of you. Now, I thank you for the ribbon but we must both pack our things if we are to leave today."

Angel had walked back to her room, not even caring whether Andrew came to fetch her or not. Something was terribly wrong for Lily to become this upset.

Within the hour, she knew the reason.

She had heard shouting and had run swiftly down the stairs until she was on the second floor, leaning over the railing. Below, Lily stood at the front door. She was dressed in a purple silk dress, and Angel's eyes had stung when she'd recognized the pink ribbon bows pinned at the bodice.

Madeleine had her dress in her hands and was crushing great handfuls of silk as she screamed at her.

When Lily had stubbornly pushed open the great wooden door, Angel had finally understood.

The carriage waiting in front had the Duke of Cuckfield's crest on the door. Four midnight black horses waited in harness, and the driver looked straight ahead, waiting.

"Let me *go!*" Lily screamed. And with a strength none of them had suspected she possessed, she pushed Madeleine away. Her friend fell heavily, and before she could get up Lily grabbed her small bag and rushed out the door, slamming it behind her.

Angel was already running down the stairs as Madeleine slowly came to her feet. Other whores had gathered at the railing, attracted by the shouting. Angel stopped at the bottom of the stairs as she heard the sound of horse's hooves clanging against cobblestone.

Lily was gone.

She was about to assist Madeleine, but something in the set of the woman's back restrained her. Madeleine slowly raised herself to her feet. She had never revealed any vulnerability to the other women at The Dark Stallion, and Angel sensed she would not welcome her help, no matter how well-intentioned.

285

She stood with her back to them, and it seemed she was gathering strength. It must have been only a minute, yet to Angel the moment would last forever, burned into her memory. Madeleine slowly turned and surveyed the group of whores with a look that expressed more eloquently than words how she felt toward them for considering this an entertainment. Feet shuffled. One of the whores coughed. Yet Madeleine stared them down, and slowly they began to move away from the railing and up the stairs into the darkness.

Angel stepped toward her then, but the anguish in Madeleine's large blue eyes told her there was nothing she could do. Heavyhearted, she returned to her room.

The knock on her door startled her out of her memories, and she sat up on her bed.

"Yes."

"Angelique, there is a man here to see you."

She stood up, smoothing her hair with her hands. Then, thinking it wise to leave her packed bag, she walked out of her room.

Andrew stood in the hallway with Jack, in front of Gwyn's old room. Janet was with them, and Angel's stomach twisted at the prospect of a confrontation with the madam. She had heard from one of the girls that Andrew had already stolen Thatch away from the brothel. It would make her leaving all the worse.

Andrew gave her a reassuring smile when he saw her, and Angel saw Janet shoot him a murderous glance. She focused her eyes on Jack, and suddenly she was no longer afraid.

"Is this true, Angelique, that you are going to leave me short a servant after all I have done for you?" Janet demanded.

She looked down at her scuffed shoes, suddenly very tired. She couldn't think of what might happen to Lily or she would burst into tears.

Then she felt a hand on her shoulder and looked up into Andrew's eyes.

"Let her speak for herself, Janet. What would you like to do, Angelique?"

Even if she had wanted to stay, she couldn't now. Not after Janet suspected she had tried to find another position. She remembered the early days, when she had first come to The Dark Stallion. It had seemed exciting and important, the most exclusive brothel in all of London. Compared to her days on the streets, she had thought she had found heaven on earth.

Now, looking around for the first time in many months that she had had the leisure to do so, she noticed the fading wallpaper, the areas of carpet wearing thin. There was a darkness, a closed-in feeling to this house, and suddenly she could not wait to get away.

"I should like to stay with Gwyn. I am going to work for Lord Scarborough." She could feel Janet's anger and knew she would never be welcome here again.

"Get your things and leave." Janet turned and walked down the long hallway until she rounded a corner and disappeared.

Just like that. She had given the woman years of service and now she no longer existed for her. After what she had seen in her lifetime, Angel wondered that it should still affect her.

"Go with her, Jack; help her get her things. I'll see to the loading of the carriage." Now Andrew was full of restless impatience, and she knew he was eager to return to Gwyn.

On the way back from her room, Angel asked Jack if she might stop at one room. She knocked softly at the door to the room Madeleine and Lily had shared. When there was no answer, she opened the door.

Madeleine lay quietly on the bed. It seemed strange not to hear Lily's light voice welcome her, not to see her pat the bed with her delicate hand and tell her to come share her chocolates. A single candle burned, and there was enough light that Angel knew Madeleine had been crying.

"Madeleine?" She set her bag down, walked over to the bed, and knelt beside it. Jack waited out in the hallway, and she silently thanked him for his consideration.

She touched her friend's cheek and spoke quickly in French. "I will pray for Lily, and I will send word as soon as I know where I am staying. We must not lose touch with each other now, not when we must help her."

There was no answer, and she kissed her friend's cheek.

"She did what she thought she had to do. I am—I am afraid for her. But you cannot give up hope, my friend. You are the bravest of us all; we must take courage from each other."

She took Madeleine's hand and squeezed it.

"Do not give up on me!" she whispered. "Madeleine, I will come and see you as soon as I can. But you must try, promise me that." Her French was soft, urgent. "I love you and I cannot bear to see you this way."

The pressure on her hand was so soft she almost thought she imagined it. Then it came again, a little more this time.

"There. You see, we take it a step at a time." She took the blanket from the foot of the bed and spread it over her friend.

"Angelique . . ." It was barely a whisper.

Angel put her arms around her friend and fought back her tears. "I know. I know how much it hurts. But we must be strong for her."

The coach rumbled and swayed, and Lily had to hold tightly to the strap. The interior was completely black, and it depressed her. She lowered the leather flap at the window cautiously, and the cold, winter air stung her cheeks and brought quick tears to her eyes. She closed it quickly.

When the carriage finally slowed, she lowered the flap again. The house in front of her seemed strangely isolated, cold and remote. There was a single light burning in one of the upper windows, and for an instant she thought he was up there, looking down at her as she stepped from the carriage.

The wind bit through her cloak, numbing her fingers through her frayed gloves as she grasped the handle of her small bag. The silk of her dress was a totally inadequate covering, and she felt vulnerable again in the same way she had when she looked her first man in the eye and realized what it was he intended to do to her.

She thought of Madeleine and the warm fire in their room. And Angelique, with her quick laughter and lively dark eyes. Lily reached beneath her cloak with her free hand and touched the pink bows.

And Gwyn. Meeting Gwyn had changed her life. She seemed such a lady, delicate and refined. Everything Lily had always longed to be. More than anything, Lily wanted to be treasured by a man, protected and cared for. She had laughed about her work at The Dark Stallion, but deep inside she had known it was doing terrible things to her.

The front door opened and a black child, dressed in loose pants, shirt, and a little turban, poked his head out. His dark eyes were questioning, as if asking her why she chose to stay outside on such an evening as this.

There was very little light in the sky, and it was getting colder. Gripping the handle of her bag tightly, Lily slowly started toward the door.

Chapter Eighteen

"Why are you frightened, Gwyn?" Andrew's voice was low. It was late at night, and they were in the bedroom of the new house.

More and more, he was able to guess her feelings. Now was as good a time as any to confront him with her fears.

"I am frightened for you. I do not wish you to see my cousin or the Duke."

"What you wish for is impossible. I will never be assured of your safety until both men have been confronted."

"What is it you plan to do?"

"They frequent one of the more popular gambling establishments. Gwyneth, the Duke is a cruel man, but a coward. He must be brought to heel. I intend to go there and confront both men. I will let them know what they can expect from me if they ever interfere in your life again."

Her insides twisted at the thought of what her cousin Edward was capable of doing. And after Angel told her of Lily's decision to live with the Duke and what kind of man he was, she had no doubts her cousin and this man fed each other's evil nature.

The only reason Andrew was involved was because of her.

"And my wish counts for nothing?" she asked softly. She couldn't meet his eyes, as she was preparing to lie to him.

"Your safety has to come first. What kind of man would you take me for if I could not protect you?"

"And if there were a special reason I did not wish you to harm yourself, would that change things?"

"No."

She decided to lie. "M'lord, I am carrying your child."

Andrew said nothing, and she could not look at him. "I am begging you, Andrew, please do not leave me when I need you so badly. I know . . . I feel something terrible is going to come of this. You do not realize the extent of their evil. I would rather live with fear for the rest of my life than never see you again. . . ."

"You carry my child?" There was such wonder in his voice she had to look at his face. And there was the expression she had always hoped to see. The hard lines softened for an instant, his eyes were warmer.

She swallowed, hating the lie even as she said it. "Yes."

"When did you realize this?"

"I did not . . . I have not . . ." She was suddenly embarrassed.

"So you have known only a little while."

"I have suspected, yes. I did not want to say anything until I was sure." She swallowed again, against the sudden tightness in her throat. "I would wish this child to have a father when it is born, and that is why I beg you—"

He took her hand in his.

"It is all the more reason for things to be settled."

Nothing was happening as she had anticipated. Her lie was making Andrew more determined than ever to have this confrontation. She closed her eyes tightly against sudden tears.

"It upsets me terribly, Andrew. I will ask you one more time—"

"I think it is your condition that affects you, nothing more. I will come out of this unscathed, and you will be safe and able to have our baby in peace." She felt his fingers brush lightly

291

over her belly, caressing gently. "He will be born in September." A teasing note crept into his voice. "Unless you are still determined to give me a daughter."

She was dangerously close to tears. "Andrew—"

"Nothing will come of this discussion. I am more resolved then ever, now that I know I have a family to protect."

Gwyn almost wept as Andrew put his arms around her. He had always been possessive of her, but now she had given him even more reason.

"You won't come back," she whispered. "I know something is going to happen. Andrew, please—"

"Shhh." He ran his finger over her cheekbone, then smoothed back a wisp of her hair. "Don't be afraid. I'll never cause you pain, Gwyn. I promised you I would take care of you and any children we should have." He kissed her forehead. "How could I harm anyone so beautiful?"

Tears welled in her eyes, and she felt one begin to spill down her cheek. "Andrew, they conspire together. I know this—"

"Calm yourself."

She had to make him understand. "My heart and life are in your hands, m'lord. If something happens to you, it happens to me. I could not—"

"Nothing will happen. You have to sleep now, Gwyn. I won't have you overtired."

She turned her face into his bare shoulder, pressed her lips against his warm skin. She had thought of Andrew facing her cousin and the Duke ever since he had told her of their association. And she had known this moment was coming.

If they should hurt him . . . Her protests were useless. His mind was made up.

"When do you go?" Her voice was muffled.

"Tomorrow night."

"And is there nothing I can do to change your mind?"

His silence was her answer.

She thought him asleep until she felt his body shift. He lay on his side, facing her.

"I should like you to know, madam, you have done nothing but please me from the day I first saw you."

"Andrew," she whispered, her throat tight. She reached up and touched the hair on the back of his neck with her fingers.

He kissed her then, with such terrifying sweetness she felt tears start in her eyes again.

"You are better than any dream, my beauty." He pulled her tightly into his arms. "For you are flesh and blood and warmth, the woman I have always desired to have in my arms. That you will bear my child makes me cherish you all the more."

"Andrew, don't—"

"I will return and we will start anew. All the hateful things we said to each other exist no more. I care for you, Gwyn, more than I have ever cared for anyone in my life."

She knew what it cost him to confess such feelings.

"Kiss me, Andrew," she said, her voice low, her lips against his ear. "Love me." The only time thoughts of their future left her was when he made love to her, and she wanted him to lift all such thoughts out of her mind.

"Always," he said softly, and as his body shifted above hers, Gwyn slipped her arms around his neck and surrendered herself to his passion.

"Would you like to visit friends this afternoon?" the Duke inquired politely as he poured Lily another cup of breakfast tea.

"Oh, *non*, Richard. I am quite happy here with you." Lily reached for a piece of sweet bread as she cautiously studied the man across from her. Madeleine had been wrong. He had acted nothing but the gentleman from the time she had entered his house. He saw to her comfort, seemed to think her interesting—he asked her many questions—and had already given her several new gowns.

She did not love the Duke. But she was still determined someone should love her. And if any gentleman ever did, she

293

would devote the rest of her life to making him happy.

"Don't you have any friends in London?" he asked again.

"Only those at The Dark Stallion," she answered before daintily biting into her sweet bread. She had never worried overmuch about her manners at the brothel, but now she watched herself, determined to make sure the Duke never regretted asking her to share his home. She wanted him to be proud of her, like Andrew was of Gwyn.

"Whatever happened to that golden-haired friend of yours? I believe her name was Gwyneth."

He asks so many questions about her.

"She moved out. The Earl of Scarborough told me he was going to set her up in a house of her own." *That should impress him, that I am on speaking terms with such fine people.*

"And do you know where this house is? Perhaps I could drive you there one afternoon to visit with her."

"That would be very kind. Angel—Angelique will let me know where she is as soon as they are settled."

She was pleased by the satisfied expression in his grey eyes. How had Madeleine ever thought they were cold?

Lily missed her friends. There was no one in the Duke's house to talk to. Whenever she was overcome with loneliness, Lily would retire to her private bedroom and try on another gown, then style her hair several ways. She had escaped The Dark Stallion just in time. Her skin was firm, her breasts still high. She would smile at her reflection in the mirror, practice several expressions, apply more rouge and a dab of powder, and wonder if the Duke found her attractive.

He had not invited her to his bed yet. She would wake up in her private bedroom and sometimes hear voices, mostly masculine, late at night.

"Where are you going tonight?" she asked sweetly.

"Out to a club." He smiled, and she caught her breath at how handsome he could look. "Ladies are not welcome. I am afraid you will have to entertain yourself this evening."

"I do not mind."

"Perhaps we could go riding in my carriage tomorrow, and visit some of your friends."

She smiled, but her lips felt stiff. Back to Gwyn again. Why had he asked her to come to his house if all he ever wanted to talk about was another woman?

"Richard, you speak as if you wish she were here in this house instead of me. Do you find me unattractive?" And she smiled, one of the smiles she had practiced in her bedroom.

He reached across the table and caught her hand. "I'm sorry. I want you to be happy here, and you have seemed lonely."

His thoughtfulness touched her. Madeleine had loved him once, she was sure of it. The fact that she never spoke of him was clue enough. Madeleine had never spoken of him until Lily had decided to come to his house.

"I am not very lonely. But perhaps I could go out this afternoon? I would like to buy you a present."

He smiled again, then leaned back in his chair. The sunlight caught his silvery blond hair, and Lily found herself staring at him.

He reminds me of someone. Who?

"Anything you desire. I will have a carriage waiting for you this afternoon."

She wanted to jump up and kiss him but knew any display of affection on her part would not please him. He was a reserved man, and she sensed his deepest feelings boiled far below the surface.

"Thank you, Richard." There was time yet. He would come to love her. He had to.

"I know he won't be back."

"You can't think this way, Gwyn. He took Jack with him. The Duke can't possibly do anything with both of them there."

Gwyn paced the large sitting room restlessly. More than anything, she longed to run outside and try to find Andrew, to persuade him not to confront the Duke. But even as the thought entered her mind, she knew Thatch guarded the door downstairs and Andrew would be furious if she were out on the street without protection.

All she could do was wait.

"He will surprise you," Angel said, but Gwyn detected the false note of confidence in her voice. "He'll be back this evening with Jack and all your fears will be for nothing."

"Do you really think so?" Gwyn whirled on her friend, the primrose yellow of her silk skirts swirling.

Angel looked down at the carpet. "No." She walked over to Gwyn quickly and took both her hands. "But we have to have hope. Sit down and let me pour you a cup of tea."

And so she sat. And drank tea. And embroidered. And watched the sun slowly sink lower in the sky.

And quietly despaired of ever seeing Andrew again.

Henry could feel his anger rising as he studied the pile of bills. Andrew was spending a fortune on the whore. His wedding plans had come to a standstill.

Wearily, he took off his glasses and rubbed the bridge of his nose. There were many times he felt he had failed his grandson. Times when he looked in Andrew's face and saw Geoffrey all over again. His son had come to ruin over his lust for a woman, and now it seemed his grandson was traveling swiftly down a similar path.

He bought her a house.

While Andrew had more than enough money at his disposal and thank God had not developed a love of cards, it was plain to see this woman had him in her hand. He was clearly infatuated with her, and Henry was wise enough to know the nature of most whores. Cold and calculating, they used their sexual skills to weaken a man, always demanding more and more financially. A woman could swiftly work her way up through society on her back if she so desired.

And if she found a man who was foolish enough.

And she has, he admitted disgustedly, pushing the bills away from him. He had thought long and hard about how he could help his grandson.

You didn't interfere quickly enough with Geoffrey, and you have lived with that pain all your life. He had argued with his son much the same way he had argued with Andrew. But his words had come to nothing the day he had seen his boy dead. Everything had stopped for Henry at that moment. There wasn't a day that he didn't see his son's face in his mind's eye. Geoffrey, with his volatile temper and quick wit. Geoffrey, the last of his children after his other son and tiny daughter had died of the smallpox. Geoffrey, who had been the light of his life.

For a time he had tried to turn Andrew into Geoffrey. There were many similarities between father and son. Yet as Andrew had grown older, Henry had thought his grandson stronger than his son.

Now he was being proved wrong.

He glanced at the bills again, reached over, and picked them up. Staring at the stack of papers, he began to formulate a plan.

Perhaps she can be bought off. I've yet to meet a whore who doesn't prefer a large sum of money to any man. He set down the bills as his mind continued to work. This time he would not wait until something tragic happened. This time he would act.

He could not bear to lose Geoffrey's son.

The Duke was furious. Edward knew all the signs. The French whore was useless. She didn't know where Gwyn was, or if she did, she wasn't telling.

"She can't possibly be that smart," the Duke muttered as he gathered the cards and proceeded to shuffle them again.

He's getting impatient, Edward thought as he watched the fine-boned hands deftly handle the cards. The last thing he should have been doing was gambling, but he couldn't refuse the Duke. He was hopelessly in debt now, and the only way he could get back in the Duke's good graces was to help him obtain Gwyn. At first, for a time, he had hoped the man would tire of pursuing his cousin. But he didn't. There was something about Gwyn that ate away at the Duke and only increased his desire to possess her.

Edward was still staring at the cards when he felt the Duke grow suddenly still beside him. Looking up, he saw Andrew Hawkesworth, Earl of Scarborough, and a blond man enter the room. The buzz of conversation died down. All of London knew of the animosity the Duke bore the Earl ever since he had publicly humiliated him at Janet's auction. Now they watched, eager to see what would happen.

And Andrew didn't disappoint them. With no hesitation in his step, he made his way swiftly around the tables directly toward the Duke.

Edward jumped at the sound of the Duke's voice.

"There are many ways to play a game, Edward. But it always helps when one of the principal players is in attendance."

And then he smiled, but it didn't reach his cold, grey eyes.

Andrew could feel the Duke's gaze the minute he entered the private gambling club. He kept his pace measured, and even as he approached the Duke's table, Jack was close behind him.

Those grey eyes were chilling as he pulled out a chair and sat down across from the Duke.

"What brings you here, Lord Scarborough?" the Duke asked, his tone bored.

"You seem to have no hesitation concerning who you harm, Richard. I realize your private life is your own—until it infringes upon a certain woman who has my protection."

"The little bride," the Duke said, a sarcastic smile touching his lips. He turned toward a thin, blond man. "His concern touches my heart, Edward."

Sleaforth. "I know your part in this, Sleaforth." Andrew watched as the blond man jerked his head in his direction.

"Pray that I don't meet you in the street, Sleaforth. I would enjoy making you pay for what you did to your cousin."

"And what did he do that was so bad?" the Duke asked. "It seems the little whore now enjoys your . . . protection."

He could feel anger rising within him, filling his blood and clouding his mind. Conscious of what the Duke was trying to do, Andrew pushed his temper down.

"I give you fair warning, Richard. If you even come close to her, you will answer to me."

The Duke idly shuffled a deck of cards. "What, Andrew, you haven't tired of her yet? Aren't you to marry Lady Pevensy? Surely you don't need two whores at your disposal."

Keep your head. The Duke was baiting him, trying to draw him into a duel. He would not give the man the satisfaction.

"As your affairs are private, so are my own. I only came to tell you this. Stay away from Gwyneth Leighton if you value your life."

The Duke was smiling now, his grey eyes almost blazing. Andrew rose from the chair. He could not wait to leave this hellish place and return to Gwyn. The smells of smoke and cologne were making him sick. Or perhaps it was the company.

His head burst with pain. Stunned for only an instant, Andrew turned and grasped the arm of a beefy, ugly man. There was a short struggle, during which he saw the Duke looking on with a satisfied gleam in his eyes. Then more hands swarmed over him, pain engulfed him.

He struggled mightily as he slowly sank into darkness.

Gwyn sat up in bed with a start. Her heart was pounding as if it were about to come out of her chest, her body was chilled by a thin sheen of perspiration. She covered her face with trembling hands.

Andrew.

The room was dark. She swung her feet over the side of the bed and reached for her wrapper. Wishing she had wings and could escape the confines of her bedroom and go to him, she ran to the window and opened it. Frigid December wind cut through her wrapper as she leaned out the window and looked across the rooftops, silver in the light of a full moon.

Something has happened to him. With utter certainty, she knew he would not be coming back this night. Staring blindly out into the sleeping city, she didn't question the source of her feelings. Lips moving silently, she began to pray.

When Andrew woke, it was completely dark. A dull pain throbbed in his head, and it hurt to move.

His senses came back slowly. He was lying on something cold. Hard and cold. Stone. The chill seeped through his shirt and breeches. His feet were bare, and something was around both his ankles and his wrists. He tested his bonds, but they were secure.

The smell. The sour stench of unwashed bodies and human excrement mingled with damp stone and mold. And blood. His own, he realized dully. He could taste it in his mouth.

There was very little sound save for the rustle of straw and what he dimly recognized as the squeaking of rats. A low moan rose from somewhere, the sound so full of suffering Andrew felt the hair on the back of his neck rise.

Goose bumps ridged his arms, and his feet had little feeling in them. He flexed his fingers into fists and could barely move them. They were numb.

With horrifying certainty, he realized there was only one place in London this could possibly be. Newgate.

Voices. Louder as they came closer. He turned his head gingerly, and his eyes growing accustomed to the darkness made out a door. There was a small, barred window toward the top, and as the voices came closer, he thought he detected a faint light outside.

He heard the sound of a key in the lock, then the scraping of the heavy door as it slowly opened on protesting hinges. Andrew blinked his eyes against the light. He heard a scratching sound and realized rats were scurrying back into the far corners. A tall man was silhouetted in the doorway next to a shorter, pudgy man with a ring of keys in his hand.

Andrew forced the words out of his aching jaw. "I demand to know why I am here. What have I done? Who is my accuser?"

"Leave us," a raspy voice commanded, and Andrew swallowed back the blood in his mouth as he recognized the Duke.

The door closed again, but not before the pudgy man gave the Duke a lantern. He set it on the floor. The flickering light illuminated the Duke's face, giving it an otherworldly quality. At this moment, he could have been the devil himself.

The light gave Andrew new knowledge. He was on his stomach, spread-eagled on the floor. Glancing at his wrist, he saw the shackles.

"A pity you lost your temper and shot Lord Cowley," the Duke said softly. "And all over a misunderstanding with the cards."

It took a minute for the words to sink in. Then Andrew pulled furiously against the shackles, his anger evident in his silent struggle.

The Duke laughed. "You didn't even call him out. His father is an extremely powerful man, you realize. He insisted you be punished."

"You liar," Andrew said, speaking slowly and clearly. "I did not shoot him."

The Duke raised one eyebrow. "Then how is it he is near death at the surgeon's? Surely he did not inflict the wound on himself."

"You know the answer to that." He was fighting to maintain his temper.

"Do I?" The Duke began to walk slowly around his prone body, and Andrew felt his stomach tighten. He tensed all his

301

muscles as the Duke stopped at his feet.

"You have been extremely stubborn, Andrew." The tone of the man's voice made Andrew bite the inside of his mouth in frustration.

"You have also angered me," the voice continued. Andrew bit his lip as he felt the Duke's cane move until it was touching him most intimately. "You made a fool of me at The Dark Stallion over that golden-haired whore. I don't forget any man who makes me the fool."

Andrew closed his eyes and pulled strongly against the shackles chaining him to the stone floor. He could feel the rough metal cutting his skin, yet he continued to strain against his bonds.

"There is one possession you have that I desire above all other things. One thing you could give me that would ensure your freedom."

He knew who the Duke was referring to and did not answer. All he could think of was escaping and ultimately killing this man.

"You know I always meant to have her. If you had only given her to me that first night at The Dark Stallion, we might never have come to this . . . misunderstanding."

Still he refused to answer.

"Where is she, Andrew? Once you tell me, you have my word you will be released."

Andrew remained silent, biting the inside of his mouth until he tasted blood.

"What, still protecting the little whore? She must be quite something in bed for you to be so loyal."

He hated hearing the Duke talk of Gwyn. Andrew began to pull against the shackles once again.

"Would that she were as loyal to you."

He continued to struggle, wanting to block that sick, seductive voice from his mind for all time.

"What is it you called her? My beauty, I believe."

Andrew slumped to the floor, exhausted. He could feel the

302

Duke, now rubbing his back. He didn't have the strength to move.

"You liked to watch her bathe. The gold brocade gown was your favorite. You taught her to play cards, and you disliked it when she called you 'm'lord' instead of Andrew."

He was perfectly still now as his dazed mind attempted to put some kind of order to his confused thoughts.

"Don't you wonder how I know this?" The Duke laughed again. "It's quite a little game they play, Edward and Gwyn. You weren't the first, and I daresay you won't be the last. Did she have you convinced she was a virgin? That's quite a good trick but easy enough to manage with a pig's bladder and some blood."

The tightness in his stomach was growing.

"What, Andrew, did she actually have you convinced Edward is her cousin? She's quite the little actress."

"You're lying," Andrew said, his voice low with anger.

"And you're going to keep her whereabouts secret from me after she betrayed you? Come, Andrew, why so noble? This time Gwyn became greedy. She wanted all the money, and Edward couldn't have that. The little slut played you out perfectly, making herself all the more desirable by refusing to become your mistress, did she not?"

The numbness in his hands and feet had been nothing compared to what was now gripping his body. Andrew was exhausted enough to begin to doubt. How could the Duke know of such private things, events that had transpired behind closed doors?

Unless Gwyn had told Edward. And Edward had told the Duke.

"Tell me, Andrew. Tell me where she is. And I will see to your release, even if young Lord Cowley should die."

Andrew remained silent, but his mind was racing. He kept remembering details of his last night with Gwyn. She was going to have his child. Had that been a lie as well?

"I will kill both of you eventually. It's just a matter of who I get first. I would think you would be eager to give her over to me, now that you know she betrayed you. You cannot trust a woman."

His thoughts were spiraling crazily out of control. *She couldn't have betrayed me. She carries my child . . .*

His head throbbed painfully, and he tried to think. He remembered his last moments with Gwyn, then riding to the gambling hell with Jack. . . .

"Jack," Andrew said quietly. "Where is Jack?"

The Duke laughed. "Your friend is safe. He was . . . injured. Not badly. Just enough to keep him off his feet for a few days."

"Now where is she?"

Andrew remained silent. And he knew the Duke was perfectly capable of forcing any manner of degradation upon him.

The fingers tightened, and he closed his eyes against the pain.

"Tell me where she is."

Still, he remained silent. He could not believe Gwyn was capable of betraying him. Once the Duke found her, it would be a matter of days before he took her life. He had heard too many whispered stories about the man's twisted appetites and his hatred of women. He couldn't betray Gwyn and give her life over to this monster.

The Duke rose. "I shall give you until morning to think about the bitch's betrayal. If you do not tell me where she is, you know what to expect. Think carefully, Andrew, and don't believe for an instant the little slut cares for you."

He swallowed against the rawness in his throat. "Unchain me and let it be a fair fight. This is the only way you could ever win, and you know it."

There was a moment of silence, then the Duke replied. "The shackles are merely a temporary measure. For your protection, of course. In case you might attempt something quite foolish."

"You bastard," Andrew whispered.

He closed his eyes as the cell door shut. As he heard the

Duke's steps fade, Andrew closed his eyes and slipped into blessed unconsciousness.

Henry opened his eyes and gazed sleepily into his valet's anxious face. The older man was shaking his shoulder quite urgently.

"M'lord, it's Master Andrew. Something has happened."

All tiredness vanished. Henry left his large bed swiftly, belted a dressing gown around his spare waist, and looked for his slippers. He followed his valet down the stairs to the library.

The sight that greeted his eyes was terrifying. Jack was lying on the sofa. His lip was split, his face discolored with purplish bruises. As he tried to ease himself into a sitting position, wincing as he did, Henry swallowed his fear.

Where was Andrew?

"The Duke," Jack said slowly. "Cuckfield has taken Andrew. I don't know where he is. We went to one of his gambling establishments. Words were exchanged. I don't know what happened. Henry, someone hit me over the head, and when I woke I was in an alley."

Henry turned to his valet. "Get Jack something to drink." He turned back to the man he had known since he was a young boy. He had always been quite fond of Jack.

"What the devil were the two of you doing tangling with Cuckfield?"

Jack took a slow, agonized breath. "It was Gwyn. Andrew wanted to settle things with her cousin and the Duke. You see, Edward Sleaforth—"

"I don't want to hear another word about that whore."

The valet returned, and Jack accepted the glass of spirits. He swallowed some of it, coughed, then swallowed the rest. Setting the glass down, he said, "It wasn't Gwyn's fault. She didn't want him to go. . . ."

"Not another word! I'm going to see her as soon as I find out where my grandson is. It's one thing for Andrew to recklessly spend his time and money, quite another for him to risk his life with a man like Cuckfield."

Jack spoke slowly, his lip obviously giving him discomfort. "I heard one of the men at the table mention Newgate. Could the Duke—"

"That man is capable of anything. You stay here, Jack. I have to find my grandson."

"You won't be able to keep me from going with you." As Henry gave him his most ferocious scowl, Jack replied, "You won't discourage me easily, Henry, and we don't have time to waste. I suggest you just give in."

The depth of Jack's friendship moved Henry, though he would have been loathe to admit it. "All right, then. Come along; we've got to find him."

Chapter Nineteen

Gwyn hadn't slept during the night, and now her fingers trembled as she tried once again to create a Christmas wreath. She and Angel had already looped the staircase with dark green holly and its bright red berries. She had asked Andrew if she might decorate the house for Christmas. It had been one of her favorite duties living with her father. And Christmas had always been her best-loved holiday.

She wanted the tables to groan with all kinds of holiday foods, and she and Angel had placed white Christmas candles everywhere. Each picture in every room was adorned with greenery, and she and Angel had sat in the parlor and stuck cloves in lemons and oranges, then arranged them in great silver bowls. She had wanted this holiday to be special for Andrew. Mistress or wife, lover or helpmate, Gwyn wanted to share a sense of creating a home with the man she loved.

She knew Andrew didn't have happy memories of the holidays. Now, trying to keep her hands busy and her mind occupied with anything but the fear that had overcome her the previous night, she sat on the floor and worked feverishly, twisting the laurel with cold, suddenly clumsy fingers.

She glanced up as Angel entered the parlor, her cheeks and nose bright pink. It had begun to snow lightly outside, and soft white flakes were quickly melting on her friend's blue wool shawl. Angel set the large basket down on the floor, then began to unwind her shawl.

"I found everything." She gave Gwyn the faintest of smiles as she began to tick her purchases off on her mittened fingers. "Pears and apples, and the nuts you wanted. More candles. Thatch is bringing up the Yule log. The parlor is cold, Gwyn. Have you let the fire go out?"

Gwyn glanced at the fireplace. She had been so intent on making her wreath that she hadn't noticed the cold. Anything to keep fear at bay.

Why hadn't Andrew come back? What had happened last night?

"Did you hear—"

"No." Angel sat down on the sofa and pulled off her mittens. "I sent a message to Madeleine and met her at the fruit stalls. She hasn't heard a thing. She's tried to see Lily but hasn't been able to." Angel arranged her dark grey wool skirt with an angry jerk of her hands. "A fine Christmas this is turning out to be."

"No one knows where Andrew is?"

"No. I tried to find Jack, but he was out. I will try again tonight."

"You cannot keep running like this. Let me get you some tea. I baked scones this morning, I think there are still a few if Thatch hasn't found them."

Gwyn started to get up off the floor when the door flew open. The movement was so sudden she fell back against the floor. A tall, silver-haired man strode in the door, followed by Jack. She heard Angel catch her breath, then understood as she saw the discoloration and bruises on the younger man's face.

"Andrew?" she asked softly, fearful of hearing the answer.

"Andrew is fine," the older man said gruffly. "He has asked me to come and escort you to a place where you will be safe."

Henry had been prepared to face the whore who had almost cost him his grandson. He would never, for the rest of his life, forget the sight of Andrew chained to the prison floor, his face as badly bruised as Jack's. After a large sum of money changed hands, Henry managed to have his grandson's shackles removed. Several warm blankets and a plate of solid food had been provided. He had barely had time to make sure his grandson was warm and well fed before he resolved to get that whore out of his life forever.

He had been prepared for a handsome woman, since the rumors flying around London had proclaimed Andrew's bordello bride was quite the beauty. But he had not anticipated seeing a face from his past, flawlessly recreated.

She looks like Beth. He had burst in the door to see a woman, dressed in palest pink, surrounded by greenery. Her silk skirts billowed out over the carpet, her blond hair hung down her back in a riot of curls.

But her face. Oval, with beautiful bones. Large, deep blue eyes. Her chin possessed a stubborn line, her brows were dark, her lashes lush. Her nose was straight and delicate. Her lips were perfectly shaped if a trifle full, and parted slightly as she looked up at him. To his astonishment and secret chagrin, Henry could understand how Andrew had lost his head in a single night.

Yes, that face is worth one thousand pounds. And every single bill on my desk.

If her face was exquisite, her body promised paradise. Delicate bones, a slender shape with full breasts and a gentle swell of hips. Small hands and feet. And that hair! It was glorious, golden-blond and thick, caught up in a pink ribbon and cascading lushly down her back to her waist. He had heard the gossip that she had been wrapped in a length of white silk as she had stood in front of the men at The Dark Stallion. Only now, looking at her, did Henry finally understand what had astounded everyone in London.

She could bewitch a man until he was no longer responsible for what he did. But what was behind that seemingly innocent face? Was she aware of the primal, feminine power she held over his grandson? Did she abuse it? Had she truly discouraged him from confronting the Duke, as Jack claimed?

She is more trouble than I ever dreamed. I fear I have intervened barely in time. Maura had been heartbreakingly beautiful. And in the end, he had lost his son. Henry distrusted beauty on this scale, as he knew from painful experience it brought nothing but tragedy.

And yet . . . As he studied her, the years seemed to fall away and he was a young man, gazing into Beth's face all over again.

How could this be? Perhaps an illegitimate child no one knew about. Jack had prattled some nonsense about her being the daughter of a vicar, but he had snorted disgustedly. A vicar's daughter at The Dark Stallion? A vicar's daughter who had managed to send his only grandson to Newgate? Impossible!

Yet he was moved by her beauty, moved in a way he hadn't been for many years. Memories assailed him, painful remembrances of decisions he should have made but for lack of courage. His father and mother had not approved of Beth, and he had wanted to please them. He had let her go, straight into the arms of another man. Over the years, he had married and continued on with his life. But a secret part of his heart had remained within that first, powerful love. Sometimes, late at night, he wondered what had become of her.

That this woman should look so much like his lost love deeply shook him. But only for the space of a minute. Then he remembered his grandson in prison and knew his decision had been the right one. He would leave Andrew in Newgate until he managed to transport this little opportunist far away from London. He would hide her where Andrew would never find her again.

Henry had had no doubts that if he had taken Andrew out of Newgate, his grandson would have walked through hell to make his way back to this woman. So he had bought Andrew protection within the corruption of the prison and had also brought in some of his own trusted men. Andrew would be safe

310

there, tucked away until he could rid him of this whore.

She stood, and he noticed a natural grace to her movements.

"You must be Andrew's grandfather. He has told me so very much about you."

Henry was determined not to fall beneath the same spell as his grandson. Yet he could see how Andrew would have been bewitched. He had not been in the presence of such beauty since he was a young man. That incandescent physical presence, combined with such grace and a gentle voice, could have guaranteed almost any young man's undoing.

"Yes, I am. Now we must move quickly and leave this place. It is no longer safe for you here." More than anything, he wanted her out of London.

"Is Andrew—"

"I will inform you of my grandson's condition once we are on the road. Madam, we do not have a moment to spare if we are to start today."

Knowing that Andrew trusted and loved his grandfather, Gwyn nodded her head. "I will certainly do what you think best." She glanced at Angel, and her friend nodded her head as well.

"Pack your things, then," Henry said gruffly. "We will leave within the hour."

The Duke walked with measured steps down the narrow corridor. It was only a matter of time before Andrew revealed the slut's whereabouts. If forcing him sexually didn't yield an answer, he knew several exquisite methods of torture that were guaranteed to loosen the lips of a statue.

He had no doubts he would have his answer within days. And he would have Gwyn all to himself.

He was frustrated, therefore, to be stopped before he reached Andrew's cell.

"Sorry, guv'nor, no one goes beyond this point." The man was enormous, his reddish hair and beard shaggy. He spoke with a peculiar inflection, and the Duke realized it was because he was missing several teeth.

"I'm sure you are mistaken. I was here the night before. There is a particular prisoner I need to speak with." He slipped several coins out of his waistcoat pocket and gave them to the man blocking his way.

The ruffian quickly pocketed them. "That was the night before. Things change, you know wot I mean?" He grinned, and the Duke was disgusted by the oaf's display of rotting gums.

"Let me past, man, or I will make you sorry—"

"Let him come." The voice that floated out into the corridor belonged to Andrew. The Duke snapped his head around. His eyes narrowed as he viewed Andrew's face at the small window in the door to his cell.

"I think the odds are better now, don't you?" Andrew asked softly. "I should like to see the outcome, with both of us on our feet. I can assure you, only one of us will leave this hellish place alive."

The Duke stood perfectly still, staring at Andrew. "How did you remove those shackles?" he asked finally.

"As you said the night before, I desire to attempt something foolish. Though I believe the murder of a man is never something one should take lightly."

"You would murder me?" he asked, his voice contemptuous.

"As easily as I draw breath."

"And you are sure you would be successful?"

"After last night, I have no doubts."

The Duke hesitated for the briefest of seconds.

"Are you afraid, now that I'm not chained? Is that how you like to fight all the time?" Andrew grinned suddenly, and the Duke ground his teeth in silent rage. The arrogant bastard! He wanted nothing more at the moment than to break Andrew to his will, make him suffer and cry out in agony.

"I was under the impression your fights were unfair. Could I

312

have been mistaken?"

"You know nothing about killing men. You talk of what you do not know," the Duke said, dismissing him. He was not going to go into that cell now. From everything he had heard about Andrew, the man was a formidable fighter.

"Then how did I manage to murder Lord Cowley? I have been told he died this morning. I would think that would be a fairly impressive record."

The Duke was silent, regretting his slip. He had been fascinated with Andrew for years. His power, his passion, the life burning furiously in his intense blue eyes. *I should have taken him last night, when I had the chance* . . . But his mind had been clouded with thoughts of the whore.

"Know this, Lord Cuckfield." Now all traces of amusement were wiped from Andrew's face, and in their place was a hatred so intense the Duke instinctively stepped back. "For what transpired between us in this cell last night, you have effectively signed your own death warrant."

"Not if I see you dance on air at Tyburn," the Duke replied. But he was deeply shaken. He had never seen such hatred in a man's eyes. Andrew was burning with it; it blazed out from his face with such intensity he could almost feel the heat of his anger. But he held his ground.

"Even you don't possess that kind of power."

"Brave words from a man behind bars," the Duke said, mocking him.

"Then come inside, and let us both see how brave we are."

"Are you suggesting a duel? In that room?" He tried to make his voice sound condescendingly amused.

"I am suggesting no weapons at all."

When the Duke did not answer, Andrew continued. "I had a dream last night. I killed you with my bare hands. Come inside, Lord Cuckfield, and let me make my dream reality."

"You know not of what you speak. I am growing tired of this conversation." The Duke looked away from Andrew, and straight into the face of the jailer. His toothless mouth was

313

wide open, his pale eyes fascinated. The Duke glanced back toward Andrew.

"There was another man," Andrew said softly. "I hated him almost as much as I now hate you. I would have killed him, given the chance."

"Then why didn't you?" the Duke challenged.

"My mother did."

The Duke felt himself flinch slightly, then cursed himself for displaying any weakness.

"I am the bastard son of a murderess. Or have you forgotten? It runs in my blood, as deeply as depravity does in yours."

"Watch your tongue."

"You'll never have her. You'll never find her." Andrew smiled suddenly. "And I know you want her because you hope she'll make a man of you where every other woman failed."

"*Damn you!*" The Duke advanced swiftly, but Andrew did not back away when he slammed his palms against the closed door.

"That's good. I want you angry. I want you angry enough to come inside." Andrew backed away from the door, then called out to the jailer. "Let him in. We're both ready now."

"No." The Duke hated himself for refusing Andrew's challenge. But a deep instinct told him the younger man would win this round. He had to catch him unawares, then finish him.

As always, the odds of any game had to be more in his favor.

Now his hatred was fueled, fueled by the way Andrew had mocked him. He would find the whore; he would have her. He would kill her first, then watch Andrew die. But Lord Scarborough would not go to his grave without knowing another man had possessed the woman he loved.

"No? Are you afraid? You weren't afraid last night; but then I suppose it is different when one of the players in the game is in bondage."

"Not yet," the Duke said softly as he backed away from the cell door. He was breathing heavily, the foul scented air

314

seemed to burn inside his lungs.

"Not yet, Lord Scarborough. But very soon."

Gwyn walked quietly through the barren rose garden. It had snowed the night before, and she was bundled snugly against the chill winter air. She had spent the morning outside watching the horses run, their tails held high, their breath flowing from their nostrils like spirals of smoke. And she had wished, as she watched the graceful animals, that she could have run with them. Anything was preferable to this endless waiting.

There was a fine tension building inside her. She couldn't stay inside, couldn't simply sit in the parlor next to the fire and concentrate on her embroidery. Ever since Andrew's grandfather had taken her to his country estate, she had felt something was very wrong.

Henry had assured her Andrew was safe before he had returned to London. Andrew had been beaten, like Jack, and Henry wanted him to have the finest surgeons available. As they were found in London, that was where Andrew was to remain. She was to stay in the country, at Andrew's request. It was all a measure of safety. Everything revolved around her protection.

She glanced up at the house, starkly outlined against the grey winter sky. Scarborough Hall, Henry had told her with obvious pride, had been built soon after the Wars of the Roses. Henry VII had been a visitor, as had several other English kings. There had been something in his tone, she was sure, designed to put her in her place. He seemed to be deliberately pointing out the vast differences between her background and Andrew's. She wondered, as she walked, why he should find this necessary. Henry must know he held the upper hand.

Since first seeing Scarborough Hall, Andrew's birthright, she had become totally resigned to playing a peripheral part in his life. She could never be anything more than his mistress.

But that didn't mean she couldn't always love him.

Scarborough Hall was intimidating to Gwyn, who was used to the home she had shared with her father. Her feet had felt cold against the Italian marble in the great hallway, even in snug woolen stockings and sturdy shoes. She had gazed up all of two stories and seen the family coat-of-arms.

Her bedroom was four times the size of the one she had at The Dark Stallion. The bed curtains were a rich red, the walls lined in matching silk. The fireplace was marble, all the furniture smooth and gleaming. Her first night, she had lain in the enormous bed, the heavy counterpane pulled up beneath her chin, and listened to the mournful winter wind outside.

She hadn't slept at all.

Andrew. Thoughts of him were her constant companion, and Gwyn wrapped her cloak more tightly around her against the wind as she continued toward the house. She walked through the rose garden every day, wondering what it would look like with a profusion of blooms. She loved to garden, but where Cook had been eager to let her help with the chores needed to maintain a garden in winter, here her suggestion that she might help was frowned upon.

She would not ask again.

Christmas passed. Her days were long. She never slept well alone in the big bed; she tossed and turned and thought of Andrew. She had written him two letters, addressed to his grandfather's London home. She had held at bay all her fears and doubts, simply asking him how he was feeling and telling him she hoped he would be healed soon.

And she remembered the last night she had seen him and how he had told her he cared for her above all others. She held that night to her heart, and it warmed her despite the chilling winter wind and the vast coldness of this estate.

She wasn't completely certain what she and Angel were to do. Henry had told her she could remain a guest in his home as long as was absolutely necessary. But Gwyn was determined to stay. She knew Andrew would come for her or at least send

316

some message. It was a quiet sort of agony, loving him and not being near him.

Now she was free to take long walks and breathe deeply of the clean country air. Now she answered to no one, did as she pleased, planned her days with complete freedom. When she remembered her confinement at The Dark Stallion and later her short stay at Andrew's private house, her time in London seemed like a dream.

She thought of how she had been frustrated, held in captivity. And she knew she would accept it all over again and suffer even more if only she would be assured of hearing his footsteps in the hallway.

And of having his face be the last thing she saw before she closed her eyes and slept.

Her attention was caught by a flash of red, and Gwyn smiled and waved as she recognized Angel at an upstairs window. Her friend was motioning her to come quickly. Gwyn wrapped her cloak more tightly around her as the wind whipped it wildly, and she quickened her step.

Once inside the great house, Angel met her in the hall.

"There is a guest coming tonight. An old friend of Henry's. Her name is Lady Caroline Pipkin, and she has known Andrew since he was a child. Do we have time to go over my table manners again?"

"As many times as you wish." Angel had been astounded when Gwyn had given her several of her gowns. They had spent many hours taking them in, fixing the hems, making sure they fit Angel perfectly.

"For you are no longer my maid. You are a woman in your own right now and must have all the things that entails."

"And I must learn how to eat my soup without spilling it!"

Gwyn squeezed her arm. "You have learned everything I have taught you quickly; I have no doubt you will be quite accomplished tonight."

*   *   *

Andrew gazed at his grandfather, the set of his jaw mutinous.

"And so I'm to stay in this cell until I promise you I will never see Gwyn again? You're mad, old man." He knew the words were cruel, but he could not believe his grandfather was being this stubborn.

"What happened to your marriage? You were to wed Belinda after Christmas, and none of the necessary preparations have been made! Are you planning on making that little whore your wife?"

"Her name is Gwyn."

"She can be Helen of Troy for all I am concerned! Your conduct in this matter has been unforgivable. If you would think with your head instead of what's inside your breeches, I wouldn't be forced to discipline you this way!"

"There was a time you didn't want me to marry Belinda."

"There was a time I didn't realize how bad things could become! Good God, Andrew, you are the last of my family. . . ."

"*Damn* this family!" Andrew was pacing the small confines of his cell, restless and completely frustrated. "And *damn you* for doing this to me! I cannot understand how you can be worried about what I do. There is no scandal I could be a part of that could possibly equal what my father—"

Henry's arm arched up, and Andrew felt the sharp crack of his fingers against his cheekbone. He did not move, did not touch his face. He simply looked at his grandfather steadily until the older man looked away.

"Grandfather, I am not—"

"She is out of your life, as you are out of hers. You are infatuated with her beauty, Andrew, and she plays you for the fool. I have removed her from that house you purchased."

"*You did what!*"

"And you are not to see her again. She is a dangerous woman; the Duke is obsessed with her. What do you know of her, after all? If you had left her in The Dark Stallion, if you had not made her exclusively yours, perhaps I could have seen—"

"You had mistresses constantly throughout your marriage. You were never happy with Grandmother. Are you asking me to consign myself to the same miserable fate?"

"I am asking you to do what you know is your duty."

Andrew remained silent, and after a time his grandfather continued, his voice softer. "She is nothing, Andrew. You will look back on this time when you are older and recognize your feelings for exactly what they are. Infatuation. Lust. She is beautiful, I grant you that, but she is nothing."

"She is everything. Everything I have ever wanted in my life. If she agrees to remain my mistress and I marry a woman you deem suitable, then why should Gwyn not have a place in my life?"

"You care for the girl too deeply. You have already made a laughingstock of this family by your performance at The Dark Stallion."

"If she has a hold on me, you can be sure every other man in London wishes those hands were holding him instead!"

"Andrew, I am not asking you. I am telling—"

He looked his grandfather directly in the eye. "She carries my child." He could see Henry visibly pale. As Andrew continued to speak, he enunciated each word slowly and carefully, consciously attempting to keep his temper in check.

"I will not abandon her. And I will rot in this cell until I can figure out a way of escaping if that is what you want. You never understood my father, and you do not understand me now. I wonder, Grandfather, if there was ever a woman in your past? Did you do your *duty* by the family?"

"You are not too old to horsewhip—"

"Do you still think of her at night, alone in your bed? Do you wonder where she is, who she sleeps with? Do you curse yourself every night in the darkness for having given her up, all in the name of *duty*?" Andrew raked his fingers through his hair, then turned abruptly away from his grandfather. "You

319

can ask anything else of me, but I am not giving her up. When I escape this place—and I will—I will search for her until I find her. I will be with her when our child is born. And if you make things difficult, I shall scandalize you further and take her as my wife!"

His grandfather wearily put his hand over his eyes. His shoulders slumped, and suddenly he looked old, every one of his years. Andrew quelled the urge to go to his side and put his arm around his shoulders. He could not give up Gwyn. His grandfather could ask for anything, but not that.

"Do you think I do not love you, Andrew?" Henry's voice was so soft he barely heard it. "Do you honestly believe I wish to see you hurt? You and Geoffrey alone are within my heart. I cannot sit back and see you make the same mistake your father made!"

"But Gwyn is no other man's wife."

"She is as good as wed to the Duke. He will not rest until he finds her. That means you will have to face him one day."

"And I look forward to that prospect."

Henry lowered his hand, shook his head. "He will kill you. And all for a girl who doesn't care about you."

"Gwyn is responsible for any goodness in me, Grandfather. When I am with her, I feel at peace. I have never felt that way around any other woman. And she is no whore. She has only known my touch."

"Even if this were true, the Duke—"

"There is a personal matter between us. It will be settled in time."

"First love doesn't last, Andrew. Life continues; we do what is expected of us. That is what endures. The years go on; you will remember this girl with fondness. . . ."

"Fond is hardly the word to describe what I feel for her." Andrew moved toward his grandfather now, knowing he was weakening slightly. He embraced him tightly, then stepped back, his hands clasping the older man's shoulders. Funny how Henry looked so small now that he was looking down at him.

"You tell me duty is the only thing that endures. I would have thought the same until only weeks ago." He kissed his grandfather's cheek, knowing Henry both loathed and loved the gesture. "What I feel for her," he whispered, "will endure."

"Andrew, I am afraid for you. When the heart loves too much—"

He smiled down at his grandfather. "You are going to have a great-grandchild."

"Listen to me. A man must keep his head three times in his life. In battle, in sports, and in love. You can be angry or passionate, but in cold blood. You are too full of emotion, Andrew, and I am afraid—"

"I will remain here if that is what you wish. But you cannot make me give her up. She will never be cut out of my heart, and I will always be a part of hers. Do not ask me to grant you this one wish. It is impossible."

Henry sighed, then turned away from his grandson. "I see Geoffrey in your face all over again."

Andrew caught his grandfather's hand. As Henry slowly faced him, he placed the older man's hand against his cheek.

"I am not my father. You have no need to worry."

Dinner was a complete nightmare. Lady Caroline Pipkin stared at Gwyn intently throughout the meal. She spilled her duck soup down the front of her gown and had to retire to her bedroom to change. Later, over an elaborate florendine of oranges and apples, Gwyn was unable to meet the older woman's eyes.

Lady Pipkin was an angular woman. Tall, all long legs and knobby elbows, she looked out at the world through a pair of glasses that perched precariously on the end of her long nose. Her hair was a soft grey, and it was only her eyes that gave her face any pretense of beauty. They were the deepest blue.

And they were avidly focused on Gwyn.

Later, they retired to the parlor. The fire crackled and hissed, and Gwyn was constantly on edge, aware of the woman's continual scrutiny. She was afraid, afraid Lady Pipkin somehow had connected her with The Dark Stallion. The story Henry had insisted they concoct to explain her presence in his home was that she was a distant country cousin. He had gone over this fabrication several times with Gwyn until her answers were smooth and came quickly to her tongue. Now she was no longer a vicar's daughter but one of a large family that lived north of London. Her father had small landholdings, and she had been married once before and now was most recently widowed.

"You look very young. How sad that you should lose your husband while still merely a child yourself," Lady Pipkin said quietly. She was knitting a shawl and did not have to look at her handiwork. Her eyes were fastened on Gwyn.

Gwyn could feel her palms beginning to sweat. Her needle pierced the linen and flew quickly as she worked. "I am eighteen years old, madam. I hardly consider myself a child."

Something in the older woman's eyes worried her. The slightest gleam of recognition. Gwyn shifted on the sofa and tried to concentrate on her embroidery.

Lady Pipkin continued the conversation, her voice smooth, almost bland. "I am quite sure I remember you. Your face is distinctive; I would not have forgotten it. Tell me, Gwyneth, have you ever been to London?"

Her needle slipped, and she pierced her finger. Gwyn stared down at the bright drop of blood as it welled up and resisted the urge to put her finger in her mouth. Instead, she sat back from the embroidery frame and kept her attention on the older woman.

"I have never been to the city," she said quietly, hating the lie as it left her mouth. "My family resides some distance north of London, and my father believed the city was not the best place for any of the women in his family."

She could feel Angel's tension. Her friend sat next to her,

mending a dress. The room was too warm, and Gwyn could feel beads of sweat gathering between her breasts. Did this woman know she had resided at The Dark Stallion? Why did Lady Caroline stare at her so pointedly? It seemed she was trying to find the answer to a puzzle within her face.

"How long do you intend to stay with us?" Angel asked, and Gwyn knew her friend was making an attempt to change the subject. "From the way you spoke of London, it seems you miss the city."

"I do." Lady Pipkin's knitting needles moved smoothly, forming stitch after stitch and row after row as the shawl took form. "I cannot understand how anyone could willfully bury themselves in the country all their life. Your father is mistaken, Gwyneth. London is quite the place for a woman. You have the face of an angel, my dear, and should be dressed in ermines, satins, and brocades. You would create quite a stir, parading along Pall Mall or St. James Street. 'Tis a pity you are shut away here. Plenty of time for that once you reach my age."

Wanting the direction of this conversation to cease, Gwyn replied quietly, "Having just lost my husband, madam, parading about London is the farthest thing from my mind." She stood up, resisting the urge to bolt from the room. "If you will excuse me, I find that my walk this afternoon tired me more than I thought. I wish to retire for the evening."

"It has been a pleasure talking with you, Gwyneth, and I shall see you in the morning. Perhaps I might walk with you?" Lady Pipkin smiled up at her.

Gwyn nodded slowly, wondering how much the woman knew—and when she would reveal her knowledge.

Henry held the letter in his hand as he stared into the fire. The handwriting was delicate, feminine, quite precise. Gwyneth Leighton was full of surprises. Andrew had informed him that the woman could read. Two letters had arrived at his

323

house over the last few weeks, evidence that she could also write. And very well.

A vicar's daughter. Her father taught her. What man would waste the time and energy to teach his daughter such advanced skills? Had she known enough to simply record a list of figures or confined her reading to her bible, he would not have been as surprised. But the letters had been eloquent. Emotional below the surface information they imparted. He had burned the first without a qualm. The last had touched him so deeply he had actually considered delivering it to his grandson.

You are becoming soft in your dotage. Without giving the matter another thought, he tossed the second letter into the flames and watched as the paper blackened and curled.

Lady Caroline Pipkin stared at the letter on the table next to her bed. She had just sealed it and tomorrow would send it to her sister in London.

And when she comes here and sees Gwyneth . . . Caroline prided herself on never forgetting a face. In her wildest imaginings she'd never believed she would see that face again. When Gwyn had first been introduced to her, she had felt a fierce surge of elation.

She had survived, after all.

But caution was necessary in times such as these, for the girl's life was still in danger. How long would it be before others recognized her? Her sister Beth would have to come quickly. She was the wiser and knew more of the situation.

Can you be sure she is who you believe her to be? But it was impossible she could be wrong. She looked exactly like . . . Caroline closed her eyes against the sharp pain. She would never forget the day she had learned of Barbara's murder.

And she had sworn she would avenge her.

I must to gain Gwyneth's trust. I was a fool tonight, staring at her so openly. The girl was nervous. Understandable, as she knows nothing. But that was always for her own protection.

She glanced at the letter again and for an instant longed for her sister Beth. *Would that she were here, right now. Oh, I am simply an old woman and I bungle things so badly.*

Caroline lay back down in her bed and stared at the dark blue canopy above. How strange life was. She had nearly passed Scarborough Hall on her way to London. She had never forgiven Henry for his callous treatment of her sister's heart but, lover of gossip that she was, she had hoped to find him here and see how he was faring. Caroline had never given up hope that one day Henry and Beth would be reunited. When her sister's husband had died almost two years ago, she had decided to try to play matchmaker.

But now she had found someone much more important.

She closed her eyes, then took a deep breath and tried to still her racing heart.

Come quickly, Beth. I fear we do not have much time.

Andrew opened his eyes when he heard the sound of footsteps in the corridor. He had to find a way to convince his grandfather to release him. Escape was much harder than he had thought. He was no Jack Sheppard, after all. He walked slowly over to the window in his door, scratching his arm idly as he walked. The angry red flea bites itched, and though scratching made them worse, he found he couldn't help himself. Why no one had thought of supplying Newgate with several cats to control the rats was beyond his comprehension.

His head ached, as did his arms and legs. He was an active man, and forced confinement of any kind weighed heavily upon his soul. He hadn't seen the sun in almost a month and was beginning to feel quite poorly.

He was not at all prepared for the sight of Belinda's face.

"Andrew! The gossip was true!" She pressed her face up to the small window, a scented handkerchief held against her nose and mouth. That same nose wrinkled in disgust as she surveyed his tiny domain.

He stared at her, suddenly revolted as he realized this was exciting to her. She was like a little girl on her way to a fair, anticipating all sorts of entertainment.

"I could not come alone, so I brought my friend Charlotte. She has never seen the inside of a prison. . . ."

He listened to her prattle for several minutes and wasn't surprised when she decided to leave shortly thereafter. As her footsteps faded away, Andrew wondered how he could have ever considered the woman as a life's partner.

Even in a marriage of convenience.

He sat back down on the pile of straw covered by a blanket. Seeing Belinda had robbed him of all energy.

But Jack had promised to come today. Perhaps he will have news.

Closing his eyes, he thought of Gwyn.

"You cannot keep him there, Henry! I saw him this afternoon and he does not look good!" Jack paced the library angrily. It was rare for him to confront Henry, but he had been shocked by Andrew's pallor and listlessness. His friend was one of the most vital men he knew, and it broke his heart to see him sitting in a cell at Newgate like some common criminal.

"He will go to her."

"He will die if you keep him there."

"You are too emotional on this subject, Jack. Surely—"

"That bastard stepfather of his used to lock him in a small room regularly. Did he ever tell you that, Henry? Do you know how much he hates to be confined?"

"He will not promise to stay away from the whore. He endangers his life every time he consorts with her. The next time the Duke will not let him off as lightly."

"Open your eyes, old man! You cannot tell him how to lead his life."

"That is enough, Jack. You have overstayed your welcome."

Outside, Jack mounted his bay mare but did not turn her

in the direction of his home.

Well, then, there's nothing else for it.

If he left London today, he could be at Scarborough Hall by nightfall.

If Henry would not let Andrew go to Gwyn, he would bring Gwyn to Andrew. He had to do something to bring some vitality back to his friend's face. Andrew would never admit what this confinement was doing to him, never back down from his grandfather's ultimatum. But Jack knew his friend.

Something terrible was happening to Andrew. And it had to be stopped.

Gwyn was walking by the lake at dusk when she saw the lone rider on a bay mare break away from the copse of oaks and chestnuts. She narrowed her eyes. There was something about him, the way the weak winter sunlight glinted off his light hair.

Jack. Dear God, Andrew.

And she began to run.

Chapter Twenty

Lady Caroline Pipkin had lived long enough to know that one sometimes learned far more about a person by listening than by asking endless questions.

Especially if one eavesdropped.

Tonight she was putting that strategy to a test.

"Newgate!" Gwyn was incredulous. "Henry told me Andrew was with the best surgeons! He said his health had to be attended to! If I had known where he was, I would have never left London!"

"Gwyn, he asks after you always. I tried to put his mind at ease by assuring him you were safe here, but I fear he is doing poorly."

"Then we will leave tomorrow. I will go to him."

"I'd hoped you'd say that. I can ready a carriage—"

"I can ride. My grey mare is here, and she will carry me to London."

"The roads are not safe."

"We will not be accosted during the day, especially if we dress as though we have little wealth."

Caroline entered the parlor then, and all conversation ceased. She studied Gwyn covertly, and a quick smile lit her plain features.

So like Barbara. The light from the fireplace burnishing that

*hair, the mutinous set of her jaw. Like a lioness fighting for its
mate. I see my littlest sister again in her eyes.*

"What is this discussion about, if I may ask?"

"We are leaving for London tomorrow, Lady Pipkin. I'm
sorry to leave you to your own devices here, but an emergency
has come up. . . ."

"My dear girl, how is your father going to take this? You told
me just the other night he detested London for the fairer sex."

Jack cleared his throat. "Her father has had a change of
heart."

"Splendid! I shall let the servants know we will be needing
my carriage. . . ."

Gwyn laid a hand on her arm, and Caroline reveled in that
brief touch. "I will be riding with Jack. I must go to London as
swiftly as possible."

Once again, those eyes. Of the deepest blue. She would give
no quarter on this issue, and Caroline had to fight against her
tears.

So like Barbara.

"You cannot object if I carry your luggage. I will give you
my sister's address, Jack, and Gwyn can stay with us if she
needs to."

"What has happened?" All conversation ceased as Angel
walked into the room. She was dressed in a dark red gown with
a deep décolletage. As Caroline surveyed the room, she noticed
the change of expression on the young man Jack's face.

He cares for her.

Jack crossed the room quickly and took Angel's hands in his.
"Gwyn and I are leaving for London tomorrow morning."

"I will go with Gwyn."

Caroline almost laughed at the highly protective expression
on the French girl's face. *Ah, how it does me good to remember.
My sister always inspired such loyalty.*

"You will ride with us?" Jack asked. He had not let go of her
hand, and Caroline was quick to notice this.

"You are not taking a carriage?" A look of apprehension

crossed Angel's face.

"Lady Pipkin is."

"I will ride with her, then. I do not . . . I cannot ride a horse."

"I will teach you when we return," Jack offered. "Now, is everything settled?"

Gwyn nodded her head. "I . . . thank you for coming, Jack."

She has never married. She has no family north of London. She has been to the city before.

Caroline lay in bed that night, unable to sleep as thoughts raced through her mind.

She loves Andrew. And she is the Bordello Bride they speak of.

Caroline had heard talk of London's Bordello Bride. Who had not? Of the auction that had scandalized a society far too rigid in its manners and lax in its morals. Swathed in a length of white silk, nearly naked as she stood in front of the most powerful men in London, Gwyn had still held her head high and stared them down.

And from what people had said, Andrew had lost his heart that first night.

One thousand pounds. How he must have desired her.

From what she had heard outside the parlor door, Henry was interfering. How like him, to hold everyone around him to the most rigid, proper behavior. If the man had done anything spontaneous in his lifetime, Caroline had never heard of it. Beth had loved him deeply. Of the three sisters, she had been the one who laughed and joked the most, sharing their mother's wit.

Until the afternoon Caroline had found her sister crying in the garden when Henry left her. Beth had never been the same. She had put on a good performance, even married a highly suitable man and raised seven children. But there had been something lacking in her, as though someone had extinguished a fire within her.

Not like Barbara, who fought to the end . . .

She would reach London before Beth left. They would have to be careful. Once Gwyn's business in the city was completed, this house would be the safest place for their niece to hide.

Gwyn barely slept. When soft rays of light glimmered on the horizon, she was out of bed in a flash. First, she bound her breasts with strips of linen. Then, after pulling on the pair of breeches and white shirt she had acquired from the stable, she surveyed her appearance quickly in the mirror. She looked like a boy, except for her hair. With it tucked up in a hat, she would pass—if no one looked carefully.

As she studied herself in the mirror, her stomach protested. With a swiftness born of knowledge and a little practice, she made it to the chamber pot in time.

That her lie to Andrew their last night together had become truth seemed to mock her. She had only realized she was with child in the last few days. It must have happened at the Inn, when she had not thought—nor had the means—to protect herself.

She pushed her pregnancy out of her mind. With Jack coming to tell her Andrew was not well . . . She couldn't think of what she was going to do. It was enough to make it through her days without succumbing to despair.

Gwyn could not understand how Henry could keep his grandson in prison. He had seemed a fair man and had treated her well, though with just a touch of condescension. Yet he had let her stay at his house.

Only because it is far from Andrew. He does not want you anywhere near his grandson, and you must face that truth.

She glanced out the window again as she pulled on the worn pair of boots she had borrowed from one of the stableboys. The sun was beginning to rise in the grey winter sky, washing it in pale, muted colors.

A soft knock broke into her thoughts.

331

"Gwyn?" Jack's voice was muffled through the door. "I'll be in the stable. Come quickly."

There was no time to think now. There was only riding to London and seeing Andrew.

He was all that mattered now.

Newgate was a hellish place, worse than any nightmare Gwyn ever had. She had thought of Andrew's imprisonment during the entire ride to London, and now, walking swiftly behind a short, squat man with a ring of keys, she knew her fears were justified.

Rats rustled away from her booted feet. Bits of straw crunched softly beneath her heels. The jailer's lantern swung in a small arc as he walked with his rolling gait, and the light sent shadows careening over the damp stone walls.

She jumped as a long, bony arm reached between the bars of a small window.

"Please," a voice moaned softly. "Please . . ."

"To hear them complain, they're all innocent," the squat man said, his voice flat.

She shuddered, wondering about the pitiful creature within that cell. Jack's footsteps were a comforting sound behind her. He had worried about how this would affect her, and she was deeply touched by his concern. She'd assured him she was strong enough.

Nothing mattered but Andrew.

"It won't be a pretty sight, Gwyn," Jack had said gently.

"I used to help my father nurse sick people. I have a strong stomach."

But nothing had prepared her for this. She breathed through her mouth so she was spared the worst of the stench. The low moans made tears fill her eyes. The building housed a living, breathing mass of human agony. They had found hell on earth, for Gwyn had never seen nor imagined a place worse than this.

"Here we are. He's up ahead—"

"*Gwyneth!*" The anguished cry echoed throughout the narrow corridor, and Gwyn felt her heart beat furiously the instant she recognized Andrew's voice.

"He's crazy, that one. Can't keep any food down; thinks he sees things wot aren't there. . . ."

"Hurry up, man!' Jack said, an edge of desperation in his voice. "Can't you move any faster?"

But the squat man continued on with his unhurried gait, the keys jingling in his hand.

"*Gwyn . . .*" The cry was soft and low now, almost a sob, and Gwyn had to fight the impulse to cry out her anguish and push the little man faster. What had happened to Andrew in this place?

"Here he is." The jailer took his time sorting the keys, and Gwyn hovered behind him, trying to see inside the small, barred window at the top of the door. But all she could see was darkness.

"He's a dangerous one, he is. Attacked one of my men the other night. I think he's gone right out of his head. . . ."

"Will you please unlock this door?" Jack said quietly. Gwyn noticed he slipped the man several coins.

"There you go, guv'nor." The door swung open, hinges protesting. "Now, not too long. I don't want you getting him all excited. Cries out all the time, he does. Keeps the other prisoners awake."

As the door swung further open, Gwyn had to fight the burning at the back of her throat. She could taste bile in her mouth as she glanced quickly around the small cell, now illuminated by the lantern in Jack's hand.

Rats squeaked and fled, then Gwyn heard rustling sounds as they burrowed into the straw that littered the floor. Andrew lay on a blanket in a far corner, his arm thrown over his eyes. Evidence of his inability to keep his food down stained the blanket and straw around him. The sharp planes of his face were obscured by a ragged beard, and his hair was filthy.

"Gwyn," Jack said warningly.

But she was already on her knees next to him, touching his brow. Her heart turned over as she realized how very hot he was. Burning.

The instant she touched him, he jerked back, then slowly struggled to a sitting position. He didn't have the strength, and she watched in horror as he fell back upon the soiled straw and glared at her, his blue eyes full of venom.

Gwyn shrank back from the look in his eyes.

"Leave me," Andrew said softly. He was looking at her as if she were a vision, something his mind had conjured forth.

He's delirious.

Her eyes filled with quick tears as Andrew drew his arm slowly across his eyes, blocking her from his sight. "How I hate you and still you torment my vision. *Leave me!*"

"Andrew." She fought to keep her voice steady. "We have come to take you from this place."

"Why did you tell the Duke?" he muttered softly. "I loved you as I loved no other and you betrayed—" His breath escaped, rasping loudly in the small cell.

"Jack, we cannot leave him here."

"I've tried to take him. His grandfather is the only one they will listen to."

She touched Andrew's brow again, but he struggled away. Gwyn stood up, reluctant to tax what little strength he had.

"How can he keep him in this place?"

"I cannot believe Henry knows how ill he is. Even when I left, he was not this way. This fever has come on him suddenly."

Andrew moaned softly, then turned on his side and clawed at the straw. Weak, retching sounds filled the silence.

Gwyn closed her hands into fists to still their trembling. "Then there is only one thing to do. Take me to Andrew's grandfather."

Henry was almost out the door when he saw Jack and a

334

young boy starting up his steps. He had heard of Andrew's condition and had just sent a request for his release. Jack was coming, no doubt, to berate him for letting his grandson fall into such a sorry state. He could not chastise Henry further than he already had himself.

When the door closed and the youth spoke, Henry stared at him in astonishment.

"Whatever you think of me, you cannot leave your grandson in such a hellish place."

"What are you doing here? I thought I told you—"

"I could not stay away once Jack told me how Andrew was suffering. He's burning with fever, and he does not know where he is!" Before Henry could even open his mouth to reply, Gwyn continued her tirade. "You may believe your grandson has made many mistakes, but he does not deserve a punishment such as I just witnessed!" Her voice broke, and it affected him strangely. "Have mercy and request his release!"

Henry glanced at Jack. The man was standing beside Gwyn, and he knew if he had not already requested Andrew's release, Jack's anger would ensure it.

"I would like a private word with you," he said, indicating Gwyn.

"And then you will release him?" she asked.

"Step into the library, please."

"Damnation," Jack said heatedly and stepped forward.

"This will take but a minute, Jack. Do not argue with me."

Once inside the library, Henry closed the double doors and faced Gwyn. Looking at her closely now, he was surprised he had mistaken her for a boy. The breeches clung snugly to her legs and hips in a most indecent manner. Yet she did not seem preoccupied with her display of immodesty; she simply stared at him as if willing him to speak.

"He would not be there but for you," Henry began quietly. "The Duke was responsible for his imprisonment. All because he wanted you."

"But surely you have the power to see to his release! He is

335

burning with fever! He does not know his own mind! I have seen others like him, and I am afraid—"

"Do you carry my grandson's child?"

She stared at him, and he saw stark incredulity on her face. He was sure she was shocked he knew.

"Your silence answers that question. Know this, Miss Leighton. Andrew's bastard will be provided for. We take care of our own. But you are never to see my grandson again. And if he should search for you and find you, you are to deny him, no matter what you may feel inside."

She was silent, her dark blue eyes wide. Watching.

"How can you be so certain I'll agree to this?" she finally asked.

Henry took a deep breath, confident he was doing the right thing. "It is the price you must pay to see to his release."

The only sound in the library was the ticking of the clock on the mantel.

"Well, Miss Leighton? You do not seem as concerned for his safety now as you did minutes ago."

The expression in her eyes told him plainly what she thought of him.

"On one condition, and surely you can grant me this," she said quietly.

"What is it?"

"I will not leave this house until I know he is well."

It was little enough to be rid of Andrew's mistress.

"As you wish, Miss Leighton. Your devotion to may grandson is quite touching."

She looked at him then, with such pain in her eyes. He almost glanced away.

"Do I have your word?" he demanded.

She hesitated for the space of a heartbeat. "Yes."

Late that same night, a coach pulled up in front of Henry's townhouse and Andrew came home. Gwyn had summoned

Thatch, and the giant carried Andrew upstairs to his bedroom as easily as if he were a child. Henry summoned his most trusted surgeon.

And the vigil began.

Gwyn ignored Henry's disapproving looks and remained in Andrew's bedroom. She undressed him with gentle hands and sponged his body free of the stench that clung to it. Twice he soiled his sheets, and she simply asked Jack to fetch her others and changed his linen. He muttered and cursed, thrashing softly beneath the covers.

She never left his side.

Gwyn knew all the signs of plague. She had seen them before, when similar illnesses had swept her father's village. The high fever and vomiting. The rapid heartbeat and quick, shallow breathing. At its worst, stupor and delirium.

And all the surgeon could do was given him laudanum to reduce his pain and quiet the delirium. The rest would depend on a Higher Power.

"How long has he been feverish?" the surgeon asked quietly. He stood with Henry and Jack at the far end of the bedroom, and Gwyn strained to overhear their conversation.

"No longer than two days. I saw him the day before I left for the country, and he was not as bad as this." Jack sounded worried.

The surgeon shook his head. "You know the symptoms as well as I do, Henry. This fever takes them quickly, and Andrew isn't strong. I've seen men go in as little as four days. If he survives longer than that, he'll have a chance."

She blocked their conversation out of her mind and looked down at Andrew's face. Again, as she had countless times, she smoothed his hair away from his forehead.

You cannot die.

He murmured something almost inaudible, and she leaned closer.

"Don't . . . want you to have to take care of me."

"Andrew, don't talk. Save your strength."

337

"Don't . . . leave me."

"Never." She smoothed his hair.

She was aware of Henry coming to stand at the foot of the great bed, but she barely gave him a thought.

"So . . . hot." Andrew's grip on her fingers tightened. "Scared."

She leaned over again, this time pressing her cool cheek against his feverish one. "I'm scared, too," she whispered. It took every ounce of her courage not to cry. She closed her eyes and tried to will some of her strength into his body. "I won't let you die, Andrew."

"Stay. Don't . . . go."

"I'm here with you. Always."

"Why did you . . . go?"

"I'm here with you now."

He seemed to relax then. But she kept hold of his hand, his fingers burning into hers. He was so terribly hot. Memories of other people she had nursed in other places flashed through her memory. The ones this sick had not survived.

Later that night he began to shake, and Jack built up the fire as she and Henry piled blankets on top of him. He protested weakly whenever she left his side, and she noticed even Henry hadn't the heart to ask her to leave. Gwyn stayed close to Andrew as the sky gradually lightened, then on into the next day. She remembered what the surgeon had said and knew the time was rapidly approaching when Andrew would come out of the fever or . . .

She gripped his hand tightly and pushed the thought out of her mind.

His eyes fluttered open in the early afternoon, and he smiled at her so sweetly she felt her throat close.

"Ba—"

She leaned closer.

"Baby," he whispered, the single word exhausting him.

Not even caring that Henry stood watching them, she placed his hand on her stomach and covered it with her own. Andrew smiled, then slipped back into sleep. He lay very still now, and she had to lean down close to him at times to make sure he was breathing. His skin felt dry, still burning with the intensity of the fever.

And she never took her eyes away from his face as her lips moved silently. Praying. Hoping.

As the sun set, she heard a slight noise at the door, then the surgeon was in the bedchamber again. He examined Andrew, then turned back toward Henry. Gwyn glanced at the man quickly and the set of his shoulders told her what he was going to say.

No. She held Andrew's hand tighter, as if by grasping him she could keep his physical presence in the room. Now all her prayers stopped, and she looked at his face, seeing all the signs she had wanted to deny.

He was dying.

She heard Henry leave the room as one of the servants began to sob. Jack came and knelt at the side of the bed across from her, gazing down at his friend with anguished eyes.

"What can I do?" he asked, and Gwyn realized he was looking to her for direction. She felt overwhelmed, suddenly realizing that if Andrew died a part of her would go with him.

"There's nothing . . ." She stopped, as a remembrance flitted through her mind. The doctor had given Andrew laudanum, but she remembered . . . When she and her father . . . But she didn't know . . .

But Cook would.

"Jack," she whispered urgently, her eyes leaving Andrew's flushed face for just an instant as she gazed into his steady grey eyes. "Go to The Dark Stallion as quickly as you can. Fetch Cook. Tell her to bring her herbs, that Andrew has a bad fever and it has to be brought down. Go quickly now, while we still have time!"

And as Jack left the room, she leaned closer to Andrew.

"You must hold on," she whispered. "Just a little longer. Andrew, *hold on to me.*"

This time she didn't see Henry.

Cook arrived within the hour, bustling into the bedroom. She took one look at the situation and organized to fight it. "I'll need boiling water. And new linen, wet with cold water. We have to bring his fever down. Gwyn, my lamb, you stay right where you are and talk to him. Keep talking to him; don't let him slip away."

She could have wept now that Cook was here, capable and strong. Shortly after the woman arrived, she had a hot herbal drink ready.

"Now we have to prop him up and get some of this down him. It will help fight the poison inside."

"Help me," Gwyn said, addressing Jack and Henry. She got up from her chair by the head of the bed, never releasing Andrew's hand. With her free hand, she indicated each man should support a shoulder.

She managed to get a mouthful down Andrew, then he choked and spat it back up all over her.

"Again," Cook said calmly. "Tilt his head back, he'll take it."

But it came back up.

When Cook gave her a second cup, Gwyn straddled Andrew's long legs. Henry's mouth opened in protest, then snapped shut.

"Andrew." Now she couldn't even see Henry's face; all her energy was concentrated on the man in front of her. "Andrew, you have to drink this!" Her fingers were entwined in his hair, and as much as she hated to, she pulled sharply. "Andrew!"

"Never tell you where she is . . ." He seemed to be drifting off, and for one horrible moment she was afraid she wouldn't be able to stop his leaving. With a determination born of complete despair, she quickly slipped her hand around his bearded jaw, then up to his earlobe, pinching it sharply.

"Andrew!"

He opened his eyes for an instant, and she maneuvered the cup close to his lips.

"Drink this, damn you! I won't let you die!"

He managed to get half the cup down before drifting away.

"Again," Cook said calmly, handing Gwyn another cup.

It was a night she would remember all her life. The intense heat from the fire, the pungent, green smell of herbs. Cook, smelling of vanilla and spices. Henry's strained face. Jack's elation as Andrew managed to drink more and more of the foul brew.

And Andrew. She couldn't stop looking at him, touching him, as if by some miracle she could transfer her determination and strength into his steadily weakening body.

They wrapped him in cool sheets, and Andrew struggled as his heated flesh came into contact with the cold. Gwyn sat on his chest to hold him still, then later she moved as Henry and Jack supported his shoulders and she straddled his legs again as Cook handed her more of the herbal drink.

Time was meaningless, measured only by each breath Andrew took, by each sip he managed to consume. Measured by each beat of her heart as she looked at the man she loved and fiercely willed him to live.

And as the sun rose the following day, Cook passed her fleshy hand over Andrew's brow and said calmly, "He'll live."

They were the most beautiful words Gwyn had ever heard. She began to shake with exhaustion, then slid slowly out of her chair and to the floor.

Henry spent the morning praying, thanking God for delivering his grandson back to him. And he knew without any doubt that but for the knowledge of the robust woman Gwyn had summoned, he would be attending to funeral arrangements.

He had walked Cook to the door after summoning one of his own carriages to take her back to The Dark Stallion. Outside,

341

as she had turned to step inside the carriage, he had detained her for an instant, then pressed a pouch of coins into her hand.

She stared at it, then smiled sadly and gave the pouch back.

"I didn't come here to be paid. I did it for that girl upstairs." When he didn't reply, the woman eyed him shrewdly. "She loves him, you know. I hear what goes on in this city, and if you're a wise man, you'll realize she's worth ten Lady Pevensys."

"I thank you for giving my grandson back to me," he said gruffly. The coins felt suddenly heavy in his hand. She continued to eye him, then surprised him by grasping his arm firmly, steadying him.

"You're ready to drop, man. Get yourself inside and lie down. Andrew will live. I've seen that fever before, and he's through the worst of it."

"I cannot thank you enough—"

"You can thank me by listening to this last bit of advice I'll be giving you. Those two belong together, and it would be a crime in God's eyes to keep them apart. You never saw the look in his eyes when they first looked upon her. And Gwyn! Well, my lamb also reveals her heart in her eyes. She wouldn't let him die this last night; she would have fought the devil himself. A love that strong is a rare and precious thing, and not to be tampered with. Not even by you."

He had opened his mouth, intending to interrupt her, and had been shocked when the woman had held up her strong, calloused hand, silencing him.

"Think about what I have said, m'lord. There are many ways for a person to sicken and die, and I have seen them all. The body is only as strong as the heart inside. Leave them be, or I am afraid you will watch your grandson's heart break. And I won't be coming back to treat him then, for there is no cure but to let him have her."

She had studied his face for a long moment, then turned and stepped up inside the carriage. Henry had stared after the coach as it clattered off down the cobblestone street.

Now, as he tiredly took the stairs one at a time, he wondered at the old woman's words.

She is a foolish creature. I loved Beth, and yet I managed to carve out a life for myself. I was responsible, dutiful . . .

The words rang hollowly in his mind. *You are tired. You almost lost him. You will know what to do later, after you have rested.*

He stopped at the top of the stairs and gazed at the door to his grandson's room. His feet seemed to move of their own accord as he walked slowly in the direction of that door. He needed to see his grandson breathing, needed to reassure himself that his boy was indeed alive.

Henry opened the door gently and slipped inside. The fire was burning brightly, and he remembered Jack tending to it before he left. The servants had been useless, frightened out of their wits at the thought of Andrew dying. He was the great favorite in the household. Henry's attention moved from the fire to the bed, and he studied what he saw there dispassionately, too exhausted to feel anything.

His grandson was lying on his back, his breathing deep and slow. Gwyn lay by his side, Andrew's arm tight around her waist. His hand rested, fingers splayed, on her belly, as if even in sleep he wished to protect the life within. Her head was turned toward him, her cheek rested against his chest. Her bright hair spilled out over the pillow. Cook must have removed her clothing, as she was obviously naked beneath the blanket.

Henry passed a hand over his eyes as they started to water.

You are tired; that is all you feel. And yet there was something about their closeness that stirred him. He studied the sleeping couple, wondering what it could be, until his eyes rested on his grandson's face.

Words Andrew had spoken during the heat of one of their arguments came back to him, haunting in their clarity.

When I am with her, I feel at peace.

Unbidden, images of Beth flitted through his memory. He

343

could remember that summer so clearly. He had felt he had the world at his feet, that all of his life should be blessed. Until the morning his father had called him into the library and demanded he finish it.

Henry stared at his grandson again. He was at peace. And he couldn't remember ever having seen him this way.

He had first seen Andrew at the age of five, when he had found out of his identity from Geoffrey's letter. He had been a dirty, frightened, impudent rascal, and hardly loveable.

As a boy, he had been wary. Tense. Andrew had moved through his house as silently as a wild animal and had rarely allowed anyone glimpses of what was inside him. His feelings had erupted in brawls and scrapping, and Henry had to keep a firm hold on his temper or he would have beaten his grandson many times. Only the welts he had discovered on the boy's back soon after he had taken him away from his sadist of a stepfather had prevented him from resorting to corporal punishment.

And then, as a young man, he had been free-spirited and wild, a darling with the ladies and a constant source of amusement and scandal. The aristocracy adored him, gossiped about his latest exploits. He had reached his zenith the night he had bought the woman beside him for such a shocking sum.

And all to simply bed her.

Yet what had Cook said just minutes ago?

You never saw the look in his eyes when they first lighted upon her.

He was tired. His legs trembled with the effort of keeping him upright. He could not possibly think of his grandson's future at this time.

His eyes darted to his grandson as he shifted in the bed, pulling Gwyn closer against him.

As if he would crawl into her skin. He thought of the one time he had loved Beth and made her his own, then pushed the thought out of his mind, annoyed by his sudden weakness. Was he getting old, determined to live in the past?

344

You promised the girl she could see him recovered. You have at least a day in which to think of this. It does not have to be decided now.

Yet even after he retired to his bedchamber, he could not forget the expression on his grandson's face.

Madeleine's boots barely made any sound against the cobbles as she walked swiftly down the dark street. Charles—Lord Hardwick, she corrected herself quickly—was asleep in his own bed after she had paid him a private visit. He had done as she had requested weeks earlier, having purchased her a fine set of men's clothing. It amused and excited him to see her dressed as a fashionable boy, though she knew he had absolutely no inclinations that way. There were countless men in London who succumbed to the Italian Vice, but not many of them frequented The Dark Stallion.

She held her breath as a group of gentlemen walked past her. They were arguing lustily, having obviously drunk copious amounts of spirits. At first, when she'd walked through London dressed as a young man and searched for Lily, she'd darted into the shadows whenever she had seen a stranger approaching on the street. Now, more secure in her disguise, she knew if she carried herself confidently, no one would approach her.

The Duke was to appear at a private home tonight. The widow who owned it had opened it for gambling, and she had heard a rumor that the Duke had purchased one of the upstairs rooms. It was said Lily would accompany him this night. Madeleine had debated the wisdom of trying to steal Lily away from the Duke's house, but she knew if she were caught there—and he guarded himself well from his many enemies—she would not remain alive.

And Madeleine was deeply afraid. Lily had visited her once at The Dark Stallion and had assured her things were working out splendidly, but if Madeleine knew one man's heart in all of

London, she knew the Duke's. He was using Lily to find Gwyneth.

It was only a matter of time before the darkness that had invaded his soul would be directed toward Lily.

The house was ablaze with lights as she walked up the front steps. Madeleine adopted the manner of a fop in public, knowing her slender build would never be believable as a man. To this end she had rouged her cheeks and mouth and had put on enough powder so that it cracked slightly when she moved her lips. Her short hair was brushed back severely from her face, and she walked with just the slightest swaying of her hips.

She was admitted without question and, drink in hand, began her search for Lily.

It did not take long. The Duke was in the largest bedroom at the top of the stairs. There were two other men at the gaming table with him, and Lily sat directly to his right.

Madeleine bit her lip against the cry that rose up at the sight of her friend. Lily was dressed in a white gown, so low one could see her dark nipples clearly. Her face was covered with powder, a white death mask. Only the smallest amount of rouge on her cheeks and lips and one beauty mark belied the starkness. But it was her eyes that captured Madeleine's attention and caused her anguish. Where before they had snapped and sparkled, with laughter always lurking in their depths, now they were dull. Glazed over with a film of pain and resignation that made Madeleine want to weep.

"Close the door, boy!" one of the men called out. He was a beefy sort, and after he glanced back at Madeleine, he directed his attention back to his cards. The center of the large room glowed with the light of countless candles. Madeleine breathed deeply to still the racing of her heart. If Richard—the Duke—should look upon her face for too long a time, he would no doubt recognize her.

She had hoped to find Lily alone and flee with her. Now she would have to wait and find time with her alone.

The Duke was concentrating on his cards, so Madeleine

wandered to the far end of the bedroom, where a long table groaning with various delicacies was spread out before her. She could keep her back to them this way and pretend she was eating.

"There!" She recognized the beefy man's voice and turned in time to see him throw his cards down on the table. "Give me what you promised me, Richard."

There was coarse laughter from the other men, then Madeleine felt her heart turn to ice as the Duke pulled Lily to her feet. The other men were clearing the table, and Madeleine knew from the scent of danger in the room what was about to happen.

"She's worthless to me in all other respects, so you might as well enjoy her," the Duke said. He lifted Lily up so she was sitting on the table, her tiny feet in their delicate slippers not reaching the marble floor. Then he bent her back and pushed up the froth of white skirts and lace-trimmed petticoats. The beefy man was already working furiously at the fastening of his breeches, his arousal all too evident.

That Lily barely resisted told Madeleine more than anything else.

Madeleine averted her eyes as he mounted her, and her gaze fell on the knife next to the large beef roast. For an instant she thought of taking it in her hand and plunging it into Richard's heart. But that would only mean she and Lily would be certainly killed.

The room was silent, save for the harsh grunts of the beefy man. The other men laughed, and Madeleine closed her eyes briefly, thinking furiously.

"I want her next, Richard."

"And you shall have her."

She felt the moment the Duke's eyes were upon her back. "Young man, I do not recognize you. Come here and join us, unless you prefer another sort of game."

She turned then and showed the Duke her face. She watched the play of emotions cross his features. Desire, slight confusion, followed by quickly dawning recognition. And she gave him a look so filled with fury and hatred she was shaking with it.

She started out of the room, knowing she would not be able to rescue Lily this night.

"Stop that man." The Duke's voice was low, filled with need.

Madeleine slipped out of the room, knowing the other men were hot after their own gratification. She could evade the Duke, as long as he did not have help.

She reached the top of the stairs as he burst out of his private room.

"Stop him!" he cried. But there was too much noise below, and no one heard him. At first.

She didn't hesitate as she vaulted up on the large, smooth bannister and slid down the staircase. There was a blur of applause and amused shouts at her daring, but she barely heard them. Landing on her feet at a dead run, she raced for the door. Several hands clawed at her and she even had to bite one, but she managed to dart out the front door and down the steps. She turned the corner, running away from the blazing lights.

And as she ran, swiftly and silently, she heard the Duke's voice ring out into the night, issuing commands.

"I want that boy found and detained! Bring him back to me!"

She continued to run, the damp night air burning in and out of her lungs, her sides aching from the exertion. Her boots were of the finest leather, and she was careful they made the slightest sound possible.

She did not look back until she was at Charles' doorstep and he was opening the door, confused, clad in only his dressing gown. He always gave his servants the night off when Madeleine visited him, thus he was alone.

In the library he gave her a glass of brandy, and she swallowed it quickly, welcoming the burning sensation sliding down her throat. Knowing she could not explain away her severe shaking and obvious pain with a simple tale, she choked out the truth.

"We will find her, then." Charles Burdett, Lord Hardwick, had long indulged her in anything she wanted. He was a basically good man, and the angry light in his eyes when she had described what the Duke had permitted Lily to endure had heartened Madeleine.

With him at her side, she would save Lily from the Duke.

He was furious, the anger growing within him until it seemed to expand and fill every corner of his soul.

Madeleine. He had desired her above all other women. Until Gwyn. Madeleine had left him, but not before confronting him with the nature of his desires. She had known too much of what boiled within him, and he had hated her for that.

Now, the thought that she had escaped his grasp much the same as Gwyn had enraged him further.

He glanced at Lily, huddled in a corner of the carriage, her fur-lined cloak pulled protectively around her. He had let five other men into his private suite, and they had all had her. He hated her now, useless to him. She had not led him to Gwyn as he had believed she would. She simply took up space at his house. She no longer even attempted to talk with him, simply staying shut in her room.

It was time to dispose of her.

He rapped against the ceiling of his carriage with his cane. Three sharp raps. His driver would understand. And it gave him a measure of satisfaction to know that the woman beside him would die this night.

He closed his eyes and smiled, lost in his private thoughts until the carriage slowed.

"Richard?" Lily seemed to have come out of her stupor long enough to realize they were not at his mansion. "Why are we stopping?"

"It is a lovely night. I thought we might walk together."

She clearly did not believe him. He was gratified by her

sharp gasp of pain as he grabbed her wrist and pulled her out of the carriage after him.

London Bridge. The Thames flowed beneath it. Though the shoreline had iced, the river was still dark and turbulent, the current rushing beneath.

A fitting end for such a useless woman.

"I wish to ask you something, Lily."

Her hand trembled in his. When she did not look at him, he stopped walking and pulled her around to face him. His hands cupped her face and he forced her eyes to meet his.

"Where is she?"

"I do not know what you mean."

He slapped her then, enjoying the sting of the back of his hand against the softness of her cheek. The large ring on his finger scraped along her skin, leaving an angry gash.

"I have no time for the games you play. Tell me where Gwyn is and your life will be spared." Though he had no intention of ever letting her live, sometimes this method worked.

"I do not know."

He glanced quickly up and down the bridge. No one was near. Grabbing her around the waist, he picked Lily up and carried her to the railing, depositing her on it with a cruel harshness. Now she clawed at his greatcoat, her eyes terrified as he pushed her, arching her back over the dark water much the same way he had held her down on the gaming table.

"Tell me where she is and you shall live."

"I do not know."

"*Tell me!*"

She looked up into his face, her eyes beseeching. "Richard, please—"

"You worthless bitch." And as he attempted to push her over the edge, the fight began in earnest.

Lily had her fingers tightly twined in the Duke's hair when

350

she felt the back of his hand crack against the side of her head. She was stunned for just an instant, but it was all the time the Duke needed. Grabbing her legs, he pushed her roughly. Her arms flailed wildly, then she was falling, her scream carried away on the cruel, winter wind.

The water shocked her, freezing cold. She thrashed her arms and legs wildly, but her silk gown and petticoats were already becoming weighted down with the brackish water. The current rushed her along, and she swallowed water as her head went under.

Fighting, she pushed to the surface again, taking deep, painful breaths of the frosty air. Branches caught at her skirts, and she realized she was near one of the arches of the bridge. Then her hands felt rough stone, and she clawed at it, managing to hold herself steady.

The stone cut into her palms, but she didn't even feel it as she tightened her grip. Her cloak and slippers had been pulled off by the current, and her feet were numb, her fingers rigid with cold. She clawed at the stone, then felt her fingers slip. The branches she grasped cut her hand, then the current claimed her again, and this time Lily knew there was no escape.

She took a deep, sobbing breath, then she was pulled under. Lily fought like a demon, tearing at the skirts that pulled her further beneath the water. But her fingers didn't seem to obey. They were stiff and clumsy, totally useless.

Her lungs felt as if they were going to explode. Lily barely recognized the last instant when she finally gave in and decided to let the dark water claim her. Her mind worked furiously.

I didn't tell him, Gwyn. I never would have told him.

Then all was darkness.

Soft knocking on Andrew's bedroom door brought Gwyn out of sleep. She raised her head, careful not to disturb Andrew, and encountered Henry's face. His expression was totally

351

devoid of emotion.

"There is someone to see you in the library." He shut the door.

Gwyn walked downstairs on shaky legs. When she entered the library, she was surprised to see Angel and Jack standing just inside the door.

"Oh, Gwyn," Angel said, her voice nasal, her eyes red and swollen. "It's Lily."

Chapter Twenty-One

Gwyn walked slowly through the rose garden, her back aching. Six months into her pregnancy, she was feeling tired and hot. The June sun was gentle, and a soft summer wind teased the skirts of her light dress. And Gwyn remembered when she had first come to Scarborough Hall and wondered what the rose garden would look like in summer.

It was glorious. But it gave her no joy.

It was so hard to believe Lily was dead. She had raced to the waterfront with Angel and Jack, and only seeing Lily's small, crumpled form, her lips blue with cold, had made her friend's untimely death seem real.

She would be ever thankful Beverly had been there. The woman had taken control of the situation and had Lily carried to her nearby pie shop. She had opened the business with money Andrew had given her for saving Gwyn's life. Once inside, Beverly had directed one of her male friends to lay Lily's body out on one of the large tables in back.

"Get her out of here, Angel," Beverly had said, indicating Gwyn with a nod of her head. "This is not a sight a pregnant woman should see."

Gwyn hadn't questioned how the woman knew. Thus they had left, but not before Angel had broken down and begged Beverly to put ribbons in Lily's hair. She also promised to send her finest gown for her to be buried in.

It was all Lily had ever wanted.

There had been no funeral, as Beverly had warned them the Duke would be less than kind toward anyone who called attention to what he had done. She had told them she would take care of Lily, and Angel and Gwyn had agreed.

Madeleine had surprised them all and suddenly accepted Lord Hardwick's long-standing marriage proposal. He had taken her away to Italy, concerned for her health. For Madeleine's heart had been broken by her dearest friend's death.

And Andrew. Not a day passed that she did not think of him. She had left Henry's house in London soon after Lily's death. He had allowed her one small courtesy, that of writing Andrew a note. She had sealed it, and Henry had promised to give it to his grandson. And she had broken her promise and given full rein to her emotions in writing. She had told Andrew how much she loved him and that no matter what might happen, she would always be his.

And she would wait for him at Scarborough Hall.

The hardest part—and she could not think of it without tears starting—had been when she had kissed him good-bye. It had been mere days after his fever had broken, and she had wondered if he would remember she had been with him. She had looked at his face for a long moment after that kiss, until Henry had cleared his throat and reminded her the carriage waited for her below.

Months later, Andrew had still not come for her.

"Hello, my dear. Are you feeling better this morning?" Elizabeth Warrick, Lady Caroline Pipkin's sister, had traveled back to Scarborough Hall with them. And though Gwyn could not understand why, she had felt at ease with the woman immediately. Elizabeth—Beth, as she liked to be called—was a great comfort to her, and Gwyn had found herself a confidante. She needed to talk to a woman who had given birth, as her time was nearing and she was afraid.

She nodded her head, and Beth fell into step beside her.

"I am worried about Angelique. She has lost weight and spends too much time by herself."

Gwyn nodded again, her throat suddenly tight. Angel blamed herself for Lily's death. She despised herself for leaving The Dark Stallion when Lily had been so terrified of her future. Though Gwyn had tried many times to convince her otherwise, even reminding her gently that Lily had insisted she leave the brothel, Angel would not be persuaded.

"I'm thankful Jack stays with her. He's been such a help to all of us here. I saw them walking the other day, and I believe he's grown quite fond of our Angel."

Gwyn placed her hand on her back and massaged the sore muscles. She felt bulky and misshapen.

"Why don't we sit down?" Beth guided her toward a stone bench, and Gwyn gratefully settled herself down on it. She closed her eyes. Depression was her constant companion these summer days, and she did not know what to do to dispel it.

Beth took her hand. "He will come for you, you know."

She studied the woman's face. It was hard to believe Beth and Caroline were sisters. Where Caroline's face was all sharp angles and strong bones, Beth's was round and soft, her blue eyes luminous in her gentle face. Her blond hair, pulled back from her face, had faded and was streaked with wisps of silvery grey. As she reached over and took Gwyn's hand in her own, Gwyn thought she had never felt a touch as comforting.

"Time is on your side, Gwyn. Time and love."

As the months passed after Andrew's illness, Henry sometimes wondered if he had done the right thing. He had opened Gwyneth's letter as soon as the carriage had driven away, and his brows had drawn together in an angry scowl as he realized the chit had broken her promise.

But it did not matter. Andrew would never read the impassioned words Gwyneth had written. Henry had listened carefully as Andrew talked in his sleep, still weakened from his bout with the fever. His grandson had relived his conversation with the Duke concerning Gwyn. Slowly, steadily, Henry had pieced together the story. If the Duke had managed to make Andrew start to doubt Gwyn's honesty, Henry would finish the deception.

He was sure it was a deception. Grudgingly, he had to admit the woman loved his grandson. He had watched her face carefully the night she had helped save Andrew's life. No whore interested solely in financial gain would have bothered.

But that did not mean she was suitable for Andrew. And Henry, believing he was protecting his grandson, found a solution. The man Henry hired to forge Gwyneth's lettering— for he was not certain that Andrew had never seen it—was one of the best, and Henry had sat with him in the library and told him what to write.

It had been a simple matter to compose a letter in which Gwyn admitted she had been in partnership with her loathsome cousin and had played Andrew for a fool. Softening at the end, Henry had let her admit she had not intended the charade to endanger Andrew's life; she had simply wanted to acquire his money.

With Gwyn out of the way, he had been convinced Andrew would go ahead with his marriage plans. And even if Belinda was a far cry from what he would have wished for his grandson, at least he had not found her in a brothel.

But his plans were going awry. Belinda had visited Andrew several days ago, one of a number of visits in which she attempted to finalize the plans for their wedding. Though his grandson spent most of his time in quiet solitude, even the servants had heard him order Belinda out of the house. He had told her in no uncertain terms they would never wed.

And now what does he plan to do with his life? The worry was never far from Henry's mind. Over supper, the only time he ever saw Andrew, he studied his grandson. More than once, Cook's warning had come to mind. For Andrew had lost his vitality. His grandson was no longer the man he had been before the fever—and Gwyn—had claimed him.

Gwyn's eyes flew open, and she reached across the bed. . . . *Andrew*.

It was just another dream.

She lay very still, and her hand reached up to gently caress her hard belly. She had been frightened at first, alone and with child. But, as Beth had said, she had time and love in abundance.

She could clearly remember the morning she had been walking by the lake when she had first felt the baby quicken. From that moment on, she'd been fiercely glad she carried Andrew's child.

Yet she wondered how he was. A suspicion was growing in her mind that Henry conspired to keep them apart. She wondered if he had ever received her letter.

She could not travel in her condition. Gwyn closed her eyes and took several deep breaths. She would rest now. But after the baby was born, she would go to London and talk to Andrew. She had to see his face. If he had decided to abide by his grandfather's wishes, then she wanted to hear it from his lips.

Until she did, she would never give up hope.

"I am thoroughly displeased with you, Belinda. You did not give the marriage a chance. You could not find a better man than Andrew."

Belinda bit her lip against the vitriolic words she wanted to scream at her father. She had told him *she* had decided to call the wedding off, to spare herself the humiliation of having been rejected. Andrew had ordered her from his room as if she meant nothing to him.

"I've heard his other woman is being kept at the country house. That will be the final insult, if Andrew decides to marry

357

this whore rather than you. You'd best attend to this, Belinda, and see he turns his eye back to you." Lord Pevensy pushed back his chair from their dining room table and strode out of the room.

And how am I to do that when Andrew has made it more than clear he wants nothing more to do with me? Belinda glared after her father, then pushed her own chair back and stood up.

There was only one possible plan of action. She would have to travel to Scarborough Hall and see this Bordello Bride. Feminine instinct told her the woman was never far from Andrew's thoughts. Perhaps the slut could be bought off.

Once she was out of the way, Andrew would indeed turn his eye back to her, and that would please her father greatly.

Gwyn was walking slowly by the lake when she saw the carriage come into view. She had heard no mention of visitors, and this arrival was clearly unexpected. Curious, she changed direction and headed back to the great house.

Inside, all was commotion.

"I insist on having the room that was mine before! I don't care who you've put there, they will have to be moved!" The woman with the commanding voice was dressed in a smart brown traveling outfit, her dark hair styled becomingly. But her pale blue eyes were peevish and her full lips were pursed unbecomingly. Beth also stood in the hall, and Gwyn almost laughed at the disgusted expression on her gentle face.

Who could this woman be?

She moved next to Beth and put her hand on the older woman's arm. To her astonishment, Beth put her arm around her waist and hugged her tightly. It was then, as utter silence descended in the hall, that Gwyn was aware of the pale-eyed woman's gaze fastened on her.

The woman studied her face for the space of seconds, then her eyes moved lower. As she took in the gentle swell of Gwyn's body, a venomous look came into her eyes.

"So you are Andrew's whore," she said softly, each word calculated to cut like the lash of a whip.

Gwyn said nothing, though she felt frozen inside. Outwardly, she simply stood her ground.

"How quickly he has tired of you," the woman continued. "For I am to marry him within the month, did he tell you that?"

Belinda. Belinda Pevensy. Gwyn felt Beth's arm tighten around her reassuringly.

"For a woman as confident as you claim to be, Miss Pevensy, you certainly seem to have a need to cut others," Beth said smoothly. "Now, what is this nonsense about changing rooms?"

Belinda's nostrils flared, and Gwyn could feel the anger and frustration emanating from the woman. "I wish to have the room I occupied before." She smiled with false sweetness, directing her next statement to Gwyn. "I visited Andrew here on so many different occasions. We used to play together as children. Where were you playing, my dear? In the gutter?"

Gwyn, surprising even herself, suddenly smiled.

Belinda was not presenting a very convincing picture of a woman secure in love.

The other woman seemed puzzled at her change of expression, and even Gwyn could not have said quite why she smiled.

"What room did you say you wanted, Miss Pevensy?" She had no desire to have her face slapped, and something told her that if she addressed this woman as Belinda, she might do just that.

"The red room. The large bedroom, the first left at the top of the stairs."

Her bedroom. "I do not see why that cannot be arranged." She turned toward Beth and questioned her with her eyes.

The older woman sighed, then glared at Belinda, clearly disgusted by her spoiled behavior. "It will be made ready."

She turned away, and Gwyn followed Beth up the stairs. She

was halfway up the sweeping staircase when Belinda called out, "Whose bastard do you carry, little whore?"

She stopped, then turned around and looked down at Belinda. Her hat was slightly askew, and she watched as the woman yanked at her skirts in frustration. And Gwyn, who had quietly observed people all her life, wondered that Andrew could have ever consorted with this woman. She looked like a little brown hen, plump and ruffled, waiting impatiently for its supper. The image was so overwhelmingly delightful that she smiled.

"And what do you find so amusing, miss? Has no one ever taught you to respect your superiors?"

Gwyn couldn't help it. Laughter bubbled at the back of her throat, and she gave in to the impulse. The soft sound wafted down the stairs, and to her horror, one of the servant girls began to snicker.

"How dare you laugh at me!" Belinda screamed, her face going bright red. "I will have you horsewhipped!"

Gwyn turned then and, throwing her long skirts over her arm, went up the stairs as quickly as her condition would allow.

Below her, Belinda continued to scream.

She carries his child. And that is the one thing I cannot give Andrew.

Belinda had requested her supper sent to her room, and now she picked over the trout with sorrel disgustedly. Even three glasses of Henry's finest sherry hadn't made a dent in her foul mood.

She had never anticipated giving Andrew children. It had not seemed to matter overmuch to him, either. She had rid herself of a pregnancy at the age of sixteen, and then again the following year. Complications had set in, and the midwife had told her she would never bear another child.

It hadn't bothered her in the slightest. Until today.

The little slut will probably present him with a fine son. She knew plenty of men professed not to care whether they became fathers, but once their first son was laid in their arms, they became great babies themselves. They saw immortality in their sons, and it made them all the more proud of their prowess.

If she gives him a child, all will be lost.

She had heard rumors that Gwyn had been with Andrew during the worst of his fever. And now the way he stayed confined in his room . . . The stupid clod was lovesick! The only thing Belinda couldn't quite figure out was why Andrew hadn't galloped straight away to Scarborough Hall and claimed the whore. Gwyneth Leighton was of such a low background she would probably agree to be his mistress.

And I could not abide that, for he would clearly prefer her over me. And that is not to be borne.

She took another sip of sherry, then belched delicately. She had been installed in the red bedroom after all, near the top of the stairs where she could see everything that went on by simply keeping her door open a crack.

At the top of the stairs. Belinda smiled suddenly as a thought entered her mind.

What if Gwyn didn't have Andrew's baby? What if something happened to her? . . .

She hugged herself delightedly, astounded at her cleverness. Lifting the glass of sherry so the liquid gleamed against the firelight, she toasted her plan and promised herself sweet, swift success.

"Heels down, toes up. Don't be afraid of her, Angel, she won't hurt you."

"But she seems so big when I am on top of her back." Angel's eyes were worried.

Gwyn couldn't help but smile. Jack was giving Angel regular riding lessons, but her friend had begged her to instruct her in secret.

"That way," Angel said, "I will not seem so stupid in his eyes."

And Gwyn had eagerly agreed. It was good to see her friend interested in life again. Angel had been deeply depressed after Lily's death and had not eaten or slept easily for the longest time. Jack had been a most sensitive friend, insisting she walk outside every day, taking her on picnics and trying to trick her into eating. The riding lessons had been another of his ploys.

Angel was still insecure, convinced anyone who looked at her could see she had once worked the streets and been a servant at a brothel. She was determined to master all the accomplishments a lady would take for granted.

Artemis, Gwyn's gentle grey mare, had been recruited for this afternoon's lesson. Gwyn was holding the reins, and Angel had just managed to climb into the saddle.

"Now, you take the reins in your hands like—"

"Gwyn, I am so scared. Could you please lead me for a minute? I have to get used to the feel of the horse, do you know what I mean?"

"I do. My father used to lead me around on our brown mare all the time." She patted her swollen stomach. "It helps the cramps in my legs when I walk, so we'll both benefit." She clicked her tongue against the roof of her mouth. Artemis's ears pricked forward, and her delicate hoof pawed the ground.

"Gwyn! Gwyn, she is—"

"No, Angel. She's playing. Come, Artemis, walk with me."

And the mare, gentle as a lap dog, began to follow her mistress.

Damn the bitch. She even has a way with horses.

Belinda watched the two women from her hiding place among the trees. She'd followed them this morning, her own mare securely tied some distance behind her.

None of her plans were working. She had tried to push Gwyn

down the stairs the other morning, but Beth had opened her bedroom door at the wrong moment.

At breakfast, she had looked for an opportunity to slip some dried herbs into Gwyn's tea. But she had never had a chance.

If this goes on too long, she'll give birth to the brat. Belinda scowled as she watched Gwyn leading her mare, Angel holding on to the saddle as she rode the animal.

Perhaps tonight, at dinner . . .

Her hand caressed the pistol she always carried when she rode in the country, and her pale blue eyes widened in anticipation. How simple! She'd never met a horse who wasn't startled by the sound of gunshot. And this little mare would frighten easily.

Pleased with her cleverness, she gripped her pistol and pointed it into the air.

"Now swing your leg over the saddle. That's it. Now dismount. Slowly, slowly. There you are!"

Angel grinned as she brushed off her skirt. "That was better than the last—"

A loud sound exploded into the air, very close. Artemis whinnied, then reared slightly, the whites of her large eyes showing.

"No, there's a good girl—" Gwyn kept her hands on the reins, and she slowly brought the animal under control.

"Good girl," she crooned.

"What was that?" Angel said. "There are no hunters this early in the year."

The sound exploded again, almost on top of them. Artemis squealed, the sound shrill and terrifying. She reared up, and Gwyn, the reins looped around her wrist, was almost pulled off her feet.

"Let her go!" Angel screamed.

Gwyn was struggling with the reins when another shot exploded. The mare bucked, then reared up. Gwyn, her hand

363

tangled in the rein, felt herself being pulled against the large animal. She lost her footing and fell to her knee.

"Gwyn!" Angel darted in and grasped her shoulder.

The mare suddenly went wild, squealing in agony. Artemis reared, and this time when her delicate hooves flashed down, she struck Gwyn's chest, then her temple.

She crumpled to the ground.

Jack heard the first shot and looked up, puzzled. No one had permission to be hunting on the grounds this morning.

Probably some poor man trying to feed his family.

When he heard the second shot, he frowned. Then, a moment later, soft screams were carried toward him on the gentle summer wind.

His heart began to pound. Turning, he raced for the stable.

"Jack! *Jack!*" Angel's face was a frozen mask of fear as she raced toward him, her skirts flying.

He dismounted in a flash. When he saw Gwyn lying in the meadow, all thoughts left his head. She was so very still. Her arms and legs were flung out about her, and she looked like a broken doll one of his sisters had once found. Blood dripped down the side of her face, the red in stark contrast to the whiteness of her skin.

"Gwyn," Angel said softly as she placed two fingers against her friend's mouth. "Jack, she's barely breathing!"

"We have to get her home," he said quietly. They weren't far from the house, but he could never carry her all that distance in time. . . .

"Angelique, hold my horse."

He saw her eyes widen with fear, but she did as he told her.

He lifted Gwyn carefully. Her body was limp, her arms and legs dangled uselessly. Swallowing against the tightness in his throat, Jack swung her into his arms and walked swiftly to his horse. He glanced at Angel.

"Hold her just an instant."

Within seconds, he was in the saddle, then leaning down and easing Gwyn up into his arms.

Angel's face had turned a sickly white. When Jack followed her gaze, he saw the dark red stain spreading over her skirt.

Gwyn's labor was hard but mercifully short. The baby, a beautiful boy, was born merely three hours after her accident. He was perfectly formed and terribly small. The cord was wrapped around his neck, so Gwyn never heard her child cry.

Belinda waited until she heard the good news, then swiftly packed her things and ordered a carriage brought around front. She had accomplished what she had set out to do. Now, she had to go to Andrew.

Jack sat perfectly still in the kitchen. He had remained outside Gwyn's bedroom door for as long as he could, but her cries had torn at his heart and he had escaped downstairs. Even in the kitchen he had heard her.

If Andrew were here. She cries his name. He could comfort her.

He was worried about Angelique. She had come to the bedroom door once to tell him there was nothing else she and Beth needed. Her eyes had been red-rimmed, her mouth set in a hard line. He had longed to take her into his arms and comfort her, but she had looked back as Gwyn had moaned softly, then quickly closed the door.

It was a hot summer day, the sun blazing in the sky and burning off the haze. And Jack cradled his head in his hands and wondered at the cruelty of a God that allowed such terrible things to happen.

He didn't know how much later it was when the door

opened. Angel walked in, then stopped as she saw him. He wanted to offer her the comfort of his arms, but something in the hard set of her shoulders restrained him.

"How is she?" he asked, suddenly afraid of the answer.

"Alive. Barely." Angel seemed to spit out the words, her tone harsh. "The baby, he is dead."

But Jack wasn't deceived by her hard tone. Something around her mouth caught his attention. The faintest quiver.

"The cord was wrapped around his neck. He was too little. If she hadn't—" She stopped, and he watched as she smoothed her finger over a china plate on the table.

"When a baby is born too early—" She stopped again.

"Angelique—"

"When a baby is born too early, it doesn't have a chance to turn. His feet came out first and the cord got tangled around his neck. He strangled to death. She wanted that baby so badly. If she had not been teaching me—"

"No, Angelique—"

"And Lily—"

She picked up the plate with a swift movement and threw it against the wall. The crash seemed to loosen something inside her, and Jack ducked as she picked up cups and saucers, crystal goblets, a pitcher, anything she could reach. Everything shattered against the wall, and she was crying and crying.

He grabbed her and she jerked away, then swept her hands over the table, dislodging bread and butter, a jar of jam, a pitcher of milk. She turned toward another stack of plates and, lifting the entire stack with arms that trembled, sent them sailing to the floor.

And in the midst of all the shattered china and crockery, she covered her eyes and wept.

He went to her then, put his arms around her, and led her to the far corner of the kitchen. And that was where Beth found them, Angel still sobbing brokenly and curled up in his lap, her cheek pressed against his chest.

*　　*　　*

Andrew was staring into the fire as his grandfather talked to him. A pain squeezed his chest and he closed his eyes, knowing what he would see. The dream again, only this time it was happening while he was awake. Blood everywhere, and screaming. He shook his head to clear the image from his mind, then covered his ears with his hands.

"Andrew?" His grandfather was studying him intently.

"Something terrible is happening," he said softly.

"Whatever do you mean?"

He walked slowly to where his grandfather was sitting and knelt down beside him. Taking Henry's hand between both of his, he looked up at the older man.

"Tell me where she is."

Henry sighed. "I don't know why you think I would know."

"Tell me."

When his grandfather didn't answer, he stood up and walked slowly out of the room.

"He is not well, Henry. Even you must see that."

Henry stared into the fire. He had sent a message, asking his most respected surgeon—and close friend—over for dinner. Now they were enjoying drinks in the comfort of his library. He wanted to talk to his friend about Andrew. The boy had lost heart. And that strange incident today—almost as if he had been having delusions again. More than anything, he was afraid the fever had affected his brain.

"He has too much black choler. It governs his mind; his mood is too melancholy. Remember his mother, Henry? It was in her blood as well."

"Do you think he would take his own life?"

"Yes, I do. All signs point to it. Does he have much religious conviction?"

"None at all, I am afraid."

"Then I must speak honestly with you, Henry. Your grandson has lived a fast life as a man of pleasure. He brings these infirmities upon himself. He needs a course of fresh air

367

and fresh milk, straight from the cow. I suggest you get him out of London and to that house of yours in the country. London has a malign influence on some men. Your grandson needs help, and you must see he receives it."

Henry closed his eyes and thought of Gwyn. *She promised.* He would see she kept that promise.

"We will leave in the morning."

"Angel," Gwyn called softly. Her friend was at her side in an instant.

"Whatever you want, I shall get it for you."

"My baby."

"Gwyn—"

"Please. I have to see him."

When they laid him in her arms, she was surprised by how tiny he was. Gwyn looked at her child for a long time, traced the inside of his delicate ear with her forefinger, counted his fingers and toes. The small amount of hair on his head was black, and Beth had told her his eyes were blue.

It seemed impossible that mere hours ago he had been safely inside her body, kicking lustily. Now he was so cold. So very still.

She felt gentle fingers smoothing her hair off her face and looked up into Beth's eyes. They were unusually bright.

"Let me take him; there's a good girl—"

"I want to baptize him."

She was met with total silence.

"I will bury him today and he will be baptized."

"Gwyneth, no one can baptize a baby once he is—"

"I will do it myself."

Angel's face appeared behind Beth. "You shouldn't be out of bed—"

"By the river, where the trees form a circle. I used to sit there while I carried him." She started to swing her feet over the side of the bed, wincing as she did so.

"Gwyn, give me the baby." This from Beth. The woman was pleading with her.

"If you do not let me do this, I will never forgive you." Something bright and hot was burning inside her body, a fierce will and determination. Though she had her own private feelings toward her God now, her child would not be put into the earth without being baptized.

Beth seemed to recognize something in her expression that would not be thwarted. "Give me your child, Gwyn. I will not betray you."

They made a strange party as they walked to the river. One man, two older woman, one girl, and a young mother carrying her child. The sun was low in the sky, and soon twilight would come to the country, bathing it in soft purple hues.

Jack carried the small oak casket in his arms. Beth had wanted him to carry Gwyn, but she had insisted she would walk. And Beth, knowing Barbara's determination was the legacy her daughter possessed, did not argue the point.

There was something so poignant in hearing the familiar words in a feminine voice, knowing only the woman who had carried the child could feel the loss in this particular way.

Gwyn's voice was low and steady as she said the words she had listened to her father say hundreds of times before. She had to pause at times; her bandaged head ached horribly. But she closed her eyes, gathered strength, and forced herself to go on.

I baptize thee, Andrew James Leighton . . .

And then, following quickly upon the baptism, Gwyn, holding her baby to her breast, spoke other too-familiar words.

She clutched him tightly against her. He was wrapped in a white blanket Caroline had embroidered, and Gwyn stroked his head softly as she continued with the service.

She spoke neither slowly nor with haste, and it seemed she had never really heard the words before. Gwyn didn't see the circle of people surrounding her, their heads bowed as they listened. She didn't see Caroline's chin quiver, or the tear that ran off the end of her long nose. She didn't see Beth enfold Angel in her arms, or Jack standing silently to the side, swallowing over and over.

She simply stroked her baby's head and offered him up to God.

It was only at the very end, when she knew she would have to put him in the ground all alone, that her voice faltered slightly.

She stood quietly as Jack dug the small grave, then gently laid her son inside the oak box. She had asked Beth to bring several things, and these went inside the coffin as well. The three pairs of booties she had knitted while pregnant. The tiny bonnet Angel had made from material left over when Gwyn had taken in a gown for her. The rattle Jack had carved out of wood.

Caroline had carried a bouquet of white roses, and now Gwyn took just one, a bud barely opened, and placed it beside her child.

She averted her eyes as Jack fitted the cover on the coffin and tapped the wooden pegs into place. Her hand reached out and found Angel's, and she knew she had to be crushing her friend's fingers.

Then Jack slowly lowered the small oak box into the ground.

After the burial, Jack covered the tiny mound with several large stones. Gwyn took the roses from Caroline and laid them on top of the grave. She stared at it, as if seeing it for the first time, then turned toward Jack, a silent appeal in her eyes.

He stepped forward, then lifted her gently into his arms. With three women following him, he slowly carried Gwyn back home.

Chapter Twenty-Two

The following morning, Gwyn knew instinctively that if she did not get out of bed she would die. There seemed to be nothing to live for. She had fallen asleep with her hand against her flatter stomach, and as she had woken this morning she had wondered why her baby wasn't moving. As her eyes opened and she slowly recognized where she was and remembered what had happened, for one intense moment she had wanted to die.

Now she dressed slowly, her fingers stiff and clumsy. Ignoring her corset, she drew on a white linen chemise and white cotton dress. It was late morning, the summer sun was already high in the sky, and she wondered at how the world could continue along as if nothing had ever happened.

A walk. A walk in the rose garden. She did not want to see people. There was a tightness within her body as she grappled with her pain, a confusion in her mind as she fought with a God who would allow such things to happen.

She was no stranger to death. But during her brief, hard labor, she had breathed a silent, agonized prayer and asked that her child be spared if she gave herself up to God.

It had not been answered.

She braided her hair, her actions wooden and unfeeling, then decided to slip outside and avoid facing either company or the smell of food. She would never eat again.

Stiffly, with carefully controlled movements, she slowly approached her bedroom door.

As Scarborough Hall came into view, Andrew closed his eyes. His grandfather had insisted they visit, but he didn't understand how this change could make any difference. They had left London the day after he had had that strange vision.

Even now, when he caught Henry's eyes on him, he knew his grandfather was afraid.

I understand you now, Mother. And as hard as I fought to remain within myself, I have found that my heart now belongs to another. I am well acquainted with your pain and why you died so long before you took your life.

He had thought of doing the same. He knew his grandfather realized this and blamed his mother for it. But when life was a continuous source of pain and it stretched out endlessly before you, there seemed no other alternative.

Just to stop the pain. To stop seeing her face—her eyes—in my mind. I simply want peace.

He opened his eyes as he felt the carriage slowly roll to a stop. Assuming his grandfather would open the door immediately, he stared at the older man curiously.

"She is here," Henry said softly.

His throat closed, and he stared at his grandfather dumbly. "She betrayed you, Andrew."

But he was already fumbling with the door. It opened and he jumped down, not caring, not looking back.

Gwyneth. He had found her.

She looked up, feeling his presence the instant before he came into sight. And for one wild moment, she thought of hiding. The rose garden was in blood, lush blossoms fully opened and facing the sun. There were petals on the ground;

372

she had vaguely been aware of their strong, heady scent as she walked.

"Gwyn?" he said softly. She watched as he stopped within several feet of her. He was hesitant. Afraid. Something in his eyes told her he had never received her letter.

She drank in the sight of him, and she wondered what had happened to the vital man who had first swept her off her feet at The Dark Stallion, who had carried her up the stairs and made love to her with such passion. Who had been unable to hurt her, even in the midst of intense pain of his own. Who had been determined to protect her.

Our love for each other has come to this. Looking at the gauntness of his face, the slightly awkward movements, she saw her own image. His eyes held the same pain. Perhaps Henry was right and they were not meant for each other. But even as the thought came into her mind, a tiny spark of her soul resisted.

His gaze was moving over her. She felt it stop as it rested on her stomach. Involuntarily, her hand came to rest on it, her fingers tightening as they clenched the thin material.

The question was in his eyes.

She took a deep breath and did not even hesitate in telling him the lie. It came to her quickly, slipping into her mind as easily as the sunlight came up over the horizon. If there was one thing she was certain of, it was that she could not continually deny this man as his grandfather had asked.

What she was about to tell him would ensure her it would only be this once.

Thus, Gwyn began the lie, not worrying overmuch about God. There was nothing more in the world for her.

"I rid myself of the baby," she said, quietly amazed that her voice remained steady. "It was an inconvenience."

The flare of deeper pain that leapt into his eyes was almost her undoing. She took another breath and sealed her fate.

"I thought there were quite enough bastards in your family, and I did not want to bear another—"

The hand that cracked across her cheekbone silenced her. The force of the slap turned her head sharply, and her eyes focused dully on a single rose. It was a deep red, and a fat, yellow and black bee buzzed gently against the velvet petals. There was no other sound in the world.

Gwyn kept her eyes averted as Andrew walked away. Only after she was sure he had gone did she allow her shaking legs to give way, and she sank slowly to her knees.

Henry was calmly seeing to the unloading of the carriage even as his thoughts were seething.

Will she break the promise? Damnation, but she has bewitched the boy!

His thoughts were interrupted as Andrew seemed to explode into the courtyard.

"Andrew! I thought we might—"

But his grandson was already untying his stallion Mephisto from the back of the carriage, and Henry had never seen such a look of despair on his face.

"Andrew, what the devil—"

He watched as Andrew vaulted up on the stallion's broad back, gripped the reins, and wheeled the horse sharply. He dug in his heels and the stallion shot forward.

"Andrew, I— *Andrew!*"

But his words had absolutely no effect.

"Keep your heels down, Angelique. And you must hold the reins tightly, otherwise you will never be able to—" Jack stopped his instructions as he heard shouting carrying clearly through the still summer air. Glancing in that direction, he watched a familiar black stallion come barreling out of the courtyard and thundering toward the forest.

"Can you control your horse for a short time?" he asked quickly.

Angel nodded her head, her gaze also following the rider's wild flight.

"I will come back for you," he promised, then he turned his horse sharply in the direction the black stallion was galloping and dug in his heels.

Patterns of shadow and light flashed crazily on the road as Mephisto floated over the packed dirt. Andrew's gloveless fingers burned with the effort he made to maintain control of the stallion. In his anguish, he thought of letting the horse have his head and run until he killed himself or, preferably, both of them.

His body burned with a fierce, primal heat as feelings he had pressed down for so very long surfaced. When Gwyn had spoken to him in the garden, something inside him had snapped. He had never truly believed she was capable of betraying him, but now her own words had convicted her. He had lain awake nights and wondered what he would do if he found she had been deceitful. But he had never believed it was possible.

Until now.

Mephisto's breath was coming in short, shallow gasps as the animal galloped faster and faster. His hooves were a blur against the ground, and Andrew thought of simply letting go and sliding underneath those powerful hooves. . . .

The sound of a horse galloping behind him caught his attention and he turned his head quickly. Jack. On his mare. The horse was no match for Mephisto, and not wanting to see his friend, Andrew dug in his heels and gave the stallion more rein.

But within minutes the hoofbeats were louder, then he could see the bay mare's finely shaped head out of the corner of his eye. Jack leaned across the short distance that separated them and reached for his reins. Andrew knew Jack could be injured if he chose to fight, and it was that knowledge that

375

stayed his hand. He watched as his friend took control of the leather reins and steadily began to slow the pace of both their horses.

Soon their mounts were walking. Andrew stared straight ahead, wondering why Jack had decided to come after him. If his friend dared to give him some religious piece of drivel concerning the sacredness of life, he would be tempted to thrash him.

Instead, Jack asked quietly, "Why are you running, 'Drew?" He hadn't used the childhood nickname in years, and the endearment caused Andrew's throat to tighten and his eyes to sting.

"My child," he began, his voice a whisper.

There was a slight pause, then Jack spoke again. Slowly, as if he were choosing his words carefully.

"I cannot know what that is like. But I do know, 'Drew, the pain will be with you forever. Now you and Gwyn need each other more than ever."

Andrew was silent, as a pain so intense it threatened to tear him apart ripped through him.

"She needs you, 'Drew. It almost killed her. When she—"

"It should have killed her. What she did—" Now his voice was harsh with suppressed pain.

Jack brought their horses to a stop. "What did she tell you?"

His laugh was bitter. "She got rid of it. She didn't want to bear a *bastard*." He looked away from his friend. Andrew felt his nose sting sharply. It hurt to draw breath, and for an instant he had the urge to cover his face with his hands and cry. The feeling shamed him.

"'Drew—" Here he could feel Jack's hesitation. "Gwyn had an accident. She was—"

"How convenient for her. I have heard of women who have—"

"*Listen to me!*" Jack grabbed Mephisto's reins, and both horses came to a halt. "It was not deliberate. I stood outside the bedroom door the day she lost the baby, and the cries that

376

came from her were not those of a woman who deliberately rid herself of a child."

"Why did she admit to it?"

There was a slight hesitation. "That I do not know. I can only tell you what I do. She loved that child. The same day he was born she got out of bed and insisted he be baptized. She did it herself. I heard her say the words and I saw the way she held that child, and with God as my witness, Andrew, she did not want to lose that baby."

He. A son. His throat tightened, making an answer impossible.

There was no sound save for the stamping of hooves and the swishing of tails. A bird twittered gently in the distance. Still, Andrew could not meet his friend's eyes.

He heard Jack expel a soft breath. Then he said quietly, "Think what you must, Andrew. But as she gave birth to your son, she cried for you." He dropped Mephisto's reins and turned his mare. He prodded her gently with his heels. The bay mare snorted, then slowly began to canter away.

Andrew stared ahead, blindly. *Why did she lie?* For as soon as Jack had told him, he knew the truth for what it was. Gwyneth was not the sort of woman to harm a helpless child.

"Jack!" he called sharply. He pulled at his reins, wheeled Mephisto around and, digging his heels into the stallion's sides, followed his friend.

Gwyn sat in the clearing, her back against the rough bark of one of the trees that formed the fairy ring. She had known this clearing would give her peace and the sight of her child's grave would comfort her. She felt closer to him here, could close her eyes and see the tiny face and hands in her mind's eye.

She had knelt in the rose garden for a long time, the sun hot on her shoulders, then had finally stood up slowly and come here—where no one would look for her.

You did what you had to. Now do what you must. There was no

377

longer any reason to stay. She had stayed to please Caroline and Beth and to await the birth of her child. Now she had to leave.

I want to leave, she corrected herself sharply. She would never be able to smell roses again without being sick. And she would never walk back through that garden. The desire to flee this house overrode all else, and her mind worked frantically as she thought of a way.

And though she had denied there was a merciful God, in the end she remembered a convent in France that Madeleine had once told her about. It seemed a fitting end to her life, now that there was nothing for her here. Her time with her father had been spent in service to others, and now she would continue that service.

She was quite sure it would be an easy choice. Both the man and the child she had loved so fiercely were gone forever. There was no chance she would be as blessed again. The only thought that restrained her was what would become of Angel. Her friend had fought so hard to make her way out of the brothel. Now she was just beginning to see what another way of life could be like. Gwyn knew she couldn't simply ask Angel to seek another restrained life.

Yet she knew she could not remain here. Andrew would come back eventually, and she could not see him again. Her lie had given her time, so she could plan her escape and never have to see him again.

It hurts too much. Every glance Henry had directed her way, each tiny inflection of his voice, had made his opinion more than clear. There was no possibility she would ever be good enough for Andrew. Now, outside The Dark Stallion, the differences in their respective positions had been brought home with crushing finality.

She would never stop loving him. She had destroyed their love with her lie, could never be with him now. Henry had seen to that, and Gwyn knew that as much as she loved Andrew, his family had been torn apart long enough. There had been nothing nearing normalcy in his life. According to his grandfather, in spoken and unspoken ways, she had contributed to that upheaval by her mere presence.

It is over. She was beyond tears and merely sat in the clearing, staring blindly ahead. Seeing nothing.

Gwyn closed her eyes and leaned her head back against the tree. Beth or Caroline would certainly lend her the necessary funds for starting her new life, and she would work dutifully until she could pay them back. And Angel—Angel would understand, as she always had.

She was still for a long time before she sensed another presence. Opening her eyes, she turned her head and saw Andrew at the edge of the small clearing.

She could not move. Her limbs felt numb as she stared at him, wondering how he had found her. And slowly, as she studied his face—for she could not seem to tear her gaze away—she sensed some of his old strength returning. His eyes seemed clearer. There was a quiet self-assurance to his movements as he started into the clearing.

He sat down next to her, and she did not have the spirit to shrink away from him. Gwyn didn't even flinch as his fingers gently touched her chin, turning her face toward him.

Andrew gazed upon her as if he had never seen her before. Gwyn could feel his concentration upon her cheekbone, where she was sure a bruise had formed. As she watched his face, tears filled his eyes. Then he lowered his lips to her cheek and kissed her.

That simple kiss on her cheek was her undoing. She closed her eyes against the quick stinging, bit her lip against the urge to cry. She hadn't been able to cry since her baby's death. Gwyn had longed for Andrew, knowing he was the only person who could truly share her pain.

He kissed her cheek again, softly, then leaned back against the tree next to her. His hand found hers, their fingers entwined. And though she did not know why or how he had come back to her after she had told him the lie, she did not question his presence. He was here, and that was all that mattered.

"Jack told me the truth."

She had no answer, so she remained silent.

"Our child—"

"A boy."

When he did not reply, she continued. "I named him Andrew James Leighton. James after my father. And I baptized him before I buried him, so I cannot believe God would deny him entrance to heaven."

"He is here?" he asked, gazing steadily at the small mound of earth.

Gwyn nodded. "I sat in this clearing while I carried him. I thought he liked it. He moved so very much, but when I came here, it seemed to quiet him as it quieted me. . . ." She stopped, her throat raw. Tight. Her eyes filled with hot tears. Gwyn leaned her head back against the tree and stared up at the leafy canopy above, a green blur. This clearing brought her peace. It seemed her life had raced along from the time she had been sold to Janet Wickens. She had forgotten how much power nature had to quiet the soul.

"What did he—what did he look like?"

It was only when Andrew asked that question that she realized he was trying to form a picture of his son. Sorrow filled her heart at the realization that Andrew had never seen his child. She had some memories, no matter how slight. And Gwyn knew her memories had helped her endure thus far.

"He had black hair," she began slowly, fighting to still the quiver she felt in her throat. "And blue eyes, Beth said. I held him in my arms for a short time." She cleared her throat, then met Andrew's eyes, her own brimming. It was as if pieces of her were beginning to loosen, to break apart. The tight knot of pain she hadn't been able to let go of was surfacing now that the one person who could understand how she felt was here.

"He was so tiny," she whispered as she felt one scalding tear run down her cheek.

He held out his arms and she went into them.

He will do it again, Beth thought as she stared out into the rose garden. Henry had taken one look at her and his brows had drawn together, his look thunderous. He had retreated to his library, disgusted with his grandson for seeking out Gwyn. Jack had told Andrew where he thought he would find her. Neither Gwyn nor Andrew had returned, and supper had been served throughout an uncomfortable silence.

I pray they are comforting each other. The time for their hurting each other is over. She knew all of Henry's objections to Andrew's loving Gwyn. Would that the man could see that his grandson truly giving his heart to any woman was a miracle in itself!

And if he knew who she truly was, even her stay at The Dark Stallion would raise no objections.

She was about to turn around and go inside for the night when a flash of white caught her eye. She squinted against the darkness, then realized she had caught sight of Gwyneth's dress. There was a full moon riding high in the summer sky, and it caught the white cotton and turned it silver. Andrew was carrying her gently in his arms as he approached the house, the look on his face tender and fiercely protective at the same time. He reminded her of a much younger Henry, and Beth felt her heart turn over.

I hope he is stronger than my Henry was. In so many ways, the two men reminded her of each other. Both were stubborn, both proud. Grandfather pitted against grandson. She wondered if the grandson would prove to be stronger in matters of the heart.

As Andrew came inside, Beth fell into step. She followed him as he approached the stairs. Her ears, ever alert, heard the sound of the library door opening.

Henry.

"Andrew, if I might have a word with you—" the older man

began from the foot of the stairs.

His grandson didn't even break stride, and Beth felt her heart swell with admiration. *Ah, perhaps the grandson is stronger already*.

Angelique appeared at the top of the stairs, and her eyes widened at the sight of Andrew with Gwyn in his arms.

"Angelique, if you would show me the way to Gwyneth's room—"

"Your clothes are in the blue bedroom at the far end of the hall. . . ." Henry began, his tone challenging.

Andrew kept walking up the stairs. He was almost to the top when Elizabeth glanced down and, out of the corner of her eye, saw Henry begin to climb the stairs.

She stopped at the top and waited for him. He reached her side, breathing heavily, and would have followed his grandson down the hall had she not laid a restraining hand on his arm.

"Leave them, Henry."

"Are you daft, woman? I cannot have him running after her like she was a bitch in heat! This has to be stopped!"

She tightened the grip on his arm as he attempted to shake her off. "Don't interfere, Henry. They need time together. They must comfort each other." As Henry's determination seemed to visibly increase, she reminded him, "They have just lost a child. Do you remember how you felt when you lost Geoffrey?"

"Woman, it is not the same thing!"

Beth knew she had opened an old wound Henry kept carefully hidden, but she refused to allow him to do more damage. She had long suspected Henry was behind the fact that Andrew had not come to Gwyn sooner. The moment she had seen the young man's face she knew he loved Gwyn and had suffered during their time apart. Now she was determined to do what she could to protect her niece. The truth about her identity would come out soon enough, and then all would be forgiven.

She held onto his arm tightly. He would have to drag her

down the hall after him if he wanted to continue with this folly. "Henry, you cannot mean that. She carried the child and grew to love him dearly. Andrew wanted that baby. Now stop this nonsense and leave them alone."

"My grandson is young and hot-blooded," Henry said quietly, his blue eyes chilling her. "He will forget her in time. She is not the woman for him."

"Rather a harsh lesson that you plan to teach him, Henry. I trust his offense warrants your punishment." Sudden hot anger at his stupidity overrode her common sense. "You treat him as if he were a boy!" The accusing words seemed to explode out of her. Beth tightened her grip on Henry's arm. He was angry with her. She was well acquainted with that anger, and though many years had passed since she had spoken with the only man she had ever loved, she was not afraid of his quiet rage. She would not bend.

Not a second time. For now she knew the price of such weakness.

"He *is* a boy. A lovesick child. He does not know what he wants, crying after her, refusing to eat. He does not behave like a man, letting that woman soften him! She weakens him!"

"Do you remember the way you once felt about me, Henry?" She deliberately lowered her voice, knowing it would humiliate him terribly if anyone were to overhear.

He didn't answer her question. "We did what we had to. We both survived. I don't understand why Andrew cannot—"

"I did not survive well, Henry."

He stopped his furiously muttered tirade and simply stared at her.

She met his gaze head on. "I have never loved another man the way I loved you. And I have never stopped loving you. Each night before I slept, I wondered at the years we wasted, all in the name of duty."

"Beth, I—"

"Did your father have to live your life? Did he see what transpired within my heart? Did he appreciate my—our pain? I

383

think not."

"Beth—"

"I do not expect you to return my affection. But I wanted you to know my deepest feelings. We made a terrible mistake, Henry. We stopped believing in each other. You, when you bent to your father's will. And I, when I married Jonathan."

He was completely silent, and she knew all thoughts of chasing after his grandson had flown from his head.

"It is the cruelest thing lovers can do to each other, don't you think? To have such little faith." She was blinking rapidly now and wanted nothing more than to flee from his side. She had thought of confronting Henry many times. Now the moment was at hand and nothing had gone exactly as she had planned it. Taking a deep breath, Elizabeth determined her niece would have the happiness she had been denied.

"He loves her, Henry. I don't even think he knows how much yet. But he is stronger than you were. He will fight you. If you deny him that love, you will watch him die, for he gathers strength from her. Did you see how he looked before he went to her? And now, the strength within as he holds her closely to him?"

She was crying, something she had sworn she would never do in front of Henry. Beth could taste the salt tears as they ran down her face. Her hands trembled, and she released her grip.

"You lost one son, Henry. In the name of heaven, do not lose a grandson and another piece of your heart."

And, turning abruptly, she stumbled away from him, tears blinding her eyes.

Chapter Twenty-Three

You have never forgiven a woman this much.

Andrew sat at the foot of the enormous bed in Gwyn's room, staring unseeingly into the fire. The only sound other than its crackle and hiss was Gwyn's slow, steady breathing as she slept.

There was still the letter between them. He had recognized her handwriting. When he had discovered she could read and write, he has asked her to show him. Her hand had been delicate. Graceful. Feminine.

He could still remember the pain he had felt when he had read her last letter. She had admitted her part in the deception.

But I trust you will believe that I only desired your wealth and had no wish to see you fall ill and suffer so. In time, I pray you will forgive me, as our paths will most certainly never cross again.

He only had to close his eyes to see that letter and relive the pain. There had been no mention of the child they had created together. No mention of where she was or how she felt. Just total admission of her part in the duplicity.

And yet . . . And yet . . .

He was startled away from his black thoughts by her soft moan. Andrew moved quickly, and when Gwyn opened her eyes he was kneeling at the side of her bed, looking down into her pale face.

"Andrew, I—" She looked wildly around the bedroom. Frightened.

"You're safe. No one is going to harm you." As she eyed him, her expression wary, he eased himself up on the bed.

"Andrew—"

He could almost see her thoughts. "I do not intend to claim any rights this night, madam, or for many nights to come. You have just suffered through birthing a child, and I am not low enough to force my attentions upon you at this time."

She closed her eyes, and his chest tightened at the expression on her face, the tautness around her mouth. Something was wrong.

Perhaps she had not thought he would ever catch up with her.

"Andrew, I must know, did you come to this house . . . for me?"

"I did not know you were here." He answered her curtly. There was a part of him that did not want her to know how deeply she affected him. He was afraid that if she knew, he would be powerless. Weak. And would go through that pain again.

You do not know who she is. Who was this woman who cried out for him while she gave birth to his child and was capable of writing him that calculated, unfeeling note?

What was within that mind? Behind those blue eyes? Had she cared for him the smallest amount? Or was she incapable of caring for anyone but herself?

"I see," she said softly. "And would you have come to me if you had known I was here?"

He thought of the hours spent in his bedroom, looking out into the sky at nothing. Of the pain that had twisted his body. Of the tears shed while lying chained to the floor in a prison cell, all because he had given her his heart and she had betrayed him.

And he thought of what she might do with that knowledge if she knew.

"No."

"Then why are you here?" Her voice was flat and toneless.

"Grandfather thought it was time for a visit."

"And do you always do what your grandfather asks of you?"

There was something in her tone that annoyed him. "No. Usually I attempt the opposite."

He watched as she swallowed slowly, then met his eyes.

"And did you receive my letter?"

"Yes."

He watched as the briefest of emotions flickered and died within those blue eyes. Her lashes lowered, and he was suddenly annoyed that she was hiding her feelings from him.

"How did you expect me to feel?" he asked suddenly.

She seemed surprised. "I would only ask that you answer me truthfully, in kind."

"*Truthfully*, Madam? Strange words, coming from you." Just the thought of that letter and all the pain it had caused was enough to make him start to tremble with rage.

He watched as she slowly raised her lashes, and the blue eyes were suddenly brilliant with emotion. "You said you received my letter, yet you claim not to know where I was. How many houses in the country do you own?"

Some instinct deep within him caught and held. For endless moments he studied her face, and he suddenly realized he was hoping, hoping she was innocent. For if she were . . .

"What did you write in your letter?" he asked abruptly.

He was surprised when a hot flush of color suffused her neck and cheeks. She could not meet his eyes.

"I said . . . many things of a most personal nature, m'lord."

"*Andrew*."

"I told you where I was. I respected and obeyed your wishes. You wanted me to leave London so I would be safe. You trusted your grandfather to take me to this place. I waited for you, Andrew, until you were feeling better and were ready to come for me."

He felt as if he were in a dream. How could this be so? There had been nothing of this in the letter his grandfather had given him.

Grandfather.

"And who did you give this letter to, Gwyn?"

She moistened her lips. "Your grandfather. He promised me I might leave you a note."

"And why did you leave?"

There was a flash of anger in those eyes, then all was restrained once again and she replied quietly, "Your grandfather told me you thought it was best."

"I see." He surprised himself by reaching up and smoothing a stray lock of her golden blond hair back from her brow. "I'm sorry to trouble you with these questions, Gwyn. I will return shortly."

"Why did you give me that letter?"

Henry had never seen his grandson in such a quiet rage. Geoffrey had never seethed like this. He recognized Andrew's anger because it was so like his own when roused.

"I did as she asked."

"That was not the letter she wrote me."

Henry's face felt tight, and he hoped his expression did not betray him, nor the sudden flush of warmth to his cheeks. "And you trust this woman, Andrew? After all she has done? You want her so badly you would forgive her betrayal?"

"She did not betray me. While we talked, she discussed quite another letter from the one you gave to me."

"I am sure she would discuss anything if she thought it might better suit her purpose."

"Then you are calling Gwyneth a liar?"

"Yes."

"And Jack?"

He was silent. What could Andrew mean by that? Jack had had nothing to do with his attempts to rid his family of that whore.

"How am I calling Jack a liar, Andrew?" he asked patiently.

"He told me how Gwyn suffered when she lost our child." Here Henry was distressed to hear the tightness in his grandson's voice. *Why did that woman ever try to bear his bastard?* His dislike of Gwyneth overrode all else and refused to let him feel even the slightest amount of sorrow for the child she had lost. If anything, he had thought it would make it all the easier for him to separate the two.

"And what has this to do with anything?" he asked impatiently. *What has that fever done to him? Now he cannot even carry on a conversation.*

"A woman who suffered so over losing a man's child could not betray that man. I know her, Grandfather. Gwyn did not betray me."

"So you are saying I did?" Now he could feel anger filling him. How had that woman managed to tell Andrew the truth?

"I am saying I want to know what was in her letter."

And Henry thought quickly of that impassioned letter and all the love it had contained. The woman had laid bare her soul, but he had felt no regret when he had flipped the piece of paper into the fire.

"I am sure I have no idea what you are talking about."

And with that reply, Henry effectively ended the conversation.

Gwyn lay staring at the ceiling. Andrew had left her, and she was sure he had gone to his grandfather.

He never gave him the letter. She knew this with a certainty now, and closing her eyes, she curled herself into a tight ball to ward off the pain.

Pain. Nothing but pain. Her cousin Edward had betrayed her. Then Henry. Lies and lies, one heaped upon the other. Was Andrew caught up in them, or was he part of this manipulation as well? Did he care for her at all?

And then, the death of her child.

From the moment she had looked at her dead son, Gwyn had lost her faith in a merciful God. Though she had baptized her child, not wanting to hinder his journey to heaven, she had also divorced herself from the faith that had always comforted her.

And what would you have me do now, Father? You taught me to believe. I find I no longer have the heart for it. I know you would tell me He lost his only son, but I do not want to hear any of it. All I know is that the child I loved will never be with me. I had so much love inside me that has turned to so much pain. And it will become bitterness in time, for I no longer believe any God exists.

The world is simply madness.

The Duke of Cuckfield sat quietly in his library, a glass of sherry in his hand. He was staring at a portrait above the fireplace, and disgust tinged his features. A similar portrait hung in his country house, Ashton Hall. He could never look upon the portraits without feeling the old, familiar emotions. Disgust and hatred. He glanced away.

I cannot find her. He had looked all over London for Gwyneth Leighton, hiring men from all walks of life to infiltrate every level of London society.

Nothing. No one had seen her.

I have to find her. He knew Andrew had not found her either. There were wild rumors racing through the city, the most promising of all that the Earl of Scarborough was actually dying. He had contracted a fever while held prisoner in Newgate, and though he had survived the initial illness, it was said by members of his household that Andrew had never quite recovered. His grandfather had taken him to the country.

All of London had looked on, wondering if Andrew would take his own life. As his mother had.

Mother. He directed his gaze back to the portrait. The woman had blond hair, so like his own, and deep blue eyes. There was a hint of stubbornness around her jawline and a rebellious gleam in the depths of those eyes.

But you didn't outwit me, Mother, for I finally found you. He
smiled. Memories of that hunt proved particularly satisfying.
He had never been thwarted before in his pursuits of either
sex. He had torn through them all, searching for that elusive
one who would give him back strength and energy, youth and
potency.

Gwyneth. She alone eluded him.

He could close his eyes and remember her on the auction
block. The moment he had seen her he had known she would
release everything locked within him. He had to have her. But
for Andrew, he would have had her that very night.

And here it was summer, and still he had been thwarted.

He took another sip of sherry, then glanced back up at the
portrait. The blue eyes seemed to be laughing at him.

"Damn you! And *damn her!"* His hand was raised in an
instant, and the glass arched through the still air. It shattered
against the portrait, the amber-colored liquid spilling over the
woman's face.

"I found you. And I will find her." His voice was low and
intense, hatred filling him as he remembered the woman in the
portrait. But as he continued to stare at the oil, he smiled. In
his mind's eye, he could still see the terrified expression on his
mother's face when she had turned and found him standing in
that cloistered garden. It was one of his favorite memories.

You never thought I would find you. I will find her, as well.

The Duke settled back more comfortably in his chair. The
way the light danced over the delicate colors, the spilled sherry
covering most of the canvas, it seemed the woman trapped in
the portrait was crying.

Gwyn sat up slowly in her bed as she heard the door open.
The light from the fire was fading, and she had blown most of
the candles out. Still, she could make out Andrew's form in the
doorway.

He closed the door, then walked to the bed and sat down beside her.

She felt the warmth of his touch as he took one of her hands in both of his. "Will you forgive me, Gwyn, if I tell you I doubted you for a time but no longer?"

She was not sure if she understood him. And a part of her did not even care. She felt numb, empty inside, unsure if she truly wanted to go on.

"Gwyneth?"

"If it gives you comfort to receive forgiveness, I will give it to you."

He gathered her into his arms, his voice rough as he whispered against her hair. "I would give anything if I could bring our son back to you."

She closed her eyes tightly against the pain.

"But I cannot. I can only hope you will let me comfort you now, as I did by the river."

"But you need comforting as well, m'lord."

She was surprised when he didn't bother to correct her. He simply held her tighter. "I would give everything I own to have been at your side when you needed me. I'll never forgive myself for letting you go through such pain alone."

His warmth seemed to be seeping into her. She held him more tightly. He was the only thing in her world at that moment.

"Once," Andrew said softly, "once you were the only one who held on to me and refused to let me go. Even though I can remember wanting to."

As he spoke, her mind went back to those horrible days so long ago in his bedroom, with Cook, Jack, and Henry close by. The smell of herbs, the heat from the fire. From the fever.

"I thought I dreamt those moments. It was your face, Gwyn, and the touch of your hands and the sound of your voice that sustained me."

She couldn't reply.

"It was merely a fever that plagued me, while you have had a

392

part of your heart taken from you."

His chest felt warm beneath his shirt. Her cheek rested on the fine material, and she could feel the beating of his heart.

"But a part of your heart is gone as well, Andrew." Her voice trembled. "I know you would have loved him."

"Let me be strong for both of us, Gwyneth," he whispered. "It is the only way I know to stop hurting."

"I feel as if—as if there is nothing inside me anymore." Now that she had given voice to her feelings, Gwyn found it easier to admit Andrew inside her heart. "Our child is gone, and my faith followed him. When I look within, there is nothing. . . . I still cannot believe this has happened. I wake at night and wait for him to move. I forget, and then I touch my belly and it is flat and I realize he is no longer inside me. . . ." She buried her face against his shoulder, her breath held tightly.

Andrew was still for a moment, then said quietly, "I am going to make things different from now on. With your permission, I will care for you."

"Andrew, you—"

"I have done nothing but cause you pain. If you had not been here, if there had been help—"

"Beth did the best anyone could. There was nothing more to be done."

"You're leaving me, my beauty. I see it in your eyes."

She said nothing, knowing it was true. Before, when her father had told her someone had died of a broken heart, she had believed him but not truly realized what it meant. It was like hearing the words as she baptized and buried her child. She had heard them so many times before, but in the clearing by the river they had meaning.

Now she knew there was no secret to dying. It was so easy.

"Will you live for me, Gwyn?" he asked softly. "I know I have no right to ask, but I will. I will fight you on this, for I cannot let you go."

"I do not know—"

"Will you try?"

She was surprised to hear fear in his voice. Tired, she leaned against him, his chest cradling her cheek, his arms supporting her suddenly heavy body.

"For me?" His voice was barely a whisper.

"Yes."

In the days that followed, Andrew bullied her back to life. Where Gwyn might have spent her days in bed, he helped her dress, and if she could not walk, he carried her down the stairs and out into the garden. And even Henry didn't say a word, so fierce was his grandson's face.

The days lengthened into weeks. Not a day passed that Gwyn didn't visit their son's grave, and Andrew was always with her. He walked her through the woods, tricked her into eating her food, even tried to make her laugh. They took a small boat onto the river one afternoon. Another morning, she picked roses for the house while he patiently held the basket. On the days she felt stronger, they rode over the grounds, Andrew taking her to all the places he had loved as a child.

He never left her side, ignoring the bedroom that had been set up for his use and remaining in hers instead. His face was the last thing she saw at night, the first every morning. He teased her, cajoled her, encouraged her. There was never the slightest hint of passion in his touch, only the most tender gentleness.

And through it all, she talked and talked and talked to him. Her feelings. Her fears. The deepest pains she had ever experienced. She gave him a glimpse into a woman's soul, and where they had once been merely lovers, now they were becoming best friends.

He let her rest, and one afternoon she was taking a nap when Andrew entered their bedroom.

"There is a guest downstairs who wants to see you."

It had been a bad day. She had cried and cried that morning by the grave, and it had exhausted her. She had known he was worried, but even with the concern on his face she had no desire to go downstairs.

Yet she let him help her dress, then he picked her up and carried her downstairs and out into the garden. It was a glorious summer day, clear and warm. Gwyn saw the man, woman, and child immediately, and her heart soared.

Madeleine.

Dinner was a festive affair. Charles Burdett, Lord Hardwick, was a man of quiet strength, and Gwyn could understand why Madeleine had accepted his long-standing offer of marriage.

But the biggest surprise had been the child. Lucy was a delicate, blond angel, her dark blue eyes enormous in her beautifully shaped face. Eight years old, she was inquisitive and intelligent. Gwyn was enchanted when the little girl answered one of Madeleine's questions in French and was astonished at the ease with which the child switched between English and French.

Later that evening, with Lucy in bed and everyone else gathered in the large library, Madeleine sat with Gwyn.

"I am so sorry about your son," she said quietly, taking Gwyn's hand in hers. "I lost a child when I was nineteen, and there is no pain to equal it."

Gwyn squeezed that comforting hand.

"And the pain will never leave you," Madeleine continued softly. "It stays with you for the rest of your life. Yet it makes you—" She paused, searching for words. "Gwyneth, the happier moments are stronger, because you know them for what they are."

Gwyn nodded. "I prayed for you when Lily died. I know you were closest to her. I miss her so much, yet I only knew her a short time."

"She is at peace now. And away from him."

Gwyn glanced up at her friend's face as her hand began to shake.

"Walk with me. Please."

She did as Madeleine requested, and soon the two women were standing within the moonlit rose garden. The summer night air was gentle against them.

"I do not know how else to say this, Gwyn, so I will tell you quickly. Charles and I stopped at his house in London for several days. I have friends. They let me know . . . the Duke is still looking for you. It is only a matter of time before he finds you."

She felt as if the balmy summer air had suddenly turned frigid and biting. Gwyn wrapped her arms around herself.

"Why does he—why won't he leave me alone?"

Madeleine's voice was harsh. "He is obsessed with you. Ever since the auction. I was there, Gwyn, and I watched him. When you walked out on that stage, he was a man possessed."

"What can I do?"

"Know he is your enemy. Watch for him. You have Andrew's protection now; he will never let anything happen to you while he lives. But the Duke is very clever and will come to you when you least expect him."

Something, the tiniest gleam of intuition, prompted Gwyn's question. "You knew him well, didn't you Madeleine?"

Madeleine was silent for a time, then said quietly, "Lucy is his child. He left me before I told him I was pregnant. Lily helped me leave The Dark Stallion. I stayed with her mother in France for a short time after she was born, then took her to a convent where my sister is a nun. I earned enough working for Janet to see my daughter twice a year. Lucy will never know who her father is."

"And Charles?"

"I told Charles I had a child before I accepted his proposal. When he suggested I bring Lucy to live with us, I knew he would make a good husband. He does not know who her father is. Charles is a powerful man. He will protect us."

"Did you love him?" She knew Madeleine would realize she didn't mean Charles.

"Very much. But he has a sickness inside him. When I met him, he was the most handsome man in London. Charming, polite, intelligent. Sensitive. But there was another side to him. It ate away at his mind all the time. I have never seen another person like him. As if he were two different people."

"You tried to help him." It was a statement, not a question.

Madeleine nodded, slowly. "I had never seen that other side. It was a sickness. He would come to The Dark Stallion and make love to me, but there was a part of him that was not there. I used to go to his house, and one time I was hiding, waiting in his wardrobe to surprise him, when he came in with a young Earl. The only true pleasure he is capable of is with men. He hated his mother and all the other women in his family. He hates all women."

"Why does he pursue me?"

"You have ignited something within him that will not be quenched."

"Is there any good left in him at all?"

"No. He is more devil than man. Like Lucifer, after the fall. There is nothing left but the shell. He is empty inside, except for the rage that feeds him."

"But I cannot believe—"

"*No!* Do not think there is anything good in the Duke. Your compassion will be your weakness. He finds a person's weakness and uses it to destroy them."

Gwyn was silent as she thought of the Duke, still in London. Still searching.

"Remember I told you you must know your enemies? You know more about the Duke than most people. Some of the ladies at court still find him most charming. But you must never forget what is truly inside."

"I won't."

"I would remain in the country for a time. I would keep Andrew's protection. The Duke has many enemies. How he has cheated death so many times remains a mystery."

"And if he finds me?"

"I pray he will not. I have seen too much of this world, and there is nothing stronger than his evil. Anyone it touches suffers. You are the only person who knows who Lucy's father is. Lily knew, but—" Madeleine's words were choked. "I never want his evil to touch her. You must understand; I tell you my secret to protect you."

"I'll keep your confidence."

Madeleine reached out and grabbed both her hands. "I loved him once, Gwyn, and that love almost destroyed me. Now, away from The Dark Stallion and the Duke, I am going to make a life for myself."

"Do you love Charles?" Gwyn asked.

"Yes. I do. He is a strong man and I can respect him. He understands me and we talk of everything. And he is good. He went with me to find Lily before—" She let go of Gwyn's hands and slowly lowered her head.

"Come." Gwyn put her arm around her friend's shoulders, and the two women walked slowly back toward the house.

Chapter Twenty-Four

"You're quiet tonight, Gwyn."

In the privacy of their bedroom several evenings later, Andrew watched as Gwyn brushed her hair. He had been worried about her all afternoon. Some days were better than others. This had not been one of her good days. And Andrew knew meeting Lucy, Madeleine's daughter, had touched something deep within Gwyn, striking a core of maternal affection. It had hurt him to watch her play with the child. He had thought of the son they had lost and how no other child they would ever have would replace him in their hearts.

Lucy had shown Gwyn her wooden doll, Arabella, and Gwyn had won the little girl's affection forever by taking out her needle and thread and quickly fashioning Arabella a dress out a scrap of red velvet. Lucy's eyes had widened in awe, for none of the doll clothing the nuns had allowed her had ever been as elegant. Andrew had watched the two of them together, their bright blond heads so close, and thought they might be mother and daughter.

She was gently raised to be both a wife and mother. Words Gwyn had said to him at The Dark Stallion were coming back to him, more and more. He envied her the ease with which she knew herself and her needs. It seemed he would never truly feel comfortable within his own skin. Since coming to

Scarborough Hall, feelings had rushed through him at a tremendous rate. He all but ignored Henry, who glowered at him every chance he could but seldom said a word. Beth followed his grandfather everywhere. Whenever it seemed Henry was ready to move in and start a heated argument concerning Andrew's conduct with Gwyn, Beth was there to soften the sting of his words or prevent them altogether. Andrew knew the older woman cared for Gwyn, and in doing so she earned a place in his heart.

"I'm tired, that is all."

"I thought we might go riding with Angel and Jack tomorrow. Would you like that?"

"Is Angel progressing with her lessons?"

He could feel the smile twitching at his lips. "Jack is quite a conscientious teacher. They spend more and more of their time together."

"They have missed supper several times in the past month. I would think they might be attending to more than Angel's seat on a horse."

Now she was smiling, and he was relieved he had found a subject she found pleasing.

He was determined to see that smile again. "I have decided, Gwyneth, that I have neglected certain parts of our relationship. So much was done out of order, due to unusual circumstances."

She had set down the silver and ivory hairbrush now and was staring at him as if he had quite lost his mind.

"Therefore," he said softly, "I have decided it is past time for me to court you. But I shall do it despite that realization."

"Andrew, you do not have to—"

"Now there are rules you must learn in order to do your part properly."

He was rewarded by the smallest beginnings of a smile. He could make her forget at times, and that was enough for him.

"First, I will shower you with gifts. The last time I did this you were most thankful and appreciative. We cannot have that."

The smile was growing wider.

"You must pout prettily and look dissatisfied. You must chastise me and tell me what foolish choices I have made, and how you would much rather have anything but whatever I have just purchased for you."

"But I have never been displeased with what you have given me."

"We can have none of that! You must learn about the game of love."

She shook her head, her golden hair falling over her shoulders and down her back in a glittering, sensuous display. She was so artlessly provocative, so innocently sensual. He could feel a tightening in his body, an arousal so strong it was all he could do not to tumble her into their large bed. But he wouldn't. She wasn't strong yet; she still hadn't healed. It would be wrong of him, and he could not bear the thought of hurting her further.

"I will never know the rules of such a game, Andrew."

"We shall pretend. It will be fun for you." He stood and approached her side. Taking her hairbrush out of her hand, he laced his fingers through hers and gently pulled her to her feet.

"Come now. When I attempt to steal a kiss, you must stop me with your fan. Then you must look away and blush, and whisper to me not to take such liberties."

She was laughing now, and he put his arms around her and, lifting masses of her hair with one hand, kissed her neck softly.

She went perfectly still as desire made its presence known.

"Andrew?" Now she looked up at him, a question in her eyes.

He backed away, letting go of her hair and watching as it fell softly around her waist. "I would not hurt you for the world, Gwyn."

She surprised him, stepping forward until she was quite close. "I have missed being close to you, Andrew."

Her words, simply spoken from the heart, fired his passion.

It was all he could do to simply take one of her hands and press it to his chest, over his heart. "We will have that again soon. For now, I am content to share your bed."

He couldn't stop looking at her, feeling he was drowning in the depths of those blue eyes. He watched as she cast her lashes downward, a blush rising in her face.

"You taught me once, at The Dark Stallion, that there were many ways a couple could seek pleasure. I would not be reluctant to share any of those pleasures tonight."

He said nothing in return, overwhelmed she should reveal so much to him.

The blush deepened. "I find myself quite shocked at my own feelings. . . ."

"Never, Gwyn." He was quick to reassure her, wanting her to always tell him what was closest to her heart. These last few weeks, when they had spoken so frankly, had opened all sorts of feelings within him. He had not been close to anyone most of his life, keeping himself secret and protected. Gwyn simply gave and gave, opening effortlessly toward him like a rose toward the sun.

He never wanted it to end.

"Though I am shocked, Andrew, in the end it is simply that I wish to be close to you again. I want to feel alive. I hope I have not offended—"

"Never." And as he cupped her face in his hands and brought her close for his kiss, he closed his eyes and gave himself over to her velvet fire.

Madeleine came awake with a start, her body bathed in sweat. She was shaking violently, and before she reached out and touched the bed curtain and smelled the familiar scents of fire and burnt candle wax, she didn't know where she was.

Her eyes grew accustomed to the dark, and she saw her husband lying beside her in the large bed. Lucy had been given the small room next door, and Madeleine listened carefully.

The adjoining door was open, and when she heard no sound, she slowly began to relax.

You thought you were with him. She ran her shaking fingers through her short, cropped hair. Then she cupped her hand over her mouth and stared at the dying embers of the fire. The room was growing cool, and she wrapped the blanket more closely around her.

It was simply talking with Gwyn that upset you. Remembering. Thinking of him the way he might have been. Richard came to her in her dreams quite often. He had made a powerful impression on her as a young girl. She had loved him enough to have his child, loved him enough to cry for his soul when she finally realized the twisted direction it was taking. He was a man who embraced evil and seemed to draw his strength from the dark side of his nature.

Gwyneth does not believe. I only pray he will never find her. Gwyneth. She had been in her dream as well. She could remember the brightness of her blond hair, the way she had held her head proudly, then turned and laughed. She had been playing with Lucy. Her daughter rarely let Gwyneth out of her sight, ever since she had gifted her with a new dress for her doll. Sometimes, watching them play together, she was struck by how physically beautiful they looked.

Something buried stirred within her, and she lay back in bed, exhausted. It was as if she had a piece of a puzzle remaining and was reluctant to put it in its place. She thought for a moment of lighting a candle, but then realized she wanted darkness. Forgetfulness. Something lurked at the edge of her memory, and she wanted to banish it.

He will never find her here. Madeleine pulled the covers up to her chin, then slid closer to the hard warmth of her husband. *And when he cannot find her, he will give up the hunt.*

But even before she closed her eyes, she knew her thoughts for the lies they were.

* * *

Angel paced her dark bedroom. She had been up most of the night, frustrated by feelings so new to her that they struggled to be born.

It can never be. Always, her mind returned to Jack. He had been by her side constantly since Gwyneth had lost her child, and now she wondered why he did not attempt to make their deep friendship anything more than it was.

You are nothing to him, that is why. Even as she thought the words, she knew they were untrue. For she had seen the way he looked at her when he thought she was not watching him. There was something in his grey eyes, a yearning so intense she would have thought he'd have yielded to it by now.

You are not good enough for him. Yet gentlemen took their pleasure with servant girls and lesser women all the time. Why had Jack not approached her in that way?

And it would be pleasure. You know that, and that is why you want him and fear him all at the same time. She had never known true pleasure with a man. Certainly some times were more pleasant than most, but she had listened as other girls talked, and Angel knew she had never experienced what they spoke of.

And probably never will. It distressed her at times. She watched Andrew and Gwyneth, saw the way they looked at each other. Once, she had come upon them in the garden. He had been kissing her gently, and the look in Gwyn's eyes when she had gazed up at him left no doubts in Angel's mind that this man had unlocked every secret pleasure within her.

And for you . . . She stopped pacing and sat down on her bed. *For you, you are lucky to be alive. And to have left the life at The Dark Stallion far behind.* She lowered her face into her hands, and the only thing she saw was Jack.

Do not wish for something you can never have. Be content with the parts of him he is willing to give you, and stop crying for the moon.

Jack lay in his bed, watching the path the moonlight made

across the carpet. He was not a stranger to such frustrated nights, having grown quite familiar with dreams of Angel that left him yearning to be close to her.

For it is more than simple desire. You know that. He was not inexperienced with women, having lost his virginity to a serving girl when he was fifteen. Later, there had been a few women at The Dark Stallion.

But none had ever affected him as Angelique.

He had been attracted to her from the start, having noticed her first at the auction when she had approached Andrew and begged him to thwart the Duke of Cuckfield. Later, he had recognized her at the club with Madeleine. He had walked her home that night and had been curious.

That curiosity had led him to find her in the garden. And stay here at Scarborough Hall once he knew she lived here.

Stronger feelings had been born when she'd opened the door to Gwyn's bedroom that horrible summer day the baby had died. He had been surprised by the intensity of her feelings and had wanted to sweep her into his arms and comfort her.

If you are honest with yourself . . . He had fallen in love with her the day she had smashed all the china and crockery. Sitting on that kitchen floor, holding her as she sobbed, he had been overcome by the strongest emotion he had ever experienced.

And now felt he could do nothing about it.

You as good as called her a whore that day in the garden. You cannot offend her further by taking liberties and assuming she will want you. But he did not want mere liberties with Angelique. He never wanted to be without her. And yet he was damned if he knew how to begin letting her know.

I cannot even force the words out of my mouth to let her know how deeply I care.

Deeply frustrated, and unhappy with his limitations, Jack closed his eyes and tried to sleep.

The sound of the door softly opening brought Henry's eyes

up. He peered over the top of his book. Reading in bed had always been a secret vice with him since he was a boy. There had been many nights he had burned the candles to stubs before admitting exhaustion and setting down a particularly compelling book.

"Beth, what the devil are you doing in my bedchamber?" For it was Beth, clad in a pale pink wrapper. Her hair was unpinned, and it flowed down her back to her waist. Her face looked pale and drawn in the soft candlelight, as if she were afraid.

She didn't answer him, simply walked slowly over to the bed. Henry put his book down and followed her progress, his attention captured.

When she started to untie the sash of her wrapper, he swallowed, then managed to force the words out of his suddenly tight throat.

"What the devil are you—"

"I'm doing what I should have done forty-two years ago if my pride hadn't blinded me. I don't intend to lose you again, Henry."

He sat up further in bed and was about to say something when she slid the wrapper off. Her nightgown was white, trimmed in lace. It seemed to float about her body, and Henry narrowed his eyes as he saw the faintest outline of her still-slender shape against the firelight.

"Do you remember that first time, Henry? It was near this very house, close to the clearing by the river."

He could only nod as she lifted the covers and slid into bed beside him.

"Elizabeth, I do not think—"

"I don't want you to think. And if you are worried about compromising me, you are certainly more than a little late."

He started to tremble when he felt her hand gently touch his shoulder. After all the years apart, her touch still had the power to enflame him. She had fire within those fingertips, and he closed his eyes for an instant, remembering.

"If there is one thing I have learned in this life," she murmured softly as Henry felt her pick up the book that had fallen against the bedclothes and set it on the small table, "it is that you must pursue your own happiness and embrace it fully."

He opened his eyes. Her face was so close to him, her eyes so very blue. She even smelled the same, faintly of lavender and roses.

Softly, slowly, she smiled up at him, and he knew she was remembering that same afternoon.

"Oh, you old fool," she whispered, her eyes brimming with tears. "Kiss me."

Lady Caroline Pipkin sat in a chair by the fire. Scarborough Hall was quiet; she was sure everyone in the great old house was asleep except for her. And Caroline found she could not sleep. Not with what she knew.

It's your own fault, you damn fool. No one forced you out into the rose garden. No one held a pistol to your head and made you eavesdrop.

It was a habit that brought more than its fair share of trouble. Several nights ago, she had followed Gwyn and Lady Hardwick out into the rose garden and sat close enough to overhear Madeleine's warning.

And so he searches for her. I pray he does not know who she really is. Once he found her . . .

She thought of what had remained of her sister, Barbara, and closed her eyes tightly, willing the horrifying memory away. If there were anything in her life she wished she could banish, that last sight of her sister . . . She tried never to remember Barbara that way, but instead thought of her as a girl, then a young woman and bride, and finally in her favorite role, that of mother.

And yet that role she had cherished most had ultimately been her downfall.

He cannot know who she is. She stared into the fire, not seeing the flames that danced gently and sent rippling shadows over the silk-covered walls. *And yet, every bit of gossip I have heard tells me he wanted her. And it was only through Andrew's courage that Gwyneth escaped him.*

She was sure of Gwyn's identity now. Though she would never have wished that it be made certain in such a tragic manner, Beth had seen the scar on her leg the day she had helped Gwyn birth her child.

There could be no doubt now. Gwyneth Leighton was not who she seemed. The girl had taken on many roles in her life, but this last and truest role might well cost her her life.

And I want to see Henry's face when he realizes the truth, for I know he does not believe our girl is good enough for Andrew. Would that he knew . . . Despite her fears, Caroline couldn't help smiling. She would certainly love to see Henry's reaction.

She turned her legs so they faced the fire. Sometimes she was so tired that she felt every year and every pain. Caroline wanted to live long enough to see her niece protected. Married. With children.

She must remain with Andrew. I have never seen two lovers who belonged to each other more than they. Henry be damned; there has to be a way.

Gwyn was safe here, hidden away in the country.

If there is a God in this world, she thought wearily, *then let Richard Trelawny be killed in London. All could be revealed then, with no danger to Gwyn.*

But Caroline had given up on a higher power many years before. She had looked upon the remains of her sister and decided no merciful God could let such a villain live. And yet Richard Trelawny, Duke of Cuckfield, not only lived, but prospered.

Wait and see. Things are not always what they seem. And talk to Beth. She will know what to do.

Gwyneth is safe now—isn't she?

*   *   *

Henry astounded everyone the following morning at breakfast by announcing he and Beth were engaged to be married. Beth had pinkened and averted her eyes. And Andrew surprised everyone by going to his grandfather's side and embracing him.

"We must have an engagement party to celebrate!" Henry announced. He looked years younger, and as Caroline studied him she wondered how he had suddenly come to the realization her sister had always been the woman for him.

"A party. That would be lovely," Beth agreed. She looked flushed and happy and, like Henry, as if the years had simply dropped away.

Murmurs of agreement raced around the table, everyone nodding their heads and smiling. Caroline was about to smile when she remembered her thoughts by the fire the previous night.

A party. People. Word could get back to the Duke that she is here. Seclusion is safest. . . .

"Perhaps we should not act hastily—" she began, but the excited buzz drowned out her words.

"Beth," she began again, looking toward her sister for guidance, "I would like to discuss—"

But Beth only had eyes for Henry, and Caroline lost her chance amidst the happiness engulfing everyone.

She glanced at her niece. Gwyn was looking at Beth, her joy in the older woman's good fortune plainly in her eyes.

Caroline sat back and sighed.

I fear it is too late. She felt carried along on the sea of enthusiasm and, with a sudden sense of foreboding, knew destiny was rushing to meet them all.

And not giving a damn if they were ready.

Preparations were made for a grand masqued ball. Henry, in a gesture totally out of character for him, insisted on helping Beth with every detail. Together, they arranged for musicians and entertainers, special foods, and costumes to be made. The ballroom was opened, invitations sent out. An air of expectancy fell over Scarborough Hall.

Madeleine left within days after the engagement was announced. She regretfully declined her invitation to the ball, telling Beth privately that she wanted to return to her husband's country house and rest. But for a very special reason.

"I am with child," she told Beth, Gwyn, and Angelique the morning she left. "It has always been a difficult time for me, and Charles insists I rest."

"He is a good husband," Beth said, hugging the Frenchwoman tightly. "I understand, and you will be here in spirit."

"Always," Madeleine agreed. Before she stepped in the carriage, she hugged Gwyn tightly and whispered, "You and Andrew will find happiness together, I am certain. As Angelique will with her Jack."

Then she was gone, along with Charles and Lucy and Arabella the doll. And all attention turned toward the engagement party.

Henry was upstairs in his bedroom. The window overlooked the rose garden, and sometimes he came here when he needed time to think. He gazed out over the garden at the profusion of sweetly smelling blooms. Beth had gathered petals yesterday for potpourri and jams, and he had followed dutifully behind, carrying a basket and watching the gentle movements of her fingers as she gathered the petals.

She has more than enough sense for both of us. Beth had swallowed her pride and forced him to do away with his. She had come to him that night and given him her heart, and he had realized afterwards that his life had always been—and would always be—incomplete without her. That morning, looking down at her in his bed, his heart had rushed to his lips and he had asked her to become his wife.

He had not even thought of his father until later.

410

A noise interrupted his thoughts, and he glanced down into the garden. Laughter. Feminine laughter, now blended with deeper masculine amusement. He saw sunlight strike Gwyn's fair hair, watched the way his grandson kept his arm protectively around her. They were walking through the garden, his dark head close to her fair one. Every action, every glance, every gesture told Henry his grandson was deeply in love.

Was I right to do what I did? Though Gwyn had not totally denied Andrew, he knew his grandson had not asked anything of her. Andrew was waiting, he knew, for Gwyn to regain her strength. And Henry had not the heart to separate the two—yet—for he knew they needed each other since the death of their son.

Beth had been fierce in her defense of both of them. And so he had done as she asked and had left them alone. But Andrew could not continue with such a girl forever.

Did you do the right thing? Wearily, he rubbed his hand across watering eyes. Beth changed everything. He could not remember being happier. He started each day with her by his side, feeling as if he could do anything.

Are you right to deny Andrew that? Father thought Beth entirely unsuitable for you.

He was tired. Laughter floated upward again, along with the heavy scent of sun-warmed roses.

You did the best you could. That is all anyone can expect.

But the words seemed hollow.

Duty.

He glanced at his grandson again, and the expression on his face tore at his heart. So Henry looked away.

"Did you hurt yourself?" Jack asked. He and Angelique had taken a picnic to the woods this afternoon, and the chubby brown mare he had selected for her had become suddenly stubborn and bucked its burden off. Now he had his arm around her and was helping her to a seat beneath a towering oak tree.

"Not badly. Just my ankle. It—*oh!*"

"Lean on me."

He guided her to the tree, then helped her sit beneath it.

"That damnable horse. How I could have asked the stableboy to saddle that one—"

"It was not the horse, Jack. I saw a rabbit. I think she was scared."

He sat down next to her. Their picnic basket was several feet away, and as he was not hungry, Jack made no move to bring it closer.

"Would you—could you put your arm around me? I feel as if I am going to faint."

He did as she requested. Angelique was always so warm. Frightened by the fall she had taken, Jack suddenly pulled her closer and buried his face in her hair. It smelled of sunshine.

"Jack?" she whispered.

He loosened his embrace and looked down at her upturned face. Something in her eyes . . . Her lips were parted slightly, her cheeks flushed. It seemed he was melting inside, yet growing stronger. Jack lowered his face slowly until their lips were barely brushing.

"Angelique?" he whispered hoarsely. His body seemed to be humming, quivering softly. He felt he was on the brink of everything he had ever wanted. "Angelique? Are you sure?"

He felt her hands on the back of his neck, fingers gently tugging at his hair. Bridging that final distance.

"Yes," she breathed softly the instant before their lips met.

Angel opened her eyes and smiled. She turned so she was facing Jack as a cool breeze touched her nakedness. The tender expression in his eyes was all she had ever wanted. That, and what had finally happened to her in his arms.

She touched his cheek, his lips, then brushed the fine blond hair from his brow. Then she kissed his temple and settled herself in his embrace.

Time passed. She was content. Finally, after waiting for so long, she understand what drove women to seek the company of men. And it wasn't merely what happened in their beds. Jack had touched something deeper within her, and she knew she would never be the same. Though she couldn't have him forever, perhaps God would not be too angry at her for stealing heaven. Just this once.

"Angelique?"

There was something different in his voice. Something that worried her. She opened her eyes.

"I love you," Jack said hoarsely.

Everything stopped.

"I—I want to marry— Will you—" He took a deep breath. "Angelique, will you—"

She put her finger to his lips as tears filled her eyes. Unable to speak, she shook her head, then sat up and wrapped her arms around her knees, suddenly cold.

He was beside her in an instant.

"Angelique, what did I—"

"Jack." She placed her hand on his arm and it seemed to calm him. "Jack, we have to talk."

"Nothing has to be said. I love you, Angelique, that's all that matters."

"No. Listen to me."

It was the hardest single thing she had ever done, telling him of her past. Unsparing of herself, she left nothing out. Faltering toward the end when she admitted her feelings for him, she was startled when she felt his lips against her back. Kissing her.

"Jack, no. I am so ugly there, the scars—"

He pulled her into his arms, and she was surprised when he moved easily above her, pinning her gently with his greater strength.

"I don't care about any of that, Angelique. It wasn't your

fault." He hesitated, and it seemed he was searching for the right words. "I do not wish to talk of your past after today. I would be . . . lying to you if I said I didn't want to be your first. But as long as we're both each other's last . . ." He let the sentence trail off, looking at her hopefully.

"But you do not understand." She could feel tears running down her face as her body started to shake. "Jack, I am never enough, just by myself. I always—I do things for people; I try to make them care for me because deep inside I never feel they will be satisfied with just me." She hiccupped on a sob, then covered her eyes with her hand. "There is never enough. There is nothing inside of me."

He was quiet for a time. Angel sighed, then tried to struggle up.

"Jack, let me go—"

"No."

There was a short silence, then she whispered, "I have never told that to anyone. How empty I am." She reached up, her hand trembling, and touched his face. "But I want you to know—what I felt for you here, what happened—" Her face felt like it was on fire, and she covered it with both hands. "What happened between us, how I—that has never happened with another man." She was so deeply embarrassed that she could barely force the last words out.

"Then, in a way, I am your first," he said, his voice low. It was filled with a peculiar, trembling sort of emotion, and Angel slowly took her hands away from her face.

"You will always be first in my heart."

"Then that's all that matters. Angel, will you—"

"*No!*"

He surprised her then, pinning her even more firmly to the damp, mossy earth. "Listen to me. I'm not going to let you go. I don't care what happened before you met me. Angelique, when I'm with you—"

"Jack, no—" She started to cry again.

"When I'm with you—what you said about feeling empty

414

inside, like there's never enough? I feel the same way. Except when I'm with you."

The thought astounded her. "But you are a *gentleman*." She blurted the words out before she had a chance to think.

"But it's still the way I feel."

"But you are not bad, Jack."

"Damnation, neither are you!"

Her eyes widened. This could not be her gentle Jack, this man shouting at her with such fury. She had never seen him lose his temper before, and suddenly she wondered what other depths this man contained.

"If we believe in each other," Jack began slowly. "If we tell each other every day of our lives that we're not as empty as we think we are—could you believe then, Angelique? For me?"

There was such yearning in those eyes. As she gazed up into his face, she felt all the walls she had carefully erected around herself begin to crumble away.

"For me?" The words were so soft she barely heard them.

"I could try." Seeing the relief and love in his eyes, Angel took her courage in both hands.

"I have loved you for such a long time, Jack."

He gathered her into his arms. "Angelique, that's all I need, all I've ever wanted."

And as his arms tightened around her, she knew she had dared to steal much more than heaven.

Gwyn was walking back from the clearing by the river when she saw Henry striding toward her. He was angry; she could tell by his brisk walk and the rigid way he held his body. Head up, shoulders stiffly back. There was no mistaking his intent. Whether or not she wished it, confrontation was inevitable.

He fell into step beside her, and she waited for him to speak first.

"You have had ample time to share your grief with Andrew."

The abrupt way he dealt with the death of her son angered Gwyn, but she bit back the hot words on the tip of her tongue and waited. Henry had not found her in order to tell her she should stop grieving.

"You will end up killing my grandson. That is your intent, is it not?"

She could endure no more. "How can you believe that of me, Henry?" She deliberately used his Christian name, refusing to utter his title. "I prayed he would live when he was brought down by fever. And Andrew has grieved as deeply as I, though it might not seem so to look at him. He never had a chance to see his son, and I know that has hurt him."

"You will kill him. Because the Duke will kill him in order to have you."

She drew in her breath sharply, but Henry continued before she could reply.

"From the night Andrew defied the Duke at your auction, my grandson's life has been in danger. If the Duke has the chance, he will relish destroying Andrew, because he made a fool of him in public. Over you."

"I had no intention—"

"I am not interested in your good intentions, Miss Leighton. I am only interested in saving my grandson's life. How much of my fortune will it take to persuade you to leave him alone?"

For one blinding moment she thought she had misunderstood him. Then anger filled her, pure, white-hot rage at this man who thought she could be bought and sold as easily as Janet Wickens had plied her trade at The Dark Stallion.

"You do not have enough money," she said quietly, a note of scorn in her voice. "And you will never buy my compliance."

"Every man—and woman—has her price. I will find yours before long. You did not keep your promise to me, Miss Leighton. I asked you to deny my grandson, and instead you bind him closer."

"Andrew has a will of his own, Henry. I have not bewitched

416

him. You are the one who refuses to see the man he has become."

"Watch your tongue, woman. You know you're not good enough for him and never have been. I was unhappy with Belinda, but had I known to what depths Andrew would sink, I would have encouraged the marriage."

Gwyn was silent but walked faster, attempting to be rid of him. Henry matched her pace easily. As they neared the house, he laid a restraining hand on her arm. She stiffened, then stopped walking. She held herself rigid, making it quite plain she held him in utter disdain.

"Andrew does not think, Gwyneth. His heart too often leads his head. You're the one with the power to help him. And if you are responsible for my grandson's death, I will never rest until I find you and see to your punishment."

"Poor Henry, trying to order the world." She saw the visible signs of his anger, the thinning lips and narrowed eyes. "Would that you could. I stopped trying long ago. You cannot control what happens to Andrew any more than I control my own fate. But you would be happier if you stopped trying."

And without waiting for his reply, she turned away and walked quickly into the house.

The Duke of Cuckfield lay on his enormous bed, his eyes closed.

She has defeated me.

All he could think of was Gwyneth Leighton. If he opened his eyes, he would see the twins he had bought for an evening's pleasure. A brother and sister, golden-haired and beautifully formed.

He had not been able to enjoy them for thoughts of her.

They were asleep now. Or wise enough to pretend. Experts at what they did, both had attended to him until it was obvious he would not be able to perform. After jumping from the bed in a rage and demanding they entertain him, he had watched—

something he rarely confined his activities to. And all the while he'd burned within at the thought of a *woman* holding such power over him.

She has unmanned me. And yet he knew if he should possess her, she would bring back what she had taken from him. And more.

The Duke moved gracefully from the bed and reached for his dressing gown. There was a bitter taste in his mouth as he crossed the opulent bedroom and stood before a large mirror in an elaborate golden frame. He stared at his face, at the white scar that ran from the outside corner of his left eye to the cleft of his chin.

The little bitch. Lily had clawed him as he had pushed her off the bridge and into the swirling water. Her nails had gouged his flesh, and he had spent much money on salves and potions guaranteed to prevent scarring. And yet there it was, a vivid reminder of that night, forever emblazoned across his face.

He abhorred imperfection in anything and could not endure it in himself. Staring at his reflection in the mirror, he could feel the hatred filling him. Glancing back at the bed, he was reminded of his humiliation last night.

The Duke walked slowly out of his bedroom and down the stairs of his silent house. Without pausing, he continued down the hall in the direction of his roses.

They will soothe me. I will find her soon and make her pay for what she is doing to me.

But nothing calmed him. He moved from flower to flower, trying to lose himself in their perfection and beauty. As his tension increased, his anger grew. Soon he was not seeing the roses, but Gwyneth. Standing on the stage, her slender body wrapped in thin white silk, hundreds of candles making the silk glow like a flame.

There was a cane at one of the small tables in the conservatory, and he picked it up, tightening his fingers around it.

*   *   *

When Edward entered the Duke's house, all he could hear was a smashing sound. Breaking glass, dull crashes, cries of pleasure. Excited with the news he had just received, Edward raced down the hall until he reached the Duke's conservatory, where the sight that greeted him stopped him.

The Duke, dressed only in a thin grey wrapper, was smashing his roses with a cane, scattering the delicate petals over the smooth marble floor. When one rose bush did not bend, he yanked it out of the pot and threw it into the fire. The flames sputtered and began to die down as they licked around the plant, watered only hours ago.

Edward watched, mouth open, as the Duke turned toward him. His normally immaculate hair was in disarray, his body was shaking with a rage so intense it caused Edward to shrink back. His eyes seemed to have sunk into his head, and they burned with a peculiar fire.

"What are you looking at?" he shouted, then brought his cane down on the marble floor so heavily the ivory split, the cracking sound echoing through the still house.

As the Duke started toward him and Edward thought of what his master had just done to the cane, he shouted his news hoarsely.

"I know where she is!"

The Duke stopped, then stood perfectly still as a slow smile spread over his features. It chilled Edward, that smile, and he was thankful it was not directed at him.

He continued, not shouting this time but talking quickly. He wanted the Duke to focus his rage anywhere else but not at him.

"Scarborough Hall. It is said Andrew keeps her there. She is in the country, with his family."

There was a strange light in the Duke's eyes, one he recognized. It made him shudder. He was off in his strange dream-world of pain and pleasure, already planning the ways he would torment Gwyneth.

And she deserves it, for all she has forced me to endure.

"I have heard," said the Duke, his tone measured, "there is

to be a costume ball at the end of this week. To celebrate an engagement. As the little whore is sure to attend, I believe we should also make an appearance. Do you not think that is wise, Edward?"

"Yes, m'lord. Indeed I do. I shall make all the arrangements myself." He would have agreed to walk across fire in order to deflect the Duke's rage.

"Very good. We will leave for the country at once."

"*Maman! Maman,* look at me!"

Madeleine laughed softly as Lucy paraded into her bedroom, her small feet in delicate dress shoes, her legs wobbly as she tried to find her balance. She was dressed in an old emerald green velvet gown, and a string of bright beads was looped around her tiny neck several times.

Charles was still asleep. They had stayed up late the night before playing cards. Lucy had entertained herself with her dolls for most of the morning, but then insisted she wanted to play dress-up with her mother's clothing.

And Madeleine, remembering how she had adored to explore her mother's wardrobe as a child, had relented.

"Do not wake Papa," she cautioned. "Who are you, Lucy?"

Her daughter wrinkled her nose in delight. "*Maman,* I am Angelique, coming down to dinner in a new dress."

And Madeleine had to choke back her laughter at the sight of her daughter's tentative steps. Angel, never shy at The Dark Stallion, was still intimidated by life outside the brothel. Lucy, a playful mimic, had captured the essence of her friend perfectly.

"Now"—Lucy was tugging her way out of an old green velvet dress—"I will be a kitten hungry for his supper."

Madeleine watched her child pretend she was a kitten, her smile soft and indulgent. When Lucy decided to pretend to be a dog, Madeleine put a finger to her lips.

"Shhh, *Minou,* you cannot wake Papa. He is very tired."

"Then I will be Gwyneth. She is quiet."

Madeleine sat back among the lacy pillows. She watched Lucy struggle into a white silk chemise. Keeping her attention on her daughter, Madeleine picked up the cup of tea Charles's maid had brought her. She would never get used to being waited upon; it made her nervous. She closed her eyes and smiled. She would spend the rest of her life making Charles happy. He was so good to her.

"*Maman!* You are not watching me!"

"Yes, I am, Lucy."

Lucy smiled. "Now I am Gwyn."

Madeleine watched her daughter as she slowly mimicked exact gestures and nuances. The way Gwyn held her head, the way she turned to answer a question. The quick smile, the graceful way of moving her hands.

"You are quite an actress, Lucy."

"That is what I want to be, *Maman*. Look at me now! This is Gwyn when she sees Uncle Andrew."

Madeleine caught her breath as her daughter's features slowly changed. Unknowingly, Lucy had caught the look of excited expectancy, the glow of sensual excitement in Gwyneth's eyes when she looked at Andrew.

But there was something more. . . .

She put down her tea, her hands suddenly starting to shake.

"Lucy." Her voice trembled only slightly. "I want you to pretend something for me."

Her daughter smiled up at her, her face childlike once again.

Madeleine swallowed, her throat tight. *It was that sensual expression, nothing more. You want to keep her a baby forever.* But even as she thought the words, she knew she was lying to herself.

"I want you to pretend you are standing in front of a room full of people. They are trying to scare you, but you are very proud and you are going to prove to them you are the bravest girl in the room."

Lucy clapped her hands. "*Maman*, you are so much fun!"

421

"Be a good girl and do exactly as I say."

Madeleine watched her daughter carefully. Lucy closed her eyes, and her small body fairly quivered with excitement.

The change was extraordinary. Slowly, slowly, Lucy began to pretend. And Madeleine saw the same proud tilt of the head. The unconsciously haughty angle of her chin. Her daughter's blue eyes flashed; her golden hair caught the early morning sunshine as it streamed in the far window.

She stood perfectly still, but it was as if someone had lit a thousand candles. The white silk chemise glowed. Lucy looked out over her imaginary audience as if daring anyone to challenge her.

There was only one other woman Madeleine had ever seen give off that incredible incandescence. One woman who had stood on a stage at The Dark Stallion and had captured the attention of every man in the room.

Her body was shaking uncontrollably. Gwyn looked so much like Lucy that Madeleine had warmed to her from the start. And that could mean only one thing.

She knew who Gwyn resembled. Who she truly was.

And why the Duke was obsessed with having her.

Book V

"My dear, you're accusing me wrongly.
You've wounded me deeply, my dove.
For you know that I feel very strongly
About acts of familial love . . ."

Chapter Twenty-Five

Gwyn stared into the mirror. Her face seemed ashen. Lifeless. Even without the slight dusting of white powder, her skin had no color. Tonight she had to attend the masqued ball and pretend she was happy, though her heart was breaking.

You must be strong. For Andrew. You cannot harm him.

She had thought of nothing but what Henry had said. He was right. As long as the Duke of Cuckfield lived, he would never forget the night Andrew had humiliated him. All because of her. The Duke had been pursuing her for almost a year and showed no signs of stopping. There could be no hope for a life with Andrew as long as the Duke was after them both.

Her hair was pinned up elaborately, feathery plumes and pearls adorning the silken mass of curls. Her dress was a concoction of lace and silk, all white. Beth had thought to dress her as an angel, and silver embroidery embellished the throat and loose cuffs of her dress. Angelique had helped her construct a pair of small wings, complete with feathers, and these were attached to a leather belt that wrapped snugly around her waist. Leather slippers completed the outfit, with tiny silver bells sewn at the heels.

But Gwyn was so intent upon her plans that she barely noticed her costume. Everything hinged on protecting Andrew from harm. She was leaving tomorrow. Gwyn would travel quickly through London and take a boat to France. Then on to the convent that had sheltered Lucy for most of her young life. She would remain there for a time. Until she was certain the Duke no longer searched for her.

When she had told Andrew of her decision, the look in his dark eyes had made her want to burst into tears. His next words had started her crying.

"What have I done?" he had asked.

"I only want to do what is best for you."

"And that is to stay by my side, where I can protect you. We were separated once, and I will never forgive myself—"

"The Duke still looks for me, Andrew. He will kill you—"

"I'm looking forward to seeing him again. There is something between us that must be settled. It has nothing to do with you and I will not have you using him as an excuse to put distance between us."

"Andrew—"

"*No.* I will not tolerate your leaving. You're afraid, Gwyn, now that we are truly coming to know one another, and of what that may lead to. I want you as I have wanted no other woman in the world. I will not have you leave me now."

She had tried another tactic. "I am not good enough for you. I am a whore. You found me in a brothel and bedded me there. I cannot hope to ever understand the sort of world you inhabit."

"Then we will create our own. And you are no whore, Gwyneth. If either of us has done more than a fair share of whoring, it has been me. I don't know what you hope to gain by playing this game with me, but be assured I won't stand for such weak excuses as these."

She knew he was going to try and stop her. Yet she had to leave. The Duke had killed before, and there was no evidence of his stopping. She was not leaving because of Henry and what he thought was right for his grandson. She simply did not want any harm to befall the man she loved.

The door squeaked slightly, and she looked up into the mirror to see Beth standing in the doorway. She was dressed as a shepherdess, complete with a staff and a toy lamb tucked beneath her arm.

"I thought you might like some company going down the stairs."

Gwyn stood up slowly, every part of her body reluctant. When she reached Beth's side, she took her hand.

"You have always been so kind to me, you and Caroline both. I do not know how I shall ever repay you."

"We think of you as family, Gwyneth." There was a slight tremor to Beth's voice, and she smiled, her eyes kind.

"Come, let us go to the ballroom and prepare to meet our guests."

Belinda rapped her cane sharply aginst the roof of her carriage. The vehicle swayed and creaked as the wheels rattled against the packed earth.

"Can't you go any faster?"

It would be her rotten luck to reach Scarborough Hall too late for the ball. She had thought about returning ever since she had left following Gwyn's accident. Fleeing to London, she had missed Andrew. She could have won him back in time, if Henry had not taken his grandson to the country.

I thought the old man did not like her. And yet he takes Andrew right to her side. He did not look that ill; he would have become better in time. All Henry has done has complicated matters.

She was hell-bent on straightening them out. When she had informed her father she was planning on attending Henry's engagement party, he had looked disgusted with her and said he hoped she would come to some decision regarding Andrew before his little whore charmed him into her bed again. And she had let her father continue to believe she was the one who was uncertain of her relationship with Andrew.

Andrew, as she had suspected, played the gentleman and never once did anything to make her father suspect he had been the one to end their engagement.

She would win him back tonight. Her costume, that of a queen, was the most beautiful garment she had ever had made. Belinda was totally confident she would turn Andrew's head and make him care for her again. And if the beauty and daring of her costume did not accomplish that end, she had one last part to her plan.

I will tell him Gwyn can no longer give him any children. He will turn to me. He has to.

Edward Sleaforth cautiously peeped out the window of his coach. The Duke had mounted his horse and now galloped away to cover the last few miles to Scarborough Hall more quickly. It had been torture, sitting in the carriage with him as they had drawn nearer. The Duke had seemed to radiate a peculiar, intense emotion, and Edward found it sapped him. And frightened him.

Suzanne sat across from him on the leather seat. She was wrapped snugly in her fur-lined cloak. Even though it was not a cool evening, she was so thin and worn she tired and caught a chill easily. Suzanne had insisted on coming along, as she wanted to see Gwyneth get what she deserved. Edward had finally relented, on the condition she adopt a disguise that would keep her true identity a secret.

Thus, Suzanne was dressed as a pirate, her pale red hair pushed up beneath a head scarf and her face concealed by her masque. She was so terribly thin she looked like a boy. He was sure no one at Scarborough Hall would guess her true identity.

He had chosen to go as a clown, and the voluminous folds of his costume hid him well.

Edward thought of the Duke, dressed as a highwayman, and of the black velvet masque that carefully concealed his features. He wondered at what the Duke had planned for Gwyneth after he managed to spirit her away.

I don't care what he does to her, as long as she is finished in the end. The bitch does not deserve to live, with what she has made me endure.

He planned on escaping this party as soon as he could, then hiding himself so well in the country that the Duke would never find him again. He still owed the man a large sum of money, so large he knew he would never repay it in this life. It was best to run while he could. Suzanne would be stranded outside of London, but he could not trouble his head over her.

Impatient for this night to be over, Edward settled back into his seat.

The Duke of Cuckfield pulled gently on his reins and the horse beneath him slowed to a walk. He was in front of Scarborough Hall now, and the candlelight in the numerous windows was reflected by the lake. Strains of music floated out into the cool night air.

He took a deep breath, enjoying the feeling of intense expectation and excitement throughout his body. Tonight. Nothing would go wrong this time. All was going to happen as planned, and before the night was out he would have Gwyneth Leighton as his prisoner.

He pulled gently on the reins again and his horse stopped. The night air ruffled the Duke's black cape slightly, moulding it against his body. Slipping his hand into one of the cape's deep pockets, the Duke grasped a black velvet masque and, with graceful economy of movement, slipped it over his face. He had studied the effect in his mirror, and he liked it. Only his eyes were visible. That and his hair, and just enough of his mouth so he could speak. His face was obscured, thus he was confident no one at this ball would recognize him.

He would slip in and take her. By the time Andrew realized she was gone it would be far too late.

The Duke lifted his masqued face toward the sky and paid silent homage to the darkness.

He had come to the end of his search.

There were too many people, the room was suffocatingly

warm, and she was tired of smiling. Gwyneth slipped out into the rose garden and walked slowly between the fragrant flowers. She hoped for a moment of respite, so she could think of what she was about to do and decide if she was truly attempting the right thing.

"Gwyneth? Will you talk to me, please?"

Andrew. As she turned, she wondered how she could ever leave him. He had discarded his masque and now stood before her. She could see the tension in his face, the rigid stance of his body. She was hurting him, all in the name of protecting him.

He had not bothered with a costume, having been so upset by her decision. His only concession to his grandfather's ball had been a masque, and now even that had been discarded.

At that moment, standing in the rose garden with moonlight streaming over them, Gwyneth looked up at this man she loved and wondered at the long distance they had traveled. She had learned of many cruelties in the world, that it was not the safe and tranquil place her childhood had promised it to be. And Andrew, who had always guarded himself so carefully, was now offering up his heart and mind, leaving himself so infinitely vulnerable.

They had changed together, and she had the sudden feeling that the best was yet to come. Was she doing the right thing by not standing and fighting the Duke? By running, would she only prolong the chase?

Andrew must have seen the indecision in her face. He stepped forward swiftly and enfolded her in his arms.

"I will not let you attempt this escape, Gwyn," he whispered against her hair. "I'd thought that, late tonight, I might announce my intentions to our guests. Only if you're willing."

She stared up at him, suddenly realizing words she had longed to hear from him were about to be spoken.

"Gwyneth." He was looking down at her now, his eyes intent. "If you insist on running from me when things become complicated, then there is only one way I can assure you'll remain by my side."

"Andrew," she replied, her voice shaking as she realized she was on the brink of the greatest discovery of all. "If your intent is what I believe it is, this is hardly the way I would wish you to express it."

He smiled then and, before she could protest, knelt quickly in front of her and kissed her hand.

"Gwyneth, I find the thought of living without you impossible. Will you consent to become my wife?" Here his voice roughened, and she felt tears spring into her eyes. "I will treasure you always and guard you with my life."

She thought of the Duke, and the threat of him seemed so near. Yet Andrew was before her, real and strong. Her hand came to rest on the top of his head, her fingers lightly touching the soft, dark hair. And she thought of the rest of her life and wondered how she could ever spend it with anyone but Andrew.

"Yes," she said quietly. "You do me a great honor by asking—"

But Andrew was already on his feet, then pulling her into his arms and kissing her with an intensity so strong she thought he would never let her go. His arms were around her tightly, the warmth of his body close to hers. It was a dizzying kiss, full of passion and promise. And a sudden, heartbreaking tenderness that spoke of commitment and a future.

All the time in the world.

When they finally broke apart, he looked down at her. "Come. Let us go inside and tell grandfather and Beth."

The thought of facing Henry stilled something inside her. The moment was too new, too special. She wanted a short time alone, to become used to the idea of being Andrew's intended bride. It was a dream she had played through her mind countless times, yet now she needed time to adjust.

"Give me just a moment alone, Andrew. I promise you, I'll come in within a quarter of an hour."

"And your answer will still be yes?" he asked.

She was surprised by the note of doubt in his voice. Gwyn

laid her hand against his cheek. "My answer will always be yes. I think it was yes from the moment I first saw you."

He took her hand and kissed her palm, then let go of it reluctantly. "I'll wait for you inside, then."

"I'll come to you, Andrew."

The Duke had waited patiently, hidden beneath the dark shadows of the hedge bordering the rose garden. He had followed Gwyn outside and had been about to approach her when Andrew appeared. Now he watched as the man he hated walked back toward Scarborough Hall. The house was ablaze with lights, and laughter floated out into the night sky.

Now. You must go to her now.

And the Duke stepped out of the shadows and into the moonlight.

"Hello, my beauty."

Gwyn started at the sound of the voice, then looked up into the warmest pair of grey eyes she had ever seen. The man's face was almost totally concealed by a black velvet masque. His mouth was firm and strong, and there was a distinct cleft in his chin.

"Hello." She was slightly uneasy, his calling her beauty. She wasn't comfortable with the endearment unless Andrew used it.

"I was about to return to the ball," she began, but the stranger moved closer and laid a hand on her arm.

"I did not mean to frighten you. I only happened to come to the rose garden to see a few minutes of solitude. I meant no harm. You are very beautiful, you must know that."

She glanced away. Though he was a guest of Henry's and she did not want to hurt his feelings, she had wanted this time alone.

"I have a great many things to think about, sir. I am afraid I would not be good company for you."

"As you wish." His tone was softly regretful.

Something in his voice stirred a memory long dormant. She had met this man before, but she could not remember where. Long ago, it seemed. Before Andrew, before Edward. Something in that voice . . .

"I know you," she breathed softly, her eyes widening as she studied him. "I'm not sure who you are, but—"

His arm came up then, so swiftly she barely saw it. Pain exploded at the side of her head. In that instant before she lost consciousness, she saw the stranger's face unguarded and recognized hatred in those eyes.

Andrew paced the ballroom like a caged bear, impatient with a world that would deny him Gwyneth's company for more than a few minutes. Almost half the hour had passed, yet she still had not returned. The ballroom floor was covered with costumed people, talking and laughing. Musicians kept up a steady stream of sound, and tables piled with every imaginable refreshment lined one of the shorter walls.

He started as he felt a tap on his shoulder and turned to find Beth.

"Andrew, your grandfather wishes to see you. In the library."

He cast one more glance out the doors into the night. *Gwyneth, don't be afraid of what we can have. Come to me.* He could not force her. Strange, how he had once told him she longed to be a wife, and now that the moment had come, she needed time.

He turned back toward Beth. "I will go to him now."

In the library, Henry paced restlessly. Would Andrew ever forgive him for the meddling he had done? He had confessed everything to Beth last night in their bed, and she had encouraged him to tell Andrew the truth.

"You cannot hope to find forgiveness from Andrew should he ever find out what you have done," Beth had said. He knew she was right. He could only give his grandson his opinion of the mistake he was making in seeing the girl.

He looked up as Andrew entered the room. Beth had been behind him, and now she smiled as she began to close the library door.

"No," Henry rasped out, his voice suddenly hoarse. "Stay, Beth. You are family now, and I wish to have you hear what I have to say."

Slowly, haltingly, he told Andrew the truth. The journey to the country he had persuaded Gwyn to take. The promise he had exacted from her. The forgery of the letter.

And the last conversation they had had, concerning the Duke.

When he finished, the room was utterly silent.

Andrew stared at the fire. When he spoke, his voice was very soft. "I am thankful you thought to tell me this, as it explains the reluctance I sense in Gwyn."

Henry flinched as his grandson turned slowly and faced him, his blue eyes intent. "I will not have you interfering again. I am no longer a child you can mould to your will. I have asked Gwyneth to marry me, and she has accepted. Hear this, Grandfather. If you force me to choose between you, I will choose her. Now you must excuse me. I wish to go to her."

Once the door shut behind Henry, he slumped into one of the brocade chairs and put his hands over his face. "What is to become of the boy if he will not listen to reason?"

"Henry." He felt Beth's hands on his shoulders, soothing. "Is it so bad he should love Gwyneth? Maura certainly wasn't an aristocrat."

He shuddered, then pushed her hands away and stood up. "And you know what happened. Beth, like must marry like! She is not good enough for him, she drives him away from me."

"No, Henry. You do that yourself."

"The fact remains he found her at The Dark Stallion. She is not fit to be his wife."

Beth took his hand and led him back to a sofa in front of the fire. They sat, then, her hand still holding his, Beth said softly, "If I trust you with a secret close to my heart, can you promise to keep that confidence?"

"Woman, this is no time for—"

"*Henry, you must listen to me!*"

He stared at her, astonished. This was not his sweet Beth. This woman was fiercely alive and determined. He remembered her spirit from so many years ago and knew he would not be able to fight her on this matter.

"Then tell me this secret that is so crucial to you." At her fierce look, he said quickly, "I promise I shall tell no one."

"Henry," Beth began quietly. "If truth were known, Andrew is not good enough for Gwyn. Now, please be still, for what you are about to hear will change your grandson's life."

"Gwyneth?"

Andrew strode through the garden, searching for her. *Perhaps she has already gone inside and you did not see her.* But he knew he had searched the crowd in the ballroom and she had not been there. *Where could she have gone?* Everything Henry had confessed explained away her reluctance, and he was eager to find her now.

He thought for a moment of the clearing by the river, and was about to change direction and seek her there when he stepped on something that made him stumble slightly.

Looking down, he saw the small wings from Gwyn's costume. They had been torn from her costume, as bits of silk and lace were also on the ground.

A fear so intense he was almost shaking began to envelop him.

He knelt down, picking up one of the feathers that had been torn loose and smashed. Glancing quickly around, his gaze fell on a black masque. A masque too large for a woman. A masque a man might wear.

In that instant, as realization hit him, twisting his insides, Andrew knew who had found Gwyneth.

"Andrew! I have been looking for you." Henry was smiling at him, but Andrew did not even see his grandfather's face.

"He's here. He has her. Shut the doors, don't let anyone leave."

"What the devil are you—"

"*The Duke!* He has Gwyn."

The smile slowly left Henry's face, but Andrew was already racing through the crowd. Exclamations of surprise drifted throughout the ballroom as he faced each tall man and demanded he remove his masque.

And then, he saw the clown. Slinking quietly toward one of the open windows. Something in the way the man moved, like a rat scuttling along a dock . . .

Narrowing his eyes, Andrew began to run.

Edward Sleaforth almost made it to the window before harsh hands grabbed him. His worst fears realized, he closed his eyes as he felt himself slammed up against the wall.

"*Where is she?*"

"I do not know—" He was silenced as Andrew slammed him against the wall once again, hard enough to hurt but not knock him into oblivion.

"Listen to me, Sleaforth. If you refuse to answer me, I'll strangle you with my bare hands. And if she dies, I'll enjoy ending your miserable life."

Edward was sweating; he could feel one fat drop sliding down his temple. "I am not responsible for what the Duke—"

Again, he winced as his back made contact with the wall.

"I don't give a damn about what you're responsible for. Tell me or I'll cut out your tongue!"

"Andrew! Andrew, don't hurt him! I'll tell you!"

Edward opened his eyes in horror. Suzanne, her pirate's scarf askew, her reddish hair starting to tumble down her shoulders, was tugging at Andrew's sleeve.

"He plans to take her to Ashton Hall. It's barely a day's ride from here to the west; the estate has been in his family's holdings for many years. He takes her there to kill her. . . ."

But Andrew released Edward abruptly, and he felt himself sliding toward the floor, his legs trembling so badly he could not stand.

"You stupid little fool!" he hissed as Suzanne squatted down beside him.

"Edward, are you hurt?"

"You had no right to tell him where the Duke has taken her!"

"Was I to stand by and watch him kill you? He's already left, as has the Duke. We can escape now, unless you're stupid enough to want to wait for Andrew to return."

Edward, realizing Suzanne had a definite point, stood up. He shrank back almost immediately as he encountered steady grey eyes. The young man looking down at both of them was dressed in livery, yet there was something about his bearing that suggested the costume was a joke.

"I think Andrew will want to talk with both of you when he returns. And God help you if she is not with him. Let me escort you to your rooms."

Moonlight flashed between the branches of trees as the Duke's horse galloped steadily. He had wrapped Gwyneth in his cloak and slung her over his mount in front of him. Once far from Scarborough Hall, he had stopped and tied her hands and feet in case she should wake. Now, one hand holding the reins and the other pressed firmly against her backside, he was filled with triumph and anticipation.

It would not be much longer. Soon she would be his.

When the first glimmerings of consciousness assailed her, Gwyn realized she was on a horse, a galloping horse. Realizing came swiftly after that. Her hands and feet were tied. There was a firm hand holding her, and she sensed cruelty in its grasp.

Her head hurt, and it took her several minutes to organize her thoughts. She could not fight him, not with her hands and feet tied and her body balanced precariously upon his horse. She could only hope to feign unconsciousness and gather strength for what lay ahead.

Her heart was racing like the horse beneath her, galloping madly away. Sheer animal fear of death had wiped everything out of her mind but a strong will to survive. But if she could not stop her heart's panicked flight, she knew the Duke would triumph.

Never. And as the horse galloped swiftly through the night, a courage such as she had never realized she possessed slowly began to fill her heart.

"My God, he must be stopped!"

Henry had raced to the stables as soon as word reached him of what Andrew was doing. Now he could see his grandson, astride Mephisto, and he knew with a certainty bordering on prophecy that Andrew was riding to his death.

"Stop him!" Henry gave one of the grooms such a look of fury that the young man raced forward and grabbed the stallion's reins. Mephisto snorted, then pawed the ground with a massive hoof. But the groom held firm, and Henry raced toward his grandson as quickly as age would allow.

"Let me go, man. I don't want to hurt you." Andrew's voice was calm, and Henry heard the words clearly in the still summer air.

"Hold him!" he cried.

But it was not to be. He watched as Andrew, who rarely raised his voice to a servant and had certainly never struck one, brought his crop down on the groom's arm. Startled, the boy jumped back, and at the exact same instant, Andrew brought the tips of his reins down on his stallion's strong rump.

Henry stared, horrified, as Mephisto shot forward, his hooves thundering against the ground. Andrew crouched low in the saddle, the whiteness of his linen shirt shot silver with moonlight.

"After him!" Henry roared, tears stinging his eyes. Beth had caught up with him now, and she grasped his arm. As Henry looked around at the stunned faces of his servants, he knew none of them would be able to prevent his grandson from racing toward the Duke.

Not caring who she was, Duchess or whore, he closed his eyes and raised his face to the moonlight, giving vent to his fury and fears.

"Damn her!"

Chapter Twenty-Six

Gwyn crouched down against the rough stone wall, the cold chains binding her wrists cutting into her skin. The room was freezing, and she was thankful the Duke had merely chained her and not taken her clothing. There was a strange bond between them; she seemed to know his mind as well as her own. He realized she would be frightened waiting, not knowing what he was going to do to her.

He was counting on that fear destroying her.

She would not let it. She still possessed her mind, though she feared she would lose her sanity if he tried to rape her. The man was a coward, for what fairness could there be in dominating a woman already held fast? The Duke did more than mark his cards and cheat at the tables. He stacked the entire deck of life so there was no chance of his ever losing.

The door to the small cell creaked open, and she met the Duke's gaze, feigning fear. She widened her eyes and forcibly trembled. He was a monster, this man so obsessed with her, and she sensed there was no room in his mind for anything but himself. Such pride could be used. If she could fool him.

"Scared?" He laughed softly, and she knew she had guessed correctly. But then her gaze dropped, and she saw the knife in his hands. Her heart began to race, faster and faster, out of control.

He is winning. You are letting him triumph.

She took a slow breath, trying to still her frenzied heartbeats. She thought of Andrew, of the expression on his face when he had looked down at her in the rose garden, and a fierce will to live rose up and choked down her fear.

When he approached her, she shrank back, wishing with all her heart she were unchained and could offer him a real fight. Gwyn could feel her heart and mind start to go curiously numb as the Duke began to slowly cut away the remains of her costume.

"Such a shame to hide such beauty," he murmured softly.

She thought of spitting at him, then realized what a useless effort that would amount to. It would only enrage him and give her less time. She had to find a way to make him unchain her.

He ripped the bodice of her dress away and she averted her head, not wanting to see the look in his eyes as he took in her naked body.

"Beautiful." The word was a hoarse rasp.

And she wondered at his words, remembering that Madeleine had told her of his preferences.

When he began to cut away her skirt and petticoats, she began to strain against her bonds, the sharp metal of the cuffs cutting into her wrists and ankles. All she could see was the top of his blond head as he bent, the knife ripping through the white silk and lace. Gwyn fought silently, determined not to give him the satisfaction of hearing her cry out. She felt something warm on her arm and looked up to see a thin trickle of blood.

Yet she felt no pain.

The last of her costume was being torn away. The Duke was breathing heavily as he divested her of her clothing. Gwyn bent her head forward, and her hair fell, offering her scant modesty. She turned her head to the side again and closed her eyes as she heard him stand up and step back, his heels sounding sharp against the stone floor.

"I have waited for this moment for so long." His voice was

low and vibrant, and at that moment if she had been free, Gwyn knew she would have tried to kill him.

"Look at me."

She kept her face averted.

Then his hands were in her hair, pulling her face painfully toward his. She opened her eyes in time to see his lips come down over hers.

Instinct took over, and she bit his lip.

"Bitch!" The blow to her head almost caused her to slip into unconsciousness. She fought the urge to leave this living hell, knowing what he could do to her while she was unconscious could be far worse than the oblivion it would afford her.

Pretend . . .

And so she hung heavily from the chains, conscious all the while of his heavy breathing and the way he was watching her.

When his hand touched her breast, she almost cried out. There was curiosity in his touch, and she wondered why he should want her when there were any number of men in London who would cater to him.

His fingers slipped lower, sliding over her stomach, her hips, then moving between her thighs.

She could not bear to have him touch her there, could feel bile burning at the back of her throat at the thought of his possession. His fingers stroked softly against the skin of her inner thighs.

Think. Carefully. If you bring up your knee sharply, you might be able to hit his head. . . .

But then his touch stopped. He pulled his hand away as if he had been burned. And Gwyn remembered the scar. Madeleine had mentioned the Duke was a man who abhorred imperfection. Perhaps she would be fortunate enough that the ugly scar on her leg would cause him to lose this twisted obsession for her.

She kept her face averted, even as she felt a strange change in the atmosphere of the small cell. Something was building. Growing. Hatred and triumph. Instinctively she knew that, had the Duke been obsessed with her before, now there was even more reason.

She looked up into his face, into the strangest mixture of desire and hatred she had ever seen.

"What is your name?" he asked.

"Gwyneth." She was amazed she was able to speak. Her heart had started to race again, as if her body were aware of something her mind had yet to grasp.

"And your father?"

"James Leighton."

"What was his occupation?"

"He was a vicar."

"In a neighboring town not far from here. A three-day journey at most."

"Yes." Again she had that strange sensation something was building, slowly and darkly. *Why is he asking me these questions?*

"And your mother's name?"

"Mary Leighton."

"Are your parents alive?"

"No."

"That scar on your leg. How did you come by it?"

Now she was truly afraid. Something seemed to dance at the edge of her mind, that same feeling she had had in the rose garden when she had listened to his voice. She knew this man. Had he held a place in her life before she could remember?

"My mother said I was burned. I stood too near the fire and—"

"Mary Leighton lied to you. And she was not your mother." He was clearly enjoying her fear and confusion. "Do you know how you came to bear that scar?"

Gwyn sensed panic rising within her, pure animal fear. She was right on the edge of knowing but pushed the thought out of her mind. *No. No.* Then suddenly it was as if her mind folded open and images she had only remembered within her dreams rushed toward her at a furious pace.

Oh yes, I remember, I remember your voice and what you did. . . .

And on top of that realization came a quick prayer, as the

441

enormity of her capture finally came crashing down upon her.

Father in heaven, protect me now, for I am in the hands of the devil himself. . . .

"I burned you. I took the hot poker and laid it against your flesh when you were two years old. If you search your mind, Frances, I am quite sure you will remember."

Frances. No, not Frances. Frannie. She could not stop her swirling thoughts, as they edged her deeper and closer to a truth she had been carefully taught to forget so many years ago.

"Frances Elizabeth Caroline Trelawny. Frances after our maternal grandmother. Elizabeth and Caroline for our aunts. Trelawny after our father." The Duke took a deep, shuddering breath. "I have looked for you all my life. I followed our mother to the convent where she was hiding, and even as I tore the life from her she refused to tell me where she had hidden you."

And Gwyn thought wildly of the golden-haired woman of her dreams. In that instant, she knew she had found her mother.

"A vicar. How like Barbara, to give you to a man of God to raise. Did he instruct you carefully and tell you of a loving God and a glorious life after death?" Gwyn felt his hand tangle itself in her hair again as he forced Gwyn to meet his eyes.

"You had best begin praying, little sister. For you will see our mother shortly."

Faster. Faster.

Andrew let Mephisto have his head, gripping the stallion's sides with bent knees. They were battling time now, in the most desperate race of his life.

His thoughts raced furiously as he urged the stallion faster. Morning stars twinkled faintly in the violet sky, and he glanced at the brightest one, hovering close to the horizon.

Hope. He had given up hoping so long ago, until a golden-haired girl who blazed brighter than any of the candles in the room had ignited emotions within him he had never thought to feel. She had argued with him, fought him, tried to reason with him.

Loved him.

No woman on earth could have feigned such passion and caring. He knew now she had been waiting to hear the most crucial of words from him. Even when he had asked her to be his bride, he had not been able to say the words. He had told her he wanted her, cherished her, desired her.

But never that he loved her.

It had came to him with a crushing finality when he had held one of the torn angel's wings in the rose garden. Had it been less than an hour ago that he'd kissed her, held her in his arms? Now he could not even be assured she lived.

She has to. For without her, there is no hope. If I lose her now, I will have lost the only dream in my life that has lived and walked and breathed. And loved me, though I did nothing to deserve that love.

He lashed the stallion with the tips of his reins. Not much further. Over this next hill and then he might see Ashton Hall on the horizon.

Faster. Faster.

And Andrew, who never prayed, opened his heart to a higher power.

Her eyes wavered open. Immediately she heard his voice and knew she hadn't awakened from a nightmare.

Andrew. She was drifting off again, remembering a private room at The Dark Stallion and the man she would always love looking down at her.

Let my last thoughts be of him. Gwyn no longer cared that the Duke would triumph.

She felt the sharp slap to her face, and it cleared her head for

443

an instant.

"I will not have you senseless! I have waited too long for this moment!"

Then he was unchaining her. His hands grasped her hair, and he dragged her out of the cell.

Andrew had heard Gwyn's scream, and the sound ripped his emotions wide open. Doors that would lead him to her side had been locked, so now he was climbing to an open window. The outcroppings of rock razed his hands, making them bleed.

He felt none of his own pain. All he could hear was her scream.

She is still alive. He thought of the Duke and the pain he had already inflicted upon her.

He will die this night.

And then he reached the open window, part of a long upper gallery, and swung inside.

"Come, come, Frannie. Don't you want to see a portrait of our sainted mother?"

He yanked at her hair, forcing her to turn and face the large portrait on a far wall. The woman who stared out at them had golden blond hair and the most alive blue eyes Gwyneth had ever seen. The painter had captured her mother's courage, and something in the portrait spoke to her now. It was as if the courage present in her mother's eyes implored her not to give up.

"I thought Barbara might like to witness her final defeat."

He held her hair so tightly that she could not move away.

"I found her, Mother. You did not hide her carefully enough."

He was talking to the portrait, and Gwyn wondered dully at the mind of a man capable of taking pleasure in defeating a woman already dead.

Before she could think further, the Duke pushed her down on the hard marble floor. His voice was a harsh rasp against her ears as he deftly began to divest himself of his breeches.

"Give me what you took from me, little whore!"

Everything she had ever felt for her brother exploded within her and Gwyn began to fight. His hands had left her hair so he might pull her more closely against the feel of his growing arousal. His touch, the hard feel of him against her sickened her, and Gwyn reached up and clawed at his face.

He slapped her, hard, but she fought her way through the pain. His hand closed over her mouth and she bit his fingers with all her strength, then tasted blood.

He raised his hand and she closed her eyes against the impending blow.

Nothing.

She felt him rise up above her, heard one crash, then another. Gwyn's eyes flew open. Andrew and the Duke were rolling over the marble floor. A table had been upended, and she realized Andrew must have bodily picked the Duke up off her and thrown him against it.

She tried to stand up, but her legs were so shaky she could not. She stared at both men. They were engulfed in a complete frenzy as they fought each other, rolling down the length of the great hall.

Then suddenly they were on their feet, circling warily, never taking their eyes off each other. The Duke struggled quickly with his breeches, fastening them.

Gwyn slowly stood, determined to fight for the man she loved.

Andrew darted away from the Duke, keeping his gaze on the man at all times. He reached her side, then swiftly took off his cape.

"Cover yourself." His voice was low as it would not carry. "Go outside and whistle for Mephisto. Take him and flee from this place."

"No." Her reply was just as fierce as she wrapped the folds of

445

his cloak around herself.

"Gwyn, if I should die, you will die as well."

"If you die, I will want to."

The Duke moved toward them, and Andrew broke away from her.

"So you have come to rescue her," the Duke called out. And Gwyn, even wrapped in the folds of a cloak still warm from Andrew, shivered at the tone of his voice.

"I'm sorry I spoiled your game," Andrew replied, his voice taut with anger. "But you did not tell me it was restricted to two players. I thought it best to even the odds."

She could see the anger in the Duke's face at Andrew calling him a coward.

"I have waited for you to come to me, Andrew, only I had thought it would be after her death. Now you will both die tonight."

"I think not." Andrew kept himself just beyond the Duke's reach as the two men circled the large hall. The match had begun.

"A foolish opinion, Andrew, as you do not know the rules." Swiftly, the Duke reached for a cane propped against a small table. With a quick twist, he opened it and pulled out a blade.

"I'm happy you feel so confident of your abilities, Andrew. It will make this fight all the more challenging."

"You always assure yourself of victory. Is that a fight at all?" Andrew did not seem nervous that he was unarmed, but Gwyn was terrified. She glanced quickly up and down the hall, then her eyes fixed on two swords on the wall, one crossed over the other. Moving silently on her bare feet, she started toward them. There was another table below. She could climb up on top of it and make sure Andrew was armed.

"It is fight enough for me," the Duke rasped. "I will kill you first, Andrew, then attend to the bitch's needs."

She was up on the table as the two men continued to talk. One of the swords came loose easily, but it was too heavy and as soon as she pulled it from its fastenings, the other came loose as well and both clattered to the floor.

The Duke turned, a look of pure rage fixed upon her. *"Gwyn, run!"*

She leapt off the table and fled, knowing the Duke had turned his fury toward her. She could hear his footsteps behind her, and she continued to race down the long hall, toward the brightness of the huge stained glass window at the end.

The sound of footsteps behind her stopped, and she turned in time to see Andrew blocking the Duke's path, one of the swords in his hand.

The Duke pivoted, his smaller sword no match for the weapons that had hung on the wall. He raced back to the table Gwyn had climbed upon and grasped the other sword.

"How does it feel to be evenly matched?" Andrew said softly, and Gwyn could see the Duke's body stiffen with rage.

"It must seem strange to be fighting a man, instead of the women and boys you usually do battle with."

"Andrew." She came up behind him and touched his shoulder gently, her fingers trembling. "Keep your head. He has done nothing to me, save to take my clothing. Do not let rage blind you."

He covered her fingers briefly with his free hand. "I cannot let that happen, not when your life would be the price."

The Duke rushed toward him and the battle began.

Gwyn stepped back, her eyes never leaving Andrew as sword struck sword, the sound of steel clanging reverberating throughout the quiet hall. Both men attacked and parried, thrust and lunged. Both were excellent swordsmen, yet she sensed a rage boiling beneath the Duke that would not allow him to fight coolly. His face was flushed; he took too many chances as he rushed at Andrew.

Andrew preferred to draw the Duke toward him. She had never seen him fight before, and Gwyn was amazed by the coiled strength and agility of his movements. There was power in his broad shoulders, a subtle beauty to the movements of wrist and arm. He was all masculine fire and grace, and as he fought the Duke, Gwyn wondered at such beauty being present within such a deadly game.

She could not keep her eyes off him, and as she watched Andrew, she began to see his plan. He baited the Duke, urging him closer rather than attacking him outright. Observing his opponent before deciding on his strategy.

Swords clashed furiously, silver flashing in the early morning light barely shining through the tall gallery windows. The two men circled constantly, then one or the other would break away. Then one, usually the Duke, would dart closer and metal against metal sounded once again.

Gwyn caught a flicker of movement out of the corner of her eye. A small black boy, dressed in loose pants, vest, and a tiny turban, stood in the main double-doored entrance. His delicately shaped features were smooth and impassive. Gwyn glanced back at the two men, and she saw the Duke's face change subtly as he saw the boy. He made a gesture with his free hand, and as she glanced back toward the doorway, the boy disappeared.

She returned her attention to the duel. Andrew was attacking the Duke more strongly now, driving him steadily backward toward the far wall. She realized he had wanted the man's rage to exhaust him. The Duke seemed to be faltering now, and Gwyn noticed bright spots of blood on the cuff of his linen shirt. She was surprised by the rush of savage delight as she realized she'd bit the fingers now holding his sword, giving Andrew a slight advantage.

The Duke suddenly rallied, with a burst of speed and strength that frightened Gwyn. The two men continued to fight up and down the long gallery. At one point, the Duke almost backed Andrew into an immense fireplace, but he sidestepped the sword just in time. A stand of pokers fell, some skittering across the marble floor, some falling into the flames. Andrew pivoted and raced down the long hall, the Duke after him.

They were beyond reason, slashing at each other now, the hatred that had existed between them for so long finally finding release in a fight to the death. Metal rang against metal, and both managed to bloody each other's shirt fronts. They moved so quickly, darting this way and that. Gwyn kept her eyes fixed steadily on Andrew and never stopped praying.

She stayed silent, standing on the far side of the gallery. She had no wish to distract Andrew or entice the Duke into doing something rash that might make Andrew more vulnerable.

Both men were by the great stained glass window, the morning light coming through the glass bathing them with brilliant color. Gwyn, even watching carefully, could not follow the swift actions of their swords.

Then the Duke lunged suddenly, and even from a distance Gwyn could see his rage had made him careless. Andrew caught him off balance, and his sword flew, slicing against the Duke. There were small, sharp sounds as something fell to the floor.

Then Andrew's laughter filled the hall.

"I thought you might be more comfortable out of your waistcoat."

And Gwyn realized he had slashed the buttons off the Duke's garments. Hatred burned in the man's eyes. She knew he could not endure being made the fool, and Andrew was doing exactly that.

Andrew pivoted again, still laughing, and ran lightly down the hallway. The Duke shrugged out of his waistcoat and flung it aside, then followed him. Now he was clad only in his breeches and a white shirt.

Andrew darted in again, and Gwyneth watched as the tip of his sword quickly grazed over the Duke's chest, through the fine linen shirt.

"For Lily," Andrew said quietly, and as Gwyn watched the blood began to stain the front of the fine shirt, she realized Andrew had carved an L into the Duke's chest.

He was furious now, his hair straggling over his face, his

hands shaking with rage. Thus, Gwyn was not surprised when he grew careless. He lunged at Andrew. But Andrew sidestepped his thrust, and the older man was caught off balance. With a quick movement of arm and wrist, Andrew knocked the sword out of the Duke's hand, then pinned him up against the wall by the large fireplace, the tip of his sword directly over his heart.

"And this is for Gwyn."

She closed her eyes before he did anything more, then cried out sharply as she felt strong hands seize her arms from behind. Her eyes flew open, and she realized one of the Duke's servants held her captive. She glanced down, her gaze encountering massive, heavily muscled legs encased in coarse cloth breeches.

She watched, horrified, as Andrew turned his head toward her cry. The Duke knocked the sword away from him as he stepped back. Two other servants rushed up to Andrew and grabbed hold of his arms, pinning them cruelly behind his back.

The Duke retrieved the sword Andrew had dropped, then placed the tip of the thin blade against his adversary's breastbone.

"It was foolish of you to come and attempt to save her, Andrew. I have been thwarted in my pursuit of her too long. Nothing you do can stop me now."

He struggled furiously, but the two men, both larger than he was, held fast.

"*You bastard!* I won your damn game and *still* you have to ensure your victory! *Let me go,* and we'll finish this fairly!"

As the Duke's back was to her, Gwyn could barely pick out the words.

"You didn't really expect me to leave anything to chance, did you, Andrew?"

*　　*　　*

He would die because of her.

The Duke will kill him, Gwyn thought numbly as she watched the tableau played out before her eyes. As if she had no will of her own, her eyes were drawn once again to the portrait above the fireplace. Her mother's brilliant blue eyes seemed to urge her to fight, and without thinking, Gwyneth began to struggle within the steely arms that imprisoned her. Her head fell back, and she gazed up at the silver-haired man who held her.

His own eyes widened as he studied her face, as if seeing a ghost from his past. Then he looked at the portrait above the fire. Abruptly, his face reflecting his fear, he released her.

Gwyneth backed away from him, not questioning her sudden release. She turned toward the Duke. He was still talking to Andrew, though she could not hear his words. There was a thundering in her ears, filling her mind as her gaze skimmed quickly over the long hall looking for . . .

Her attention was caught by several pokers that had fallen by the fire. There was one in particular, the tip of which rested within the flames and glowed white-hot.

Moving as quietly as she could, Gwyneth approached the fireplace.

Everything he had ever hoped for was within his grasp. He would kill Andrew first, but not before tormenting him a moment longer.

"This will be your own private hell, Lord Scarborough, for you will die knowing I have her."

The fool still struggles to save the bitch. Andrew's attempts to wrest himself from the grip of his manservants amused him greatly. He pressed the point of the sword sharply against Andrew's breastbone, then smiled. Blood seeped out, staining the front of his shirt.

"Would you reconsider, Andrew? Many a young lord finds

his tastes change when he is confronted with his own demise."

Hatred glowed within the depths of Andrew's blue eyes, and the Duke decided it was time to finish him.

"Thus, the game has been played, Andrew. And you have lost."

Something heavy slammed against the Duke's leg, then he was burning, screaming. The sword fell out of his hand and he turned to confront a woman with wildness in her eyes, a glowing poker held firmly in hands wrapped within the folds of a black cloak.

"*Bitch!*" He lunged at her, but she dropped the poker and darted to the side. He stumbled and fell heavily, dangerously close to the fireplace. Regaining his balance in an instant, he struck out at her, but his hands clawed at air. She was running now, and his body trembled with hatred as he scrambled to his feet and rushed after her.

Her hands had been shaking so badly that she had barely been able to lift the poker. But once it was in her hands, a rage she had never known she possessed had filled her soul, and she had swung it against the Duke's legs with all her strength.

It did not seem to have made a difference. *But Andrew is still alive. Even for a moment longer. He lives. . . .*

She glanced back quickly as she ran, and saw he was coming toward her, running faster than she. Gwyn redoubled her efforts. The sun tinted the stained glass window at the far end of the gallery hundreds of different colors, the pattern emblazoning the floor her feet skimmed over so quickly.

The scream caused her to look back.

The Duke was writhing as he ran, rage mottling his face. For one impossibly long, suspended moment she didn't understand, then fire shot up from his back. He turned, spinning crazily as he ran the length of the long gallery, and Gwyn saw that his shirt was on fire.

452

But I did not do that. . . . Then she remembered. He had fallen near the fireplace but jumped back so quickly it had seemed the fire hadn't touched him.

He screamed again as flames licked over his bloody body, fanning brightly as he ran. And Gwyn turned and raced ahead, knowing from the hatred in his eyes he was determined she should die with him.

The window loomed up in front of her, the colors blindingly brilliant. She could hear his breathing behind her, feel his touch in her hair. . . .

There was a crashing sound, breaking glass, unbelievable pain as she felt strands of her hair being pulled away. She stumbled, closer to the sunlight pouring in through shattered glass. The Duke was falling, his body a blazing ball of fire, as he screamed and screamed.

She averted her gaze before he reached the earth, wanting to look anywhere but down. Her glance fell on the upper part of the stained glass window, undamaged. And there, pictured in vivid colors, was an angel falling through the sky.

Lucifer.

She was trembling and could still hear the flames softly crackling below. Gwyn walked slowly away from the window, her mind numb.

Someone touched her, caught her up in strong arms. Someone embraced her tightly, as if willing her to come back from the frightening place her mind had resided in so briefly.

Andrew.

He was trembling as he held her, and she put her arms around him, pressing herself tightly against him.

"I was so scared. . . ."

His lips were moving over her face, her cheeks, her temples, then finally claiming her in a desperate kiss. She felt warmth begin to bloom in her body once again. It seemed a lifetime ago that he had held her in his arms in the rose garden.

*　　　*　　　*

The sun was higher in the sky as Andrew directed the servants disposing of the Duke's remains. He had wanted to severely punish the men who had held both of them captive at the end, but Gwyneth had managed to dissuade him.

"They were frightened of him, Andrew. He would have beaten them—or worse—if they had not obeyed."

And it had been true. After the sound of screaming and shattering glass, several servants had peered out from around the doorways, then shrunk back. The older servants had stared at Gwyn as if she were her mother back from the grave. And she had understood, walking toward them slowly and holding out her hand.

"Come out. I will not hurt you."

And they had, slowly at first, then the weaker had gathered strength in the fact that nothing seemed to happen to those who revealed themselves.

While Andrew had attended to the Duke's burial, Gwyn had remained with the servants. She had wanted to reassure them.

An older woman entered the great hall, her eyes searching until her gaze came to rest on Gwyn. She walked quickly to her side, fell on her knees, and kissed her hand.

"There is no need to do that. I won't hurt any of you."

Then the old woman had surprised her, standing and pulling her into a fierce embrace.

"Oh, my darling Frances! I never hoped to see you alive again, after Lady Barbara was murdered. We thought Richard had found you as well."

As they spoke, Gwyn learned that the silver-haired man who had restrained her at first was this woman's husband.

"And who might you be? I'm afraid I do not remember you."

"Faith, that you should forget the woman who helped bring you into the world and took care of your every need! My name is Dierdre, and I was your mother's maid from the time she was a girl. Your mother knew she had brought a devil into the world, but an angel as well."

"My brother—" she said slowly, then turned and stared at the broken window.

"A monster," Dierdre said, crossing herself. "He had the most unnatural affection for your mother. When you were born, he was beside himself with rage. Couldn't stand anyone else taking her attention away from him. Lady Barbara knew she had to protect you, Frances. I suggested she take you to the vicar."

"He wasn't my father," Gwyn said slowly.

"No, but he was a dear friend to your mother and promised to love you like his own. Your father died in a dueling accident a month before you were born. His gun misfired." Her brow furrowed. "Frances, what madness possessed you to come to this house?"

"He—he brought me."

The woman's mouth gaped open. "And did you know he was your brother?"

"Not 'til this night."

Quickly she recounted how the Duke had looked for her and finally spirited her away from Scarborough Hall. Dierdre seemed pleased by this last piece of information.

"Your mother hated Henry Hawkesworth for what he did to her sister. But she would have loved his grandson. The two are very different men, I'm sure you've noticed. He will protect you the way your mother would have wished. She fought for you, Frances, you must never forget that. 'Tis a pity you never knew her."

"Would you tell me about her? Someday?" Gwyn could not keep the quaver out of her voice.

"You stand before me, Frances, and I see my Barbara all over again. You have the same fire in your eye, that same will to fight." The rheumy old eyes suddenly twinkled. "I suspect you know that woman in the portrait better than you think."

*   *   *

455

She met Andrew outside as he and several servants were finishing the burial. And then, with arms around each other, they walked in back of the great house and sat down on the stone steps leading out into an immense garden.

"I thought I had lost you," Andrew said quietly.

"Never."

He was holding her hand and they were facing each other on the stone steps, warm from the summer sun overhead.

"There are so many things I wish I could have done differently with you, Gwyneth."

"I have the same feelings."

"Grandfather told me everything. The promise. The letter he forged. The last offer he made you."

"He loves you, Andrew. He wanted the finest woman for you, there is no sin in that."

"But I have had the finest woman by my side all these months and never realized it until now."

"I don't believe that's true. You have always been kind to me, Andrew. You have asked me to be your wife, and I have said I will marry you."

"But I never told you—" And here she could sense his fear. "I never told you how I truly felt about you."

"We have the rest of our lives for that."

"It's so difficult for me to say. You deserve a man who can say those words to you more easily than I."

"But he might not mean them, Andrew."

When he did not reply, she said, "There is something I must confide in you."

"No." His voice was low and intense, and he took her other hand in his and faced her squarely. "I am—I have to—I am going to tell you how I feel about you before I lose my courage. Gwyneth, somehow you have always lived in a secret place in my heart. I've searched for a woman like you and never thought of finding her until that first moment I saw you. I will confess, it was your face and form that attracted me first, for I

456

did not believe a woman with your beauty could possess a spirit as fine. But I have been waiting for you always, to make my life complete. Without you, I feel there is less of me."

"Andrew—" she began.

"I do not understand how I can be unafraid of fighting a duel or racing a horse. I can do many things, but the thought of laying my heart and soul at your feet terrifies me."

"You are a brave man to admit to that feeling."

"There is nothing brave about me. I have bullied and tormented you, made you a prisoner in my bed, forced responses from you before you were comfortable with me. I treated you as a whore, as a mere mistress—" Here his voice broke. "And still you cared for me."

"I do, Andrew. Very much."

"I have never been given a love like that. Yet I took that caring and accepted it as my due, never thinking what it cost you."

"You have asked me to be your wife. I believe that is a statement of faith in your feelings for me."

"But the words have to be said. I *want* to say them. Gwyneth, will you believe me if I tell you I have never told another woman of feelings such as these?"

"I believe you. But Andrew, before anything more is said, I must tell you—you do not truly know who I am. I must tell you now—"

"*Damn* who you are! I don't care! You have a finer spirit and more heart than any woman I have ever known. And I would consider it an honor if you would consent to wed me."

She smiled up at him. "I will."

"Then—what I want to tell you—what I meant to say before we talked of other things—"

His hands were practically crushing her fingers, his eyes were agonized. And she had never loved him more.

"Help me, Gwyneth," he said softly.

"Oh, Andrew, I love you, too."

Then he kissed her, a kiss that made her forget they were

sitting out in the open. Her arms came up around his neck, she leaned into his warmth and strength, and forgot everything but the man in her arms.

When they broke apart, she leaned against him, their foreheads touching.

"Here now, I will not have you compromising Lady—"

Gwyn turned quickly, giving the old maidservant a slight shake of her head. The woman studied her for the briefest of seconds, then began to smile.

"Is there anything you might need?" she asked.

"My lord and I are quite exhausted from the events of this day. Could you show us to a suite of rooms, so we might rest before attempting the journey back home?"

Andrew's fingers tightened against hers, and Gwyn merely smiled.

After they had reaffirmed their love for each other in the way most lovers do, Gwyn closed her eyes and moved closer against Andrew.

"I do love you, Gwyneth," he said softly.

"I know."

"I hope the words will come easier with time."

"You have shown me your love in countless ways. Since you came to the country, I have never doubted you."

"Sleep, Gwyn. I will be here when you wake."

She was almost asleep, her fingers tightly entwined in his, her cheek resting against his chest, when the sound of his voice stirred her.

"What was it you wished to confide about yourself, Gwyn? You said it was something important."

Her eyes remained closed, and a soft smile touched her lips. Turning her head, she kissed his chest, then his neck.

"It was nothing. Nothing at all. There is only this." She kissed him again, then her smile grew wider as he gently rolled over so he was looking down at her. He kissed her again, and she could feel the familiar velvet fire beginning to bloom within her heart once again.

He broke the kiss, and everything she had ever wanted to see in his eyes was there. Touching her cheek gently, Andrew smiled.

"There is only you, Gwyneth. Only you."

Now you can get more of HEARTFIRE right at home and $ave.

Preview Four Brand New ZEBRA *Heartfire* Romance Novels...

FREE for 10 days.

No Obligation and No Strings Attached!

❤

Enjoy all of the passion and fiery romance as you soar back through history, right in the comfort of your own home.

Now that you have read a Zebra HEARTFIRE Romance novel, we're sure you'll agree that HEARTFIRE sets new standards of excellence for historical romantic fiction. Each Zebra HEARTFIRE novel is the ultimate blend of intimate romance and grand adventure and each takes place in the kinds of historical settings you want most...the American Revolution, the Old West, Civil War and more.

<u>FREE</u> Preview Each Month and $ave

Zebra has made arrangements for you to preview 4 brand new HEARTFIRE novels each month...FREE for 10 days. You'll get them as soon as they are published. If you are not delighted with any of them, just return them with no questions asked. But if you decide these are everything we said they are, you'll pay just $3.25 each—a total of $13.00 (a $15.00 value). **That's a $2.00 saving each month off the regular price.** Plus there is NO shipping or handling charge. These are delivered right to your door absolutely free! There is no obligation and there is no minimum number of books to buy.

TO GET YOUR FIRST MONTH'S PREVIEW... Mail the Coupon Below!

Mail to:

HEARTFIRE Home Subscription Service, Inc.
120 Brighton Road
P.O. Box 5214
Clifton, NJ 07015-5214

YES! I want to subscribe to Zebra's HEARTFIRE Home Subscription Service. Please send me my first month's books to preview free for ten days. I understand that if I am not pleased I may return them and owe nothing, but if I keep them I will pay just $3.25 each; a total of $13.00. That is a savings of $2.00 each month off the cover price. There are no shipping, handling or other hidden charges and there is no minimum number of books I must buy. I can cancel this subscription at any time with no questions asked.

NAME

ADDRESS   APT. NO.

CITY   STATE   ZIP

SIGNATURE   (if under 18, parent or guardian must sign)   2133
Terms and prices are subject to change.

EXHILARATING ROMANCE
From Zebra Books

GOLDEN PARADISE   (2007, $3.95)
by Constance O'Banyon

Desperate for money, the beautiful and innocent Valentina Barrett finds work as a veiled dancer, "Jordanna," at San Francisco's notorious Crystal Palace. There she falls in love with handsome, wealthy Marquis Vincente — a man she knew she could never trust as Valentina — but who Jordanna can't resist making her lover and reveling in love's GOLDEN PARADISE.

MOONLIT SPLENDOR   (2008, $3.95)
by Wanda Owen

When the handsome stranger emerged from the shadows and pulled Charmaine Lamoureux into his strong embrace, she knew she should scream, but instead she sighed with pleasure at his seductive caresses. She would be wed against her will on the morrow — but tonight she would succumb to this passionate MOONLIT SPLENDOR.

TEXAS TRIUMPH   (2009, $3.95)
by Victoria Thompson

Nothing is more important to the determined Rachel McKinsey than the Circle M — and if it meant marrying her foreman to scare off rustlers, she would do it. Yet the gorgeous rancher feels a secret thrill that the towering Cole Elliot is to be her man — and despite her plan that they be business partners, all she truly desires is a glorious consummation of their vows.

DESERT HEART   (2010, $3.95)
by Bobbi Smith

Rancher Rand McAllister was furious when he became the guardian of a scrawny girl from Arizona's mining country. But when he finds that the pig-tailed brat is really a ripe, voluptuous beauty, his resentment turns to intense interest! Lorelei knew it would be the biggest mistake in her life to succumb to the virile cowboy — but she can't fight against giving him her body — or her wild DESERT HEART.

Available wherever paperbacks are sold, or order direct from the Publisher. Send cover price plus 50¢ per copy for mailing and handling to Zebra Books, Dept. 2133, 475 Park Avenue South, New York, N.Y. 10016. Residents of New York, New Jersey and Pennsylvania must include sales tax. DO NOT SEND CASH.

FIERY ROMANCE
From Zebra Books

AUTUMN'S FURY (1763, $3.95)
by Emma Merritt

Lone Wolf had known many women, but none had captured his heart the way Catherine had . . . with her he felt a hunger he hadn't experienced with any of the maidens of his own tribe. He would make Catherine his captive, his slave of love — until she would willingly surrender to the magic of AUTUMN'S FURY.

PASSION'S PARADISE (1618, $3.75)
by Sonya T. Pelton

When she is kidnapped by the cruel, captivating Captain Ty, fair-haired Angel Sherwood fears not for her life, but for her honor! Yet she can't help but be warmed by his manly touch, and secretly longs for PASSION'S PARADISE.

SAVAGE SPLENDOR (1855, $3.95)
by Constance O'Banyon

By day Mara questioned her decision to remain in her husband's world. But by night, when Tajarez crushed her in his strong, muscular arms, taking her to the peaks of rapture, she knew she could never live without him.

SATIN SURRENDER (1861, $3.95)
by Carol Finch

Dante Folwer found innocent Erica Bennett in his bed in the most fashionable whorehouse in New Orleans. Expecting a woman of experience, Dante instead stole the innocence of the most magnificent creature he'd ever seen. He would forever make her succumb to . . . SATIN SURRENDER.

Available wherever paperbacks are sold, or order direct from the Publisher. Send cover price plus 50¢ per copy for mailing and handling to Zebra Books, Dept. 2133, 475 Park Avenue South, New York, N.Y. 10016. Residents of New York, New Jersey and Pennsylvania must include sales tax. DO NOT SEND CASH.

THE ECSTASY SERIES
by Janelle Taylor

SAVAGE ECSTASY (Pub. date 8/1/81)   (0824, $3.50)

DEFIANT ECSTASY (Pub. date 2/1/82)   (0931, $3.50)

FORBIDDEN ECSTASY (Pub. date 7/1/82) (1014, $3.50)

BRAZEN ECSTASY (Pub. date 3/1/83)   (1133, $3.50)

TENDER ECSTASY (Pub. date 6/1/83)   (1212, $3.75)

STOLEN ECSTASY (Pub. date 9/1/85)   (1621, $3.95)

Plus other bestsellers by Janelle:

GOLDEN TORMENT (Pub. date 2/1/84)   (1323, $3.75)

LOVE ME WITH FURY (Pub. date 9/1/83) (1248, $3.75)

FIRST LOVE, WILD LOVE
(Pub. date 10/1/84)   (1431, $3.75)

SAVAGE CONQUEST (Pub. date 2/1/85)   (1533, $3.75)

DESTINY'S TEMPTRESS
(Pub. date 2/1/86)   (1761, $3.95)

SWEET SAVAGE HEART
(Pub. date 10/1/86)   (1900, $3.95)

Available wherever paperbacks are sold, or order direct from the Publisher. Send cover price plus 50¢ per copy for mailing and handling to Zebra Books, Dept. 2133, 475 Park Avenue South, New York, N.Y. 10016. Residents of New York, New Jersey and Pennsylvania must include sales tax. DO NOT SEND CASH.